The Muckers

Director's Choice

Our Director's Choice program is an opportunity to highlight a book from our list that deserves special attention.

Discovered in Syracuse University Libraries' Special Collections, William Osborne Dapping's previously unpublished manuscript, *The Muckers: A Narrative of the Crapshooters Club* is a long-lost and singular firsthand account of the author's youth as a member of a boys' street gang in 1890s New York City. The publication of Dapping's story represents the commitment of Syracuse University Press to preserving the history, literature, and culture of our region, as well as our mission to promote the scholarship of the university. I am delighted to add this book to our New York State collection and showcase one of the many treasures Syracuse University has to offer.

Alice Randel Pfeiffer
Director, Syracuse University Press

The
Muckers

A Narrative of the Crapshooters Club

William Osborne Dapping

Edited and with an Introduction by **Woody Register**

Syracuse University Press

For a listing of books published and distributed by Syracuse University Press,
visit www.SyracuseUniversityPress.syr.edu.

ISBN: 978-0-8156-3440-9 (hardcover)   978-0-8156-1063-2 (paperback)
978-0-8156-5362-2 (e-book)

Library of Congress Cataloging-in-Publication Data
Names: Dapping, William O. (William Osborne), 1880–1969, author. | Register, Woody,
    1958–, editor.
Title: The Muckers : a narrative of the Crapshooters Club / William Osborne Dapping ;
    edited and with an Introduction by Woody Register.
Other titles: Narrative of the Crapshooters Club
Description: First edition. | Syracuse, New York : Syracuse University Press, [2016] |
    Includes index.
Identifiers: LCCN 2016039311 (print) | LCCN 2016039484 (ebook) | ISBN 9780815634409
    (hardcover : alk. paper) | ISBN 9780815610632 (pbk. : alk. paper) | ISBN 9780815653622
    (e-book)
Subjects: LCSH: Dapping, William O. (William Osborne), 1880–1969—Childhood and
    youth. | Gangs—New York (State)—New York—History—19th century. | Boys—New
    York (State)—New York—Biography. | Boys—New York (State)—New York—Social
    life and customs—19th century. | City children—New York (State)—New York—Social
    life and customs—19th century. | Poor children—New York (State)—New York—
    Social conditions—19th century. | Slums—New York (State)—New York—Social
    conditions—19th century. | Dialect literature, English—United States. | Yorkville
    (New York, N.Y.)—Social life and customs—19th century. | New York (N.Y.)—Social
    conditions—19th century.
Classification: LCC HV6439.U7 N4368 2016 (print) | LCC HV6439.U7 (ebook) | DDC
    364.106/609747109041—dc23
LC record available at https://lccn.loc.gov/2016039311

Manufactured in the United States of America

published with the help of a grant
Figure Foundation

breathing home runs in a vacant lot

For Julie

Contents

List of Illustrations   *xi*

Acknowledgments   *xiii*

A Note on the Text   *xv*

EDITOR'S INTRODUCTION

The Charm That Truth Never Lacks
*A Brief History of William Osborne Dapping
and His Crapshooters Club*
WOODY REGISTER   *3*

THE MUCKERS: A Narrative of the Crapshooters Club

1. Foreword   *51*
2. Introductory   *53*
3. Dugan's Cellar   *58*
4. The Crapshooters' Housewarming   *69*
5. An East Side Surprise Party   *77*
6. Mickey's Lecture on "How to Get a Job"   *87*
7. Mickey's Scheme, and a Visit to a Bowery Museum   *94*
8. The Dewey Baseball Team   *111*
9. Miggles   *125*
10. The Club Attends a May Party in Central Park   *129*
11. The Last Raid on the "Cherry Bunk"   *142*
12. An East Side Excursion   *148*
13. Burglarin'   *157*

14. Fresh Air Kids   164

15. Mickey Sent to the George Junior Republic   185

16. Hallowe'en   195

17. Letter from Mickey in the George Junior Republic   204

18. 'Lection Time   208

19. Mickey In-Wrong Again   220

20. Ragamuffin Day   222

21. Spike's Comment on Religion   229

22. Not to Be Opened until Christmas   232

23. Christmas Graft   236

24. New Year's Callin'   242

25. Riley's Christmas   252

    Index   263

Illustrations

1. William O. Dapping, author of *The Muckers* and "college man," around the age of 20   5

2. Dapping with other leading citizens of the George Junior Republic, ca. 1897   10

3. Dapping's photograph of the Heucken & Willenbrock lumberyard   23

4. William R. "Daddy" George, founder of the George Junior Republic, ca. 1900   27

5. Thomas Mott Osborne, board chairman of the George Junior Republic, ca. 1900   35

6. Thomas Mott Osborne with his favorite citizens of the Republic   37

7. Boy citizens of the George Junior Republic, ca. 1900   60

8. William R. George and the Republic's baseball team, ca. 1895   112

9. Dapping's photograph of tenement backyards in Yorkville, ca. 1899   132

10. A pauper shown the meaning of "nothing without labor," ca. 1901   191

Acknowledgments

This project started a number a years ago, leaving me happily with many people and organizations to thank. I am grateful for the funding support from the Central New York Humanities Corridor Libraries, the Appalachian College Association, the Associated Colleges of the South, the University of the South, its Center for Teaching, and the University Research and Faculty Development Grants Committee. The Special Collections Research Center of the Syracuse University Libraries, the Division of Rare and Manuscript Collections at Cornell University's Carl A. Kroch Library, and the William George Agency in Freeville, New York, have generously allowed me to reproduce materials from their collections in this book. Of the many friends I have made and relied on during my ongoing research on the boys and men of the George Junior Republic, I am especially thankful for the support and encouragement of Lucy Mulroney, Nicolette Dobrowolski, and the generously helpful staff in Special Collections at Syracuse, including former director Sean Quimby. I am grateful to Elaine Engst, Eisha Neely, Hilary Dorsch Wong of Cornell's Rare Books and Manuscript Collections. At Syracuse University Press Suzanne Guiod has been supportive, patient, and firm, all of which I have needed. Kay Steinmetz provided much-needed editorial insight and placed the manuscript with Sara Cleary, whose superb copyediting made a difficult job manageable. Mona Hamlin's expertise and enthusiasm have been evident in marketing Dapping's book. My months in Syracuse were memorable and always warm thanks to the hospitality of Carol Faulkner and my dear friends Johanna Keller and Charles Martin. I am indebted to David Connelly, a fellow student of Thomas M. Osborne, who shared his research and put me in touch with Trish Sprague, archivist at the William George

Agency. Her help has been essential and generously given. Amy Shrager Lang and an anonymous reviewer of *The Muckers* manuscript shared valuable insights, advice, and encouragement. I benefited, as always, from my team of inspiring friends: Danny Anderson, Bruce Dorsey, and John Sullivan. At Sewanee I thank Tanner Potts and DebbieLee Landi for their smiling support and forbearance, Leigh Lentile (one of the best friends a scholar could have), and Liesl Allingham, who was there for me with the German language. Andrew Huebner provided uplifting support early on, and Ernie Freeberg has been a rock of friendship throughout. Lacy Broemel was a collegial fellow researcher, and Victoria Miglets transcribed the original manuscript with care and patience. Sophie Register made a difference by giving bountiful loving support from afar. Julie Berebitsky made and continues to make all things possible and joyful for me.

A Note on the Text

A variety of challenges arose in editing *The Muckers*. To start, most of the surviving pages, although typewritten, are century-old carbon copies; in places words are blurred or faded, making them difficult to decipher. Handwritten or typed-over corrections sometimes are illegible. In addition to its material condition, the draft may be clean and finished, but it still is a draft; it was not professionally edited and thus contains a number of spelling and punctuation errors, irregularities, and omitted words. In one case (Chapter 16), Dapping used the wrong name for one of his characters. Finally, the body of the book is presented in the street voices of the Crapshooters. Words typically are spelled phonetically to convey the sound of mucker speech. For instance, New York is spelled "N'York" (or in some cases "N' York") to convey how the boys pronounced the two words as one. The terminal "g" almost invariably is missing from words: "nothing" becomes "nothin'" or "nuttin'"; "lying" and "going" appear as "lyin'" and "goin'." But there are exceptions when New York is properly spelled or "nothing" appears both with and without a "g" in the same chapter (see Spike's speech in Chapter 3).

In preparing the manuscript for publication I have endeavored to make the text accessible to twenty-first-century readers while maintaining the original so far as possible to preserve Dapping's intended message and the integrity of the document as a draft manuscript. Some punctuation has been corrected and spellings modernized or edited for uniformity. Contractions have been modified (replacing "did n't" with "didn't"). The occasional instances of "N' York" now appear as one word, "N'York," and the various spellings of "youse" and "you'se" are spelled "youse." Indecipherable or missing words are in brackets.

Two major editorial changes have been made. First, Dapping compiled his glossary of slang words and phrases in a freestanding section at the end of the book; these have been transferred to chapter footnotes for the reader's convenience. Second, the entirety of Spike's narration in the original manuscript (Chapters 3 through 25) was contained within quotation marks. Dapping likely did so to maintain the illusion that he was not the author of Spike's speech, only a listener transcribing it. To assist today's reader, those quotation marks have been removed; only spoken dialogue is set in quotation marks. The sections of narration by Spike and other Crapshooter boys have been set in a distinctive typeface to differentiate them from the author's prose.

Editor's Introduction

The Charm That Truth Never Lacks

A Brief History of William Osborne Dapping and His Crapshooters Club

WOODY REGISTER

In the decade after 1899, when the aspiring young author William Osborne Dapping was writing his sketches of New York City's fearsome gangs of street boys, he was conscious of entering a crowded literary and socio-logical field. For more than half a century the most high-minded social reformers, the most respected sociological investigators, and the most opportunistic of the daily press's headline hunters had studied "the prob-lem of the slum" and "the children of the poor." They produced a massive library of graphic and shocking descriptions of the "hordes" of "street urchins" and "gutter-snipes" who roamed the city at will. In some ver-sions they resembled an occupying army of wild and nomadic "Arabs," in others the pathetic victims of a heartless Dickensian world or a swarming pestilence of ravenous locusts gnawing away at the foundations of social order.[1] Those lurid images and uncontested truths in the early 1900s are not to be found in Dapping's exposé on the same subject, *The Muckers: A Narrative of the Crapshooters Club*. He had no patience for these renditions of what he termed, ironically, "the so-called slums." He dismissed them as written "from the outside, in harrowing and sensational detail, or in

---

1. Timothy J. Gilfoyle, "Street-Rats and Gutter-Snipes: Child Pickpockets and Street Culture in New York City, 1850–1900," *Journal of Social History* 37, no. 4 (2004): 853.

picturesque and exaggerated dialect, to entertain and amuse the reader."
The Muckers was altogether different, he explained in its early paragraphs.
It was based on "inside sources" and so could rightly claim "to show for
the first time" what the gangs of rowdy boys from the slums—the ones
who called each other *muckers*—were truly like. His scenes, he said, may
lack the sensation and hyperbole of the usual fare, but they possess "the
charm that truth never lacks."[2]

The Muckers, excavated from the archives and published here for the
first time, more than a century after Dapping completed it, delivered on
its promise of an alternative portrait of the city's poor populace that con-
formed to the author's understanding of the truth. The book's twenty-
three chapters are narrated in the first-person voice of "Spike"—so called,
he explains, "because I was handy with me mits." Each chapter is an
episode in the escapades, mischief, or outlawry of a gang of adolescent
boys who gave themselves the swaggering title of the Crapshooters Club.
What Dapping did not reveal in his text was the nature and identity of
his inside source or how he gained access to him. Or, to put it more accu-
rately, what he deliberately concealed was that he was not a link to that
source but himself the insider. He was the American-born son of a poor
German immigrant, and he was a mucker from the tenement neighborhoods and dangerous classes of New York City. He had run with a gang of
"hard blokes" or "tough characters" until the age of sixteen, when he left
the slums on a path of regeneration that led to Harvard and eventually a
distinguished journalism career. He wrote the first chapters at the age of
nineteen. *The Muckers* was his story, and Spike his alter ego.

It is hard to exaggerate the rarity of a firsthand account of working-
class boy life like *The Muckers* or to overstate its contribution to our
understanding of one of the important yet elusive aspects of late nineteenth-century history. The American metropolis in this period—whether
New York City, Boston, Philadelphia, or Cincinnati—was literally a city of

2. William O. Dapping, "The Muckers: A Narrative of the Crapshooters Club," unpublished manuscript (ca. 1910), p. 4, William O. Dapping Papers, Special Collections Research
Center, Syracuse Univ. Libraries. Future references will use WOD for Dapping and WODP
for Dapping Papers.

1. William O. Dapping, author of *The Muckers* and "college man," around the age of 20. William R. George Family Papers, no. 800. Division of Rare and Manuscript Collections, Cornell University Library.

children. When school was not in session, the streets of major industrial cities, where work spaces and play spaces overlapped and kids and adults battled each other for control, were thronged with children, especially boys like the Crapshooters: shining shoes, hawking newspapers, running errands, raiding peddlers' carts, playing games, pulling pranks, and generally sowing mayhem in the lives of adults, irrespective of their class. Unless these boys were arrested or had their exploits sensationalized in the newspapers, they left few written traces of their lives before adulthood. For one, they were not just children, but children of the poor. Powerless people of any age were not expected or encouraged to be writers, much less the authors of their lives. Other people with education, wealth, and experience possessed the authority to tell their stories for them. In addition, writes historian Timothy Gilfoyle, the "world of the street child was organized, in part, around an unwritten, oral culture." Boys like that did not use, need, or produce materials in print. The street-boy's eye view of *The Muckers*, then, is an exceptional find. Of those very few instances in which boys' actual experiences or voices have survived on paper, none equals *The Muckers* in the density and variety of its information about the poor boys in New York City's immigrant neighborhoods. Nor do any match the depth and complexity of its rendering of how muckers saw themselves, the world they inhabited, and the "better class" of people who regarded them as dangerous. Finally, no other social reform text from the period has its insubordinate attitude and slyly seditious humor. Most of the literature about the problem of the slum was written to persuade minds and to stir the heart, but until its very last chapter *The Muckers* eschews sentimentality. Its tone is frank, self-assured, rude, unapologetic, and offensive by the standards of its day. "Youse guys probaly think I dont know nothin' because I dont know how to speak swell English," Spike introduces himself. "Well, believe me, I'm no dub; even if I cant sling words." The confusing chain of double or triple negatives in actuality conceals a provocation. Who, Spike impertinently asks, is the real *dub* (slang for "fool, ignoramus"): the privileged reader or the underprivileged mucker? Who, he asks, deserves pity and needs help?[3]

Although we cannot be certain, the version of Dapping's book published here appears to be the final of two extant drafts that were transferred to the Syracuse University Libraries after his death in 1969.[4] It is not a

---

3. David Nasaw, *Children of the City: At Work and At Play* (New York: Oxford Univ. Press, 1985), 17; Ann Fabian, *The Unvarnished Truth: Personal Narratives in Nineteenth-Century America* (Berkeley: Univ. of California Press, 2000), xi–xii, 1–7, 78; Gilfoyle, "Street-Rats and Gutter-Snipes," 853. I am grateful to Amy Shrager Lang for emphasizing the near absence of sentimentality in *The Muckers*.

4. WODP contain two undated typescripts, one incomplete and the other complete, both titled "The Muckers, A Narrative of the Crapshooters Club." The typescript published here is the complete and likely the final version. It includes a notation, "Mailed to Mr. Large in New York City before he sailed." WODP contain a letter to Large, 16 Apr. 1912, expressing

novel, but a collection of mostly freestanding episodes or sketches portraying the antics and opinions of the gang. Its members—the leader Spike plus Mickey, Butts, Shorty, Red, Blinkey, and Riley—are fictionalized representations of boys from the poor but striving German and Irish families who lived in Dapping's tenement neighborhood on the Upper East Side of New York City. The book is not a rough draft, but a polished work of social reform literature, written by a young man acutely and personally aware of what it meant to be poor in America at the turn of the twentieth century.

The Muckers belonged to the Progressive Era, the period from about 1890 to 1920 when a vast wave of intense reform agitation swept the nation in response to the social conflicts and upheavals brought by rapid industrial and urban growth. The women and men who instigated these actions—large and small, national and local—were motivated by a variety of concerns. Some focused on the corruption of urban politics and the growth of massive industrial monopolies, whereas others campaigned against the disease- and crime-breeding conditions of modern cities or labored to bring the rapidly growing population of foreign immigrants more fully into mainstream American life. Across the spectrum of interests, progressives offered modern methods of social investigation, planning, and efficiency to clean up the disorder in American life and restore harmony to the republic. They also built new public and private organizations to fund and harness their knowledge and direct it to solve social problems. Reformers ultimately defined an enlarged arena for state action and intervention in Americans' lives to ensure their health and the welfare of the nation. The endeavors also created conditions under which strong emotional and affective bonds developed between reformers and those they were trying to reform. Such ties were especially evident where children were concerned. Children, particularly those of immigrants, attracted a disproportionate share of the attention because, as everyone agreed, America's future would be determined by the kinds of citizens

concern that his response to the manuscript may have sunk with the *Titanic*, placing the completed manuscript around that time.

its youngest grew up to be. How children played, worked, and studied was no longer a matter of private decision-making; with the future of the nation at stake, some reformers agitated successfully to build schools or playgrounds, whereas others pursued more aggressive means, such as anti–child labor laws, to free the children of the poor so they could grow up responsible and patriotic adults. They demanded, writes historian Paula Fass, that "school augmented by play, not exploitative work, should be the domain of childhood."[5]

Dapping was a child of the Progressive Era and at an early age stepped into the very center of the reform arena, first as an object of others' philanthropy, then as a regenerated subject, and ultimately as an ambivalent commentator on the reform movements of the period. Between his birth in the city's Lower East Side in 1880 and his first efforts to publish his stories in 1899, the population of New York City (that is, Manhattan) grew more than 60 percent to 1.8 million. Foreign immigrants accounted for most of the new population, and Germans, like the Dappings, were the single largest segment. In 1895 the Dappings were among the 1.3 million people, nearly all of them immigrants and their American-born children, crowded into the city's 40,000 slum tenements, the four- to six-story multifamily dwellings that lined the streets of some of the most densely populated and poorest neighborhoods in the nation.[6] These social conditions, which had been growing since the Irish immigration of the 1840s, stimulated urgent investigations into the "problem of the slum" and debates among Americans who were not poor about the nature of Americans who were. By the 1880s propertied and respectable New Yorkers regarded the ubiquitous "urchins" and "gamins" like Dapping and the gangs they formed as the nucleus of most evil in the modern city, from disease and crime

5. Two recent surveys of the Progressive Era are Rebecca Edwards, *New Spirits: Americans in the "Gilded Age," 1865 to 1905* (New York: Oxford Univ. Press, 2011), and Maureen A. Flanagan, *America Reformed: Progressives and Progressivisms, 1890s–1920s* (New York: Oxford Univ. Press, 2007). Paula Fass, "Foreword," in *Children and Youth during the Gilded Age and Progressive Era*, ed. James Marten (New York: New York Univ. Press), vii–viii.

6. Jared N. Day, *Urban Castles: Tenement Housing and Landlord Activism in New York City, 1890–1943* (New York: Columbia Univ. Press, 1999), 8.

to political corruption and public immorality. The foremost authority on the subject, Jacob Riis, rejected popular prejudices and theories of inherited criminality and sympathized with children who could not help who their parents were. He also admired street boys' resourcefulness, plucky good humor, and noble-savage code of honor among thieves. Nevertheless he, like most others examining the modern city, believed boys like Dapping were the preeminent threat to social order and decency. Without vigorous reform intervention, they were fast on their way to becoming brass-knuckled, beer-swilling "young rascals" who were "ready to cut the throat of a defenceless stranger at the toss of a cent." Today, Riis warned, "We have the choice of hailing him man and brother or of being slugged and robbed by him" tomorrow.[7]

Dapping chose to write *The Muckers* and add his voice to the mix for complex reasons, many of which grew from the accidents of his personal history. The decisive stroke of fortune occurred in 1895 at a Methodist Sunday-school meeting in the city, where he met and fell under the spell of William R. George.[8] That summer George was starting the George Junior Republic, which almost immediately emerged as one of the era's most celebrated and highly publicized experiments in rescuing boys from the slum. Dapping voluntarily left his family in New York City and traveled two hundred miles north and west to a village near Ithaca to enter George's program. Uncommonly intelligent and ambitious, he embraced the Republic idea and quickly rose to positions of leadership. He also attracted the favor of Thomas Mott Osborne, the Republic's wealthy patron. Osborne unofficially adopted him when he finished at the Republic and was educating him to enter Harvard when Dapping began writing the Crapshooters volume. The details of Dapping's life in these years placed him directly on the fault line of the urgent Progressive Era debates about the dangerous classes of the urban and immigrant poor. From

7. Jacob A. Riis, *How the Other Half Lives: Studies among the Tenements of New York* (New York: Charles Scribner's Sons, 1914), 217–25, quotations appear on 222, 220; Jacob A. Riis, *The Children of the Poor* (New York: Charles Scribner's Sons, 1902), 6.

8. WOD, "The George Junior Republic," Dapping scrapbook, William George House Library, William George Agency, Freeville, NY (hereafter cited as Dapping WGHL).

2. William O. Dapping (left) with other leading citizens of the George Junior Republic, ca. 1897. William R. George Family Papers, no. 800. Division of Rare and Manuscript Collections, Cornell University Library.

where he stood at the age of nineteen, able to look back at his mucker past and forward to his future as a regenerated man, Dapping possessed the unusual perspective of a reformed rowdy, an array of experiences to bring to those debates, and the material support of a wealthy philanthropist to assist him in doing it.

Dapping accepted environmentalist theories of criminality and did not dispute the predictions that Riis, George, and Osborne made about what becomes of street boys in the absence of better influences. But his portrait of muckers challenged the more familiar alarmist literature from the period by adding his own voice and perspective as a "reformed" subject. *The Muckers* is not an uncomplicated, unmediated, or naïve "voice from below." After all, Dapping already was "rescued" at the time he began writing the stories, and he revised them during his Harvard years. The older he got, the greater was the distance between his youth on the streets and his later reflections. Whether he was writing at nineteen or older, the stories in *The Muckers* were works of Dapping's imagination and as literary as other contemporary fictional accounts of "the other half," including Stephen Crane's work of realist fiction, *Maggie: A Girl of the Streets* (1893). Their value consists in how Dapping not only represents the boys' lives in the slums but also reveals the subjective experience of being a reformed subject. Dapping was determined to submit *The Muckers* to the debates about the "problem of the slum" as something other than proof that a boy from the "dangerous classes" can be saved, which was the role his benefactors usually assigned him. He also wanted to use *The Muckers* to write his way to respectability and acceptance as an author and thereby free himself from the anchor of his low origins.

The following pages explore how the recovery of *The Muckers* complicates and enriches our understanding of the history of the Progressive Era. With so few materials to work with, scholars have had difficulty giving the perspectives and experiences of the poor as much consideration as they have that of the reformers, who produced extensive published materials.[9] Dapping's manuscript is a wealth of fresh information about the lives of poor boys and provides new insights into how they were equal opportunity exploiters, willing and able to use urban political machines and high-minded reform endeavors for their own purposes. The chapters describe the boys' world of the slums, including the rituals, pastimes, and dialect of their street culture.[10] The glossary of some 500 slang terms that Dapping provided for his polite readers underscores the distinctive language of street boys. It also reminds us of the most basic difficulties well-meaning philanthropists encountered in communicating with boys, who used language to identify outsiders, shield themselves from intruders, and cement their secret fraternity. *The Muckers* adds the voice and viewpoint of the "reformed" subject to the more familiar literature and scholarship on the period.

Beyond the contribution of this information, and just as important, *The Muckers* recovers the history of Dapping himself. In addition to saving his valuable manuscripts, Dapping wrote hundreds of letters to

---

9. Excellent examples of scholarship that incorporates the voices and experiences of poor and working-class girls or boys are Mary E. Odem, *Delinquent Daughters: Protecting and Policing Adolescent Female Sexuality in the United States, 1885–1920* (Chapel Hill: Univ. of North Carolina Press, 1995), and Timothy J. Gilfoyle, *A Pickpocket's Tale: The Underworld of Nineteenth-Century New York* (New York: W. W. Norton, 2006).

10. Nasaw, *Children of the City*, 24.

Osborne and his family, most of which have been preserved and allow us to plot the history of his sketches and to recover his perspective on the reform journey from the slums to respectability. That history should be recovered not because he became an important figure or because his journey upward from the slums confirms the openness of American society. It should be told because Dapping and *The Muckers* have conjoined histories. Viewed together, they help us understand what that trajectory meant to him, what was gained and what was lost in his upward mobility, and the "complex ambivalence" visible in the balancing act of claiming the authority to tell his own story without revealing that it was his story to tell.[11] An introduction to *The Muckers*, then, should begin with its inside source, the mucker himself.

In his writing on the poor, Jacob Riis was determined to puncture the self-satisfaction of the "better half" who believed they had much to offer the suffering ragamuffin children. Give the boys a vote, Riis provocatively suggested, and allow them to choose between their "old life with its drawbacks, its occasional starvation, and its everyday kicks and hard knocks" and the better life with "the good clothes, the plentiful grub, and warm bed, with all the restraints of civilized society and the 'Sunday-school racket' of the other boy thrown in." He predicted, "the street would carry the day by a practically unanimous vote."[12] Riis's astute observation is important to keep in mind in the case of Willie (as his family called him) Dapping. Poor as his family was and determined as he was to get to the Republic, it is too simplistic to say that he left them in 1896 to escape the joyless grind of poverty. Hunger, material discomfort, illness and death, hustling for money to survive, begging charity agencies and churches for help through hard times—these were not abstractions for the Dappings. Misery visited them often, and they, like most tenement families, scrambled to survive the vacillations of fat and lean times. They depended on

11. I have been influenced here by Allyson Hobbs, *A Chosen Exile: A History of Racial Passing in American Life* (Cambridge: Harvard Univ. Press, 2014), 11. Quotation from Gavin Jones, *Strange Talk: The Politics of Dialect Literature in Gilded Age America* (Berkeley: Univ. of California Press, 1999), 136.

12. Riis, *Children of the Poor*, 7–8.

Willie to support the household with whatever cash he could pull in from selling newspapers, running errands, or fetching growlers of lager for an infirm neighbor. But even with all these "drawbacks," as Riis called them, Dapping and other boys like him, once they were in the streets, enjoyed an extraordinary freedom to do as they pleased and to choose the kinds of jobs they wanted. The streets were where muckers like Dapping wanted to be—playing, making money, and, in general, happily escaping the eyes of parents and the constraints of poverty. As Spike boasted, rich folks had nothing on boys like him: "In the first place, I'm me own boss—an' that's all I want. I dont take no guff from nobody. . . . So long as I can earn me three squares a day, find some place to sleep at night, and get a heap o' fun along with it, I'm satisfied. Look at me. I aint worried about nuttin!" (Chapter 3).

Most middle-class Americans would have seen in Spike's vision of ambition, his attitude toward work, his frank pursuit of pleasure, and his understanding of self-sufficiency a neat summation of the evil the slums cultivated in children. One of the most significant inventions of the nine-teenth-century bourgeoisie was its separation of childhood from labor, which historically had been necessary to keep children fed and sheltered and to prepare them for adulthood. The Victorians enshrined a new understanding of childhood as the age of tender innocence divorced from the adult world of work. In the ideal, children were nurtured by a virtu-ous mother within the protective confines of the home and shielded from the dangerous streets and marketplace. Over the course of the nineteenth century, writes historian Steven Mintz, the middle-class belief that "every child had a right to a childhood free from labor and devoted to educa-tion" became the standard of all Americans regardless of class or eth-nicity. Reformers put the power of government behind this new "pattern of childhood" in the form of state (but not federal) laws regulating child labor practices and mandating school attendance.[13] Having and want-ing to make money did not rob Dapping and children like him of their

13. Steven Mintz, *Huck's Raft: A History of American Childhood* (Cambridge: Harvard Univ. Press, 2004), 152–53, 180–83.

childhood or turn them into tragically premature and immoral adults. As Riis argued, New York's slum children had as much fun and amusement as any child with a toy-equipped parlor or grassy park at his disposal. Looking out over the city streets, which were crowded with exuberantly active children, it could be hard to distinguish mischief-making from moneymaking, those at work from those at play. Hawking newspapers or running errands allowed them to roam the streets in and beyond their neighborhoods, to hustle "mazuma" (money) without constantly being supervised, and to slip off at will to shoot craps, smoke a "butt," or just loaf and swear with other muckers on their employer's dime. These were among the reasons why, once he had left the slums and its poverty, Dapping grew homesick at times and would "sigh for N.Y. City" and long for his family. Misery alone cannot account for his decision to leave.[14]

The first reason Willie Dapping had to work was because his father was unable to keep a paying job. The only reliable income he provided was a monthly pension of four to six dollars he collected as a disabled veteran. In the eyes of the nation he adopted as his home, the record that William (born Wilhelm in 1844) Dapping accumulated over the course of his life was marked by unsteady employment, physical disability, an unmanly reliance on charity and money earned by his wife and children, and a shameful weakness for what his son called "cursed liquor." That record composed the portrait of a near lifelong failure: a "broken" not a "self-made" man. He bore the stamp of the pauper.[15]

It is safe to say that William Dapping had higher expectations for his future when he arrived from German Westphalia in May 1864 in the midst of the American Civil War. He was twenty years old, one of 491 traveling steerage aboard a Prussian ship, and one of some 1.5 million mostly poor, German-speaking people who immigrated to America between 1840 and 1865. He was literate with some education and declared himself

14. Nasaw, *Children of the City*, 47; WOD to Thomas Mott Osborne, 21 Dec. 1897, box 38, Osborne Family Papers, Special Collections Research Center, Syracuse Univ. Libraries. Future references will use TMO for Osborne and OFP for Osborne Family Papers.

15. WOD to TMO, n.d. (30 Nov. 1901?), box 43, OFP; Scott Sandage, *Born Losers: A History of Failure in America* (Cambridge: Harvard Univ. Press, 2005), 236–37.

a "merchant" from the provincial town of Höxter.[16] Some nine months later, however, he was not in business but in the Union army, following the path of many Germans before him. Alien men who intended to be naturalized were subject to the military draft, but Germans volunteered more enthusiastically than any other immigrant population, in part because of their unionist and even antislavery sentiments and their conviction that as soldiers they would earn a place of respect in their new country. The army also meant regular pay, perhaps a more decisive incentive for young immigrant men like Dapping, newly ashore with few English language or marketable skills. When he enlisted, he could not have known the war would last only another two months and that he would be confined for its duration to a regiment stationed in New York Harbor. Dapping never saw combat or rose above the rank of private in his three years of service, most of it in postwar South Carolina. He effectively missed out on the battlefield experience that a generation of white men, north and south, held up as the full measure of their manhood. Perhaps feeling that inadequacy, he invented a heroic past, later telling his son that he fought and was wounded in the war. He even gave him the pistol used to shoot him.[17]

Dapping was wounded, and badly, but in 1871, long after Appomattox. Months after his first discharge in 1868, he reenlisted with his old regiment and soon was promoted to quartermaster sergeant in charge of his company's supplies. In June 1871, while stationed in the western Indian Territory, Dapping found himself and a fellow soldier courting the same woman. His rival shot him and the bullet struck his right arm,

16. For information on Dapping's immigration, see ship's manifest for the *Hansa*, 1864, New York, *Passenger Lists of Vessels Arriving at New York, New York, 1820–1897*, mic. ser. M237, 1820–1897, roll 240, line 42, list no. 363, digital image, Ancestry.com, accessed 7 Mar. 2016, http://interactive.ancestrylibrary.com. On his education, see Affidavit of William Ewald, 26 Aug. 1902, in William Dapping, Federal Military Pension Application—Civil War and Later Complete File, National Archives and Records Administration (hereafter cited as NARA).

17. Stephen D. Engle, "Yankee Dutchmen: Germans, the Union, and the Construction of a Wartime Identity," in *Civil War Citizens: Race, Ethnicity, and Identity in America's Bloodiest Conflict*, ed. Susannah J. Ural (New York: New York Univ. Press, 2010), 16–17, 24–27, 31; David W. Blight, *Race and Reunion: The Civil War in American Memory* (Cambridge: Harvard Univ. Press, 2001), 84–97; WOD to TMO, 29 July 1901, box 45, OFP.

smashing the humerus. No one thought Dapping at fault, and he appeared to recover, but the bullet remained in his arm for the rest of his life. A year after his honorable discharge, Dapping applied for an "Invalid Pension," explaining that his injured arm was mostly useless. At this point, he was employed "Keeping [a] Lager Beer Saloon" on the Lower East Side. Native-born Americans had a nativist expression for Germans—"Damned Dutch"—that was shorthand for the beer-loving, clumsy, and lazy foreigner. The awkward circumstances of Dapping's wound and his postwar employment matched the stereotype, which may explain the difficulty he had convincing the commissioner of pensions that his claim was worthy. It took another ten years before officials relented with a half-pension of four dollars per month.[18] In 1895 the monthly allowance rose to six dollars. Dapping appealed for a full pension in 1899 because the "stiffness of [his] right arm . . . prevents him from doing any kind of work." A young physician examined him and found nothing unusual; the request was denied. He died a little more than two years later.[19]

The pension doctor who examined Dapping likely regarded his application as a telltale sign of pauperism. Most Americans in the nineteenth century believed there were two kinds of poor people: the honest poor who could not help their condition, and the dishonest poor who could. The first kind—the blind, widows, orphans, blameless victims of incapacitating calamity—needed and deserved assistance. The other kind was the able-bodied poor, or paupers, whose need existed only because of their laziness or "vicious habits." By the end of the nineteenth century,

18. Statement of US Army surgeon S. D. Cowdrey, in W. B. Hazen to Adjutant General, US Army, 14 June 1873; service record of Charles Backer/William Dapping, War Department, Adjutant General's Office, 26 Feb. 1902; discharge record, William Dapping, 5 Nov. 1871; D. Mortimer Lee to W. B. Hazen, 28 May 1873; Hazen to Adjutant General; William Dapping to Generals Office, Washington, DC, regarding pension claim no. 176,910, 20 May 1883; declaration for an invalid pension, 1 July 1872, all NARA. On stereotype, see Engle, "Yankee Dutchmen," 27.

19. William H. Glasson, *Federal Military Pensions in the United States* (New York: Oxford Univ. Press, 1918), 135–36; original invalid pension, 1, 12, and 19 June 1882; declaration for increase of an invalid pension, 19 May 1899; surgeon's certificate in the case of William Dapping, applicant for increase, no. 212,069, 23 Oct. 1899, all US Pension Office, NARA.

charitable relief organizations in the United States had reached the consensus that pauperism was a growing and corrosive social problem. In New York and other cities, charities began cooperating with each other and "scientifically" organizing their programs, exchanging information on the people they served and using in-home investigators to ensure that loafers and "professional" indigents were not abusing the system. In the charity organizers' view, helping those who did not need help did far greater harm than unmet poverty because it encouraged people to live off "handouts" when they were fully capable of supporting themselves. The rich, with their tenderhearted but undiscriminating charity, were as much to blame as the wicked poor; both contributed to an advancing social plague of idleness, improvidence, and dependency among able-bodied poor people. Charity workers and pension doctors were on the alert for men like Dapping, who, in their minds, had been unmanned from years of living off "handouts."[20]

What was worse, six children lived in the Dapping household before Willie left for the Republic. The modernizers of social welfare in the Progressive Era were less judgmental than earlier generations of charity workers in blaming poor people for their problems; they recognized that severe economic depressions and technological innovations caused unemployment and poverty far more often than individual moral failings. The new generation of philanthropists and social reformers reoriented their focus away from helping the poor in general and toward saving children as the better way to attack poverty and its associated problems at the roots. To achieve their goals, "child-savers" sought and achieved an enhanced interventionist role for state and private agencies in regulating or promoting an array of economic and social practices that affected the welfare of children. They embraced new scientific theories of child psychology and promoted health and sanitation practices that reflected the growing influence of the medical and scientific professions. In general, their strategies emphasized prevention and sought to keep children

20. Michael B. Katz, *In the Shadow of the Poorhouse: A Social History of Welfare in America*, 10th ann. ed. (New York: Basic, 1996), 17–19, 75–86.

in a family environment instead of institutionalizing them. Even with greater acceptance of environmental causes of poverty, charity agents maintained their focus on the problem of the able-bodied poor and pauperism. They presumed that unfortunate children absorbed the indolent habits of a malingering father, spreading the contagion of pauperism into the next generation and magnifying its effects. By this standard, the Dappings were practically an incubator of social disorder: the social damage of pauperism potentially multiplied by the six children in the household. The family found themselves in the crosshairs of the heightened focus on child welfare and the continued concern about pauperism. The "family has long been known to" us, an official with the New York Association for Improving the Condition of the Poor wrote in 1903. Records at the Junior Republic reported that the Dappings belong to "the improvident class" who are "constantly endeavoring to live upon charity."[21]

The surviving evidence suggests that life was not always this way for Mathilda Lauterbach Dapping and that she married William in April 1875 with reason for optimism. She was born in West Point, New York, in 1854, her German-born father a musician in a military band linked to the life of the academy. By 1870 the Lauterbachs were living in New York City's *Kleindeutschland*, or Little Germany, on the Lower East Side. Little Germany was the third largest concentration of German-speaking people in the world, and its flourishing popular culture of beer halls and gardens, theaters, and festivals necessitated bands and orchestras for concerts and dancing, which meant plentiful work opportunities for musicians. The family was hardly middle class (the daughters and mother all had to work), but the musician Justus probably was able to maintain them in

21. Katz, *In the Shadow of the Poorhouse*, 109–50; Walter I. Trattner, *From Poor Law to Welfare State: A History of Social Welfare in America*, 6th ed. (New York: Free Press, 1999), 100–103; M. Fullerton to Ware, Commissioner of Pensions, New York Association for Improving the Condition of the Poor, 10 Jan. 1903, NARA; on the "improvident" Dappings, see "H. (W. Dapping)," in "Student histories 1898–1900," box 263, OFP. Michael Katz observes (p. 19), "it is only a slight exaggeration to say that the core of most welfare reform in America since the early nineteenth century has been a war on the able-bodied poor: an attempt to define, locate, and purge them from the roles of relief."

respectable, modest circumstances in the Seventeenth Ward. That part of Little Germany had newer brick and stone tenements several cuts above those in the older, overpopulated areas to the east and south, where poor and unskilled laborers predominated. In 1870 the Lauterbachs dwelled among families headed mostly by skilled artisans and tradesmen, often German-born. They were poor, but it is easy to imagine they regarded themselves as people of cultivation.[22] The patriarch, surveying Dapping's prospects in 1875—educated, a fellow soldier whose rank as quarter-master sergeant augured a future with a bookkeeper's clean collar—may have been able to see past the arm the younger man avoided using.

William and Mathilda Dapping lived for most of the next eighteen years at different addresses on East Sixth Street, never far from the Lauter-bachs. The narrow range of their mobility appears a sign of stable poverty. The four-dollar monthly pension probably covered few of their expenses. The first child arrived nine months after the wedding, and nine or more births followed, each one exacting the immediate cost of a midwife and the enduring expense of another mouth at the table. At least four of their children died, burdening the family with sorrow as well as medical and burial expenses. Willie was born in 1880, and the last surviving child, Robert, in 1893. Although a decade younger than her chronically under-employed husband, Mathilda turned thirty-nine that year and could not have welcomed that birth with unqualified joy. Within a year the family

22. Date of birth 19 Mar. 1854, New Jersey State Department of Health, Medical Certificate of Death for Matilda [sic] Dapping, 23 July 1935, NARA. The family surname can be found under two spellings: Lauderbach and Lauterbach. Under Lauderbach, for his activity at West Point, see *Returns from U.S. Military Posts, 1800–1916*; mic. ser. M617, roll 1413, digital image, Ancestry.com, accessed 6 Mar. 2016, http://interactive.ancestrylibrary.com. According to 1870 census data, Matilda was a "flower maker"; 1880 census: wife Maria "tending a grocery store" and daughter Justine "works at factory." See Ninth Census of the United States, New York State, New York County, 19th Electoral District of 17th Ward, 27 Dec. 1870, pp. 47–48, digital images, and Tenth Census of the United States, New York State, New York County, Sup. Dist. No. 1, Enum. Dist. No. 262, p. 31, digital image, all Ancestry.com, accessed 7 Jan. 2016, http://interactive.ancestrylibrary.com. On *Kleindeutschland*, see Stanley Nadel, *Little Germany: Ethnicity, Religion, and Class in New York City, 1845–80* (Urbana: Univ. of Illinois Press, 1990), 105–8.

followed many other poor Germans who were moving far uptown to Yorkville in part to get away from the Eastern European Jews moving into
Little Germany, but also to find newer and less expensive housing.[23]

Today Yorkville is home to an affluent and cosmopolitan population,
demarcated roughly on the south and north by streets numbered in the
seventies and nineties, Third Avenue on the west and the East River on the
east. At the time of the Civil War the city's edge of intense development
halted more than a mile to the south, and Yorkville was a rural village of
modest houses. In the 1870s, the city ingested the village whole. The arrival
of large-scale manufacturing and later the extension of elevated railroads
on Third and Second Avenues drew poor and working-class Irish, German, Jewish, and other immigrants from abroad and other parts of the
city. Although less infamous than the Lower East Side, Yorkville from
the 1880s on was a center of the city's immigrant working-class life. The
future Yankee baseball great Lou Gehrig (born Heinrich Ludwig Gehrig)
lived with his German immigrant parents on Ninety-Fourth Street. The
extended Jewish clan of the Marx brothers was on Ninety-Third Street,
"poor, very poor" and "always hungry." The Dappings started out in a
practically new five-story tenement on Eighty-Ninth Street.[24]

---

23. Dapping's residential address and clerical occupation are listed in the annual editions of *Trow's New York City Directory* (New York: Trow's Directory, Printing, and Book-
binding Co.). See, for instance, *Directory for the Year Ending May 1, 1886*, p. 420; on the move
to Yorkville, *Directory for the Year Ending July 1, 1894*, p. 307, digital images, Ancestry.com,
accessed 5 Jan. 2016, http://interactive.ancestrylibrary.com. The Dappings' surviving children and their birthdates appear in Department of the Interior, Bureau of Pensions, ques-
tionnaire, 4 May 1898, NARA. Two Dapping girls, one three years old and the other three
months, died in 1878 and 1879. See records of Matilda L. and Mary E. Dapping (interment
nos. 192284 and 196746), compiled by Green-Wood Cemetery (Brooklyn) Genealogy Team,
April 2016, in author's possession. WOD mentions the deaths of his "little brothers" in a letter to TMO, 1 Mar. 1903, box 50, OFP. On Yorkville, see Nadel, *Little Germany*, 161–62.

24. Kenneth T. Jackson, ed., "Yorkville," in *Encyclopedia of the City of New York* (New
Haven: Yale Univ. Press, 2010), 1428; Larry R. Gerlach, "German Americans in Major League
Baseball: Sport and Acculturation," in *The American Game: Baseball and Ethnicity*, eds. Lawrence Baldassaro and Richard A. Johnson (Carbondale: Southern Illinois Univ. Press, 2002),
44; Harpo Marx with Rowland Barber, *Harpo Speaks!* (New York: Limelight Editions, 1985,

The new residences in Yorkville were considered "better-class," but the change in address may not have signaled upward mobility for the Dappings. The 1880s wave of new German immigrants and older generations of immigrants and their American-born children from the Lower East Side composed the clientele for this new housing. In 1899, when the physician judged the pensioner fit to work, the Dappings lived among families headed by employed and unemployed cigar makers, carpenters, stonecutters, livery drivers, brass polishers—a step lower on the working-class scale, perhaps, from earlier days in the Sixth Street neighborhood of Little Germany. Dapping told a census taker in 1900 that he was a book-keeper and had not worked in a year and that his wife and two older daughters sewed to make money. His annual pension income of $72 was a fraction of the $591 that American men made on average in 1900. Supplemented by the earnings of Mathilda and the two older daughters, the family was able to keep the same address for several years, but their stability was fragile. A calamity could instantly render them destitute, as it did in late 1900, when the oldest daughter's attack of acute appendicitis reduced them to begging a church mission society for help.[25]

Under circumstances like those, charity workers looking through the lens of pauperism were liable to see trouble in the making in the older, self-confident, and evidently intelligent son Willie. The fact that William R. George recruited him to the Junior Republic indicates as much.

1961), 19. For Eighty-Ninth Street residence, compare the insurance maps from 1891 and 1896 in "Outline and Index Map of New York City, Manhattan Island," plate 31, and "Insurance Maps of the City of New York. Surveyed and Published by Sanborn-Perris Map Co., Limited, 115 Broadway, 1896. Volume 8," plate 162, digital images, New York Public Library Digital Collections, accessed 15 Apr. 2016, http://digitalcollections.nypl.org.

25. Nadel, *Little Germany*, 161–62; M. Fullerton to Ware, 10 Jan. 1903, NARA; information on Dapping neighborhood from Twelfth Census of the United States, New York State, New York County, Borough of Manhattan, Sup. Dist. No. 1, Enum. Dist. No. 830, 7 June 1900, sheets 11A, 11B, 12A, digital images, Ancestry.com, accessed 7 Jan. 2016, http://interactive.ancestrylibrary.com. On income, see Mario Maffi, *Gateway to the Promised Land: Ethnic Cultures on New York's Lower East Side* (New York: New York Univ. Press, 1995), 180n6. On illness, see WOD to TMO, 21 Oct. and 10 Nov. 1900, box 43, and ca. 30 Dec. 1900, box 40, all OFP.

George boasted that his program, alone among those targeting slum children, wanted not the best, but the city's worst boys. The "types" the Republic sought, a contemporary explained, were "the street idler, the leader of the 'gang,' the bully who is the terror of his neighborhood, the boy who is unmanageable at home." Although Dapping detested the "bad boy's Republic" reputation of George's program, *The Muckers* leaves little doubt that in 1895–96 he matched a less sensationalized version of that description. (Osborne claimed Dapping "was just beginning a fine criminal career in the City before he came to Freeville" and was lucky to have avoided jail.) Dapping was under no illusions about his family's mean existence or his father's condition, but his embrace of the "mucker" label indicates his resistance to an identity wholly determined by his poverty or the way "outsiders" judged the family's failures.[26]

The Upper East Side neighborhood of Yorkville where Dapping and the Crapshooters "hung out" was one of the city's fastest growing areas with a booming residential market. Ehret's massive Hell Gate Brewery and its rival Ruppert occupied three city blocks on Second and Third Avenues and produced the "kags o' booze" or "buck-beer" that lubricated the city's social and political operations. On the riverbank to the east were busy commercial docks and the big Heucken & Willenbrock lumberyard at the end of Ninety-Third Street. Newly built tenement houses filled in the spaces between these structures.

The official green space nearest Dapping's tenement was almost a mile to the east in Central Park. The muckers' play spaces were the streets; their hideaways were in the city's neglected gaps and cavities, like the "damp, dark and dirty" cellar the Crapshooters made their clubhouse (Chapter 3). As middle-class observers witnessed children playing in the grimy streets, darting in and out of traffic, fighting and roughhousing, they pitied them

26. William Reuben George, *The Junior Republic, Its History and Ideals* (New York: Appleton, 1910), 10; Walter Shepard Ufford, *Fresh Air Charity in the United States* (New York: Bonnell, Silver & Co., 1897), 59; on "bad boys," see William R. George and Lyman Beecher Stowe, *Citizens Made and Remade: An Interpretation of the Significance and Influence of George Junior Republics* (Boston: Houghton Mifflin, 1912), 65–90. On WOD before the Republic, see "H. (W. Dapping)," OFP.

3. William O. Dapping's photograph of the Heucken & Willenbrock lumberyard on the East River in Yorkville, where the muckers "dove from the highest lumber piles" into the river. William R. George House Library, William George Agency.

their lot—deprived of the childhood right to nature and, as the playground advocate Joseph Lee said, "to explore, to dig in the ground for treasures, to climb a tree and discover a new world." The Crapshooters eagerly played the part of the pitiable gamin; they boasted they could melt the heart of a charitable "Sund'y school dame" and win a free vacation in the country just by whining they were "a club o' hard workin' boys what had never seen no country an' that we was all in poor healt'" (Chapter 14).[27]

Poor as they were, and capable as muckers were in exploiting the sympathetic prejudices of the privileged, Dapping and his friends were not denied a childhood by a blighted urban environment (as he makes clear in

27. Lee quoted in Jack M. Holl, *Juvenile Reform in the Progressive Era* (Ithaca: Cornell Univ. Press, 1971), 77.

his letters and *The Muckers* narrative). Children piled out of the tenements and onto the sidewalks and streets to play, girls mostly on the stoops and boys in the street. Boys playing baseball or other games in the street were subject to arrest, which made vacant lots the most coveted, if officially forbidden, spaces. Only a scattering of lots (each 25 feet wide and 100 feet deep) remained on the narrow cross streets by Dapping's day. Lots were private property and trespassing was prohibited, but wooden fences were easily scaled and a lookout stationed to watch for the neighborhood cop. An empty lot, Spike explains, was a mucker's paradise "full o' rocks, tin cans, contractors tool boxes and abandoned dump wagons still left to play in" (Chapter 8). Nominally cleared of refuse, they became rough baseball diamonds, battlefields for turf wars with rival gangs, and arsenals of debris to hurl at enemies. Dapping's good fortune was to live one tenement down from six contiguous vacant lots, which created 150 feet of uninterrupted space on Eighty-Ninth Street. This open territory in all likelihood was the "peachy lot, with a high board fence" described in *The Muckers*, where the Crapshooters "useter to run like we owned it" (Chapter 8). In his sketches (Chapter 12) Dapping also writes of fishing from the busy commercial docks in the filthy East River, soothed by the sound of swearing longshoremen—an urban inversion of the pastoral the author likely intended to rattle reformer sensibilities.[28]

Few other scraps of information about Dapping's youth in Yorkville have survived in the archival record. He wrote of attending school at P.S. 77 several blocks from his home, but as yet there is no evidence he went beyond the age of fourteen, which was the state-mandated minimum. His family was Protestant, probably Lutheran, in a neighborhood with many Catholic Germans.[29] Neither church nor formal education figured importantly in his Yorkville life, or in *The Muckers*. Spike's comment on religion

28. On the Eighty-Ninth Street lots, see 1896 "Insurance Maps of the City of New York," plate 162; on street play and its illegality, see Nasaw, *Children of the City*, 22–28.

29. On his school, see WOD to TMO, 21 Sept. 1899, box 40, OFP; on New York laws, see Thomas E. Finegan, *A Textbook on New York School Law* (Albany: Matthew Bender, 1918), 184. Dapping's father was buried in the city's Lutheran cemetery: New York State Certificate and Record of Death, William Dapping, Nov. 1901, NARA.

explains his view and, in all likelihood, how he met George at Sunday school: "We went to church when we felt like it an' that was on'y when they was somethink doin', like a strawb'rry festival or a magic lantern show" (Chapter 21). There were more things doing outside of school and church walls.

Dapping found ways to make money to assist his strapped family, but also to buy his share of the pleasures the city offered. For city boys of Dapping's day, writes historian David Nasaw, there usually "was more than enough work to go around" for those willing to hustle. Dapping likely started out a "junker," or scavenger, plundering the neighborhood for anything that could be sold, in Spike's words, "to the junk peddlar fer a dollar" (Chapter 10). Dapping's letters allude to selling newspapers, the most prevalent type of boy labor in the city. The "newsies" who hawked the dailies' afternoon editions in congested downtown areas had to be tough, savvy, and pushy to mark their turf, fend off competitors, and wile customers for sales and tips—all tough-boy skills that Dapping possessed. He also worked as an errand boy, including, for a time, at the downtown establishment of "Johny" Miles, the millinery wholesaler. Miles was a penniless Irish orphan who became one of the city's most visible hustlers. He made his fortune, as his sales motto stated, by "pushing to the front," and he spiced his monologues on life and business with snappy sales jargon: crackerjack, grit, ginger, pluck, and persistence. Miles was legendary for glad-handing salesmen with cheap ten-cent cigars, which Dapping recalled purchasing for him. If a boy wants "to dynamite [himself] a rung higher" in life, Miles opined, he must be "on deck at all times . . . always look cheerful . . . put on the elastic step and get a two-minute gait on . . . like a young colt."[30] The milliner surely shared this wisdom with Dapping, who must have struck him as his kind of coltish hustler.

30. Nasaw, *Children of the City*, 88–100, quotation on 88; Mintz, *Huck's Raft*, 142, 207; WOD to TMO, 5 Dec. 1899, box 40, OFP; quotation from "'Johny' Miles, Merchant Who Began with $50, to Retire," *New York Times*, 20 July 1913; on WOD working for Miles, see letter to TMO, 23 Feb. 1904, box 53, OFP; on cigar prices, see "High-Priced Cigars," *New York Sun*, 22 Sept. 1883. John Miles's motto appears on his Wholesale Millinery Goods company envelope, ca. 1906, in author's possession.

Getting hired by the amiably self-important Miles shows how certain kinds of men were attracted to Dapping. The boy likewise was drawn to this kind of man—aggressive, forceful, charismatic, evangelical in their devotion to the gospel of hard work, and in no way like his weak and incapacitated father.

The "child-saver" William R. George was an even higher expression of the vigorous manhood that pushed to the front. Dapping met George in June 1895 at a Sunday-school class at the Methodist Episcopal Church of the Savior on East 109th Street. "He was tall and athletic in physique," Dapping recalled in a school essay. "He was frank, vigorous, a disciplinarian, keen to remove embarrassment, and sympathetic—indeed one longed to confide in him." The firmness of George's handshake left the boy's fingers tingling. The date they met, Dapping wrote, should be "printed in heavy type" in his biography.[31] Within days of their introduction, Dapping's life assumed a markedly different course.

An examination of George's influence helps us understand not only the stories in *The Muckers* but also how Dapping achieved the distance and the impetus to write a book that both honored and talked back to child-savers. George was born in 1866 on his family's farm in West Dryden in upstate Tompkins County, only miles from where he founded the Freeville Republic. The Georges maintained a modest, respectable, and intensely Methodist household. Their only child's life was mostly carefree and work-free until 1880, when his father, weary of farming, moved them to New York City. George, already a dreamy loner, made few friends. He spent his idle hours reading and making up stories, or wandering the city's poorest neighborhoods trying to befriend the slum boys, studying "the social conditions of the great city." When he grew older and with his father's help, he made a stab at business, manufacturing jewelry cases and other specialized boxes, but his real interests were less commercial and had rougher edges: the male fraternity of the militia that he joined, bouts of boxing, and the companionship of tough slum boys. In 1888 George was swept up in an evangelical revival among

31. WOD, "The George Junior Republic."

4. William R. "Daddy" George, founder of the George Junior Republic, ca. 1900. William R. George Family Papers, no. 800. Division of Rare and Manuscript Collections, Cornell University Library.

Methodists, and two years later he declared his "life henceforth for the salvation of children in the slums of the city of N.Y." He did not share the doctrinal priorities of the city's established missionary societies, which also favored children who already were good. George preferred a more roughhouse form of ministry with slum boys, especially the much-feared members of street gangs. In 1877 the *New York Tribune* newspaper began sponsoring "Fresh Air" charities that took urban children into the countryside for weeks at a time to liberate them from the foul and unnatural conditions of the city. In 1890 George secured funding and organized his first group of Fresh Air children, but he unnerved his fellow philanthropists when he stocked his ranks with "the particularly 'tough' sort" of city boys. When the camp season ended, George spent the rest of the year neglecting his business interests as much as possible to "chum" with "tough specimens" like the Duffyville Gang in Harlem and the Graveyard Gang on the Lower East Side, endeavoring to turn them to "the path of good citizenship."[32]

George's attraction to gangs indicates that, in actuality, he was less a child-saver than a boy-saver. Like other students of childhood, George believed the gang in itself was not evil; a gang, as Dapping explained in his *Muckers* introduction, manifested boys' "natural impulse to associate with each other." The era's leading scientific authority on such ideas was G. Stanley Hall. The pioneering psychologist posited that the different stages of an individual's maturation from infancy to adulthood "recapitulated" the successive stages in the evolution of human societies. From individualistic, primitive, and savage beginnings (childhood), the human individual progressed to a period of tribal communalism (adolescence) and then to the highest stage of an advanced and integrated urban-industrial civilization (adulthood). In the final stage the tensions between primitive, selfish individualism and tribal, communal domination of the individual were resolved in effectively socialized persons. Adolescent boys, according to Hall's theories, belonged to the less advanced middle stage of tribalism, a natural educational period of boisterous play and gang association. To try to destroy the gangs, according to this theory, would do far more harm than good. Whether in legitimate or illegitimate gangs, boys developed and expressed admirable and desirable qualities—esprit de corps,

32. William R. George, 1889 memo book, box 61, William R. George Family Papers, 1750–1989, no. 800, Division of Rare Books and Manuscript Collections, Cornell Univ. Library (hereafter cited as WRGFP); Holl, *Juvenile Reform*, 77–81; George, *The Junior Republic*, 8; William R. George, "Daddy's Book," 25, 30–35, 52, ca. 1929, box 56, WRGFP. The best scholarship on George are Holl, *Juvenile Reform*, and Kevin P. Murphy, *Political Manhood: Red Bloods, Mollycoddles, and the Politics of Progressive Era Reform* (New York: Columbia Univ. Press, 2010), 125–44.

steadfast loyalty and friendship, a willingness to sacrifice oneself for the group, a nascent sense of natural justice—that a civilized society sacrificed at its peril. In his article "What to Do with a Boy," the journalist Lyman Beecher Stowe explained: "it all comes in the last analysis to putting a boy in a gang, turning 'the gang' toward helpful purposes, and making use of the boys' loyalty to keep them straight."[33]

But George's focus on gangs was more than theoretical. He sought to win their approval through feats of masculine aggressiveness, like boxing, as a way to gain admission to their street fraternity. Once among them he reveled in their rough, intimate camaraderie and friendship. Scholars like Kevin Murphy have shown that opponents of social and political reform routinely attacked reformers as sentimental and weak, and in the case of male reformers, more like women than real men. George and his allies were especially sensitive to charges that the Republic's methods and goals were sentimental and utopian—that the children were playing games. They struck back by asserting the realism and scientific rigor of the Republic. Reformers also fended off charges against their virility by seeking and gaining the approval and fellowship of hobos, tramps, criminals, and boy gangsters. George was not a child of privilege, but he labored to integrate his reform work and his image with activities and relationships that appeared unambiguously masculine: military training, outdoor work, rough team and individual sports, and acceptance by the city's most feared gangs of boys. But George also desired the warm and intimate friendship of boys and he used the power of his personality to draw boys closely to him across the barrier of class and ethnicity; at the Republic, he wanted all citizens to call him "Daddy."[34]

Dapping met George at an opportune moment. By 1895 his work with gangs and the summertime Fresh Air camps had earned him a reputation as one of New York City's most committed child-savers, but George also felt the five years of experimenting with Fresh Air camps, Sunday schools,

33. On Hall see Howard Chudacoff, *How Old Are You? Age Consciousness in American Culture* (Princeton: Princeton Univ. Press, 1989), 66–68; Lyman Beecher Stowe, "What to Do with a Boy," *World's Work* 26 (June 1913): 195.

34. Murphy, *Political Manhood*, 1–37, 128, 133.

and organized activities for slum boys had failed truly to convert them to the bedrock values of individual responsibility, independence, thrift, respect for law, and patriotic devotion to America's forms of government. In a matter of days, he told Dapping, he was launching a daring new enterprise, a Junior Republic, based on uncompromising adherence to two principles: that children learn how to be citizens by governing themselves under laws they themselves create, and that they learn the value of honest labor by receiving nothing—no food, room, or clothing—without first working for it. George designed his *junior* republic to simulate the larger republic, only without the institutions and practices that had corrupted the nation's social, political, and economic order. At its core, George's program—in method and principle—was as innovative and even radical for its time as it was old-fashioned and conservative. "The plan at once set me to bubbling with anticipation," Dapping recalled. When the first Fresh Air campers under the new Junior Republic system boarded the train for Freeville on July 9, Dapping was among them.[35]

Over the course of its first decade, the child inmates, who were called "citizens," usually were twelve to sixteen years old upon entry. They arrived in mostly extrajudicial ways. Separate juvenile systems of justice for youths under the age of eighteen were only just developing in the United States. Most young offenders passed through the judicial processes for adult offenders. Although the Republic was subject to state regulation, it was privately funded and had no formal relation to the state system. Courts assigned approximately a third of the Republic's population. More often, private welfare agencies in New York City (and later other cities) referred children there, or relatives or guardians of unruly children who heard George speak or read about the Republic in newspapers and magazines appealed to have their child taken in. Not all were poor. Some children from middle-class families entered the Republic, and George

35. Holl, *Juvenile Justice*, 43; Rebecca M. McLennan, *The Crisis of Imprisonment: Protest, Politics, and the Making of the American Penal State, 1776–1941* (Cambridge: Cambridge Univ. Press, 2008), 330–31; WOD, "The George Junior Republic."

boasted that rich boys needed its discipline, too. Many citizens were like Dapping, handpicked by George or Osborne because of their attractive rough edges. In its early years the Republic had one young citizen who had committed murder, and many others who had done nothing worse than been unruly. By whatever route its citizens got there, the Republic soon was in demand. Osborne wrote to George in 1904 that requests were coming from "Parents & guardians—Judges & Pastors all clamoring for admittance to the G. J. R."[36]

The Republic's population included both sexes, but in reality the program was for boys, admitting girls to perform the domestic labor suited to their sex and to keep the male citizenry from channeling their "natural" sexual desires in "unnatural," or homosexual, directions. George had little and Osborne absolutely no interest in reforming "bad" girls. An all-male Republic, George insisted, "can never expect to reach such high standards of mental, physical, and moral perfection as those which have girls as citizens, any more than a town composed solely of cowboys and miners or a military camp of soldiers can be an ideal community."[37]

More conventional was the socioeconomic structure, which hearkened back to an imagined preindustrial past when men were free to rise or fall and knew their survival depended on themselves alone. George sympathized with poor people, but also claimed to see pauperism's insidious effects on the camp children, who abided by rules only so they could load up with free secondhand clothing and sacks of potatoes at the end of their country sojourns. Under the Republic's slogan "nothing without labor," George instituted a primitive economy with its own tin currency; children who arrived with American coin in their pockets were as good as penniless and had to auction off the contents of their suitcases even to

36. LeRoy Ashby, *Endangered Children: Dependency, Neglect, and Abuse in American History* (New York: Twayne, 1997), 81–84; Holl, *Juvenile Reform*, 9. For the profiles of Republic boys, see photo album, ca. 1898, box 133; for the boy murderer, see "No. 28"; TMO to William R. George, 31 May 1904, box 4, all WRGFP.

37. Murphy, *Political Manhood*, 142–44, quotation on 143. For TMO's position on girl citizens, see TMO to D. F. Lincoln, 24 Dec. 1901, box 215, OFP.

eat. Anything beyond that—including shelter against upstate New York's brutal winters—they had to work for.[38]

George's decision to teach the children self-discipline and self-respect by permitting them to govern themselves was more innovative. George turned to self-government models when he saw that maintaining order through violent force—the method common at more traditional reformatories—was working against him. The alternative he devised effectively shifted responsibility for preserving order from a single sovereign power (himself) to the collective will of the "governed," the children, who then owned an interest in the protection of their safety and property. The Republic's constitution was written by the boys (girls initially could not vote), who ran and held offices, legislated by town meeting, held court and tried criminal defendants, and maintained their own police force and jail. Making them their own governors was designed to transform the boys and, eventually, the girls into conservative defenders of the status quo who sided with law and order and identified with the victims of crime rather than its perpetrators.[39]

Dapping argues for the effectiveness of the Republic's dual dimensions in the letters Mickey writes to the Crapshooters after getting "pinched" by the cops and sent there by a judge (Chapters 15, 17, 19, and 24). Mickey's conversion, after a series of ups and downs frequently related to smoking "butts," demonstrates how the Republic was supposed to work. The wise-cracking prankster and chief philosopher of how to make the most of a job without actually working (Chapter 6) appalls his mates when he reports that he was a new man: "a willin' to obey the law, a willin' to quit smokin', a willin' fer to be a cop! An' worse yet, he was willin' to work!" The Crapshooters regard such actions as traitorous.

Mickey's new loyalty to himself and the Republic, instead of the Crapshooters, may sound too good to be true, but Dapping would have pointed to himself and some of his friends as evidence that it did work. Regardless,

---

38. George, *The Junior Republic*, 15–16; for George's explanation of how he arrived at the design of the Republic's economy, see 56–62.

39. Murphy, *Political Manhood*, 138–40.

the Republic's sociopolitical and economic order made it unlike any other solution to "the problem of the slum" in its day. It departed from the authoritarian "spare the rod" discipline that was common in juvenile institutions of the time, and it allowed the citizens to set the punishments, which sometimes were harsh and violent. It enlisted children's participation in their education as they learned cooperative, democratic principles by experience in a community setting, a methodology akin to Progressive innovations in formal education at the time. As conventional as it was, "nothing without labor" was highly unusual in shifting control of the economic order to the Republic's inmates and encouraging them openly to accumulate wealth and power. Self-government did much the same with political power. The children, of course, were not totally in control in either realm; ultimate authority rested with George, who was the legal custodian of its citizens, and the Republic's other administrative authorities. The Republic had no walls to confine the children, and it compelled no one to work. That said, it hunted down those who escaped its boundaries, and it jailed vagrants and sentenced them to hard labor and thin rations. Its techniques were coercive and its goals were in line with what middle-class Americans valued, but compared with other Progressive Era juvenile programs, the Republic's transfer of significant power to the children was radical for its day.[40]

From the outside looking in, Dapping's career at the Republic, more than Mickey's, validated the effectiveness of its methods and the social contribution of its results. When George began the Republic experiment in 1895, he tried to continue the Fresh Air camps, which served hundreds of children each summer, while simultaneously instituting a small year-round program. During the first summer, rivalries between Fresh Air and year-round citizens over power and leadership proved insurmountable; the last Fresh Air session was in 1897. Dapping attended the summer camps under the new principles in 1895 and 1896 and joined as a year-round citizen (the Republic's twenty-fourth) in September 1896. From the

---

40. Holl, *Juvenile Reform*, 173; Robert B. Westbrook, *John Dewey and American Democracy* (Ithaca: Cornell Univ. Press, 1991), 93–111; McLennan, *Crisis of Imprisonment*, 330–31. Sexual crimes (attempted sodomy or masturbation) were harshly punished: see Glen Wilson to TMO, 7 May 1899, box 39, and WOD to TMO, 27 May 1899, box 37, OFP.

moment Dapping landed in Freeville, George recalled, he "was instantly engrossed in everything that pertained to the business and political life of the little colony." By the time he left two years later, he had served as the elected judge of its courts and president, started its newspaper (*The Citizen*), overseen its library, and played on its sports teams. He and other leading citizens traveled throughout New England and New York to donor events, where they appeared with George or Osborne to represent the marvelous transformations the Republic worked in boys like them. "Looking back over the years," wrote George, "I say unhesitatingly that Dapping was one of the most useful citizens we ever had in the Republic."[41]

In actuality, though, Dapping and George were at odds during most of his tenure at the Republic. Most frequently they sparred over the extent of the citizens' control over the Republic; Dapping pushed further than George was willing to go to make the Republic "republicy"—the citizens' term for government absolutely "of the youth, for the youth, and by the youth." Dapping "cherished the principles of self-government literally and he observed me like a watch dog," recalled George. The struggle for power was complicated further when Thomas M. Osborne was recruited in late 1896 to help the organization through a critical period of harsh publicity and near financial ruin. Osborne became chair the next year of a new and enhanced board of directors to whom George now had to defer. In the meantime he developed an attachment to George's young antagonist. By February 1897 Osborne and Dapping were exchanging letters and in May he invited the boy to spend the weekend with his family to discuss his entering Harvard.[42]

Dapping was smart enough to sense that George, even with his charisma, was no match for the patrician, wealthy, and cosmopolitan Osborne. Born in 1859 Osborne grew up in Auburn, a small city west of Syracuse and about thirty miles north of Freeville. His father, David M. Osborne, built a

---

41. Holl, *Juvenile Reform*, 115–19; "William O. Dapping," *The Citizen*, July 1915, 61–62; George, *The Junior Republic*, 68; George, "Daddy's Book," 178–79; on Dapping's enrollment, see "H. (W. Dapping)," and ledger "List of G.J.R. Citizens," p. 2, box 71, WRGFP.

42. George, "Daddy's Book," 179; Holl, *Juvenile Reform*, 126–28; TMO to WOD, 24 Feb. 1897, box 210; WOD to TMO, 31 May 1897, box 37, OFP.

5. Thomas Mott Osborne, board chairman of the George Junior Republic and "daddy" of William O. Dapping, ca. 1900. William O. Dapping Papers, Special Collections Resource Center, Syracuse University Libraries, Syracuse University.

large and successful company that manufactured agricultural machinery; his mother, Eliza Wright Osborne, linked him to the New England reform aristocracy, including the feminist Lucretia Mott (his great aunt) and the abolitionist William Lloyd Garrison (by marriage). After Harvard, where he made its exclusive clubs, and the death of his father in 1886, Osborne unhappily assumed management of the company he regarded as a dreary business affair. He cared far more about the music of Beethoven, amateur theatricals, the fight against political corruption, and, in secret, donning a disguise and masquerading as a hobo or tramp to fraternize with lower-class men. Osborne never remarried after his wife died in 1896, leaving him with four sons. He continued to do his duty at the company, attended to his sons, masqueraded, and became more active in the reform branch of the Democratic Party, but the Junior Republic was his consuming passion. "I have never felt the call of duty more keenly than in regard to these poor children," he told an associate in 1898.[43]

By children he meant boys, and of all the boys at the Republic, Dapping mattered the most to him. He must have recognized in Dapping a potential agent who could report on the Republic in his absence. But there were other motivations at work. In his introduction to George's book, *The Junior Republic, Its History and Ideals* (1910), Osborne called the Republic "a laboratory experiment in Democracy," the importance of which went far beyond the lives there. "The future conduct of charitable institutions all over the world I believe hangs on the success of this experiment," he asserted in 1898. Dapping was one of many Republic boys whom Osborne took in and made a test case in the experiment of applied democracy. "I find the study of the boyish mind at the Republic is most interesting," Osborne stated in 1899, but like many Progressives of his day, he was after more than clinical insight. He sought, to use historian Mark Pittenger's words, a "mix of science and sympathy," gathering cold information and generating human warmth; he wanted unsentimental facts as well as requited love. Like George, he prized the acceptance, friendship, and physical touch of tough boys. "Every time I go to Freeville and talk with the boys and shake their dirty little hands," he wrote, "it makes me feel that I am really doing part of my share toward uplifting humanity."[44]

43. Rudolph W. Chamberlain, *There Is No Truce: A Life of Thomas Mott Osborne* (New York: Macmillan, 1935), 32–33, 91–92; Murphy, *Political Manhood*, 144–50; TMO to E. Lawrence Hunt, 30 May 1898, box 223, OFP.

44. TMO, "Introduction," in George, *The Junior Republic*, x; TMO to Hunt, 30 May 1898; TMO to George P. Baker, 20 Feb. 1899, box 223, OFP; Mark Pittenger, *Class Unknown: Undercover Investigations of American Work and Poverty from the Progressive Era to the Present* (New York: New York Univ. Press, 2012), 9; TMO to A. G. Agnew, 21 Apr. 1900, box 213, OFP.

6. Thomas Mott Osborne poses with some of his favorite citizens of the Republic drawn closely around him, including Jean Volland (who became his personal valet), standing to his far right, and William O. Dapping, above to his right, wearing a Clinton Liberal Institute jersey. Osborne Family Papers, Special Collections Resource Center, Syracuse University Libraries, Syracuse University.

Winning Dapping's love was important evidence of the effectiveness of the Republic's methods of reform.

But there always were two parties in these friendships. The alliance and friendship between the patrician and the mucker worked in both directions. Dapping, it seems, recognized the shifting balance of power at the Republic and hitched his future to Osborne, using him against George and leveraging his emotional capital—the mucker's affection that Osborne sorely desired—to draw the wealthy philanthropist more closely to him. Dapping was obligated, as all citizens were, to call George "Daddy." Over the course of a year and numerous letters, long private conversations, and weekends with the Osborne family, Dapping carefully maneuvered himself into a more intimate relationship with Osborne. In December 1897, he decided on his own to change the salutation of his correspondence from "Dear Mr. Osborne" to "My Dear 'Daddy' Osborne." "I hope you will not be offended," he wrote. "I address you thus, because you *are* a 'Daddy' to me and I like it for a change." Within the year he took the additional step of making Osborne his middle name. Dapping left the Republic at the end of October 1898, moved in with the Osborne family, continued the schooling for Harvard, and began writing stories about his youth in Yorkville.[45]

In the summer of 1899 Dapping (now going by Will instead of Willie) turned nineteen years old and imagined himself as someone with stories to tell. He never revealed if writing the sketches was his or his "daddy's" idea. When Osborne pitched them in May 1900 to Frank W. Garrison at the *New York Evening Post*, he indicated that the author—"one of the Republic boys, in whom I have been much interested"—had taken the initiative. Osborne underscored the unusual and revealing "side lights that [the sketches] cast on the social problem." There have been "all sorts of study of the slums from the outside," he continued, but "this is about the first time we have ever had the thing from the inside." Osborne assured Garrison the text was entirely the boy's and "founded strictly on fact," although he conceded that it was "remarkable that a boy who has had so little education and reading could write so well." The *Post* later published a selection of the sketches—the only ones that ever appeared in print—on three successive Saturdays in August 1900 under the title, "The Crap-Shooters' Club. By an Ex-Member." The author was identified as "G.E.M.," a coded pseudonym using the last letters of Dapping's name in reverse order. In spite of this initial success and Osborne's enthusiastic lobbying, some of the era's leading magazines and publishers showed no interest in publishing the rest in book or serial form. *The Muckers* is a later version, but the incidents correspond to those circulated in 1900. What changed was how Dapping told the stories.[46]

45. On addressing Osborne as "Daddy," see WOD to TMO, 7 Dec. 1897, box 38, OFP; on adding Osborne to Dapping's name, see TMO to William Everett, 6 Apr. 1900, box 224, OFP. Dapping's departure date appears in ledger "List of G.J.R. Citizens," p. 2.

46. "The Crap-Shooters' Club. By an Ex-Member," *New York Evening Post*, 11, 18, 25 Aug. 1900. The five sketches in the *Post* are Chapters 3, 4, 6, 10, and 18 in *The Muckers*. TMO to Frank W. Garrison, 1 May 1900, box 213, OFP. For rejections, see Lawrence F. Abbott to

Osborne insisted the sketches were "not a work of imagination," but the opposite was true. Their artfulness is evident in his introduction for the *Post*, vouching for the "Crap-Shooters' Club" as "an undoubtedly truthful account." His word was an example of what Ann Fabian calls "devices of authentication." The practice she describes dated from earlier in the nineteenth century when publishers used various stratagems to document the truthfulness of poor people's narratives of their lives as beggars, convicts, or slaves. In some instances, figures with impeccable credentials contributed statements of verification. A well-known example is abolitionist Lydia Maria Child's testimony in Harriet Jacobs's slave narrative: "The author of the following autobiography is personally known to me, and her conversation and manners inspire me with confidence." Osborne similarly lent his prestige to fend off doubts that a slum boy could have written the sketches and to keep the meaning of the astonishing revelations within the boundaries of respectable reform literature. Later, when Dapping began revising the sketches, Osborne urged him not to alter the manuscript lest he "spoil the flavor—the very mistakes and bad constructions that you will want to prune away are the very character of the papers." Osborne, it seems, worried that improving the prose would render them less credible as the work of an ex-slum boy. There was a political struggle here, too, as Osborne sought to confine Dapping's message to the envelope of his social reform agenda.[47]

TMO, 10 Dec. 1900, box 43; Charles Miner Thompson to TMO, 18 Dec. 1900, box 43; Margaret Deland to TMO, 6 Apr. 1900, box 41; Samuel Hopkins Adams to TMO, 16 Nov. 1900, box 43; WOD to TMO, 15 May 1904, box 54, all OFP. The last chapter of *The Muckers*, "Riley's Christmas," originally was an independent story that *The Youth's Companion* accepted but never published. In his last year of college, WOD published it as "Crampy's Christmas" in *Harvard Illustrated Magazine*, for which he served as an editor; see WOD, "Crampy's Christmas," *Harvard Illustrated Magazine*, 6 (December 1904): 53–60.

47. TMO to WOD, 17 May 1900, box 225, OFP; Osborne's introduction, "Crap-Shooters' Club," 11 Aug. 1900; Fabian, *Unvarnished Truth*, 7, 29–38, 98–109; TMO to WOD, 5 Nov. 1903, box 218, OFP; Lydia Maria Child, "Introduction by the editor," in Harriet Jacobs, *Incidents in the Life of a Slave Girl* (New York: Oxford Univ. Press, 1988), 7; William L. Andrews, "How to Read a Slave Narrative," National Humanities TeacherServe, accessed 14 Apr. 2016, http://nationalhumanitiescenter.org/tserve/freedom/1609-1865/essays/slavenarrative.htm.

The most obvious imaginative decisions Dapping made involved choosing a voice or perspective from which to tell the inside story, and selecting how to identify himself. He wrote the *Post* sketches in the omniscient third-person voice of the reformed *"ex*-member." A revised (and incomplete) version, which likely dates from his college years (1901–5), abandoned the "ex-member" device for a straight third-person omniscience that follows the friendship of Spike and a book-smart but clueless settlement house worker, "Mr. Colledge Guy," to whom the mucker tells the inside story of the Crapshooters. The third (and complete) revision, mostly likely produced between 1905 and 1911, is the one published here in full. Aside from a short introduction, Dapping raised Osborne's ante, eliminating virtually all polished "Colledge Guy" prose to allow Spike to tell his stories straight to the reader in the first-person dialect of the streets.[48]

We do not know what Osborne thought of this redesign of the message and envelope and can only surmise why Dapping elected to make the changes, but his choices affected the impact of the text. In the *Post* version, the ex-member employs a narrative tone of judgmental mockery or ironic slyness, perhaps to connect with the educated reader by talking down to the Crapshooters. The second version, with the "Colledge Guy" Boylston and an omniscient narrator more distanced from the action, has a no less personal, but more aggressive edge. The tone may reflect Dapping's feelings of alienation at Harvard, where he had to listen to enlightened students hold forth philanthropically on the "social question" even as they held his slum past against him and denied him admission to the higher echelons of social life. Spike destroys Boylston's pet theories and "methods of ameliorating the condition of the poor" that he acquired in college, then puts the "Colledge Guy" through a crash course on the slums "direct from the ranks of the submerged." By the third version, Boylston had disappeared as a character, and Spike held center stage,

---

48. The incomplete "Colledge Guy" and first-person manuscripts of *The Muckers* are in WODP.

speaking directly and impertinently to his presumably educated reader after the author briefly vouched for his character.[49]

Dapping won a more immediate victory over Osborne in 1900 on the matter of identifying himself as the author of the *Post* sketches. At the time, Dapping was enrolled in boarding school, the Clinton Liberal Institute in Clinton, New York, still working his way toward Harvard, and he did not want the students to learn his past. "Daddy," he wrote, "you do not know how embarrassed I feel over it." Osborne tried to be persuasive, but effectively demanded Dapping reveal himself as author. The value of his sketches as actual, not imagined, pictures of slum life, he explained, "would be materially increased if people have some idea as to who writes them." Dapping responded in a jovial, but no less adamant way, inviting Osborne to choose "a nom de plume" that "would be suitable to carry during my literary career." Osborne was displeased, but Dapping's identity remained "a private affair."[50]

We are the beneficiaries of Dapping's not-so-small victory. Speaking of antebellum slave narratives, Ann Fabian has observed that "the stories told by former slaves did not always end with the narrators' incorporation into a free society; they ended with narrators on the lecture circuit—no longer enslaved, to be sure, but suspended somewhere between slavery and freedom." Dapping would have understood Fabian's point. Osborne's efforts to name Dapping were for his purposes, not the author's, and comparable to putting him on the lecture circuit as proof of the Republic's and Osborne's good work. Dapping's anonymity was an assertion of his right and power—that is, of what he had been told the Junior Republic promised him—to control the stories he told, irrespective of his daddy's interests.[51]

---

49. WOD to TMO, n.d. [24 Nov. 1902], box 49, OFP; WOD, "The Muckers, A Narrative of the Crapshooters Club" (third-person narrative), unpublished manuscript, n.d. (ca. 1905), p. 17, WODP.

50. WOD to TMO, 13 May 1900, box 41; TMO to WOD, 17 May 1900, box 225; WOD to TMO, 19 May 1900, box 41, OFP.

51. Fabian, *Unvarnished Truth*, 85.

Moreover, rather than discrediting or diminishing the historical value of his work, the concealment of his identity in all probability enhanced it, especially as, over time, he pushed Spike to the center. The cover freed him from having to put his stories in the mold of American fables of humble origins and self-creation; nor did he have to tailor them to the standard fearmongering literature on the slums. In many ways, he was a Horatio Alger story: a boy from the depths whose hustle and honorable character wins the patronage of a wealthy sponsor who helps him rise to a position of respect. Unlike the hero of *Ragged Dick* (1868) or Alger's other boys on the smooth way up, Dapping was an actual person. He knew from personal experience how it felt to be treated in print as a "specimen" and what the "better class" of people thought about boys like him. Outsiders, he reminded Osborne in 1902, can never know "the lacerations which our hearts undergo" when decent people learn of his low background and their faces involuntarily disclose their pity and disgust.[52] Spike could demand a respect that Dapping did not dare ask for himself. His concealed role also enabled him to tell the stories with an unapologetic frankness and bravado that ordinarily were impermissible when the poor addressed their more privileged counterparts. In many instances Spike speaks in a jaunty braggadocio; in others, in a matter-of-fact or didactic tone (explaining carrier pigeons or how to play "migs" or marbles, for instance, in Chapters 14 and 9), interrupted occasionally by expressions of wonder and impatience at just how little educated readers know about the world around them—in effect, what dubs they are.

Of course, after the *Post* stories, almost no one read Dapping's sketches. Samuel Hopkins Adams, the muckraking journalist then at *McClure's*, said "they are too wordy to be sketch literature of a high order." *The Atlantic* editor Horace Elisha Scudder found them "interesting but not especially valuable," and passed. Anonymity caused its own set of problems. Lawrence F. Abbott of *The Outlook* urged him to revise them as a street-boy version of Booker T. Washington's inspiring autobiography and make them a tale of social mobility from the depths. Dapping, it appears, refused to use

52. WOD to TMO, [24 Nov. 1902], OFP.

his up-from-the-slums story as leverage. Such critiques leave the impression that Dapping's weaknesses were psychological and stylistic, when the more important factor may have been the perceived immorality of his text. Abbott said the sketches described "certain phases of life" that were unfit for his publication. An editor at *The Youth's Companion* was more direct: "We have too many careful mothers who would like neither the morals nor the slang of these lively young people, and who would not at all appreciate their great sociological value and human interest."[53]

Both editors were saying that Dapping's sketches, although not strictly fiction, were nonetheless "pernicious" literature. Despite the rise of literary naturalism and realism by the end of the century, the widely shared belief in America, writes literary scholar Larzer Ziff, was that "the office of literary fiction in general was to present to the reader the social world as it should be rather than as it was." Furthermore, as a writer in *Scribner's* stated in 1874, the point of literature for young readers was "to train up a generation of virtuous men and women."[54] Dapping's refusal to present his stories as straight autobiography left them somewhere in the gray region between fiction and nonfiction. Although Osborne maintained they were unvarnished fact, they resembled the much-loved "bad boys" of nineteenth-century American fiction, like Thomas Bailey Aldrich's *The Story of a Bad Boy* (1870) and Mark Twain's *The Adventures of Tom Sawyer* (1876). However, the precocious lads in those books were from the middle, not the poorer classes, which made it possible to believe their childhood mischief over time would mature into the pep and ginger that served adults well in a market society. The enterprising mischief of the Crapshooters— cutting down the tenement house wash-lines so housewives would pay the boys to restore them (Chapter 10)—had "bad boy" ingenuity, but no independent narrator to represent a moral compass. A reader of *The Muckers* might strongly detect in the merry and often illegal adventures of the

53. Adams to TMO, 16 Nov. 1900; Deland to TMO, 6 Apr. 1900; Abbott to TMO, 10 Dec. 1900; Lawrence F. Abbott to TMO, 26 Dec. 1900, box 43, OFP; Thompson to TMO, 18 Dec. 1900. *The Outlook* was then serially publishing Washington's *Up From Slavery*.

54. Larzer Ziff, *All-American Boy* (Austin: Univ. of Texas Press, 2012), 32; "Literature for Boys," *Scribner's*, Jan. 1874, 370–71.

Crapshooters a more subversive mockery of traditional authorities—parents, adults, government, church, the gospel of work, and the law—and a tempting alternative to the ultimate path of decency and virtue. Moreover, Spike and his mates are never apologetic or remorseful about the cruelties they inflict or the crimes they engineer. And they are never effectively punished for their actions in either a legal or cosmic sense. They always get off. The system is no match for them. No higher authority in heaven or anywhere else intervenes to enforce the moral order.[55]

And then there was the issue of "the morals and the slang." In part, the problem was that *The Muckers* is shot through with profane, vulgar, and foul language and scenes. The boys window-shop for "guns, daggers, blackjacks an' other playthings like them" (Chapter 7). The taboo word "hell" appears in some exclamatory or descriptive form twenty-one times (and "damn" once). Readers today should be forewarned that the Crapshooters think along hostile dividing lines of age and ethnicity. Parents are not respectfully father and mother, but "old man" and "old woman." The text contains a profusion of derogatory epithets and racist and anti-Semitic terms that are used against any and all groups, including their own: Chinky, Ginney, Dago, Sheenie, Kuyk, Mick, Dutch Heinie, and more. Nearly every chapter contains a reference to men and women downing beer or being intoxicated, and Dapping draws from an array of offensive terms to describe the inebriated state of the Crapshooters and others: pifflicated, pickled, plastered, canned, ossified. The boys run errands for "the yaller-haired actress what we calls The Fairy," a prostitute. Spike spends a blasphemous chapter (21) defaming all religions as "nursin' a soft graft, an' shootin' hot-air an' bull-con fer to keep it agoin.'" All of these words, situations, and opinions were not just forbidden in polite company; they described a moral order turned, seemingly, upside down.

Mickey changes, of course, but the others swear they never will. And why should they? The Crapshooters may be raiding the local grocers for their housewarming party, but the cop who should be watching for thieves is too busy enjoying the apple he has pilfered, and the "Irish biddy" who

---

55. Ziff, *All-American Boy*, 1–7, 40–58.

squeals on them is herself stealing from the merchant. Mame Donegan thinks she has arrived in Yorkville society, but everyone knows her husband is a "cheap skate booze fighter." The "bum's rush" defined by Spike captures the routine sadism of the cop on the beat. Country boys are not rural innocents, just lamer con artists than city boys. Muckers are caught playing baseball and hauled off like "terrible criminals" to court. The boys admit they are looking for "great graft!" wherever they can find it; there is no special reason to spare Christmas parties for poor children. They even steal ice from the undertaker's wagon. But everyone else is looking for graft, too, especially the "graftin' polytishan." The adult world is arrayed against muckers, but Spike is not without a moral sensibility: "Ye' noodle tells ye' when ye' done wrong. Ye' noodle tells ye' what's right" (Chapter 21). As Dapping explains at the start, the Crapshooters are "a terror to all whom they disliked, good fellows to those to whom they took a fancy." A "good fellow" abided by a code of honor. He may have stolen or vandalized, but instead of violence he used his wit and cunning—and his fleet feet when he needed them—to foil the cops and greenhorn grocers, to escape an enraged farmer whose orchard they have looted, and to make an easy killing—not to get rich, but to lavish his windfall on his "bo's." Mickey takes the fall for the rest of the gang and holds no grudges when he gets arrested (though never convicted) for the toy store burglary in Chapter 13. Mickey was the ultimate "good fellow." In the end, his loyalty to his gang may be more impressive than his conversion to law and order.[56] It is little wonder Dapping had such difficulty finding a publisher.

The Muckers also is an example of what literary scholar Gavin Jones has called the "strange talk" of dialect literature, a genre prevalent at the turn of the twentieth century and about which middle-class Americans were distinctly ambivalent. Mindful of popular demand for such literature, publishers solicited works featuring the authentic speech of rural and urban folk (for example, that of Twain and Stephen Crane). They also worried that exposing educated readers to "strange talk" contributed to the degradation of manners and morals of the respectable classes. Richard

---

56. Gilfoyle, *A Pickpocket's Tale*, xv.

Watson Gilder of *Century Magazine* knew his readers were "trying to bring up their children with refinement, and to keep their own and their children's language pure and clean." *The Muckers*, if read in an unapproved way, provided a virtual guidebook for the popularization of slang expressions among the upper half. Gilder, it appears, was among the editors who declined to publish Dapping's sketches.[57]

Scholars have usually regarded dialect fiction as conservative and reactionary, but other assessments are possible. For instance, Gavin Jones argues that Stephen Crane's use of the profane dialect of the urban poor in *Maggie* "assaulted the naive, patronizing values" in the reportage on the dangerous classes. *The Muckers*, as I have shown, was similarly disruptive on a number of fronts, but pointedly so in Dapping's refusal to clean up its language or constrain the boys' voices with a refined and judgmental narrator. Consider the title: a slang term that circulated—like the people who used the word and those whom the word described—in the immigrant slums of late nineteenth-century American cities. Most educated people would not have recognized the word, or, if they did, used it. *The Century Dictionary* in 1897 defined slang as the gutter "jargon" of "thieves, peddlers, beggars, and the vagabond classes generally." Such "low-bred" language, Edwin Herbert Lewis warns in *A First Manual of Composition* (1902), "embodies ideas that no gentleman ever entertains." Dapping was well schooled in the class politics implicit in the prohibitions of slang. As he wrote in an earlier draft of *The Muckers*, educated persons who used street jargon effectively threw their "dignity and class superiority to the winds." Still, Dapping occasionally dropped a mucker word or phrase into his letters, likely sensing that Osborne found pleasure in the rough play of street language. Even in these cases, though, Dapping was aware that slang was unbefitting the man he was endeavoring to become and kept the jargon at a safe distance, quarantined in quotation marks and qualified by disclaimers: "as they say it in slang." Dapping also knew from experience that the word "muck" was impure and unclean in itself because of its

---

57. Jones, *Strange Talk*, 1–13, quotation on 51; TMO to Richard Watson Gilder, 12 May 1900, box 213, OFP.

more familiar and general usage. Muck was the dung of farm animals or, in the case of the metropolis, the waste deposited by the vast fleet of horses (128,000 in 1910) hauling streetcars, wagons, cabs, and fire engines through the city streets. An offensive and inescapable fact of daily life, it assaulted the senses of urban Americans irrespective of wealth. Men who handled muck—or boys who thought nothing of grabbing a handful to hurl at an enemy—were filthy; they absorbed all its unpleasant qualities and sensory associations, which was why respectable people of means paid others to deal with it for them. Perhaps the title, in its assault on the senses and sensibilities of its potential readers, was a way for Dapping to take off the mask of Spike and speak directly—even defiantly—to those who thought they knew the poor.[58]

Dapping's sketches had another chance in his third year at Harvard, but the publishing house went bankrupt. He revised his sketches into *The Muckers*, but there is no evidence he ever came that close again to publication. After Harvard Dapping worked for the Osborne newspaper in Auburn until his retirement. He died in 1969, shortly after his eighty-ninth birthday. He and his wife, Ina, who predeceased him, had no children. The long obituary in the Auburn newspaper is the most thorough telling of his life ever published, but for all the wealth of information, it is a thin history. It names his parents and mentions that the late Thomas M. Osborne had been "instrumental in helping Mr. Dapping get an education," and that Dapping "was practically a member of the Osborne family." It misleadingly reports that he gave "up employment in New York City to join the late William R. George . . . in setting up" the Republic. He won a special Pulitzer Prize for reporting on a prison riot in 1929 and became a respected newspaper editor and prominent Roosevelt Democrat.[59] Perhaps

58. Jones, *Strange Talk*, 2–13, 134–36, 138, 141–50, quotation on 138; "Slang," *The Century Dictionary and Cyclopedia*, vol. 7 (New York: Century Co., 1897), 5683; Edwin Herbert Lewis, *A First Manual of Composition* (New York: Macmillan, 1902), 63; WOD, "The Muckers" (third-person narrative), p. 7; WOD to TMO, 31 May 1897; "Horses," *Encyclopedia of the City of New York*, 612–13.

59. WOD to TMO, 6 Mar. 1904, box 53, OFP; "William Osborne Dapping," *Auburn Citizen-Advertiser*, 2 Aug. 1969. The bankrupt publisher was D. Lothrop & Company of Boston.

as he once and maybe still wanted it, the "low" origins that got him to the Republic and beyond are hinted at but not stated in his obituary.

At the time of his death very few people would have known about the history behind his achievements, the manuscripts preserved in his files, or his intention to deed them to the Syracuse University Libraries. We are fortunate they have survived, although their preservation was not an accident. We can hear Dapping and the lost voices of the Crapshooters of Yorkville now only because he—not Thomas Osborne or any outsider or child-saver—decided to preserve this insiders' version of the truth about the so-called slums.

The Muckers

A Narrative of the Crapshooters Club

1.

Foreword.

In the NEW YORK WORLD of recent date appeared the following item. It constitutes an admirable sample of the manifestation of the gregarious instinct in boys in the form of the "club." No comment is necessary.

— • • —

JUVENILES HAD "CLUB" HIGH UP IN AIR

LOFTY ABANDONED BROOKLYN "L" STATION[1] THEIR RENDEZVOUS UNTIL RAID

Snugly curled up in bundles of straw, five boys, the oldest sixteen, were found asleep in the abandoned elevated railroad station at Fortieth street and Third avenue, Brooklyn, the highest point on the line at dawn yesterday. The youngsters had been using the station as a clubhouse for some time, despite the fact that just below their lofty nest was the new station in which a ticket agent is on duty at all hours. They managed to reach their perch by climbing up the iron girders, a height of fifty feet, instead of using the stairs.

At the Fourth avenue police station they said that they were ——, aged sixteen, —— and —— aged fifteen and thirteen, ——, aged fifteen, and ——, aged thirteen.

Residents of the neighborhood recently complained of sounds of revelry by night, but the seat of the noise could not be found until the

---

1. "L" Station. "L" used here is an abbreviation of the word "Elevated." [Dapping prepared a separate glossary of approximately 500 slang words and phrases (such as "L" Station) to assist readers unfamiliar with street dialect. For the published edition of *The Muckers* I have repositioned the definitions and translations in footnotes. My annotations are enclosed in brackets.—Ed.]

Brooklyn Rapid Transit set Special Officer Pfanenschlag to watch. His vigil was rewarded Wednesday night when he saw a light shining in a crack in the disused station.

At first Pfanenschlag saw only five rolls of straw. He shuffled his feet and then five pairs of startled eyes peeped up at him. The next moment the five bundles of straw unfolded and that number of frightened youngsters pleaded not to be "pinched."[2] They said there were a dozen other "members" of the club.

The walls of the "club" were adorned with gay posters and bits of looking glass. A shelf held some dime novels. The "furniture" consisted of soap boxes. The boys were sent to the Children's Society, except ——, who was arraigned in the Fifth Avenue Court, where he pleaded not guilty to a charge of disorderly conduct. He was held pending an investigation.

2. *pinched.* Placed under arrest.

2.

Introductory.

The foregoing is not the only kind of human interest story that frequently appears in the public press concerning the street boy, for there often issues an edict dealing with the next stage of gregarious manifestation— the street gang. Then one reads the dictum of some police commissioner or magistrate: "Death to the gangs. The gangs must go!" For some time thereafter there follows a series of battles between policemen and gangsters in which deaths sometimes occur and broken heads are many. In due time delegations of "hard blokes"[1] are "settled up the river"[2] in Sing Sing prison for long terms, or are put "over on the Island," Blackwell's Island, in the East River, for shorter periods in the penitentiaries. In spite of such occasional crusades, however, with scores of arrests and many convictions, the net result is very discouraging to public officials, and the problem seems to get more and more beyond control each year. Today the police seem content if they are successful in keeping the gangs within the bounds of their respective neighborhoods and out of conflict with the better members of society. Sociologists study the problem and offer scientific remedies, such as the wiping out of the "double-decker" and "dumb-bell" tenements[3] and the establishment of public playgrounds, which certainly mitigate the evil, if they do not cure it.

1. *hard blokes.* Designation used by young men to indicate tough characters. Generally self-applied with air of bravado.

2. *settled up the river.* Sent to Sing Sing prison, on the Hudson River near New York. "Settled" means sent to prison.

3. [*double-decker and dumb-bell tenements.* The notorious "dumb-bell" tenement was proposed by philanthropists as an improved housing model and widely adopted. The

Where tenements are thick the gang thrives. The herding together of many families through economic stress can perhaps be abolished only by the removal of that stress. Certainly children born into such an environment find little chance for legitimate expression of their natural impulse to associate with each other, and seeking relief in alleys or backyards where they are forced to congregate in the absence of adequate playgrounds they are inevitably forced into channels that lead to demoralization and crime. Doubtless the warfare between police and dwellers in the so-called slums will be perpetual, and the denizens of Whitechapel, the Paris apaches, and the East Side thugs will continue to furnish sensational "copy" for the newspapers.

How do these gangs grow? Where do they begin, in their small way, to develop embryo hold-up and second-story men? What are the steps that lead the mischievous boy onward to become a rowdy, petty thief, thug and ultimately a full-fledged criminal? Who are the tender lads who recruit these vicious, brutal gangs, who join the ranks of the Car Barn Gang, Tanner Smith's Gang, the Humpty Jackson's, the Lush Lobs, Jimmy Shields' Gang, Gas House Gang, Corcoran Roost Gang, Canary Island Gang, San Juan Hill Gang, the Graveyard Gang, the Jungle Gang, and so on ad infinitum?[4]

New York City has known for many years the depredations of the above mentioned gangs, which, as training schools, have graduated burglars, pickpockets and highwaymen who do not hesitate to commit violence if interfered with in their criminal work.

Much has been written from the outside, in harrowing and sensational detail, or in picturesque and exaggerated dialect, to entertain and

---

windows of its interior rooms opened on an enclosed courtyard airshaft, which was supposed to enhance ventilation. The design actually created a fire trap and served more often as a dump for garbage and waste.—Ed.]

4. *Car Barn Gang, etc.* These gangs are named after local names, individuals who lead them, or characteristic traits of the members. The *Lush Lobs* alone require explanation. The word "lush" means a hard drinker, and the word "lob" is a monosyllabic contraction of the word "lobster"; hence "Lush Lobs," drunken lobsters. [These are the names of actual gangs in New York City in the early 1900s.—Ed.]

amuse the reader; but nothing has come from the inside, excepting the occasional episode that some police reporter, having treated some gangster "white"[5] and gained his confidence, receives in confession, and then generally spoils [it] by playing it up into "hully gee!"[6] stuff that reads well but loses the charm that truth never lacks. The following pages purport to show for the first time from inside sources how young boys, living in the unwholesome environment, not only of New York's East Side but of any thickly populated section of the great city, naturally gravitate toward this criminal life. Incidentally the writer hopes to suggest an effective and wholly new method of reform, through the encouragement of the gregarious instinct of juveniles under the principles governing the Junior Republic.[7]

We are to narrate the commonplace and other adventures of The Crapshooters Club. Perhaps it would be well here to inform the reader that "crap shooting" is a gambling game played with a pair of dice. Although originally popular with negroes it has become a favorite pastime with all street boys, and in fact has found enough favor in more elevated stations to alternate with draw poker in more exclusive society.

Commonly, however, "big crap games," as gatherings where over a score of boys wrangle and gamble over the "bones" are called, take place on street corners where oncoming police are at all times visible, or in side alleys where the players are free from molestation. As in other forms of gambling all is not left to chance, and professional crap-shooters sometimes "ring in"[8] loaded dice that turn up the desired combination of pips.

5. *To treat "white."* To deal with honorably, to do a favor for.

6. *hully gee.* Among tough characters, the words "Holy Jesus" have become a blasphemous exclamation, as indicated. Gangsters recognize the exclamation as descriptive of exaggerated toughness.

7. *The Junior Republic.* An institution founded in Freeville, New York, by William R. George, as the result of several years of experimenting with so-called bad boys, by which boys and girls now conduct a juvenile republic that is turning out first class American citizens from material that is commonly regarded as hopeless. Its wonderful results in this direction have attracted worldwide notice and the idea is soon to be adapted in Great Britain to meet with the ideals of the British constitution.

8. *ring in.* To produce surreptitiously.

The youngsters with whom the following pages deal selected for their "monaker"[9] the title of "Crapshooters" not because of any distinguished success in this form of play, nor because they intended to follow it as their sole activity, but merely because it was typical of one of their pastimes, and in their own sphere carried some dignity.

The members of The Crapshooters Club were like most East Side boys of the class—profane, neglected, independent, shrewd and capable of turning more tricks than a conjuror, frequently as skilful at gold-bricking[10] an experienced official as in winning the smiles of a Lady Bountiful, a terror to all whom they disliked, good fellows to those to whom they took a fancy, and always ready to engineer any prank that promised anything from petty loot to a mere laugh.

Crooked? Yes, but only in the sense that they are victims of environment, like trees planted under a gate. They rendezvoused in doorways, on street corners, or in side alleys where exits were many. Here they planned escapades, smoked cigarettes, and swore, and shot craps to their hearts' content. When the "cop"[11] strolled down his beat and looked in on them they scattered in laughable panic. When the policeman moved on down the street they re-appeared, like timid mice returning to a plate of cheese. When they were absent from their usual haunts, it was a safe bet that some tenement janitor, Chinese laundryman, or greenhorn grocery clerk[12] was suffering torment at their hands. The next best bet was that they were down the avenue, prowling in some cellar, or investigating a back yard with the sole object of purloining anything eatable or that might be disposed of as junk.

The members of The Crapshooters Club were known only by their nicknames, which had become attached to the respective owners in some

---

9. *moniker.* A nickname.

10. *gold-bricking.* To deceive. Based upon the game of the confidence man who sells a valueless commodity to some gullible stranger in the guise of a highly valued article.

11. *cop.* A policeman. Also called "copper."

12. *greenhorn grocery clerk.* An East Side type, usually a German immigrant from the low countries ("Plattdeutsch") who, unable to speak English, runs errands for grocers and is the target for much annoyance from street boys.

physical characteristic, some habit, or episode in their careers. These "monakers" generally stuck to them, and would remain in all probability to be catalogued as aliases when destiny brought them before the Bertillon clerk[13] in some institution where the law demanded that they be "mugged"[14] and given a niche in that hall of infamy, the Rogues Gallery.[15]

There were seven members of The Crapshooters Club—Spike, Blinkey, Shorty, Mickey, Red, Butts and Riley. Spike was their leader and dictated the crude organization that governed them. Subsequent pages give the narrative of The Crapshooters Club.

13. *Bertillon clerk*. The clerk of the Bertillon measurements in that system of identifying criminals.

14. *mugged*. When a criminal is photographed for purposes of identification he is said to be "mugged." Two photographs, front view and profile are usually made, and placed on a card with Bertillon measurements and data for filing in the Rogues Gallery.

15. *Rogues Gallery*. The collection of photographs of convicted felons found in all police headquarters, detective agency, important prisons, State capitols and in the clearing house for same in National Bureau of Identification in Washington. [In the Bertillon system of identification, criminals were photographed and their features precisely measured; the archived information was used to target repeat offenders, preventing them from using aliases if arrested again. The New York City Police Department had the first Rogues Gallery in the 1850s, a display of notorious criminals. The National Bureau of Identification, founded by the International Association of Chiefs of Police, was a clearing house for distributing Bertillon records to police agencies.—Ed.]

3.

Dugan's Cellar.

Youse guys probaly think I dont know nothin' because I dont know how to speak swell[1] English. Well, believe me, I'm no dub[2]; even if I cant sling words. What I aint got in learning I've made up in experience, an' it'll take a good one to goldbrick me. I may look like a kid,[3] but I aint no spring chicken, at that. I can show some people cards and spades[4] about some things. In the first place I'm me own boss—an' that's all I want. I dont take no guff[5] from nobody, not even from me old man. He used to say "Money is the root of all evil—but gimme lots o' the root!" No, that aint original with him. He copped that from a vaudeville actor. But I say: "Not fer mine!" So long as I can earn me three squares a day, find some place to sleep at night, and get a heap o' fun along with it, I'm satisfied. Independence aint confined to the rich. Look at me. I aint worried about nuttin! I'm no more askared of losin' me job—when I got one—then I'm askared to sneak up an' swipe[6] an apple off'n a Ginney stand.[7] If I get fired from one job it aint long before I'm holdin' down another. But this aint what I started out for to tell you!

1. *swell*. Elegant, stylish.
2. *dub*. Fool, ignoramus.
3. *kid*. Youngster, inexperienced boy.
4. *show cards and spades*. To excel, to demonstrate wide knowledge of.
5. *guff*. Scolding, advice.
6. *swipe*. Steal.
7. *Ginney stand*. An Italian is called a Dago or a Ginney. A Ginney stand is the term applied to a fruit stand conducted by an Italian.

You want to know about the Crapshooters. Well, this bunch I'm telling you about hung out[8] up in Yorkville. You know where Yorkville is? Uptown—east o' Third avenue, capitol somewhere on Eighty-Sixth street. We used to get our orders from the cops of the East Eighty-Eighth street station.

We had a fine bunch of rough-house artists. I was leader. I was called "Spike"—because I was handy with me mits,[9] I s'pose. In them days any fellow who could scrap[10] was called Spike something or other. Well I had trimmed nearly every guy[11] me size in Yorkville, and was some scrapper. So the boys called me "Spike."

There was Blinkey, too. He was another scrapper. Once done a three-round bout at the Shamrock Amateur Athletic Club an' got his name in the sporting extras. He had a bum[12] eye, too; but he could always see an openin' to land a punch. He was our funny-man and had it like a bushel basket over[13] all the vaudeville fellows at impersonating Sheenies,[14] Dutch Heinies,[15] and Chinks.[16] He wasn't very good on Harps[17]—because he was an Irishman himself, I guess. We called him Blinkey because he had a scar over his left eye that made him blink and squint. His last name was Paterson, I think. Cripes sakes![18] We never knew each other's last names anyway except when one of us croaked[19] or got pinched! It was just "Well Bo,[20] how goes it?," or Red, Butts, Mickey, Shorty and so on.

8. *hung out.* Rendezvoused.

9. *handy with the mits.* Skilful at boxing or fighting with fists

10. *scrap.* Fight.

11. *guy.* Person, fellow.

12. *bum.* Bad, defective; lazy person when used as noun.

13. *to have like a bushel basket over.* To greatly excel.

14. *Sheenies.* Persons of Hebrew extraction.

15. *Dutch Heinies.* Persons of German extraction.

16. *Chinks.* Chinamen.

17. *Harps.* Irishmen.

18. *Cripes sakes!* Blasphemous exclamation—from "For Christ's Sake." When used never means more than mild surprise or interest.

19. *croaked.* Died.

20. *Bo.* Name genially applied to a stranger. From "hobo," tramp.

7. The closest we have to a portrait of the Crapshooters are the boys of the George Junior Republic (pictured here ca. 1900 with William "Daddy" George)— "muckers" from the city streets who were terrors to their enemies, "good fellows" to their friends, and "always ready to engineer any prank that promised anything from petty loot to a mere laugh." William R. George Family Papers, no. 800. Division of Rare and Manuscript Collections, Cornell University Library.

"Shorty." He was another candy kid![21] A little sawed-off and hammered-down runt! He'd let you kid[22] the life out o' him, and never get sour. He could roll the bones better than a coon.[23] He busted more crap games than any six guys that ever played the game in our ward. Some fellows said that they had got hep[24] to Shorty usin' loaded dice now and then. Well maybe he did, an' maybe he didn't. It aint fer me to say! If he did he certainly got away with it,[25] and as that's the way they measure

21. *candy kid*. Applied as mild approbation.
22. *to kid*. To tease, to annoy, to "jolly."
23. *coon*. Negro.
24. *get hep*. To learn about, to discover.
25. *to get away with*. To succeed, usually by questionable means.

success in everything elst, why blame him! And maybe he couldn't spiel[26] some on the mouth harmonica! Say, that guy was a real musician. And you ought to have heard him tear off the latest songs and popular hits on his accordeen! You've heard an accordeen, aint you? Well Shorty had one the swellest makes o' them tenement house pianos. It had bells on, and when he got to a good place in the song he rung the bells. He made a hit with all the crows[27] in the neighborhood and got bids[28] to all their parties. He sure was a shine![29]

And Mickey! Say, he knew more about joints[30] worth hitting than all the crooks[31] in Sing Sing. He could spot a flatty[32] a mile away, and no plain clothes cop ever got into his range without Mickey bein' the first to pipe him off.[33] Mickey was the official yarn-spinner of the club. We'd often get together somewhere and listen to him as he told us about Jesse James,[34] Carl Greene, Nick Carter, Old King Brady[35] and all the rest of them phony-detectives[36] what we thought was genuine. Gee, how many times didn't the bunch git up, move to make a big haul, buy guns, railroad tickets, lassoos and them long pants with the hairy leggings what cowboys wear, and all of us shake the dust of good old New York from our feet an' dig fer Wyoming! It's funny we never done it, at that! Probaly because we had some doubts about the truth o' them dime novels. Mickey had over a hundred of them novels hid in his woodshed,

26. *spiel*. To play, to talk. A speech or tune when used as a noun.

27. *crow*. Girl; not intending disparagement and always used to indicate the gentler sex.

28. *bids*. Invitations.

29. *shine*. A popular person, a Beau Brummell. Sometimes used disparagingly to indicate an effeminate or stupid person.

30. *joint*. A place.

31. *crook*. A thief.

32. *flatty*. A detective; policeman in civilian attire.

33. *pipe off*. To espy, to recognize.

34. *Jesse James*. A noted bandit and desperado.

35. *Carl Greene, Nick Carter, Old King Brady*. Detective heroes of dime novel fame.

36. *phony*. False, counterfeit.

and certainly was a dime novel fiend if they ever was one. He always had a hump in his back pants pocket where the cops carry their guns, but Mickey's hump wasn't from totin' a gun.[37] No it was on'y a dime novel folded up and handy fer his spare moments.

And then there was Red. Old brick-top, positively the laziest lobster[38] I ever knew! That kid could smell work farther away than a Dutchman could smell limburger cheese. But he was a good scout,[39] just the samee! He was always game fer any rough house that the bunch got mixed into, and he'd never welch[40] on any man.

Butts comes next. He was a card![41] Got his name goin' round the streets under the elevated railroad stations, outside theayters, subway entrances and such places sniping butts.[42] D'ye ever snipe butts? That means to wait until nobody is lookin' and then pick up the ends o' cigars what rich guys chucked away.[43] Buttsy would bring in a whole cigar box full sometimes, and they was some real Havanas in them, too.

Then finally there was Riley. Poor little Riley, on'y a kid. He was a daring cuss,[44] but he didn't have no noodle[45] on his shoulders and come near gettin' the whole outfit pinched many a time. I think he had the con,[46] poor kid. These is all they was to our crowd.

•◆•

Well as I was sayin', we started The Crapshooters Club all together one night. We was all sitting on the railing in front of the store where we hung out, and were having a spittin' match. Red had got into an argymint with Shorty because Shorty spit out of turn and it landed on Red's

---

37. *tote a gun.* To carry a revolver.

38. *lobster.* A friendly salutation.

39. *a good scout.* A good fellow.

40. *to welch.* To go back on, to be a traitor to.

41. *card.* An amusing fellow.

42. *sniping butts.* Picking up discarded cigar and cigarette stubs.

43. *chuck away.* To throw away.

44. *cuss.* A fellow. To cuss means to swear.

45. *noodle.* Head.

46. *con.* Consumption, tuberculosis.

hand when he was measurin' the distance he had just spit himself. They got so riled up that I had to butt in.[47] "Aw, what's the use a chewin' terbacker when you got to spit the juice!" sez I, puttin' an end to the scrap by shovin' them apart. Then comes Buttsy, Johnny-on-the-spot.

"Cut out the scrappin' bos," he yells, "I got a scheme." He moseyed up[48] and we surrounded him. Then he says: "Say blokes,[49] why dont we get up a club like them Tammany guys got on Eighty-Sixth street? Of course we aint as old as them guys and dont vote, so there wont be any graft[50] to support us, but if we had a club we could meet every night, say down in Dugan's cellar. There we could talk over our plans without havin' any o' them fly cops[51] rallyin' us all the time! Hey? Wot do youse guys think o' that plan?"

"You got the right dope,[52] Buttsy" says I, and the rest of the guys jumped at the idea like Sheenies after money. "We're on, we're on!"[53] they yells, and inside of ten minutes we had all snuk down into the cellar, and were gropin' around in the dark, pilin' dusty boxes and furniture up against the door before we struck a light. It sure was necessary to barricade yourself in that joint, believe me.

Of course you dont know nothin' about Dugan's cellar, so I got to put you hep to a few things fer to begin with. It wasn't a very swell joint but it come in handy fer our crowd. It was our castle. Once inside nobody could get us. If any stranger put his nut[54] into the door like as not he'd feel the weight of a brick against his noodle. If the cops or Dugan himself tried to get us it was skidoo[55] fer us through our secret passages. We paid no rent an' had the fun o' takin' a chance o' havin'

47. *butt in.* To interfere, to be meddlesome.

48. *to mosey up.* To shamble, to shuffle.

49. *blokes.* Fellows, comrades.

50. *graft.* Illegitimate gain, something obtained unfairly or corruptly.

51. *fly cop.* A meddlesome or dictatorial policeman.

52. *dope.* Idea, plan, intention. Also a drug as opium, morphine, cocaine.

53. *We're on!* An exclamation indicating that a bargain is closed.

54. *nut.* Head. Used interchangeably with "noodle."

55. *skidoo.* A slang expression meaning to flee, to drive away.

old Dugan rap us over the nut when we used to sneak in. We wasn't a-skared of him once we was inside but it was in gettin' in and out where we run our chances. Pat Dugan was as gentle as a steam shovel if he ever laid hands on ye', and we allus knew what was comin' to us if he got his hooks on[56] one of us after he found out that we was usin' his cellar fer a club room. But we wasn't goin' around with a brass band tellin' everybody on the block that we had a club house, and managed to steer clear of Dugan all right. The joint we occupied was a suite of three rooms intended by the landlord to be rented to some coal-and-wood dealer, junkman or guy of similar perfession. He could use the big room fer a place of business and the inside rooms fer livin' quarters, if he could stand it. One room was fitted with a chimbley flue, sink and cold water faucet. The floors were laid on the wet bottom of the cellar and everything was damp, dark and dirty. They was small grated windows near the ceiling that let in a little light when they was washed, and fresh air and stray cats when they was open.

So far as livin' in the place was concerned, it sure was a bum joint. The sign "Basement to Let" got old and weather beaten workin' overtime up on the street tryin' to attract some dub to hire the rooms. But no one never come to rent the old hole.

In the biggest room Dugan stored old window blinds, frames, timbers and any old kind o' junk. The rats, cockroaches, thousand leggers and other kinds o' vermin had a monopoly in stayin' there until we butted in and scared most o' them away. But when we was out the stray cats continued to come in and crouch in the dark corners waitin' fer a rat or a mouse to streak acrost the floor an' get nipped.[57] Before the time when we took possession of the place fer our club we used to go down only once in a while, like when we played hide-an'-seek, or when some cop chased us and kep' hot on the trail, makin' it wise fer us to make ourselfs scarce fer awhile. Well to come back to where I left off.

56. *get one's hooks on.* To lay hands upon.
57. *nipped.* Caught, arrested.

As I was sayin'—after we got the door braced against any butt-er-in-sky[58] Mickey struck a match, thawed out the end of a candle, and glued it on a overturned barrel. Then all sittin' around the spooky light I took charge and made a speech.

"Now youse guys listen," says I, an' with that I wades in. "All blokes that's got any kind o' gumption[59] have clubs o' one kind or another. Fer instance in the Sunday schools they calls 'em Boy's Brigade or Watchful Eye Society. In the high schools they calls 'em 'frats' and the college boys calls 'em the Alpha Skeltas or the Pi Eyes. Other guys have the Elks or the Masons or the Knights o' Columbus, or the Eagles or the Owls or the What-Nots! And then they have Tammany clubs on'y five blocks apart from the Battery to Harlem. An' think o' the athletic and social clubs, and mixed ale[60] and pinochle[61] clubs! Hell, fellows we're dead slow in not havin' our own club!"

That settled it, fer I could see they was all crazy to get up a club right away; but I went on. "You see, bos, if we get up a club we can go on the crook, raise hob[62] any old time, duck[63] down here when the cops make it warm fer us instead of blowin' over into[64] some other ward, and then if by any chance any of us gets pinched we can all stand together and try and get out the fellows what gets landed. We can hold our meetings right here, and nobody will know nothin' about them. We all know how to get into this dump without a lantern to light the way. We can go out an' swipe cans of sardines and salmon, smoked herrin's, pickles, condensed milk and other kinds o' grub,[65] and have feasts here every night. Hey!"

The idea looked good to me and I was feelin' enthusiastic.

---

58. *butt-er-in-sky.* A person who interferes.

59. *gumption.* Pluck, initiative, enthusiasm.

60. *mixed ale.* A combination of beer and ale.

61. *pinochle.* A card game popular among the Germans.

62. *raise hob.* To play pranks, create a disturbance.

63. *to duck.* To dodge.

64. *to blow over into.* To flee into.

65. *grub.* Food.

"You're all right, Spike," says Mickey, "and I think you ought to be put up fer floor manager or president or somethink," he says, noddin' to the bunch in reckonition o' me speech.

"All right, then," says I before they could change the dope. "All those in favor of havin' a club, and me fer the main guy[66] say 'Aye.'" They all fell fer[67] me, and yelled "Aye" so loud that I had to warn them right off the bat that they'd put a crimp in the club at the start by lettin' Dugan know we was down there. Then we'd get the Bum's Rush.[68]

Did you ever get the Bum's Rush? No? Well I have, an' I dont like to get beat up in that way. Maybe you'll be committin' some great crime, like standin' in a doorway, or settin' on a stoop, or peekin' into a flat-house letterbox, and a cop nabs you. He'll take you by the ear, twist it good and plenty, drag you half way down the street till he forces the water to run in your eyes. Then he'll swing up behind you and hand you a good swift kick that'll make you remember his No. 11's sure until the next time. I have got the Bum's Rush from cops, janitors, watchmen, landlords, grocery clerks and other guys and know what it is. That's why I did not want our bunch yellin' too loud. Well, havin' been elected leader I takes me place on the clean side of an ash barrel an' with lots of dignity, I says: "Gents, what's yer pleasure?"

"Me pleasure is to drop a rotten beef liver down into Sing Lee's Chinky laundry," says Riley, tryin' to start something.

"Ye're out of order," says I. "Fade away,[69] Riley," and with that I rules: "The next question we got to settle is what are we going to call this club?"

Then Blinkey has to start in with some comedy. He says: "I move that we call this club the Beer Swiggers Union."

"Chop it,"[70] says I, from me perch on the barrel showing by the tone of me voice that I didn't want no kiddin'.

---

66. *main guy.* The leader.

67. *to fall for.* To be fooled by, to be hoodwinked, to accept.

68. *Bum's Rush.* Ignominious ejectment.

69. *fade away.* A command to subside.

70. *chop it.* A command to desist, to "cut it out."

"That's right, Spike, muzzle him. You're too flippy[71] anyway, Blinkey," chimes in Butts from behind a packing box. Then Shorty takes a hand in the game.

"Mr. Chairman," he says, "I move we call this club The Crapshooters Club. There aint none in the whole bunch what's a slouch at[72] rollin' the dice, and we want a name suitable fer all."

"Now that's talkin' some," says I; and then we chewed the rag[73] fer hours. I tried to get everything goin' accordin' to parlemantery law but them guys was indifferent. We got along orderly, though, and finally I called 'em to order to sum up everything.

"Well fellows. This is about what we done tonight! First we are to be known as The Crapshooters Club. Second, I am to be leader an' everything I says, goes. But I wont say nothing what youse guys dont want. Last we have these rules, which aint goin' to be writ down so youse better all listen.

"Rule 1. All guys must be here every night and be willin' to do what the majority wants.

"Rule 2. Nobody can tell nobody else about this club or about where it meets; and if he does he's going to get two blinkers[74] from me outside o' what the club votes to do to him.

"Rule 3. We got to make a raid on some joint at least once a week and have some kind o' grub here on Saturday nights. All other rules will be made hereafter. That's all."

After that we sets to work to dig out furniture fer our clubrooms. Shorty cops[75] a oil stove from some woodshed and brings that in. The stove, not the woodshed. We puts that in the innermost room where Red, who made a bluff[76] at being some class[77] in the line o' cooking

71. *flippy*. Flippant.

72. *to be a slouch at*. To be sadly deficient in.

73. *chew the rag*. To discuss, to converse.

74. *blinkers*. Black eyes, resulting from an assault.

75. *to cop*. To take, to steal.

76. *to bluff*. To pretend, to exaggerate one's ability or powers.

77. *to have class*. To possess distinguished excellence.

was appointed club cook, and took charge of it. Butts drags in some old busted chairs, and they was placed around the rooms, and the joint begun to look pretty nifty.[78] Then Shorty comes back from a second expedition draggin' a old mattress what he swiped out of a tenant's woodshed. He threw it out on the middle of the floor, and everybody dives fer a soft place on it. They wasn't room on it fer all, and a scrap started. Riley was the first guy froze out of it. He got mad an' appealed to me.

"Mr. President," says he, diggin' down into his shirt, "I move that this mattress be chucked out of the clubroom because it's lousey!"

Well bo, it 'ud a done yer heart good to see the way them guys scrambled off'n that mattress! Then we had to have a examination of it, an' it sure did look buggy; but the motion to chuck it out was lost by one vote, so it had to stay. After that a motion to adjourn was made and carried, and we blew out the candle, and one by one snuk up into the street. That's how we got started.

78. *nifty.* Neat, attractive, desirable.

4.

The Crapshooters' Housewarming.

Saturday night soon come around. First avenue as ushal was jammed with hawkers, peddlars, Sheenies a yellin' out their wares, women an' kids an' wops[1] buyin' stuff, and pilin' in and out of the stores, or linin' up on the curb to make bargains with the push-cart guys. Of course you been there, and know what it's like, but fer a stranger it must seem like—gosh, I don't know. Everything bustle, bargains and hullabaloo!

Well, it was just about this time that the honorable members of The Crapshooter's Club was stealthily droppin' in, one by one, down into Dugan's cellar, gettin' ready fer the inaugural blow-out.[2] There was to be a banquet, but first we had to swipe the stuff that was to go into our menu.

Red was in charge of the larder, but on goin' to the cupboard he found it like Mother Hubbard's—there was nuttin' to it! As soon as I got there I announced me orders, which was to this effect: "Every guy wants to outdo himself tonight. This is the first blow-out of this club and we want some class to it. Each bloke wants to do his best an' see how much he can swipe. The programme is this—first we hit Davey's store, and after we have lifted all there is around there that is loose or if they get wise to us, we go on to Rafter's store. Who ever gets chased or gets away with the goods must come back to Dugan's cellar, usin'

---

1. *wops.* Foreigners, European immigrants.

2. *blow-out.* Feast, entertainment, function.

69

a roundabout way if he thinks he is bein' follered. We ought to get a pretty good bunch of eats[3] in the swag[4] from them stores, and on the way back a couple of us can stop at Dutch Miller's grocery store an' get away with a couple o' bottles o' soda water. It's gettin' late, so—on our way!" With that we gets out on the street, and starts down First avenue.

Davey's is a great big cheap grocery store, and on Saturday nights it is packed with East Side housewifes buyin' groceries fer a week. Outside the store they have great, red tubs. One'll be full o' cans o' corn; another'll have cans o' salmon, another pickle bottles, sardines, catsup, washin' soda and so on.

We scatter as we drift down the avenue. Too many of us guys in one bunch looks suspicious. When we got near the store—oh joy! There on the curb was piled up a pyramid of small, wooden pails decorated with labels showin' clusters of flowers, fruits an' berries! We knowed at a glance what them labels meant. Jelly! "Them's our meat!"[5] we says quiet to each other. How the grocer left them out on the curb subjeck to the tender mercies of any muckers[6] like us that come along is explained this way. The wholesale grocer's wagon had been along that afternoon and left them there, and them Plat-deutsch,[7] greenhorn, grocery clerks was too busy to take them inside. Consequently some of them pails went South[8] with some of our push when we come that way.

I never seen such a slick job done before, neither. I have saw many good jobs pulled off, some right under the cops' noses, but none ever raised so much respeck in me as the trick that Shorty and Riley put over.[9] We had hardly got in front of the store and none of us had even took a look in to see whether anybody was watchin' when Shorty steps up to

---

3. *eats*. Eatables, food.

4. *swag*. Loot, stolen articles.

5. *to be one's meat*. To be desirable for conversion to one's use.

6. *muckers*. Tough characters, street boys, gamins.

7. [*Plat-deutsch*. Or "Plattdeutsch," also "low German"; a variation of spoken German in northern regions that resembles Dutch.—Ed.]

8. *to be taken South*. To be stolen.

9. *to put over*. To accomplish against great odds.

one o' them red tubs, digs down into it an' picks up a lot of articles like he was the proprietor's own son fillin' an order, and walks off whistlin'. Nobody but thought that he was payin' good money for them articles.

At the same time Riley, pretendin' he was an errand boy fer the grocer, pushes through a crowd o' wimmin as was examinin' the jelly labels, picks up a pail in each hand, and goes follerin' Shorty down the avenue.

Mickey an' me were behind ready to spill any o' them Dutch hunyacks[10] if they got wise and took after them to grab them, but nobody was on to the game, and we all kep' on walkin' until they turned down a side street, and were safe on that job.

Shorty and Riley went on to Dugan's cellar with their plunder. They had done their share and on'y had to wait fer the rest of us to hold up our ends. Me and Mickey joins the rest of the bunch who was still hangin' around Davey's waitin' fer a good chance.

That bold work done by the other guys put it up to us pretty hard. I, meself, was just screwin' up courage to walk half-way into the store where there was a ten pound can with a glass front showin' some nifty, fruit crackers. I was about to nail that can when I heard Buttsy's voice yellin' "cheese it, the cop![11]" and of course it was dig out! We beat it[12] at top speed down the avenue never stoppin' to see whether we or the cop was gainin', an' stopped on'y when we was out of breath. As a matter of fact the cop what caused the stampede never even knowed that we was pipin' off the place, and he kep' on his way, swingin' his club gently as he strolled down past the store chewin' an apple that he picked off some Ginney's fruit stand.

After we got together again we hiked it fer Rafter's. There we found a dandy "show."[13] That means everything easy fer us to steal anythink. I walks up to a pile of packages, lifts up a few kind of easy so as not to tumble down the whole pile, and starts to walk off. Then a big Irish biddy, who was fussin' around with her basket when I done it, an' was

10. *hunyacks*. Foreigners.

11. *cheese it, the cop!* A warning of danger.

12. *to beat it*. To run away, to flee.

13. *show*. Opportunity to rob. Stage performance.

probably crookin' somethink her self, seen me and starts to yell. She goes into the store to put up a holler,[14] so the rest o' the guys tells me to blow. I makes fer the gutter an' starts beatin' it hotfoot fer other territory. I got a good start, an' when the clerks come out all they see was the direction I took. Mine, too was a safe getaway.[15]

It was nix[16] fer the rest there that night and after hangin' round near that store waitin' fer a chance fer a longtime they give it up, and goes back to Davey's.

Butts again takes his place to "lay keegie,"[17] but there was no good show fer so long that the word was passed to hit 'em up, caught or no-caught. When fellers decide to do that they are desperate, an' they was waitin' so long that they had begun to get cold feet.[18] So jump in, sink or swim, was the order!

Blinkey and Red accordingly led off, swooped onto them tubs, shoved a couple o' old wimmin over into them in their hurry, grabbed a mess o' junk, and lit out down the street, with a strappin' Dutch grocery clerk at their heels.

The remainin' Crapshooters chased along behind the Dutchman ready to hand him somethink[19] if he caught Blinkey or Red. He had no chance, though. His long apron tangled around his legs, and he was no ten-second man, at that. After he run five blocks he got winded, set on the curb and wiped the sweat off'n his face. They come along and was goin' to punch him, just fer fun, but they wasn't borrowin' trouble, then.

Butts and Mickey was the last guys to show up[20] at the club-rooms, and they was empty-handed. They was no kickin' though, fer they done their share layin' keegie fer the rest. But I sent them out to see whether

---

14. *to put up a holler*. To give the alarm.

15. *a getaway*. An escape.

16. *nix*. Nothing.

17. *lay keegie*. To lay on the lookout, spying for police or other persons who are liable to interrupt a robbery.

18. *get cold feet*. To lose enthusiasm, to become cowardly.

19. *to hand one something*. To assault.

20. *to show up*. To put in an appearance.

they couldn't swipe a few bottles of soda water from Dutch Miller's store, just up the street a ways. We had all kinds of grub, but nary a drop to drink. While they was on this job[21] we lit a couple of candle stumps in the inside room and set around watching Shorty throw sevens and 'levens with his favorite pair of dice. We was all interested in his classy crapshootin' when suddenly footsteps was heard on the stone stairway leadin' down into Dugan's cellar.

"Pinched already!" says I in a sorrowful whisper while we doused[22] every light and clim' up fer the airshaft windows from where we had a secret way of reachin' an alley and then to the street. Before diggin' out, though, we listened again.

We heard clinkin' bottles and our fears skidooed, fer it was Mickey and Butts comin' back. They'd forgot to give the street signal. I opened the door and gave them hell fer not whistlin' up on the street—one long, one short—the advance. They give the secret inside rap, all right, one, then three, but they never let us know whether they was friend or foe when they come down from the sidewalk. We was pretty keen about discipline then. After we barricaded the door again we lit the candles again. Butts sets down a lot of bottles, and turns to the rest of us.

"Now dont youse fellows kick because we brung back seltzer water instead of soda water. Dutch Miller was standin' right in the door-way and we could not wait all night fer him to get out of our way an' give us a chance. So we had to try something elst. Mickey suggested that we try the row of woodsheds in the cellar of the Sheeney flathouse down the block. So down we goes. He clim' over the partitions and hands out what he finds. It was them bottles. Four of them is seltzer, the other is somethink elst. I dont know what. It's got a Dago name[23] on it an' must be somethink Kosher[24] fer them Sheenies. The label says its mineral water, so instead o' chuckin' it away, I kep' it."

21. *job.* An employment. A robbery.

22. *doused.* Extinguished.

23. *Dago name.* Italian or foreign.

24. *Kosher.* Orthodox Hebrew.

"Let's see it," says I. I see it says "Hunjady"[25] on the label, and that was too many fer me.[26] I didn't know nothin' about it so I hands it over to Shorty who wanted to inspect it. He knowed what it was right away. He says: "I know what that is. I used to work in a drugstore an' we sold quarts an' quarts o' that stuff. It's expensive stuff an' doctors recommend it. I think it costs half a plunk[27] a bottle. Its mineral water what comes from Germany and makes sick people strong."

With that the whole push[28] wanted to open it up and swig[29] it off right away, but I ruled it fer the last, because it was so expensive.

Well, we sure had a swell banquet. Red was cook, and he announced the list of plunder. Say bo, maybe there wasn't some class to it! And more 'n you could eat, too! Red says: "Here is one pail of apple butter, and one pail current jelly—these to the credit of Brother Riley!"

"Yea bo!" yells the crowd.

"An' here's six cans o' nice oil sardines, what Shorty nipped[30] fer us."

"He's a good kid!" says Butts.

"Here's five packages o' stuff what you put on cakes. Let's see what you call it? The printin' says: 'Shredded cocoanut.' Then we got three cans o' Columby river salmon, and them two big bottles o' Pride o' Long Island catsup, which Red hooked.[31] Fer drinks we got these bottles o' seltzer an' that expensive mineral water, what Shorty says makes you strong. Aint this a swell lay-out?"

It was gettin' late and everybody was hungry, so we got busy. Red opened up the cans with Mickey's old rusty, cheese dagger,[32] tore off the paper from all the packages, and handed all over to me as president.

---

25. [*Hunjady water.* The boys stole bottles of Hunjady János "natural purgative water," a laxative.—Ed.]

26. *too many fer me.* Beyond my comprehension.

27. *half a plunk.* Fifty cents. A plunk is one dollar.

28. *push.* Crowd, gathering, mob.

29. *to swig.* To drink.

30. *nipped.* Here means "stole."

31. *hooked.* Stole.

32. *cheese dagger.* Any kind of pocket knife.

Well, I first divvied up[33] the shredded cocoanut. It was bum stuff. All cut up fine, packed together and sweet. Would have made pretty good plug chewin' terbacker fer dudes. It didn't go well with our gang. Some et some but most chawed it up into gobs, an' threw it at each other or plastered up the walls with it. It was mighty satisfyin' but didn't make very good eats.

Then we pitched into the rest. We divvied everything on the square.[34] After openin' a can o' sardines I take one fish, drink a sip of oil an' pass it on to the next guy. He done the same, an' passed it to the next, an' so on until we cleaned out all them six cans. Sardines was one of our favorite things to swipe. Then come the salmon, each guy dumping out a handful. The catsup went next, each guy bein' allowed to take one big swig out of the bottle each time it was passed. Maybe that catsup didn't go fine with that salmon! Then we drunk the seltzer, each guy swiggin' out of the nozzle. We raised holy terror with that seltzer, squirtin' it out of the siphons. Then come the jelly! We made pasteboard plates out of the shredded cocoanut boxes and scooped out all we wanted to eat when the pails was passed.

"Too much is plenty," says Blinkey, plastered up to the ears with apple butter and current jell'. We had so much that the guys got lawless. They smeared it around and got so fresh[35] that I had fer to call them down.[36] We'd forgot about the mineral water when Riley, scrapin' jelly off'n his pants in the other room by the aid of a stick an' cold water from the sink shouts: "Open up that mineral water, Spike, what makes ye' strong. I want to get a pull at that before we close this banquet!"

I ripped off the tinfoil, dug out the cork, an' took a good, healthy pull at the bottle. That was all I wanted. It was the punkest[37] tastin' stuff

---

33. *divvied up*. Divided. To "divvy" is to divide, to share.

34. *on the square*. On honorable terms, fairly, honestly.

35. *to get fresh*. To become mischievous, bold.

36. *to call down*. To reprimand, to caution.

37. *punkest*. From "punk," an adjective commonly used to mean distasteful, worthless. Also as noun to mean "bread."

I ever drunk! It must a been stale, fer it was bitter and warm. "I'm poisoned," says I, runnin' fer the sink.

"No y'aint," says Shorty, "that bum taste is what makes it valuable. Course it's bitter an' salty; but it's good fer ye." With that he takes a good swig.

Well, them yaps[38] really drunk up all that mineral water, twistin' their faces into knots, but swallerin' it because Shorty says it cost four bits[39] a bottle.

At midnight we still had lots o' apple butter left but they didn't waste it when I adjourned the meetin'. They took it up on the street with them, and findin' most of the house doors closed they smeared the knobs and stuffed the keyholes with the apple butter, like it was axle grease. An' it might have been, from the taste it was beginnin' to have about this time.

We went on down the street passin' old man Doyle, the night watchman at the cigar factory. He was sittin' out smokin' his pipe. He sizes us up kind of suspicious.

"Out kind o' late, aint ye?" he asks.

"We're goin' to bed now, Pat. We're good boys," says Mickey, thinkin' of gettin' up early next mornin' fer mass. Mickey was a regular church guy. Onct was a choir boy.

"Well good night to ye'," he says, "an' may ye' have pleasant dreams."

But we didn't have no pleasant dreams that night. Somethink we et or drunk gave us all a awful bellyache. Me own private opinion is that it was that expensive mineral water!

---

38. *yaps.* Simpletons, "easy marks."

39. *bits.* "Two bits" equal 25 cents. "Bit" means term in prison.

5.

An East Side Surprise Party.

Ye' never heard about Mame Donegan's surprise party? Well, that's funny; I thought the whole East Side heard about it. Why it started a race riot, an' got into the newspapers! Sure I'll tell it. Ye' see, bo—it was this way. Shorty comes slidin' down into Dugan's cellar one night, with a little o' the green in his eye an' some tremor o' jealousy in his voice. He says kind o' sourly: "Say fellers, there's goin' to be a surprise party fer Mame Donegan next week Wensdy, an' nearly every yap in the ward has got a bid—all exceptin' us. No, excuse me, Mr. Riley's the on'y one in our whole push what's been invited."

Well it did cause some rumpus in our set to get turned down like that. We wasn't big, howlin' swells[1] ourselves an' didn't think much on the society gag,[2] but it seemed to be rubbin' it in when a gal[3] we all knowed and whose old man[4] was on'y a cheap skate[5] booze fighter,[6] anyway, give us the go-bye like that.

"I think we ought to get square,[7] fer that," says Shorty, ranklin' no doubt over the fact that he an' his bloomin' accordeen wasn't to be prominent in that party.

1. *swells*. Aristocrats.

2. *society gag*. Society game, society as a pastime.

3. *gal*. Girl.

4. *old man*. Father.

5. *cheap skate*. A pretender.

6. *booze fighter*. A toper, drunkard.

7. *to get square*. To even up an account, to revenge one's self.

"That's what,"[8] says I, lookin' at Riley, the on'y Crapshooter honored with an invitation. He looked sick but his loyalty to the gang showed right up.

"T' hell wit me invitation," he says, "if them Micks aint got no use fer youse guys, why I aint got no use fer that invitation. Let's get square by breakin' up their party," he says, comin' out flatly on our side.

"Ye' got the right idea, Riley," says I, pokin' him playfully in the solar plexus. "We'll rig up some sort of job on those harps."

Then a bright idea come out of Riley's noodle.

He says: "I tell ye' what, fellers, here's a good gag to woik." Riley talks real New York, says, "Oh Poicy, take your goil to choich," instead of speakin' good lingo, like me. I say: "Oh Percy, take your girl to church." But that aint here nor there. Riley says "woik" when he means "work." So he says: "Here's a good gag to woik I'll accept the invitation, put up a big bluff[9] that I'm interested, find out all I can about it, an' youse guys, on the outside lookin' in an' me inside lookin' out, will give them the surprise that they aint lookin' fer. I'll give the signal from inside when they are about to surprise Mame, and then one o' youse guys can run down into the basement, turn off the gas at the Donegan meter, an' throw the wrench away. That's the way we can get even with them tarriers."[10]

"An' when darkness comes wit' me and a bunch of crows mixed up together in that parlor, say maybe I wont get me money's wort," adds Riley, wipin' a smile off'n his face.

With that he goes up to the street to rubberneck[11] around and see what he can find out. He goes plumb into a bunch of crows that was holdin' a gabfest[12] on Mame Donegan's front stoop. When they pipes

---

8. *that's what.* An abbreviated phrase meaning: That's what I believe, that is my opinion.

9. *put up a bluff.* Pretend.

10. *tarriers.* Irish person, playfully intended.

11. *to rubberneck.* To be unduly inquisitive.

12. *gabfest.* Conversation.

him off as he comes down the line one o' them skirts[13] yells, "Oh Jim Riley, I got somethink fer you" and hands him his invitation. She pipes him off with such twinklers[14] that he goes into a trance, and chewed the rag with her so long that somebody ups and yells: "Break away there!"

Riley ducked down out o' sight into Dugan's cellar a few minutes later, an' handed me his invite. It said:

Dear friend.

We wish to cordially invite you to a surprise party to be given in honor of Miss Mame Donegan on Wednesday night. Please bring two bunch bananas or two lbs. dates.

Yours, the Committee.

P.S. Please bring your girl.

"Will ye' listen to that," says Riley. "Bring ye' goil! Jest as if I ever had a goil! Why I don't even look at crows, I aint got no use—"

"Chop it," says I, "get off of that stuff,[15] Riley. We all knows who's the lady's man in this Crapshooter's club. Now tell us what ye' know."

He sets down on a soap box to make his report.

"Well, it's goin' to be a great shindig![16] The more I think of it the more I wonder why they left out havin' an awnin' over the doorway and an I-talyan orchestry. Foist it's exclusive! On'y goin' to have fifteen fellers an' fifteen crows. All must come up to the Donegan apartments an' hide in the parlor behin' the chairs an' sofa right after seven o'clock on Wensdy. Mame wont be there, o' course. She'll be up in Harlem payin' a visit to her aunt that afternoon an'll be expected home about half past seven. When she gets home to her own flat the guests 'll settle down quiet in the parlor, the gas will be low, and Mame's old woman[17]

---

13. *skirts.* Girls.

14. *twinklers.* Bright eyes.

15. *get off of that stuff.* Desist.

16. *shindig.* Party, entertainment, function.

17. *old woman.* Mother.

will lead her inside, toin up the light, an' the whole push yells 'surprise! surprise!' an' hands out the josh[18] to Mame.

"Then they plays kissin' ring, t'row down the pillow, and other kinds o' them mushy games.[19] About half past ten supper will be soived. They ordered t'ree crates o' soda water, couple a gallon of ice cream, a whole raft o' cake; an' besides all that they serve up all the grub what the guests bring.

"Now as I'm the inside conspirator, here's me dope! I'll go up oily wit' the guests, present me invitation, an' mix in. Youse guys hang around in front o' the house until ye' sees Mame comin' home. After she starts upstairs one o' youse ginks[20] run down into the basement an' be ready wit' a wrench at the gas meter to toin it off when I gives the signal. Me signal 'll be meself puffin' hard on a cigarette out'n the Donegan's front window, an' youse guys can see me from the other side o' the street. After ye' toin off the gas be sure to make yerselfs scarce, because they'll be pretty mad if they get hep.

"And say bos, I got another bright idea!"

"Holy gee, your noodle is workin' overtime tonight," says I.

Then he goes on. "I loined that the ice cream was ordered around in the confectionary store on Second avenue, an' theys goin' to send two o' the boys around fer it when theys ready fer it. Now why'n hell cant two o' youse guys floss up[21] a bit, shine ye' shoes, wash ye' faces, put on clean collars—in short impersonate dudes an' go round about eight o'clock, say ye' was sent by Mrs. Donegan an' bluff[22] the Dutch confectioner into givin' ye' the ice cream? It's a lead pipe cinch[23] to put that over!"

Well, say, this extension of the original plan made a hit right off, and we sure didn't think fer a minute o' passin' it up.[24] In fact, I puts it before

18. *hand out the josh*. To tease, to tell fables.

19. *mushy games*. Effeminate sports or games.

20. *ginks*. Fellows.

21. *floss up*. Dress up, wear neat clothing.

22. *to bluff*. To deceive.

23. *lead pipe cinch*. An exclamation used to indicate absolute certainty of accomplishment.

24. *to pass up*. To ignore.

the club as a reglar motion and it was carried without a kick. "Leave that to me and Blinkey," says I. "We'll kidnap that ice cream or youse guys can lambaste[25] us with bed slats. I can see us eatin' them Neapolitan bricks *now!*"

Well on Wensdy night Mame come home on schedule. We seen her half a block away, an' some o' the guys follered her home. She lived in one o' them regular East Side flat houses, six stories high, two families on a floor, seven rooms through, dumb-waiter, air shaft, 'lectric bells and speakin' tubes. Mame lived on the fourth floor, east. The airs her old woman put on had started feuds with most o' the neighbors, and things was ripe fer hell raisin' when that swell party was pulled off that night. Owin' to the fact that Mame's father wasn't much on society an' generally come home late an' then with a skate on,[26] he wasn't put wise[27] to the birthday surprise party. In fact they expected to have it over by the time he come navigatin' into port. It aint customary fer East Siders to let in the old man on such doin's.

Well once we seen Mame disappear in the doorway we all lined up on the opposite side o' the street an' gazed up hard at the windows where Riley was to tip us off to start something. It seemed like that crow never would get up there. Up in the Donegan apartments everything was dark an' quiet as the grave. About five minutes passed. Then suddenly there was a light lit and the girls and boys begins to yell: "Surprise!" Up goes the window and out pops Riley's noodle. He puffed a butt[28] so's It glowed like a torch.

Zip! Down goes Shorty into the basement, a turn o' the wrist and he was out in the street again, joinin' us guys acrost the street. Up in the Donegan's parlor it was dark again. But there was no graveyard silence now. Oh no!

Them nice Sunday school boys what was too good fer the Crap-shooter's class could turn a trick, too. When they found themselfs in

25. *to lambaste.* To assault.

26. *with a skate on.* Intoxicated.

27. *be put wise.* To be informed.

28. *butt.* Cigarette stub.

pitch dark wit' fifteen nice crows tumblin' around they sure didn't sit still waitin' fer Mrs. Donegan to find another light. No sir. They knocked over the furniture, kissed the other fellers' crows, tore down pictures from the walls, pasted[29] each other over the head with sofa pillows, an' Riley was in the middle o' the mob howlin' like a wild tiger an' handin' an occasional fist full o' knuckles to any o' them nice Sunday school boys what come clost enough fer a collision. When Mrs. Donegan finally found a candle, lit it, an' come in from the kitchen Riley heaves a sofa cushion at her and she beats it back to the kitchen. She didn't try no more fer to restore order, but sent Mame down fer the janitor. He got lambasted, too, when he come in, but after goin' down to the meter finds out that a prank was played an' tells Mrs. Donegan.

She flared up and blamed it on the family that lived on the floor below. They had not took kindly to the racket over their heads that night, so the suspicion fell on them fer turnin' off the Donegan's gas.

Well after the janitor got it goin' again one o' them fellers who had brung his accordeen, an' couldn't play fer old hats,[30] got busy an' pumped out Sweet Rosie O'Grady, Sweet Molly O, an' Turkey In The Straw, Riley doin' a buck an' wing.[31] The neighbors enjoyed it I don't think!

About this time we begun to think o' that ice cream, so me and Blinkey spruces up a bit and goes moseyin' around to the confectioner. We each screwed up our nerve and put on a good front.

"Good evenin' sir," says I. "Me and me friend here came round fer the ice cream what was ordered fer Mrs. Donegan. Is it ready?"

"Yes it iss, but I must got to haf 25 cents deposit for the can," he says.

---

29. *to paste.* To strike.

30. *couldn't play fer old hats.* Expression indicating inferior ability.

31. [*Sweet Rosie O'Grady, Sweet Molly O, an' Turkey In The Straw.* A variety of popular songs that came out of New York City's Tin Pan Alley, Broadway and 14th Street, a district where after 1890 leading music publishers and songwriters were located. A "buck and wing" was a high-energy tap dancing feature of popular minstrel ("blackface") and Irish performers at the turn of the century.—Ed.]

Well we was up against it. We hadn't looked fer anything like that. I didn't have a red cent[32] an' Blinkey didn't even have a plugged nickel. While I was scratchin' me head thinkin' what to do, Blinkey points up at some candies in a jar an' asks the Dutchman:

"How much is them mellow juicy peps[33] a pound?"

"Mellow juice vot?" asks the Dutchman, lookin' hard at the row of jars to which Blinkey was pointin' with one hand, his other hand bein' busy stowin' chocolate nut-bars into his jeans[34] from off'n the counter.

"Dem aind vot you said," says the Dutchman, "dem is shust ordinary vintergreens drops."

"Oh, my mistake," says Blinkey, appearin' kind o' sorry in troublin' the Dutchman. But it was his kiddin' the confectioner that give me a chance to stack the deck[35] fer the next play, as well as give Blinkey his chance to lift some nice candy.

"Well," says I, "Mrs. Donegan never said nothin' to us about any deposit. We'll go back an' get the dough."[36]

When we got outside I left Blink on guard to watch fer any genuine agents in case Mrs. Donegan sent them around, and ducked fer Dugan's cellar. "Youse guys shell out[37] a quarter right away. The Dutchman wants a deposit!" I says, out-o'-breath, and they all coughs up[38] small change fer me.

I got back to the store and me an' Blinkey tackles the feller again. We gives him the quarter, picks up the pail an' walks out. It was dead easy.[39] Like takin' candy from a baby.

---

32. *didn't have a red cent.* Absolutely without means, destitute.

33. *mellow juicy peps.* Fictitious name for candies.

34. *jeans.* Trousers, pants.

35. *stack the deck.* An expression from card playing meaning to pre-arrange the cards to bring about a desired result. Here means an effort to gain time to meet the contingency.

36. *dough.* Money.

37. *shell out.* To deliver, to pay up.

38. *cough up.* Same as "shell out."

39. *dead easy.* Absolutely without difficulty.

Instead o' goin' to Donegan's that pail went to Dugan's cellar. Now this story dont end here. We thought it did, but it didn't. We smuggled the pail of ice cream down into the clubrooms, and bestowin' silent blessin's on the absent Riley we put away that ice cream. I et near two quarts meself. When we finished it we took a sneak up the street again, an' hung out on the curbstone acrost from the Donegan's house. About eleven o'clock we seen old man Donegan come out o' the corner saloon pie-eyed.[40] He come unsteady down the street lookin' hard to pick his own house out o' the row of identickle flathouses. We steered him right, rung hell out of his own door bell and started him upstairs. Then we run acrost the street again an' waited fer trouble. It come soon enough.

Riley told us about it when we seen him again. It begun as soon as old Donegan poked his nut inside the door. He had on just enough edge[41] to be quarrelsome, an' when he learned that they was havin' a party without havin' first consulted him he starts in to chase the guests out'n the parlor. "I'll show who's boss in this shanty," he says, an' Mrs. Donegan begins to cry. She seen that a family brawl was goin' to break up the party. "What'll I do?" she asks Riley who was rubberin' out in the kitchen.

"Leave the old man to me," says Riley, an' she done it.

Donegan still was thinkin' about cleanin' the house[42] with the crowd in the parlor when Riley greets 'im.

"Good evenin', Mr. Donegan, nice party ye're daughter's havin'," he says, an' before the old boy could get on his feet Riley goes on.

"Did ye' hear how the people downstairs insulted ye' wife?" he asks. Then he tells how them "malicious neighbors" turned off the gas, an' worked up Donegan into such a rage that it was sure time to fly the storm signals. Just when somethink was about to bust in comes the two boys what Mrs. Donegan had sent fer the ice cream. They says that the Dutchman swore he sent it around two hours ago. Donegan butts in[43]

40. *pie-eyed*. Drunk.

41. *have an edge on*. Intoxicated.

42. *to clean house*. To drive out, to eject forcibly.

43. *to butt in*. To interfere, to meddle, to break into the conversation.

on this an' listens to their explanations. Then he decides to go around an' see the Dutchman himself. Hopeful that after he had straightened out this matter he'd drop in at the bar on the corner, an' ferget to come back, Mrs. Donegan orders the feller with the accordeen to strike up a grand march, and all come marchin' in an' sits down to the table.

It was a mighty nifty lay-out. They was cold ham, pertater salad, chicken san'wiches, candies, nuts, raisins, fruit, cakes, jam, dates an' other good eats, and everybody was laffin', an' snapcrackers was snappin', soda bottles poppin', nuts crackin' an' all was havin' a swell time an' waitin' fer the ice cream. But nix![44] It never come.

Pretty soon they was a noise in the hallway, an' some heated argymint. In comes old man Donegan, a cop, an' the German confectioner. Riley almost fainted. "Here's me finish," he says, thinkin' as how the cop had got wise to the kidnappin' o' that ice cream, an' was comin' to pinch him. But that wasn't what they was after. Accompanied by Donegan the Dutchman went around the festive board, the guests all a-skared, lookin' into the face of every bloke in the room. Riley met him with a marble stare, an' stopped shiverin' in his boots when the Dutchman passed him up. When the inspection was over the confectioner said that the guys what called for the ice cream wasn't there. Donegan said he didn't believe no fellers ever come an' got the stuff. The ice cream guy answers back somethink about that he would not let no drunken Irisher swindle him.

"Biff! Bing!" Before the cop could block him Donegan had swung his mitts,[45] an' landed twice on the Dutchman's physog. Then come the claret![46] Insistin' that the cop arrest Donegan on a charge of assault an' battery, the Dutchman put up such a holler that the whole flat house turned out.

When Mrs. Donegan sees her husband puttin' on his togs[47] gettin' ready to go with the cop, she throws a fit,[48] goes into hysterics an'

44. *nix!* An exclamation of absolute, imperative negation.
45. *mitts.* Hands, fists.
46. *claret.* Blood.
47. *togs.* Clothing. Coat and hat.
48. *throw a fit.* To go into hysterics, to become greatly excited.

Mame, takin' her cue from the old woman, faints. It was a fine finish! The guests got into a panic, grabbed their hats an' coats an' dusted fer the street[49] where they dressed an' went home. Riley copped a couple pockets full o' candy from the tables in the excitement an' skidooed with the other guests. It was sure the most surprisin' surprise party ever pulled off in Yorkville!

I spose youse guys want to know what happed to Donegan. Well nuttin'. The desk sergeant cut 'im loose when they got him over to the police station. But it wasn't the last he heard o' that surprise party. Next day it got all around[50] the neighborhood that the Donegan's had their gas turned off by the gas company because they didn't pay their bills. It was rumored too, that the landlord had served some kind of paper on Donegan. Mrs. Donegan wouldn't show her face on the street.

The Dutchman a week later found out his mistake when they picked up his empty ice cream pail in an alleyway. He felt so sorry that he took around a peace offering in the shape of a big box o' bonbons. But he didn't find the Donegans in. They had moved away to the Bronx.

49. *dust fer the street*. To run for the street, to escape.
50. *got around*. Was gossiped.

6.

Mickey's Lecture on "How to Get a Job."

We was talkin' about jobs down in Dugan's cellar one night. Not "put-up jobs"[1] but real jobs—positions, occupations an' such like. Some of the guys thought that the best way to succeed in life was to get one job an' stick to [it] so's they couldn't pry you loose without dynamite. I, meself, didn't think so, because a guy has got to travel aroun' to find out what kind o' work he can do best.

"You're wrong on that," says Shorty. "Remember the old philosoffers says: 'The rollin' stone dont git no moss!'"

"Oh, git off'n that philosoffer stuff," says Mickey wit' disgust, "because dem guys dont allus know what they's talkin' about. The rollin' stone may not gather no moss, but how about the rollin' snowball? Dont it gather no snow? An' talkin about thinks in motion—dont rovin' bees git the honey? Chuck that philosoffer dope into the discard, and use ye' noodle. Apply common sense!"

Shorty faded away.

With that Mickey has the floor all to hisself, an' he give a spiel about gettin' jobs that was really some class. He says:

"Youse guys is allus askin': 'How's a feller goin' t' get a decent job, an' hold it?' The trut' is that youse blokes what's all the time whinin' about not bein' able to get a job is too damn lazy t' woik if ye' get a job. An' it's my opinion that ye'll never get none. Jus' let me give ye' my experience o' the question.

1. *put-up jobs.* Conspiracies, usually pranks.

87

"As ye' all know, I was lately workin' fer the printer down on Franklin Square.[2] I t'rew up that job, an' I had me reasons. Sure I was a little sorry, because I was 'beer-boy'[3] in that factory. I carried two sticks, ten cans each, some beer, some ale an' some soup. Had 'em filled over in Pearl street every noon. Think o' that fine graft! I got me lunch allus from the free lunch counter.[4] But this was the on'y thing about the job I liked. Ye' never could get a day off, an' had to woik over time fer nothin'.

"But youse guys is probaly already t' ask me: 'What fer did ye' t'row up ye' job, then?' Well, the because why is jus' this! It was ruinin' me healt'. I was gettin' run down. Folks said I begun t' look like a lunger.[5] The factory work was too hard on me, an' besides the job was too dirty. I had t' wash me face every night because o' the ink. I'd been thinkin' about quittin' fer some time so las' Saturdy I walks int' the office an' asks the bookkeeper fer me dough.

"'What for?' says he.

"'Cat's fur! D'ye' ever see it on a dorg!' says I.

"'Are you quittin' ye're job?' he says.

"'You're on!'[6] says I. 'I'm sick o' this job, an' I want me mon.'

"He wouldn't pay me until he seen the boss, and they got to talkin' about dockin' me[7] fer not givin' a week's notice. Well I took no chances o' their gettin' int' me[8] like that so I slips a five-dollar micrometer into me pocket to see what they does. They cought up,[9] an' after I got me salary I returns the micrometer to the bookkeeper, an' says ta! ta! to that job.

---

2. [*Franklin Square*. The publishers Harper & Brothers had its large headquarters on Franklin Square near Pearl Street, close to the foot of the Brooklyn Bridge.—Ed.]

3. *beer-boy*. Errand boy who acts during the noon hour in factories to go out to saloons with long sticks from which are suspended the cans, or "growlers," to be filled with beer.

4. *free lunch counter*. A table supplied with food free to customers in saloons and grog shops.

5. *lunger*. Pronounced "lung-er." A consumptive.

6. *you're on!* Exclamation commonly used to mean "you understand."

7. *to dock*. To take some penalty from one's pay. Cutting a salary.

8. *get into me*. To defraud me, to get ahead of me.

9. *cough up*. Pay up.

"When I gets home I chucks me pay envelope wit' t'ree dollars in it on the table, an' remarks to the old woman: 'Well, I t'rew up me job, t'night. I'm goin' to take a rest now. Go down t' Palm Beach or 'lantic City.' Me funny stuff didn't go fer nix wit' the old woman. She blew up[10] like a subway explosion. Before the smoke had cleared away I promised to dig right out, bright an' early Monday mornin' an' look fer a new job. On Sunday she hands me the 'want' section o' the Sunday paper. 'Make out a list of places where they want boys, an' tomorrow go to all o' them until ye' get a new job,' she says. She adds: 'If ye' come home without a job ye'll either be put out o' the house or we'll send ye' up to the House of Refuge[11] or some other place fer bad boys.'

"I tells her t' dry up, an' takes the quarter she give me fer carfare. The next mornin' she drags me out o' bed before daylight an' starts me off downtown. I was out so early that I had first whack at the milk bottles, an' I drunk the cream off'n all between me house and the elevated railroad station.

"The first place on me list was a shoe factory down in Canal street. I took the elevator an' went upstairs. They was about skeenteen[12] fellers ahead o' me. Most o' them was Sheenies, Dutch kids an' Ginneys. I got in line but seein' a lot o' Sheenies up in front I goes up, shoves the first one out an' takes 'is place. A little Dutch guy in front o' me grins an' says: 'Huh! Before you wass behind, but now you are first at last!'

"'What kind of a job is this?' I asks him.

"'They want lasters'[13] he says.

"I didn't know a 'laster' from a 'firster.' I was thinkin' o' pullin' up a bluff. I have saw many a amateur talk an' act like a thug on the baseball field jus' t' make people think he played like a professional, an' I knowed

---

10. *she blew up.* Evidenced a violent outburst of rage.

11. *House of Refuge.* Institution for delinquent children on Randall's Island, East River. [The New York House of Refuge, founded 1824, was one of the city's oldest juvenile institutions and in the 1890s was located just north of Yorkville.—Ed.]

12. *skeenteen.* Indicates an indefinite number.

13. [*lasters.* Mickey is referring to the operators of machines that fastened the upper leather of a shoe to the sole.—Ed.]

that a bluff will take a guy a long ways. But me bluff was called too soon when a big, husky foreman ast me if I ever had experience, an' I says 'no.'

"'Then beat it[14] out o' here,' says he. An' I did, believe me. I didn't like the idea o' workin' wit' Sheenies and Ginneys, anyway.

"Next I took a sneak up into a place on Mercer street where they makes flowers and feathers. The smell o' that place told me it was Kosher, an' I sticks me face into the door jus' long enough to say: 'Nay, nay Pauline, not fer mine!'

"Well, I went to half a dozen other places, an' believe me, there is twenty boys scrappin' fer every job that's advertised. I seen that somethin' would have to happen mighty soon if I was to get a job. Then I gets a new idea. I chucks me newspaper list away[15] an' starts up fer Wanamaker's department store.[16] I had decided to take a job as salesman or stock boy.

"When I got up there I met a guy outside who says:

"'You lookin' for a job here?'

"'That's what I am,' says I.

"'You dont get no job in that place unless you have on a collar an' necktie,' says he.

"'What's the matter wit' mine?' I asks.

"'I dont think they'd get by, in there,' he says.

"Me collar was somewhat on the blink,[17] not havin' seen the laundry fer a mont' so I goes over to Third avenue, buys a new collar, puts it on, and makes me toilet in front of a mirror in the window o' a saloon. Wit' me new regalia I goes into the big store.

"'Hey kid!' says I to one o' them kids what runs around from counter to counter when them crows yells 'cash! ca-sh!' 'Hey kid, where do ye' go to get a job in this joint?'

---

14. *beat it*. Command to get out.

15. *chuck away*. To throw away.

16. [*Wanamaker's*. The pioneering merchant John Wanamaker of Philadelphia opened a New York store in 1896 on Broadway between Ninth and Tenth Streets and expanded with a new building in 1907, one of the city's most magnificent shopping emporia.—Ed.]

17. *on the blink*. Soiled, unsatisfactory.

"He took me to a office where I finds another mob o' guys, all ahead o' me. I waits an' waits and fin'ly a floor manager comes up, chews the rag with me, an' says 'you'll do.'

"He gimme a slip o' paper an' tol' me to take it to the top floor, where I would be given me instructions. I goes up, an' glory be! What do you spos'n they done. They took me pedigree, hands me one o' them round, shiny badges with a number on like them cashboys wore, and sent me down to report to the sup'rintendent!

"'I see meself in hell, first, before I wears one of them tin badges,' says I, an' I gets me hat when nobody was lookin', an' resigns that job without writin' out me resignation.

"'Here,' says I to the kid what opens the street door, 'give this badge to his nibs, with the pink whiskers over there by the counter!' and I was hot-footin' it fer Broadway.

"Now, most guys would o' given up by this time—an' that's where I make me strong point. Dont give up, but go right on an' tackle every place you come to, whether they advertised fer a boy or not! Like as not they's about to advertise fer a boy an' you're there to save them the price o' the ad. I started in and asked in every store I come to, headin' down town. 'Want a boy?' I says, stickin' me noodle into every doorway and pipin' off the boss. O' course most o' them didn't want no boy. But most o' them was interested an' told me to come around soon again if I failed to land.

"I struck one place and got next to the boss. He was a kuyk![18] Generally I dont like to work fer Sheenies but I was tryin' to satisfy the old woman, not meself. He wanted a errand-boy, an' likin' the looks o' me biceps he says he'll take me right off.

"'How much carfare d'ye allow?' I asks.

"'Ten cents below Canal street and above Twenty-Third street, nothin' between,' he says.

"'Punk[19] enough,' says I.

---

18. *kuyk.* A Hebrew.

19. *punk.* Bad, uninviting.

"'What's the salary?'

"'Two and a half a week,' he answers.

"'In $5 gold pieces?' says I.

"He didn't like me sarcasm an' after hirin' me had the nerve to ask me fer a 'rec.'[20]

"'I don't furnish no recommendations on two-dollar-and-a-half jobs' says I, an' with that he cans me.[21] I got mad an' says 'G'wan ye' cheap-skate Mock.[22] Fer two cents I'd yank [your] lilacs!'[23] He started to send fer a cop so I pushed over a stack o' boxes near the doorway and dusted down Broadway.

"When I stops again I looks fer some other joint where I might land a job. Right in front o' me is a hat store. In I goes an' butts into the boss. He listens to me spiel, takes me into his office, sends fer the shippin' clerk an' in five minutes I'm hired. I never struck such a snap job in me life. I get me t'ree an' a half a week, an' knock about ten bucks[24] in carfare. I show up fer work each day about seven-thirty or eight—the rest o' the time I'm either deliverin' bundles or soldierin'.[25] It's about half an' half. I'm s'posed to go out o' the store with me bundles by the back way, but when the boss is in the store I goes out the front way. I waits until he is busy with customers, an' then goes along by him, gruntin' and groanin' like me bundles was killin' me. He has to make a bluff in front o' his customers so he ushally says: 'Well, me boy; where you goin?'

"'Way down town' I says.

"'Got enough carfare?'

---

20. *rec.* Recommendation.

21. *cans me.* Discharge me.

22. *Mock.* Hebrew. Corruption of "Moses."

23. *lilacs.* Whiskers.

24. *knock about ten bucks.* Withhold about ten dollars, etc.

25. *soldiering.* Loafing. [When laboring people sought to control the pace at which they worked, their bosses, who wanted them to work faster, accused them of "soldiering," by which they meant loafing.—Ed.]

"'I need ten cents more' says I. Then he digs right down into his jeans, pulls out a quarter an' hands it over to me, sayin': 'Never mind the change, keep that fer ye' self!'

"Every few days they sends me down to Dun's an' Bradstreets[26] fer to find out if any o' them guys what has their names on the list the bookkeeper hands me is 'dead-beats.'[27] It takes t'ree hours sometimes to get me report so all I has to do is to sit around with other ginks shootin' craps or readin' dime novels. It's a great graft! When me statements is ready I shoves 'em into one pocket, puts me penny-dreadful[28] into the other pocket o' me pants, an' takes a nice ride up Broadway on the back of a truck an' charges the bookkeeper carfare fer it.

"Some days when I wants to get home early I picks out a nice uptown trip, frames up[29] a list o' jumps chargin' a nickel carfare fer each, walks or steals rides fer most o' them, an' knocks about half a dollar in carfare. Now fellers, that's the kind of a job youse can strike jus' like me. Jus' go walkin' down Broadway an' go rubber-neckin' into every store, an' you'll find a job if ye' really want one."

26. [*Dun's an' Bradstreets*. Dun & Bradstreet was a credit-reporting agency that provided businesses with information about persons wishing to borrow or purchase on credit.—Ed.]

27. *dead-beats*. Debtors, impecunious persons.

28. *penny-dreadful*. Penny novel. [Another name for dime novels, the cheap, mass-produced works of sensational adventure fiction that targeted reading audiences of working-class men and boys. Middle-class Americans believed that reading dime novels corrupted boys and made them wish to be outlaws. Possession of a dime novel was a crime in the George Junior Republic.—Ed.]

29. *frame up*. Arrange to suit one's purpose.

7.

Mickey's Scheme, and a Visit to a Bowery Museum.

Red was broke, out of a job an' ready to join the Down-an'-Out club.[1] He come down into Dugan's cellar where me and Shorty was havin' a quiet smoke, one afternoon. The rest o' the club guys had gone down to Tony Pastors theayter[2] on billboard tickets.[3] Red was blue! Get that? He was so clean busted that he couldn't o' joined a crap game if it was on'y a penny a shoot. Fact was he hadn't even et no grub that day, cause he hadn't the price.

"Hell man, go up to some hot-dog joint[4] an' line ye' stummick wit' coffee an' crullers!" says Shorty, stakin'[5] him with a dime.

When he come back he was a new man. He t'rew himself on the mattress an' yawned.

"Shorty, I'll pay back that dime jus' as soon as I kin invent some way to raise money without doin' any woik!" he says.

"Say, you aint no Thomas Edison," says I.

"Remember, Necessity is the mother of Invention," says Shorty, who reads other books besides dime novels.

---

1. *Down-and-Out club.* Imaginary group of the hopeless and destitute.

2. [*Tony Pastors theayter.* Tony Pastor's Theater was on Fourteenth Street. In the 1880s and 1890s the "father of vaudeville" established variety theater in fashionable neighborhoods and made the entertainment more suitable for respectable audiences.—Ed.]

3. *billboard tickets.* Special tickets issued for bill posters and window privilege in advertising a show.

4. *hot-dog joint.* Restaurant. "Hot dog" is word used always for sausage.

5. *staking.* Lending, regardless of terms.

"Yes, an' she's got some queer kids," says I. "When Edison an' such guys invents anythink that brings in the mon'[6] they calls it Industry, but when you an' me invents some game fer producin' the mazuma[7] they calls it Crime."

"If I was on'y rich an' prosperous!" sighs Red.

"Prosperous!" says Shorty. "Say, aint you an' me seen the day when we had money to burn?[8] Aint we had slathers[9] o' it at times? Where is it today? Say, prosperity puts more of us blokes on the blink than poverty! Can a guy drink hisself to deat' 'nless he's got the mon' to pay fer the booze?[10] You remind me o' them fellers what's all the time goin' round lookin' fer Christmas trees to pick off the things what other guys hung on them. Take my woid fer it Red, the on'y way to get anything worth while is to sweat fer it."

Red let them words soak into his noodle fer some time. He was framin' up somethink that kep' him in a trance. Then he opens his mush[11] with a yell.

"I got it. The greatest scheme ye' ever heard of! I'm goin' to be rich in a hurry. I'll have enough dough to break every crap game in this ward! My scheme 'll bring me mazuma every day in the year! My scheme—"

"Aw you're jus' like the Socialist labor party," says Shorty, "allus got great ideas but they never woik!"

"Let 'im spit it out," says I, interruptin', "maybe his idea 'll pan out."

"Well, here's me plan," says Red, when we set back to listen. "Of course youse guys knows the system they have around in the big meat market on Second avenue—how when a guy buys anythink he gets his meat and a little ticket, an' is exspected to pay up to the crow what sits at the cashier's desk? Well, me scheme is this, nothin' more nor less. I waits until the store is crowded, goes in an' buys me meat. Gets it tucked

6. *mon'*. Abbreviation for money.

7. *mazuma*. Money.

8. *money to burn*. Money in abundance.

9. *slathers*. Boundless quantities.

10. *booze*. Intoxicating drink, generally whiskey.

11. *mush*. Mouth.

under me arm, takes me ticket, an' then instead o' goin' to the cashier's desk I puts up a good front an' walks out o' the store with the crowd. Its dead easy, 'specially on Saturdays, when the market's crowded. Ye' see how great me plan is! Everythin' to gain and nothin' to loose! All I have to do is to get people to let me runs their errands to the butcher!"

"It listens good,[12] but believe me, you poor mutt![13] It aint goin' to work like you think it is," says Shorty. "That butcher guy might be asleep a little while an' let ye' beat the system, but believe me, that system was put in to beat crooks! The cashier would find out that somebody went south with some o' the cash when the registers are figgered up, the proprietor would put a 'flatty' in the store, an' once ye' get nailed at that kind o' crookin' it'll be the Juver[14] or the House o' Ref fer you, an' the Crapshooters wont see you again fer many, many moons. Man, ye' must be foolish to think they wont get hep to ye're game! What d'ye' sposn that little bells rings fer, when they ring up yer order? Why simply to put the cashier next[15] that somebody'll soon come her way to pay up! Take my advice, play that game mighty careful!"

"Well, youse guys may be from Missouri; but I'll show ye'," said Red.

• ◆ •

Red worked his scheme overtime the next Saturday. He come down to the club rooms that afternoon with the airs of a millionaire. I never seen him with such a swelled head before! He says:

"Well, youse guys from Missouri[16]—here's how me scheme worked!" an' he pulls out a pocketful o' chicken feed.[17] "Here's five dollars an' thirty-five cents I raised today beatin' that system."

12. *listens good.* An exclamation often used, meaning: "it sounds reasonable" or "it is agreeable."

13. *mutt.* Dog. Fellow.

14. *Juver.* For Juvenile Asylum, institution for juvenile offenders. [The New York Juvenile Asylum, founded 1851, was located in the Washington Heights area of northern Manhattan. Unlike the House of Refuge, which treated delinquents, it rescued runaways and homeless children from the city's streets.—Ed.]

15. *put next.* To inform.

16. *be from Missouri.* To be skeptical, demanding positive proof.

17. *chicken feed.* Small coins.

"Well, kid; how d'ye' do it?" says the bunch.

"I done it like I said I'd do it. First I buys a nice, lean ham fer Mrs. Lahey, the janitor. I flim-flammed[18] 'em out of ninety cents on that. When I went in to buy it I goes right up like the old wimmin an' digs me finger nails into the meat on the counter like I was a critic o' tender an' juicy meats. I orders me ham an' puts it in a basket I had brung along. Out'n the corner o' me eye I pipes off the chances fer a getaway,[19] fumbles around me basket until I sees a good chance, an' walks out. It was as easy as divin' off'n the dock in swimmin' time. Onct I got me head wet I felt like stayin' in all day. The water was fine. I delivers the ham an' then runs an errand fer the yaller-haired actress what we calls The Fairy. She wanted a roast o' beef. I was a little leary[20] on that trip, because I thought that may be they had got hep to me first job. But I pulled that off jus' like I was pickin' up me winnin's in a crap game. Me technique was gettin' polished. Well to make a long story short I pulled in between five an' six bucks,[21] an' I've come down here now to invite the whole push down fer a visit to the Globe[22] an' we'll see Carrie Stanley this week in 'Deadwood Dick.'[23] I'll t'row in the eats, too an' blow youse all to a regular at Beefsteak John's."

The Globe was a museum down on the Bowery. It aint there today because the Bowery is goin' on the blink these days. In them days they was the old Globe near Houston street an' the Gaiety down near Grand street. Between they was snake shows, Bosco who eats 'em alive, the Australian What-is-it?, an' some o' them wax-figger anatomy shows. Today they's nothin' on the Bowery. Its simply on the blink!

18. *flim-flammed*. Swindled.

19. *getaway*. An escape.

20. *be leary*. To be frightened.

21. *bucks*. Dollars.

22. [*Globe*. The Globe Dime Museum on the Bowery offered cheap variety entertainments that catered to audiences lower on the social scale than Tony Pastor targeted with his more fashionable theater further uptown.—Ed.]

23. [*Deadwood Dick*. The show was based on the popular dime novel outlaw, who was featured in more than thirty works the writer Edward L. Wheeler produced between 1877 and 1884 for Beadle & Adams, publishers of cheap fiction.—Ed.]

It wasn't more'n half an hour before our whole push was unloadin' from the elevated road at Houston street. It was a little early so we go's scoutin' around on Great Jones street to see if they was anythink we could pry loose. Riley gets his hooks[24] into a packin' box and makes a getaway with a box o' brass buttons what they uses on sailor suits. Ye' couldn't hock[25] 'em in the best hock shop on the Bowery fer fifteen cents. I didn't see the least use o' swipin' them. Mickey was there with an idea, though. He took a couple o' them buttons, laid them on the cartrack an' let the heavy cars flatten 'em out. They was just the right size an' heft to go in the penny-in-the-slot macheens, an' we sure done a rushin' business flattenin' out that box o' brass buttons and feed 'em into all the slot macheens that stood on the street. We got enough chewin' gum to supply the club a week, an' had a lot o' buttons left, at that! Them brass sailor buttons is about the on'y things I ever seen that could beat the slot macheen. Ye' got to use the medium size. If ye' use the large size they wont go in the slot, an' if ye' use the small size they aint heavy enough to do the business, but it works fine with them medium size ones. You try it sometime!

Well when we got t'rough with this pleasant interruption we goes to the dear, old Globe. It was a great old joint in its day. People come to that museum from all over the world. Lookin' out over his audience the perfessor who lectured over the freaks there could see Jackies from the Navy yard, reglars from Governor's Island, Chinks from Doyers street, gamblers, bookmakers, pimps an' cadets,[26] dive keeps, show people, working men and working women, Harps from Sullivan street, Ginneys from Mulberry street, Dutch heinies from First avenue, Frenchies from over Sout' Fifth avenue, all kinds o' down-an'-outs that lived on

---

24. *hooks.* Hands.

25. *hock.* Pawn.

26. *cadets.* Procurers, "white slavers." [In the early twentieth century, concern spread throughout the United States that men were forcing young white women into prostitution, a practice called "white slavery." Cadets entrapped the women, and pimps managed the prostitution rings.—Ed.]

the Bowery, an' muckers[27] like us guys, the honorable members o' the Crapshooters Club.

Anybody who ever useter go on the Bowery wont never ferget them bells in front of the old Globe. They clanged day and night, first one bunch then another, an' the cable gongs, the trolley bells an' the rumbling elevated didn't have nothin' on them old dime museum bells fer racket! They sure got the crowds up to pipe off them great signs. They allus had a Dutch band hidden up behind some shutters over the entrance in competition with them bells. It was a dead heat, at that!

Well on this particular night they had a flarin' canvas with a picture of The Wonderful Horse With The Human Feet. Its feet was jus' like your'n or mine—in the picture! The big attraction, though, was shown on a picture that run clean acrost the building. It was seven beautiful ladies, the champeen pie eaters of the great nations. It said they was all engaged at great expense fer this series o' pie-eatin' contests. But I'll let the lecturer give his spiel when we get inside. Admission was one dime. We had some trouble gettin' in though.

Red, who was blowin' the crowd off[28] an' stood treat steps up to the ticket office, plunks down seventy cents and gets seven tickets. But the guy at the door, who had a big, rattan switch, stops Shorty.

"Hay, you—get out o' here. You aint sixteen an' you cant go in without parent or gardeen!" he says.

Oh moicy, Poicy! Wouldn't that frost ye'r punkins? Shorty needin' a gardeen! An' he as wise a gazaybo as ever went into that museum! Well we all put up a kick, an' told the guy that if Shorty wasn't goin' in none of us would, an' we wanted our money back, too. Then he changes his mind, the fat slob![29] He let's us all pass through an' we goes upstairs. This was the main lecture hall. Freaks was settin all round an' we pipes off the perfessror as he steps down from the side platforms to climb up on

27. *muckers.* Street boys.

28. *blowing off the crowd.* Standing treat.

29. *slob.* Fellow, with idea of contempt. Unkempt, dirty person.

the big stage at the end. He was a funny old dub, skinny an' as bald as a billiard ball. His noodle was as shiny, too; on'y he kep' it covered with a skull cap. He wore spectacles an' carried a cane. He was allus wipin' off his glasses with a nose-rag[30] that stunk with perfumery. Gimme anythink but a man what uses perfumery! I feel like pastin' a guy in the mug[31] every time I smell perfumery on him. Up our way perfumery is used on'y by niggers an' wimmin. Well old ivory top raps on the wall with his cane fer silence an' hands out this spiel:

"Ladies an' gents. I takes great pleasure in introducin' to ye' notice the woild renowned champeen pie-eaters of the great nations of the globe. On me extreme right sits Norah, champeen of Dalway, Dublin an' more recently of all Ireland."

(Norah, in green satin short skirts and Irish costume stan's up an' lets the crowd inspect her until the spieler goes to the next crow.)

"On her left we have Princess Alice, from dear old London, champeen of all England and of the larger colonies, as can easily be seen by an inspection o' the medals upon her breast. The young lady would be pleased, I am sure, to exhibit her trophies to anyone in the audience," he says, noddin' at her. She nods back, an' Mickey makes her lean away over so's he can rubber at them.

"Them medals is phoney!" he says out loud when he got through, but the perfessor never heard him, he goes right on to the next young pie-eatin' dame.

"This beautiful young lady hails from gay Paree and has won many contests in France. At her side is La Belle Fanny, the fair daughter of Uncle Sam just arrived from a series of contests in the West where she won many victories. She is a fitting representative of the land of the fair an' the home of the brave," he says, lookin' toward our bunch as a cue to cut loose wit' applause. We done it all right, all right, even if we did roast[32] the show. While we was listenin' to the lecturer Mickey pulls out

---

30. *nose-rag*. Inelegant word for handkerchief.

31. *mug*. Face, mouth.

32. *roast*. Ridicule, make sport of.

o' our crowd after borrowin' a couple o' pins an' says he [will] come back. We judged that he must o' busted his pants, or somethink. Well the barker[33] goes on with the spiel.

"Here we have Gretchen, champeen of Berlin, the home of good beer and, gents, I know you'll join me in the wish that I had one now," he says, grinnin' and holdin' up both hands to measure up the size of a regular Bowery schooner.[34] He give "Angelina," a Ginney who represented Italy, an' the last gal what he called a "dark-eyed seen yora from Spain," a send-off and wound up wit': "I assure ye', ladies an' gents, these bewtiful champeens have been secured at tremendous expense by our agents in Europe, an' have just arrived on the palatial greyhounds of the ocean durin' the past week!"

"What kin o' bull con[35] ye' givin' us? I bet ye' one dollar against a plugged nickel that none o' them dames ever seen the outside o' Sandy Hook!"[36] yells Shorty to the perfessor.

"Dont interrupt the performance, or ye' 'll have to be put out!" says the spieler, lookin' around fer one o' the museum's bouncers.[37]

"The contest will now begin," he announces, an' everybody in the lecture hall crowds up in front to see the champeens go to it.

By this time Mickey had come back, an' he was grinnin' all over. "Say," he says, "ye' know that t'ree-legged boy down on the platform near the doorway? Well he's a fake.[38] I tested him out meself an' found out that one of his legs is phoney. I done it by shootin' bent pins at his legs. I hit the middle leg t'ree times an' it never moves, but once, when I missed that an' hit one o' the other legs he grabs at it like he was stung, an' complains to the fat lady settin' on the next platform. Then I makes me self scarce, bein' certain that his middle leg was phoney."

33. *barker.* Lecturer, "professor" in a dime museum, or side show.

34. *schooner.* A large goblet.

35. *bull con.* False information.

36. *Sandy Hook.* The outer bound of New York harbor.

37. *bouncers.* Men employed in public halls, saloons and similar places because of their strong-arm ability to eject persons not wanted.

38. *fake.* False.

That guy, Mickey, allus *was* a inquisitive guy!

Well, when the spieler says: "The contest'll now begin" all them dames stands up, shakes out their skirts an' bows. Then they gets down on their knees with the hands behin' their backs an' leans over a board on which they was a fi' cent pie be-front each dame.

Takin' 'is turnip[39] out'n 'is pocket the perfessor says: "Ladies an' gents. This bout will last until the first pie is et! The winner thus scores one point. At the end of this week the nation having the most points will be awarded the priceless diamond medal offered by this management. Are youse ready!" he yells, raisin' a blank cartridge-pistol over his nut.

He pulls the trigger! Bang! The crows of all nations was at it! Talk about excitement! Them pies slipped all over the board an' the champeens wasn't allowed to touch 'em wit' their hands. They dug their physogs right in an' it was great sport. The poor Ginney gal what represented Italy had a custard pie an' it got over the edge an' fell wit' a flop on the floor. She was disqualified but maybe we didn't do a thing to that pie. The crow what stood fer America had no chanst at all. The sucker[40] runnin' the pie-end o' the contest had slipped her a berry-pie with juice what ran all over. O' course she got beat and when the perfessor announced that Germany won we hissed like hell. Fer bein' so patryotic the perfessor gives us all the pieces o' busted pie what was left, an' we divvied it up square. Then the bell rung and a barker yells out that the performance in Hall No. 2 was now about to start, so up we goes like a ton o' bricks fallin' down stairs.

Now this floor o' the museum didn't have much good stuff. On one side was a row o' pictures which ye' looked into, sort o' panoramic. On the Bowery end was a stall with that wonderful horse wit' the human feet. That was the biggest fake in the place. All it was, was a pony what had toes carved on its hoofs. Any bum blacksmit' could take any old nag an' cut toes on the front of the hoofs an' call it a horse wit' human feet, if he had noive enough. O' course it was alive, all right, all right; but that

39. *turnip.* Watch.

40. *sucker.* Fellow easily deceived. Term of disparagement.

dont make no difference. It dont hurt a horse to have his feet carved. An' couldn't they chloroform it if it did hurt? An' yet them museum guys had the noive to print a sign and hang it out there on the Bowery with a picture of a real horse wit' real pink feet like a human bein'! I could open a museum meself, wit' them kind o' freaks! Well the on'y thing wort' seein' up there was the Punch an' Judy show, because they lets ye' t'row things at Punch whenever he sticks up his nut. Well now, whenever they comes to the place where Mrs. Judy says to Mr. Punch: "Here now, take care of the kid'" an' she hands over the baby to Punch an' he says "All right" an' takes the kid, well all us fellers gets ready then, because Punch throws the baby out to the crowd as soon as Judy goes down stairs. Well now, whoever gets the kid when it is chucked out has the right to t'row it back wit' all his might as soon as any one in the Punch an' Judy show sticks up his noodle fer to begin actin' again. Well this time Shorty got the kid but instead o' t'rowin' it back right away he held it until we could get a lot of apple corksies,[41] banana peels an' peanut shells. Well when the Hangman comes in to hang Punch we all took sides wit' Punch and let the Hangman have everythink! Shorty hit him so hard with the kid that it ripped the curtain an' when that shower o' apple cores, peanut shells, an' so on come down on the feller inside who was runnin' Punch an' Judy he rung down the curtain.

Well then we goes upstairs to the top floor, Chamber o' Horror. Here they had a collection of wax figgers showin' guys bein' murdered, other guys being tortured, an' wax faces of prominent guys like Lincoln, George Wash'nton an' Doctor Munyon.[42] There's hope!

Every hour, when the show down in the theayter in the basement of the museum ends, they rings a big gong upstairs an' the guy in charge opens up a brass door-gate an' down comes the whole push lickety-cut,[43] pell mell jabbin' each other wit' their elbows and scrappin'[44] fer

---

41. *corksies.* Apple cores.

42. [*Doctor Munyon.* Dr. James Monroe Munyon, manufacturer of Munyon's Homeopathic Home Remedies, was famous at the turn of the century for his patent medicines.—Ed.]

43. *lickety-cut.* In utter disorder.

44. *scrapping.* Fighting.

front places in the theayter. Ye' see those guys what pay on'y a dime aint allowed to set down in the theayter, all seats bein' reserved. Reserved seats costs a nickel apiece, an' if ye' dont buy none ye' got to stand up all t'rough the performance.

Well Mickey was blowin' us that night so we done it up brown[45] an' after we bought seats we butted and elbowed our way for-ard an' set ourselfs right down clost to the stage. I dont know whether ye' ever seen that theayter; but if y'aint seen it I'll say that it was a pretty[46] bum joint. It was a boxlike room and at some time way back when the Dutch settled N'York it must a been frescoed. The walls was faded and yeller wit' age above the wainscot, and down near the floor was brown wit' dried tobacco juice squirted by a t'ousand audjinces. They was no windows. The on'y air what come in was when the doors at the Bowery end was opened after the hour performance. Inside the air smelt like sawdust, stale beer an' powder smoke. The powder smoke come from the gun-play.

On that old stage many a great actress had done their acts. Fer instance Fannie Herring! She was the idol an' queen o' the Crapshooters club. Then they was Carrie Stanley! She come a clost second. An' Weber, the comedian, a guy what they say graduated to Broadway in after years.[47] Them dear old names was known to every East Sider. Fannie Herring was a brunette an' Carrie Stanley was one o' them peroxide, strawberry blondes.[48]

Well now the show what I am tellin ye' about was called: "The Stirrin' Melodrama, Deadwood Dick, or Run to Eart' at Last." We'd all read Deadwood Dick in our dime novels an' knowed all o' them characters on the program. Well now, Fannie Herring was down as "Madge, a cowgirl, the ranchman's daughter." She was a sort o' Annie

---

45. *do up brown.* Do up completely.

46. *pretty.* Used here in the sense of nearly, almost.

47. [*Carrie Stanley, Fannie Herring, [Joe] Weber.* Both women were popular theatrical actresses. Joe Weber and Lew Fields were a famous vaudeville comedy team and opened the Weber and Field's Music Hall in 1896.—Ed.]

48. *peroxide blonde.* Hair chemically bleached.

Oakley or female cowpuncher. The orchestry was a fiddler an' a feller what banged the box.[49] They crawled up out'n a hole under the stage an' played a overchure. Then come act 1.

The scene was out on a road in Colorado somewhere. They was a gang o' tough lookin' nuts[50] standin' around, pullin' at their villainous whiskers an' discussin' plans fer a hold-up. The mail coach was to pass there that night wit' on'y t'ree passengers, a wealt'y mine owner, his bewtiful daughter, an' a Chink. They allus has a Chink in them wild west plays. Now somebody had put them robbers hep to the fact that the driver of the stage-coach was guardin' a casket full o' gold an' diamon's what belonged to the swell skirt inside the coach. Well the crooks gave out that they was goin' to cop the casket an' kidnap the crow an' her old man, an' hold 'em fer ransom an' make her marry the leader. Well them guys had cooked up a pretty mean job, an' we hissed 'em when they went off threaten' to come back at stage coach time.

Now as soon as they went away out jumps Madge from behin' a rock. She was simply a peach.[51] She stood there with a cowgirl's suit on, slouch hat, rawhide whip, Colt's 38 in her holster an' cursin' them guys what just went off.

"No, youse dont, ye' black-hearted scoundrels; not if I'm alive to frustrate yer dastardly plans!" Then down come the curtain. We whistled an' clapped an' stamped fer her. It was one o' the swellest scenes I ever seen!

Well we chewed gum an' et peanuts while the pianner guy banged out another overchure. Then come the second act.

It was s'posed to be midnight on the stage. Robbers could be saw sneakin' around findin' places where they could be hunky-dory[52] until the mail coach comes along. They seemed to be on'y dark shadders an' it was awful spooky. Well now pretty soon one o' them bandits come up an' standin' on a rock puts his hand over his eyes, palm down, like

49. *banged the box.* Played the piano.

50. *tough nuts.* Vicious characters.

51. *peach.* A pretty girl.

52. *hunky-dory.* Snugly concealed, in a place of safety.

they was a sun shinin', an' he peers hard down the canyon. "It's a comin, boys!" he says, an' ducks behind a rock. We was all rubberin' hard into the wings where we heard footsteps approachin' on horseback. Then the fiddler begun to go "tunk! tink! tink! tunk!" on his violin makin' that kind o' music what shows somethink is approachin'. We set there breat'less an' at last the mail coach appears.

"Bang! bang!" goes the revolvers an' "T'row up ye're han's!" yells the robbers swarmin' all around.

"We are held up!" says the millionaire's daughter, stickin' her bun[53] out'n the winder.

Then Red-eyed Ike, the bandit king, steps up chesty,[54] an' puttin on airs says: "Sir, you an' ye're daughter is me prisoners. Make no attemp' to escape. We are dead-shots. Ha ha!" an' he touches his holster. Then he drags out the Chink an' make him dance a jig like he was shootin' up some tenderfoot. Well after the Chink done some funny stunts like that they cut him loose to starve to deat' in the desert, an' mountin' imaginary broncos they goes off to the mountains over in the direction o' Bleecker street. Now after they made a safe getaway in comes Madge, gun in each hand, an' ridin on a real pony. Beind her come her lover, Deadwood Dick an' his band, supers dressed like cowboys. They was come fer to make a rescue.

Now Deadwood Dick was also a bandit, but he was a good outlaw. He useter help the sheriff catch other bandits, probaly t' break up the competition. Well Madge was his gal, so he come to the rescue. When Madge finds that the robbers have went she comes down to the footlights. She says:

"Alas Dick, we are too late. They have flew to the mountins, to their rocky dens an' craggy fortresses. What shall we do. We cannot let them die like dorgs! What shall we do!"

Dick didn't seem to know what to do so he took Madge in his arms an' kisses her sayin': "Madge, you're a brave goil!" at which we clucks

---

53. *bun.* Head.

54. *chesty.* Puffed up with importance.

our tongues an' makes a noise like kissin' an' whispers "Break away, Dick, she et onions fer supper!"

Well now in comes Hop Lee, the Chink, an' he tells Deadwood Dick in pidgeon English where the bandits are. Well they all sets out in hot pursute.

The third act takes us to the mountain retreat of the robbers an' when the curtain went up we seen the bandit king layin' on the ground near a campfire. Near him the captive maid was reclining on a old sofa couch listening to the bandit king while he was entreatin' her to marry him an' accept all of his wealt'.

"Leave me," she cried, "I dee-spise you, you cowardly wretch! I would die rather than become the wife of a dastardly viper, like you! Away, you dee-spick-able wretch, you loat'some creechure!"

"Outside o' that he's all right, aint he?" says Shorty, in a stage whisper.

Up to this time the villin took this roastin' an' abuse without objectin'. But at last, havin' her in his power he t'rows off his mask an' shows hisself in his true colers.

"Then, by heavens! If ye' refuse me I'll kill ye're farther!" The old guy shuddered when he heard the t'reat, an' crouched low over by the fire where he sat holdin' his sad, white whiskers. The robber drawed his weepons an' walks over to the old man. He puts his gun clost to the old guy's noodle.

"Oh dont! Please spare me farther, an' I'll do anythink ye' say!" screams the gal. But, no, the robber is crule an' he's jus' about to cut out the old man's giz[55] when a commotion is heard. On all sides the robbers come runnin' in shoutin': "We are bee-trayed!" The fiddler plays violent, an' biff, bang in comes Deadwood Dick brandishin' a brace o' six-shooters an' yelling: "Surrender!"

"Never! Never!" yells the outlaws an' Dick's gang then kills all o' them with blank cartridges. That is all exceptin' the captain. That guy seein' they was no escape pulls out a silver-plated bowie knife an' rushes over to the side of the bewtiful dame whose old man he had been

---

55. *giz.* Gizzard.

threatenin' to kill. "I die, but she dies too!" he says an' wit' that he raises his hand to plunge the knife into her heart.

"No ye' dont! Drop that knife or ye're a dead man!"

It was Madge who spoke, an' Red Eye Ike was lookin' down the barrels o' two 38's when he come to. He slowly opened his paws an' let the knife drop harmless to the groun'. His black mustachio whiskers parted an' a oath an' a hiss was heard. "I s'render!" he says.

Well that scene brung down the house. They eng-cored it again an' again, an' before the show could go on they had to have every member walk across be-front o' the footlights an' get all the applause or hisses that was comin' to them. Oh, it was a grand show an' we sure thanked Mickey fer stakin' us to the price o' it!

Then come the last act. It was in the parlor of the mansion of the rich mine owner in N'York. It was a reglar Fifth avenue joint. All the guys wore dress suits an' they was a butler buttlin' to them an' passin' around cigars. The dames wore their glad rags[56] an' they was some swell skirts, there, believe me! They was to be a double weddin'—the mine owner's daughter and the young superintendent o' the mines, an' Madge an' Deadwood Dick.

Well now before the ceremony the old mine owner comes in an' fer weddin' presents hands out bundles a stocks an' bonds an' bundles o' coin to all four what's gettin' married, an' then all set down to the weddin' feast. Just as the old guy raised a glass o' champane to toast the brides in comes a cop with Red Eye Ike. He takes off his handcuffs an' lets him make a speech, tellin' where the hidden gold is kep'. Then Ike commits suicide, an' the curtain comes down wit' everybody happy.

"All out! All out!" yells the theayter bouncers, an' quick as they can they gives us all the bum's rush out onto the Bowery an' gets everythink ready fer the next performance.

After we got out o' the show we starts fer Beefsteak John's joint fer that reglar dinner what Mickey was to blow us. When we got there the place was crowded so we goes down to P'body's. Beefsteak John's was a

---

56. *glad rags.* Sunday-go-to-meeting clothes. Best clothes.

swell hash-house, with porcelain sign in front an' a 'lectric griddle in the window. But P'body's was down a basement an' wasn't so swell, bein' advertised by a sandwich sign man. Well we wasn't particular about the kind o' eats so long as we gets them, an' down we piles into P'body's.

We set down to a long table an' a guy that looks like a hobo[57] wit' a dirty towel comes over an' asks us what we want.

"D'you sling the hash[58] here?" asks Mickey.

"You're on," he says.

"Well bring along seven reglars,"[59] says Mickey. Two more o' them waiters come over an' helped the first guy to deliver the goods. A reglar dinner costs fifteen cents an' they gives ye' the money's wort'. Ye' get a plate o' crullers, a bowl o' coffee, liver an' bacon, spuds[60] or cabbage, an' choice o' puddin' or pie. Well our guys had a fine time talkin' over the show an' puttin' away their eats, an' we leaned back like them guys in the business men's lunch rooms, pickin' our teet' an' chewin' toot'picks like we dined in hash-houses[61] every day.

Now while we was enjoyin' ourselfs an' sat there contented Mickey got another idea into his noodle. I see a gleam o' deviltry in his eye but I didn't get wise. Not then. He picks up his hat an' says:

"Say fellers, I'll be back in a minute. I'm goin' upstairs to buy a pack o' butts."

Well now he was gone long enough to buy out a whole cigar store, so I, not havin' a red cent to me name thinks it a wise move to get out o' that rest'rant. I takes me chance an' pickin' up me hat an' coat from the rack says: "Well fellers, I'm goin' up to join Mickey" an' wit that I hurries up to the street.

Now the fun o' this game consists in not bein' the last guy. When I got out the five guys left looks at each other an' then all gets a hunch[62]

---

57. *hobo*. A tramp. Member of the "Society of Casual and Intermittent Workers."

58. *sling hash*. Wait on table.

59. *reglars*. Regular dinners.

60. *spuds*. Potatoes.

61. *hash-houses*. Boarding houses, restaurants.

62. *hunch*. Suspicion. Intimation.

at onct that somethin' was up. In a minute Butts was missin'. Then they was four. Red was edgin' over near the door when one o' the waiters got wise to the game, an' rushes over to the door an' coops up all four jus' as they was gettin' ready to break fer the street.

"Youse mutts dont beat this rest'rant," says the waiter, callin' the other waiters an' threatenin' to give the boots to[63] all four. Well after takin Red's hat, coat an' necktie an' holdin the other t'ree guys as hostage he lets Red go up to see if he can find Mickey who had the cash. Well by this time I found the lobster[64] hidin' behin' an Elevated post, an' comin' acrost with the dough I goes down an' gets the bunch out o' hock.

When we got out on the Bowery again we all had a good laff, an' then strolled down towards Steve Brodie's joint[65] lookin into the hockshop windows at the guns, daggers, blackjacks an' other playthings like them.

63. *give the boots to.* To kick.

64. *lobster.* Fellow. Used in a bantering sense among associates. As a term of contempt when applied to a stranger or enemy.

65. [*Steve Brodie's.* Steve Brodie claimed to have survived a jump off the Brooklyn Bridge into the East River in 1886, though many doubted he did it. Once famous, Brodie opened a popular saloon and briefly had a theatrical career playing himself; he died in 1898. See Dennis Hevesi, "Off the Brooklyn Bridge and into History," *New York Times*, 23 July 1986.—Ed.]

8.

The Dewey Baseball Team.

Spring come around an' it was gettin' to be pretty punk stayin' down there in Dugan's cellar. We on'y went down there nights when it rained an' the drip splotched agin the windows an' made a nice tickly noise what made ye' feel comfortable when ye' was inside. We sure knowed enuf to come in when it rained.

Well now that warm Spring air come oozin' down between them barren tenements, an' begun to get the housewifes to put out the flower pots. Down in the bottom o' the airshaft where we had our secret escape from Dugan's cellar some beans a layin' there in the doit sprouted an' out on the street pavement oats what had fell out'n the dray-horse's feed-bag an' escaped them hungry sparrers shot up blades o' grass in the cracks between the cobble stones. But they was other signs that summer was comin' in. It was the itchin' in the palms o' the hands to make a guy feel like throwin' a baseball.

Maybe you dont know it, but I want to say right here that city guys'll play baseball if they have on'y a side alley with room on'y fer a home plate an' one base. Most guys play on the street an' duck when the cops comes. Us guys in Yorkville had a couple o' vacant lots full o' rocks, tin cans, contractors tool boxes and abandoned dump wagons still left to play in, in them days, so we was very lucky. Up the block a ways from Dugan's cellar they was a peachy lot,[1] with a high board fence. Well we knowed how to scale it or tunnel it, and all the time use-ter to run like we owned it. If any o' the neighborhood kids was playin'

---

1. *a peachy lot*. Here a vacant lot admirably convenient.

8. William R. George (center rear), founder of the George Junior Republic, surrounded by the Republic's baseball team, ca. 1895. William O. Dapping stands to
his right. William R. George Family Papers, no. 800. Division of Rare and Manuscript Collections, Cornell University Library.

there an' we wanted it, all we had to say was: "Beat it!" an' everybody
skidooed fer us.

Well we had rights to it anyway, because we was the best ball players
in that block an' done most o' the work in cleanin' up tin cans an' rubbish
what the wimmin throwed out'n the windows o' the houses alongside.

Now if you come along there late in them Spring afternoons when
the working guys in the Crapshooters club got home an' joined the
neverworks, an' if you glued yer eye to a knothole in that fence you'd
a seen as clever a bunch a ball tossers as ever heaved a pill.[2] They was

2. *heaved a pill.* Threw a baseball.

us guys, a practicin'. Ye' could hear the crack o' the bat, the yells when a guy made a good play an' the swearin' when a guy made a bum one. Of course this is on'y *if* ye' put ye're lamp[3] up to a knothole. The chanst was that ye' wouldn't hold it there long, cause why, one o' us guys would heave a handful o' sand at ye' from the inside. Not that we had nothink against them guys what rubbered at us. We was glad to have them. But when one guy rubbers everybody elst wants to rubber, an' in five minutes everybody on the block[4] begins to look fer knotholes, an' by this time some fly-cop gets hep that we're inside the lot again commitin' the dastardly crime o' playin' baseball what aint doin' no harm to nothin' an' he goes after us, breaks up the game an' pinches any guy what he gets his mitts on. So that's the because why we had to soak anybody what rubbered at us from the outside. If they wanted to see us they should a clim' over an' took chances o' gettin' pinched like the rest o' the push.

Now if you read them there Sundy papers, sportin' page, ye'll find lots about such teams a ball players. They have hundreds o' them teams an' even if they have on'y back lots to play on sometimes they develops players what breaks into the major leagues, an' let me say right here that more'n one guy gradjated from a Harlem lot to the Polo Grounds, which is the name o' the baseball park o' the National League, an' which us guys has seen a thousand times from Coogan's bluff,[5] which is jus' ferninst it.

Well now them rival baseball nines on the East Side has got anything stopped[6] that I knows of fer startin' a real scrap. I'll seen more heads busted in baseball than in polyticks. Around our diggin's in Yorkville they was teams from the little "Dooley Kids"[7] average ten years, fitted

3. *lamp.* Eye.

4. *block.* Street.

5. [*Coogan's bluff.* In Dapping's day fans of the New York Giants baseball club watched games for free standing atop a rocky hill overlooking the Polo Grounds ballpark. Today it is in the city's Highbridge Park, north of East 155th Street.—Ed.]

6. *to have anything stopped.* To excel, to be superior to.

7. [*Dooley Kids.* The reference may be to John J. Dooley, a powerbroker in New York City's Tammany Hall Democratic political machine.—Ed.]

up with real uniforms by Alderman Dooley up to them fast, semi-pros, the "Excelsior At'letics" what had their name in the Sundy sportin' column every week an' play games wit' teams averagin' 18 or 20 years fer anythink from a kag o' buck-beer[8] to twenty-five simoleons,[9] winner to take all. An' maybe they wouldn't get pickled[10] when they won a kag o' beer!

At this time it was April, an' our bunch of muckers sure wanted a nine. Well, we had on'y seven members o' the Crapshooters club an' bein' a close corporation we didn't like to let any other guys get too clost to us. So we didn't call it that but instead called in honer o' Admiral Dewey. It was called the "Dewey Dew-drops" because Shorty, our pitcher, had a drop curve[11] that got the name o' "dew-drop."

Well we took in two guys what Shorty knowed. One was Dutch Whitey. He was a nice German guy what we always kidded because one day when his old woman was hangin' out'n the window buyin' a bunch o' banannas from a peddlar he yells up to her: "Mamma, can I have a ban-anna? My bellyache's all gone!" an' we heard it, an' ever since called him "Whitey-with-the-bellyache." He couldn't scrap much, so the name stuck to 'im. Well the other guy's name I cant remember. Every night jus' before it begun to get dark an' it was possible to get our nine together we practiced in that lot.

We got team work goin' an' along about May Shorty an' me went into executive session to challenz some other team. Now this was no easy job, this drawin' up a challenz. We hadn't crossed bats with[12] no team yet, an' didn't know whether we had a bunch o' bone-heads[13] or a

---

8. *buck-beer.* A special brew of beer sold in the Springtime and said to have an extra powerful "kick" over ordinary beer. Always advertised with an illustration of a rampant he-goat.

9. *simoleons.* Dollars.

10. *pickled.* Intoxicated.

11. *drop curve.* A curve in a pitcher's delivered ball that causes it to drop suddenly as it approaches the batter.

12. *crossed bats with.* Played a game of baseball with.

13. *bone-heads.* Blockheads. Here means stupid players.

mob o' Honus Wagners.[14] Runnin' a good baseball nine is no soft snap. One bum player can spoil a team, jus' like one sour nut 'll queer a whole mess o' fudge candy. We was takin' no chances. Shorty knowed of a nine over on Eighty-Fourt' street. They was called the Hobson Juniors, an' he said they was composed [of] soft things and Geese[15] an' that we could try out our gang o' sluggers[16] on them. Well we drawed up a chal-lenz an' sent it over to their manager by Butts.

When Butts got back he said they said all right, we'll accept ye're challenz, an' that they would put up two-an'a-half plunks[17] guarantee if we put up our'n, winner to take all. Buttsy stayed over there an' spied 'em off while they practiced an' he said they had a hot team an' would play rings aroun' us. Well now wasn't that fine news to bring back after we was lookin' fer soft pickin'? The game was for Friday afternoon an' we lost no time gettin' ready fer that bunch of kuyks, the Hobson Juniors.

Well the great day come. The Dewey Dew-drops was early on the field an' Shorty, who was elected captain, walked around givin' orders while the little kids carried his bat an' shagged balls[18] fer him. Well here was our line-up:

Shorty was pitcher; Butts, lanky and wit' a long reach was catcher; Riley, shortstop; Mickey, first base; Blinkey, second base; Spike, third base; an' Red, Dutch Whitey and the other guy was coverin' the outer garden.

So we heard the ringin' sound o' baseball bats bein' pounded on the pavement outside the lot an' a few minutes later them Hobson Juniors throwed their bats, an' mitts an' themselfs over the fence an' made invasion o' the Dewey Dew-drops home grounds. We seen they

---

14. *Honus Wagner.* A noted ball player, distinguished for his batting ability. [The short-stop Honus Wagner, the "Flying Dutchman," played professional baseball from 1897 to 1917, most of that time for the Pittsburgh Pirates.—Ed.]

15. *Geese.* Hebrews.

16. *sluggers.* Hard hitters.

17. *plunks.* Dollars.

18. *shagged balls.* Retrieved hit or thrown balls.

had a bunch o' kuyks with them an' thought that the game was goin' to be a little Sundy school affair in which we was goin' t' eat 'em alive.

But oi-oi! Moisy![19] We seen diffrent when they trots out on the diamond an' starts fer to practice an' warm up. I sees at a glance that we wasn't up against no tall-grass[20] bunch o' rubes,[21] so I goes up to the corner saloon an' gets "Paddy, the Devil," who helps out there as a substitute bartender, to officiate as empire.[22] Paddy was a neighborhood character an' we choosed him fer empire an' stakeholder, because we knowed we could depend on him. Well I framed it up with him that if them Sheenies put the kibosh on[23] us in the early part o' the game, an' it begun to look like we was trimmed that along toward the last innin' I'd get some guy on the street to yell "Cheese it, the cop!" an' we'd all duck on the false alarm. That would break up the game an' Paddy could call it off an' give back the money, half an' half.

After Paddy got the Hobson's money safe in his jeans Shorty, as captain o' the Dewey Dew-drops, gives up his right to last innings an' our bunch started in with a smashin' battin' streak. We got four runs, an' the Hobsons got nix. Well we got one more in the second an' the Hobson's got another goose egg. Our rooters begun to line up on top o' the fence an' yell an' kid the Hobsons.

Well in the third inning the Hobsons decided to start kiddin' an' when Shorty started in to pitch they lined up an' gave a good loud grunt at every heave that Shorty made. Then they jeered, then they begun to tell Shorty he had a glass arm, that he was sufferin' from "Charley-horse,"[24] an' before we knowed anythink poor Shorty was startin' on a balloon ascension. With four grunts he shot four bum ones toward

---

19. *oi, oi, Moisy.* Euphonious expression of mingled doubt and satisfaction.

20. *tall-grass.* Green, from the country.

21. *rubes.* Rustics.

22. *empire.* Always used erroneously, for "umpire."

23. *put the kibosh on.* Defeated, humiliated.

24. *Charley-horse.* Term applied by professional baseball players to malady similar to rheumatism affecting a throwing-arm.

the pan[25] an' the batter walked. The next guy met the ball on the nose an' it went sailin' to the far corner o' the lot. Then another gink waited an' walked. A couple more toyed wit' his delivery an' when the innin' ended the score was Deweys 5, Hobsons 6. What do ye' know about that, hey? In one little inning they clouted[26] us fer six runs!

Well if Shorty was up-in-the-air in the pitcher's box he was more rattled at the bat! The first one put over by the Hobson pitcher cut the plate an' Paddy yells: "One strike!" A volley of jeers met that. Then an out-curve tempted Shorty to swing an' he missed. "Strike tuh!"[27] yells Paddy, imitatin' Hank O'Dea.[28] Then the Hobson's captain got Shorty's alley by yelling: "Oh, look at the iron batter!" That insulted Shorty an' throwin' down his bat he rushed at the Hobson captain. There was no stoppin' a one round bout an' we all picked our men an' had a good old round robin scrap. When it come to usin' the mitts them poor Hobsons weren't in it. Well Paddy got the bunch untangled after a little while an' Shorty went back to bat. He pasted out the first ball thrown but it was copped by an outfielder. Two more guys went out in order and when that innin' closed the score was Hobsons 7, Deweys 5.

In the next innin' Shorty an' Butts arranged a new set o' signals. Them Hobsons had been bitin' on out curves, but got onto the signal an' passed them up. Well now they bit again an' Shorty struck out two an' the third flew out easy to an infielder. Then they was another balloon ascension. Our first man up hit the ball hard an' it went over a fence into the yard. That counted fer a home run, an' started another scrap because we hadn't made no ground rules. When Paddy decided that the run counted the Hobson pitcher blew up, an' we lambasted him all over the lot. Before he come down again we annexed five runs and

25. *pan.* Home-plate.

26. *clouted.* Batted, hit.

27. *Strike tuh!* Strike two!

28. *Hank O'Dea.* A famous umpire in professional baseball. [Dapping misspelled the name of Henry "Hank" O'Day, a baseball umpire who "tolerated no demonstrations against his decisions." See "Henry O'Day Dies; Baseball Umpire," *New York Times*, 3 July 1935.—Ed.]

at the close o' the innin' the score was Deweys 10, Hobsons 8. Now, what do ye' know about that!

Them poor guys went to bat feelin' punk but they did not get back any lost ground the next innin'. We got three more runs an' with a lead o' five runs everythink was over, we thought.

"Dont forget that the game aint won till it's over," says Mickey an' in baseball ye' never know what's goin' to happen. To cut it short I'll say that after a couple o' argymints wit' the empire an' some scratch hits the Hobsons got a few more runs.

When the nint' or last innin' began the score stood 13 to 10 in favor of us Deweys. Bein' superstitious Shorty wanted us to get another run. "We cant win on thirteen. It's a hard luck number," he said. Well we couldn't connect with the ball in our half an' the Hobsons come to bat fer the last time.

Say bo, it was the greatest finish I ever seen. On'y it wasn't a real finish. Now them Hobsons knew that it was their last chance an' they got up some do-or-die spirit. The first guy at the bat got pale around the gills when he realized the responsibility on him. He slashed at the atmosphere twict and when the third ball came toward him fanned out. It was sad, an' our push yelled so they could be heard down by the East River. Out on the street passin' truck drivers halted their nags an' stood up on the seats so's they could rubber over the fence an' watch the game. Pedestrians stopped an' shoved each other to peek through the cracks. It was the excitin'est game ever pulled off in that lot!

"Batter up!" yells Paddy, an' the second guy steps up to bat.

Now this second guy met the first ball Shorty sent to him. It was a hot grounder an' it went to Riley's butter-fingers an' he fumbled it. To make matters worse he heaved it wild over the first baseman's nut. Another Hobson steps to bat, hits a measly[29] infield twister an' the whole bunch gets to bootin' the ball.[30] Result, two Hobsons on base, second an' third. Then comes another slugger. He sends in both men an' gets to

29. *measly.* Trifling.

30. *booting the ball.* Kicking the ball and throwing it wildly.

second on a clean hit. Remember, bo; here's where we stand: Deweys 13, Hobsons 12, man on second an' on'y one out. Then comes the Hobson captain to bat. The fence by this time is lined wit' rubbernecks what clim' up to see the excitement.

By this time I was beginnin' to wonder where that guy was that I told to give the "Cheese it" yell if it looked like we was goin' to get the hook throwed into us.[31]

Now that Hobson captain stood there calm, disregardin' the kiddin' that our whole push was slingin' at him, and when Shorty sent a swift, straight ball toward the pan to fool him he simply leaned against it with the full heft o' his body an' that ball went sailin', sailin! I did not wait to see it come down. It was a sure home run an' it meant victory fer the Hobsons—if the game ended. But it didn't. Jus' then I heard the yell:

"Cheese it, the cop! Cheese it, the cop!"

Well bo, if they was an eart'quake that very minit they would a been less excitement. The guys on the fence dropped off'n it like rain drops off'n an umbreller. I stopped long enuf to laff at me own joke. But on'y fer a minute. Soon I seen a cop's hat over the top o' the fence. Then I see his physog, an' in a minute old Forty-brass-buttons[32] was inside the lot an' lookin' over the crowd to see which guy he'd cop first. A minit later another cop got his fat, old carcass over the fence. They meant business, sure enough. Well it was a case of beat it fer the back fences. The poor guys in that lot sure cut a funny picture. All run around like cockroaches in a sink an' the cops didn't know which to grab. The Crapshooters, of course, went hotfoot fer the cop-ladders in the back fence. Cop-ladders is holes cut into the fence like steps at certain places that we knowed, and our push dug for them. Mickey, the bonehead, fergot his coat which he left on the ground near first base, so he sneaks back to get it. A cop seen him an' gives chase. Mickey got back to a cop ladder but some o' them Hobson Sheenies had got

---

31. *got the hook throwed into us.* Ignominiously routed.

32. *Forty-brass-buttons.* A policeman.

tangled tryin' to climb out an' Mickey was almost up the fence an' safe when that copper nabs him an' pulls him back into the lot. Pinched, fer him!

All the guys what the cops gathered in were taken out onto the street, one cop passin' them over to a cop on the other side. Mickey was the only member of the Crapshooters club to get pinched. He come near makin' a getaway, too. When they was all in line, about ten o' them, he drops his hat an' steps back to pick it up; but one o' them bulls[33] seen him an' grabs at him before he could beat it. Most o' the kids was squealin' an' bawlin', an' sisters were goin' into hystericks an' mothers were comin' down pleadin' but it was no use—all o' them terrible criminals was marched off to the police station. There they was put in the cops' room fer ten minits, an' then they cut most o' them loose. All what blubbered[34] got free, but Mickey was made out o' different stuff. He never opened his mush fr'm the moment he was pinched. He knowed if the crows seen him cryin' on his way to prison they'd put him down fer squealer.[35] He'd take his medecine an' get sent up to the Juver' or to the House o' Refuge, before he'd squeal.

That's what got Mickey in wrong.[36] When he was lined up before the desk sergeant he didn't let out a peep, while all the rest was shiverin' with fear and moanin' dolefully. Mickey was just mum. The sergeant tried to put over some bull con on the kids.

"Well, been playin' in the lots again, have yer? And after my men have given yer so much warning! Here are all the property owners complainin' about the noise you boys make, an' my men tryin' to keep you in order, and here you are, violatin' the law again. I guess I'll have to send you all up for five years," he says, while the kids all shudder and start their howlin' over again—all exceptin' Mickey.

"Ye' cant do it," says Mickey, "You aint got no right to send us up fer playin' ball."

33. *bulls.* Detectives, also policemen.
34. *blubbered.* Cried.
35. *squealer.* One who goes back on his principles or friends.
36. *get in wrong.* To make a tactical error, to blunder.

That gets the desk man mad an' after cuttin' the other kids loose he says to Mickey: "Aint I had you in here before? I guess you're a tough nut, an' I guess I'll hold you." With that he nods to a turnkey an' down goes Mickey into the cooler.[37]

In them days they was no juvenile court so Mickey goes into a reglar cell. He set there thinkin' it over. "Hell," he says, "if I made meself out a cry-baby the cops would let me off. But what would the fellers say? They'd say: 'Mickey, ye're a squealer!' No sir. I could do the baby act, but I wont. I'll take a chanst on the judge. I'll think up somethin' nice an' pathetic an' spring it on him when I'm hauled up. If it works, all right! If I dont get away with it, all wrong. I'll take me medecine!" So Mickey had a great experience out of it. He told us all about what he done in there after he got out o' that scrape, although the Crapshooters club expected that he'd go up till he was 21. Mickey said: "After that screw[38] locks me in me cell I set still fer a long time. It was dark and the only light was a gas jet down the line. I couldn't stand fer that silence fer long so I got up an' rubbered around. The cells was cages an' I seen a guy stretched on the floor in the next cell. He was a bum, an' was paralyzed drunk. I calls in to him: 'Hey, Jack; what yer pinched fer?' (Whenever a man in the underworld does not know a fellow passenger, he always addresses him as 'Jack.') Well that guy was plastered to the ears[39] an' never opened his mush. He lay like he was dead. I give it up. Then I waited about fifteen minutes more. Gosh, that silence was killin' me! Then I yelled: 'Hey, keeper, hey?' When he come I tried to get him to talk to me.

"'Hey keeper, wont ye' let me walk around the corridor?' I asked him.

"'Cant do it. It's against the rules,' says the turnkey.

"'Well say, got a match?'

"'What do ye' want with a match?'

"'To light a butt,' says I, gettin' out the makin's[40] of a good smoke.

---

37. *cooler.* Jail.

38. *screw.* Jailor, keeper.

39. *plastered to the ears.* Dead drunk.

40. *makin's.* Cigarette fine-cut tobacco and paper used in making a cigarette.

"'It's against orders to permit smokin', so I cant give you a match,' he says.

"'Ye' aint askared that I'll set the cement floor on fire, are ye',' says I. Then I asks fer a drink an' he let me out to get a drink. When I come back that bum was sittin' up in his cell yawnin' an' stretchin' himself. I was glad he was awake.

"'Hey Jack, what ye' pinched fer?' I ask him again.

"'What's that to you?' he says, kind o' sassy.[41]

"'Well ye' needn't get hot under the collar about it,' says I. Then I pulled out a plug a chewin' terbacker that I had in me pocket an' offers him a chew. He takes me plug, tears off a big gob an' hands it back. I asked him fer a match an' he digs out a greasy stump from a pocket in his vest an' hands it through. I lit up me cigarette, pulls over me stool to the side of the cell next to the hobo's cell an' we talks about things. Like the rest o' his kind he had the old hard luck story. He says:

"'I'm a hard workin' man, but I been out o' work eight months because o' sickness. This mornin' I starts out to find a job an' drops into a saloon jus' to get a glass o' beer. When I pays up the waiter says I give him a counterfeit nickel, an' I says he lies. With that he throws me out an' I hit him with a beer glass. Then a gang jumps all over me, throws me into the gutter an' along comes that cop an' pinches me. Here I am, alone, up against it, dead broke, an' no fren's.'

"'I shouldn't think ye'd want ye' friends to find ye' here,' says I. He didn't answer.

"'They'll probably put me away over on Blackwell's Island fer sixty days,' he says.

"'An' me, they'll probably send me up till I'm 21, me about five years fer playin' baseball, an' you on'y two months fer fightin',' says I.

"Well we sat there talkin' when there was a commotion upstairs an' down they come luggin' an excited Dago.[42] He was wailin' about his stand, they'd pinched him fer havin' a pushcart fruitstand without

---

41. *sassy*. Saucy, impudent.

42. *Dago*. Applied exclusively to an Italian on the East Side.

a license. Ye' see them Wallyoes[43] useter buy a license, one guy would use it until a cop on a beat knowed that he had it, then he'd lend it to another Ginney an' so they'd pass it on, one license bein' sufficient. But the cops got wise an' caught this Ginney without his license. After the Ginney quieted down the turnkey got us supper, coffee an' sandwiches, an' then we turned in fer the night. I was awful tired an' had done all the worryin' about the future that was necessary so I curled up on the smelly cot an' went to sleep. Well I woke up after a few hours because I wasn't alone in that bed. The cells were lousey. Them bugs bit like they was big as lobsters. I throwed all o' me bedclothes out through the bars into the corridor. They's nothin' nowhere so dirty as them police station cells. They disgraced the city more than we done. I was a happy guy when I seen the first streak o' dawn an' knowed that I would soon get took up out o' that place to court.

"After we et a bum breakfast o' 'ham-and'[44] we lined up fer the Black Maria.[45] I had often seen the Black Maria as it come up Second avenue with the fingers o' human beings stickin' out o' the ventilation slats, an' I had run alongside often an' heard the guys inside yellin' an' cussin', but I never thought I'd get a ride meself some time. Well I stepped in lively an' proud, took me seat an' leaned back, an' after the other guys shoved in they shut the door and we was left in darkness. In a few minutes we was on our way down to court an' got tumbled together pretty much on the way down. Well on the way down I was thinkin' of some way o' gettin' influence workin' fer me an' a bright idea came into me nut when I thought of havin' Riley get his uncle what was an alderman to butt in fer me. They's nothin' them politicians cant do. Well now, I was in that there courtroom about half an hour when me name was called. I felt pretty shaky when I went up to where a jailor pointed out, but I cheered up when to me great surprise I seen Shorty an' Riley settin' there dressed in their glad rags like they was

43. *Wallyoes.* Italians.

44. *ham-and.* Ham and eggs, announced in cheap restaurants as "ham-and."

45. *Black Maria.* The closed wagon for transportation of criminals.

attendin' a funeral or a surprise party. I seen that there was somethin' doin'. Well the judge says:

"'Young man you are charged with disorderly conduct and resisting an officer, are you guilty or not guilty?'

"'Guilty, ye're Honer, but I got somethink to say fer meself,' says I.

"'Go ahead, let me hear what you have to say,' he says.

"'Well, ye're Honer, I was on'y playin' ball an' I dont think that's no crime nor disorderly, an' as to the charge o' resistence all I can say is that when the cop arrested me I dropped me hat by accident, an' when I stopped to pick it up, the cop thought I wanted to break away an' soaked me over the nut with his club. Ye' can see by this bump on me nut where he hit me!' I says, turnin' me noodle so's he could see a bump I got there when a foul ball hit me in the game.

"Well now, before the judge fell fer me story he called up that there cop, an' chewed the rag with him fer a few minutes about me case. Then he said:

"'I find you guilty of disorderly conduct, and impose a fine of five dollars. Can you pay?'

"'Yes sir, Ye're Honer,' I says without havin' the least idea where them five bucks[46] was comin' from. I stepped aside an' was just about to go back to the pen when Shorty come down the aisle an' slips a mitt full o' small change to me. 'Here's the money,' he says. I counts it and turns it over to the clerk o' the court an' beats it from that joint as quick as me wobbly pins[47] 'd carry me. Shorty an' Riley follered me out. We wasn't on the sidewalk when I asked: 'Where'd ye' get the dough?'

"'That's the baseball guarantee. When the game was busted by the cops an' everybody ducked we went after Paddy, the Devil, and he forks over[48] the mazuma to us, declarin' us the winners. So we come here to help ye' get out when it looked like ye' was in fer keeps!'"[49]

---

46. *five bucks*. Five dollars.

47. *wobbly pins*. Wobbling legs.

48. *forks over*. Surrenders possession of.

49. *in fer keeps*. In permanently.

9.

Miggles.

Miggles[1] is played in miggle-time. Miggle-time is when migs is out. Migs is marbles, but all marbles aint migs, because they is migs, croakers,[2] Chiner alleys,[3] an' realers,[4] an' then they is glass alleys[5] an' imitations,[6] too. Teeny-weenies is called "pee-wees." But when ye' play marbles they all is called jus' "migs." Them toystore guys has all grades from the baked clay migs what sells twenty fer a cent up to them peachy, bull-eye, pigeon-blood realers what sells twenty cents fer one. An' the because why is that them realers is made out'n a rare kind o' stone called "on-nyx." Miggles bust easy an' dont last long when ye' play with them, an' bein' so cheap we didn't care nothin' fer them an' all we used 'em fer was when we happened to be playin' up on the roofs an' some guy rubberin' over the cornice happened to see a cop walkin' his beat on the street below an' then we'd try an' bounce a miggle on his nut. O' course after ye' done it ye' got to duck because sometimes they comes up to the roofs lookin' fer ye'. Well that's all miggles is good fer.

We useter have our pockets filled with them other migs, though, in miggle-time. Croakers, Chiner alleys an' realers is round but them cheap

1. *miggles.* Marbles.

2. *croakers.* Hard baked marbles in brown and blue clouded porcelain.

3. *Chiner alleys.* China alleys, porcelain marbles with longitudinal and latitudinal lines.

4. *realers.* High-priced agate marbles. Called "realers" probably because their high cost brought forth many types of glass imitations.

5. *glass alleys.* Glass marbles of all kinds.

6. *imitations.* Glass imitations of agate and onyx marbles.

migs is lopsided an' split, an' anyway they bust after ye' have took a few shots with them. My advice to ye' if ye're a goin' to play miggles is to buy croakers, alleys an' realers, 'spechially buy a realer of good size fer a "shooter."[7] A realer is heavy, hard as stone, an' when it hits the pot it sends them marbles scatterin' all over. Them what bust has got to be replaced by the guys what own the busted ones. With a realer ye' dont even have to "punch"[8] to get in a hard shot, but if ye' use a cheaper marble the chanst is ye' likely to bust ye' shooter.

Maybe you aint never played migs? I never seen a guy yet what didn't play migs when he was a kid. But if you aint done it let me say that you play it by makin' a hole, not too deep, but jus' deep enough to hold the migs what each guy has to put in. That hole with the migs in it is the "pot."[9] Then they make a ring around the pot-hole, an' after the pot is made up each guy shoots at the pot from toye,[10] which is on the outside line. In shootin' ye' aint allowed fer to "punch." Punchin' is swingin' ye're arm around an' sort o' throwin' ye' shooter at the pot instead o' shootin' from ye' hand held still, an' givin' force to ye' shot with ye' thumb. This is the way ye' shoot. Ye' take a good realer if ye' got the price, ushally twenty cents, an' put it on ye' right hand restin' against the middle an' index fingers right where they sprouts from the hand. Then ye' draws back ye' thumb like a trigger, an' lets fly. The more strengt' ye' got in ye're thumb the harder ye' can shoot. If ye're a Southpaw[11] ye' reverses this. Allus before shootin' blow ye' breat' on the shooter. It brings luck. Also grunt.

Now in shootin', if ye' hits the pot all migs what ye' shoot out an' what go outside the ring is your'n. If ye're shooter stays in the pot ye' can

---

7. *shooter.* Marble used as missile in striking other marbles in the center of the ring in the game of marbles.

8. *to punch.* To use the force of the arm instead of the power of the fingers in projecting the "shooter" marble in playing the game. Punching is contrary to rules.

9. *pot.* The accumulation of marbles in the center ring to be shot at and won by the players in turn.

10. *toye.* The bounds or limits.

11. *Southpaw.* A left-hander, usually applied to a left-handed pitcher in baseball.

"baby"[12] an' sometimes clean up the whole pot. Babyin' is puttin' English[13] on ye're shooter so when it hits a mig it knocks it out'n the hole but stays spinnin' in the hole itself, an' so gives the same guy another shot. But if ye're own shooter goes outside the pot but still inside the toye mark, well, every other guy gets a shot at ye' an' the guy what knocks your shooter out'n the bounds makes you fork over all the migs ye' got in that game. Well ye' keep on shootin' in turn until the pot is empty. Then ye' starts over again. D'ye' get me on this? P'raps ye' dont. Well all I can say is that its pretty hard to learn a dub unless he can see a game bein' played.

Sometimes they has a penalty called "knuckles down." Then the guy what loses must put his fist down over the pot-hole, an' the other guys take shots at his knuckles from acrost the other side o' the pot-hole. If ye' shooter drops into the hole ye' must put down ye're own fists to get shot at, too. My advice is allus to aim up so's to hit the top o' the knuckle. This hurts most, an' ye're own shooter allus glances up an' dont fall into the hole. Realers is best fer knuckle-shootin' because no matter how hard ye' hit a guy's knuckles it never makes no moons in the realer.

A moon is what comes into a realer when ye' make a hard shot against another realer or bouncin' it on a stone sidewalk. Ye' can see how many moons is in a realer by soakin' it all night in butter. Ye' can allus tell if a realer is old by countin' the moons in it. If a guy wants to trade ye' a realer with a lot o' moons in it dont do it unless ye' got some kind of lemon[14] ye' want to unload on him. Otherwise ye'll get stuck. A moon is really a crescent shape bust or fracture in the realer.

Miggle-time is in the early Spring an' tops ushally comes with it. If ye' like tops dont get none o' them cheap kind. What ye' start spinnin' by twistin' ye're fingers an' then keeps a goin' by hittin' it with a whip. Buy a boxwood, hard-peg, what ye' wind around with a string an' then chuck down hard on the sidewalk, the string unravelin' an' settin' it to spinnin'. To make it spin a long time allus be sure to spit on the end of

12. *to baby.* To play the game in such manner as to nurse an advantageous position.

13. *English.* In marbles the quality that makes a marble spin after contact with another marble instead of rolling away from the place where the collision occurred.

14. *lemon.* Something undesirable.

the string before windin' it. A great game to play is "split top." In this game ye' chooses up to see which guy is first up. Well now the first guy spins his top, an' then the second guy throws his own down as hard as he can on top o' the one what's spinnin', an' tries to hit it on the noodle to split it in two. If he dont succeed well the next guy tries an' so on until some guy's top get's busted. Stone sidewalks is best fer playin' with tops but dirt alleys or alongside fences o' vacant lots is best fer playin' miggles.

This reminds me that if ye're foxy ye' can get more assorted miggles through a "miggle-trap" than through bein' a shark at[15] straight playin'. We made about a dozen "miggle-traps" up outside our lot an' what migs we got we shared up on the square between the members o' the Crapshooter's club.

Miggle-traps was kept secret because if most guys knowed about them they'd do like we done, an' never have to buy no marbles. This is the way we done it.

Along the fence by the vacant lot they was a stretch o' hard dirt where all the guys on the street played miggles. Well by rollin' marbles we tested where all the low places was when migs rolled out'n the ring, an' at them places we dug little holes in the ground, like mouse holes, runnin' deep an' coming out down the bank on the other side o' the fence inside o' the lot. Well at the outlet we had rocks piled so's ye' wouldn't notice it. Well when some greenie was up there shootin', like as not his shooter, a twenty-five cent realer, would roll into that hole on the first shot, down it would go an' good-bye fer his marble. It would run down the channel underground an' land under the stone pile an' one of us guys there watchin' the traps would pocket it long before the guy was able to climb over the fence to look inside the lot. We useter entice suckers what had fine realers to come over an' play outside our lot, an' sometimes our own migs went down the trap just like we was come-ons.[16] It's great sport watchin' traps, like huntin' Easter eggs.

---

15. *being a shark at.* Proficient, very skilful.

16. *come-ons.* Bait, persons acting innocent victims to aid in carrying out a fraud or swindle.

10.

The Club Attends a May Party in Central Park.

Shorty come down Dugan's cellar one Saturday night a couple o' weeks after Mickey was pinched an' brings this news: "Hey fellers, what d'ye' think! The crows up the street are all talkin' about havin' a May Party, Riley's old woman is bossin' the job, an' our whole push is in on the bids."

"I'm on," says I. "We'll help Mrs. Riley run that thing an' be in with both feet when it comes to the ice cream an' grub."

"—an' kissin' all the peachiest crows in the party," says Shorty, who was some lady's man, believe me. He sure run me a clost second when I was out in Second avenue society, which I broke into onct in a while.

"They's one crow ye' wont kiss, Shorty; that's Big Liz!" says Red, grinnin' at the rest o' the club. Shorty cussed her out. Ever since she near chewed an ear off'n Shorty's head onct when he got into an argymint with her he was dead leary[1] o' that crow. She was a big, husky dame, well set up an' good lookin' an' well able to take care o' herself if any bloke got fresh to her. She could scrap like a real "pug"[2] an' when her mitts failed her she was there with the hatpin. She could lick[3] most fellers of her own size an' the crows o' the neighborhood either stayed away from her or become her devoted slaves. She took quite a shine to me, an' Shorty didn't quite like it.

---

1. *dead leary.* Afraid, shy of.
2. *pug.* Abbreviated word, used for "pugilist."
3. *lick.* Thrash.

129

Butts was nix on the female dope. He never had no use fer any crow, an' he put up a kick about havin' the club go to the party. "Aw, what's the use o' us guys goin' to that skirts'[4] party? All the crows'll have their old women there, an' they wont let us take 'em out row-boatin' or cuttin' didoes in the grove," he objects.

"You dry up,[5] Buttsy! Jus' cause you aint got no crow to go with aint no reason why we should stay home. Nix on that. If you want a gal come along, I'll give ye' a knockdown[6] to anything from a pie-face to a queen! An what's more I'll tell her not to shake ye' until the day is over," says I.

"Well," he says, "I'll go; but believe me I've got to scrape up some dough. I'm broke." Well now, he wasn't the only guy in the Crapshooters club that was busted at that time, an' we all discussed ways an' means fer some time. Butts decided to nip a quarter onct in awhile from his mother's old coffee pot where she kep' her small change. He also knowed of a cellar of a empty house where he could saw off a couple o' yards o' lead pipe an' sell it to the junk peddlar fer a dollar. Shorty didn't have to do no worryin' because next day after church he went over an' started a crap game with the young guys what come out an' by night he cleaned up[7] three bucks as easy as takin' candy from a kid. Mickey an' me got up an old game which hadn't been worked around our diggin's[8] fer a long time. The next day bein' Sunday we waited 'til night an' then took a sneak[9] up the block, clim' over the fence at the vacant lot, got up the back fence an' discreetly shinned up a dozen wash line poles down the street an' undid a number o' lines from their fastenin's. We was on the job early next mornin', Monday bein' wash-day, an' believe me we done a rushin' business as "line-up" men.[10] Ye' see

4. *skirts.* Females.

5. *dry up.* Used imperatively to command silence.

6. *knockdown.* Introduction.

7. *cleaned up.* Got possession of.

8. *diggin's.* Headquarters, rendezvous.

9. *took a sneak.* Sneaked, made a surreptitious visit.

10. *line-up men.* Men who go around the backyards repairing wash lines.

them wimmin what found their lines busted didn't know how it come about an' as it was necessary to fix 'em right away they hired us guys when we went back in the yards yellin': "line-up! line-u-up!" an' we annexed from fifteen cents to a quarter a job accordin' to the height that we had to go up on the pole. Well the other guys raised their money by coppin' lumber at places where they was puttin' up new buildin's, choppin' it up into firewood an' sellin' it at ten cents a barrel.

Well Riley's old woman sure was bossin' that party an' on Monday she sent Riley down to the Arsenal,[11] where the park department has its offices, an' he got a permit fer havin' a May Party on Nort' meadows in Central Park. Well they was lots o' work to be did. Chief was the makin' o' the May pole. Youse guys probably dont know what a important matter this is. The May pole is the chief think in a East Side May Party an' every old woman on the block pipes it off to criticise it. They's more jealousy over the looks o' May poles than they is over the physogs[12] of their own babies. Ye' could tell Riley's old woman that her baby had a pie face an' flannel-mouth, an' she'd on'y laff; but ye' tell her that her May pole looked like a Ginney barber-shop pole an' she'd lam ye' over the nut with it. Well she put in yards an' yards o' red, white an' blue bunting, an' then some. She sewed an' twisted an' tacked an' stuck up a beautiful canopy fer the King an' Queen o' May. They was twenty streamers fer the maids o' honer to hold an' a swell gilt paper crown fer the poor feller what had to be King. She wanted Riley to be this but he wouldn't stand fer it.

Now the rules o' May Parties is that each crow an' feller pays ten cents, which is fer the ice cream an' cake what him or her gets at the party. In addition each carries his own lunchbox with his eats. Well them parties is allus held on Saturday's in May because they aint no school on that day. In June they call's 'em June Walks. Friday night before is the worst time because everybody wants to know what the weather

11. *Arsenal.* An old arsenal in the lower end of Central Park near Fifth avenue, used for administrative purposes.

12. *physogs.* Faces.

9. William O. Dapping's photograph shows the web of washlines in the backyards of tenements in Yorkville, ca. 1899. William R. George House Library, William George Agency.

is goin' to be. An' if the evenin' paper says "rain" well nobody better hang around one o' them May Party headquarters, because he's liable to get his block[13] knocked off. Well Riley's old woman had good luck, an' when she read the paper it says: "Clear, warmer, southerly winds."

13. *block.* Head.

The day dawned fine an' the sun shined down swell as us kids all got ready fer to go to that May Party. Riley's old woman as proud as a fat peacock waddled around an' got all the kids in line. Out'n every window in the street hung them old women what hadn't been invited, all pipin' off the crowd to see if they wasn't somethink to roast.[14] The girls was dressed in white an' wore them blue an' white caps what they sells in the candy stores fer a nickel fer May Parties, an' the blokes wore the same kind, on'y red an' white. Well they put one feller with one crow, but the Crapshooters passed up[15] this arrangement. We had other work to do. We had to gather up the lunch boxes an' take 'em when the names was wrote on 'em, an' pack 'em into baskets an' pile the whole outfit in a delivery wagon. Then Mrs. Riley appears carryin' the May pole, which had some class! She brung it down on the sidewalk an' showed it off an' then puts it in Riley's mitts, because he had fer to carry it over the nut of the King an' Queen. Then the Dutch band shows up an' the procession starts.

Well the parade went around the block which is the custom like at funerals an' other society events, an' by the time we come 'round the second time we got straightened out into a procession that sure was all-to-the-candy. The jealousy o' them wimmin what was left behin' was worth all the trouble fer Mrs. Riley an' she was tickled to deat'. Well the fellers an' crows, holdin' hands, follers that Dutch band over to Fift' avenue, apast Andy Carnegy's swell joint[16] an' up to Ninety-Sixth street entrance o' Central Park. There they uncoupled that Dutch band because they don't allow Dutch bands to play in Central Park, an' I cant say as I blames 'em, at that! Well after we showed a park cop our permit an' shook them Dutch heinies after they promised to come back at five o'clock to meet us at the park gate an' lead the procession home again we went on over to the Nort' meadows. Say, aint Central Park simply swell? Cripes, it was swell that mornin'! A guy was cuttin' grass an' ye'

14. *to roast.* To criticise or ridicule.

15. *passed up.* Ignored, disregarded.

16. [*Andy Carnegy's swell joint.* The industrial magnate Andrew Carnegie moved into his mansion on Ninety-First Street and Fifth Avenue on Central Park in New York City in 1903.—Ed.]

could smell it great. Gee bo! It's me fer Central Park whenever I get the chanst! Well we marched over to a grove o' maple trees an' pitched camp there fer our party. I knowed they was maple trees because I onct drawed pictures o' them leafs in school. Red bet me a dime they was oaks an' I took him up an' won. Nothin' like bettin' on a sure think!

Well as soon as Mrs. Riley had laid out our ground an' put up our May pole an' started the kids a playin' bean-bag, baseball, ring aroun'-the-rosie, an' so on what does we pipe off but another May Party marchin' acrost the meadows right fer our grove. "Well, what d'ye' know about that!" says I to Mrs. Riley, an' she begins to get ready fer a scrap. When they come nearer we seen they was kuyks an' we made up our minds that none o' them Lexin'ton avenue ginks[17] could put anythink over on us. Some fat Sheenie wimmin led that party, an' they sure weighed in fifty poun's apiece heavier than our dames. They started right in fer to pitch camp in our grove, an' when I seen one o' them young motzer eaters[18] put their May pole on our ground I goes over an' hits him a paste in the eye. Well he drops the May pole an' starts to blubber, an' them wimmin come fer me. I ducks an' Riley goes in an' tears down their pole. By this time some o' them Sheenies surrounds Riley an' hands him a few uppercuts before the rest o' the Crap-shooters hears the war-cry an' wades in. Well the engagement become general an' pretty soon we hears the cops' whistles blowin' an three or four comes up, one o' them mounted an' ridin' right on the grass. Well them wimmin chewed the rag wit' the cops an' projooced the permits an' finally the cops decided that the place was big enuf fer both parties, an' threatened to pinch us all if we got to scrappin' again. Well we won because their May pole was all shot to pieces while our'n didn't even lose a streamer. We got square other ways, too. We had to go fer our drinkin' water acrost the place where them kuyks was settin, an' we allus spilt some water on their grass so they couldn't set down. They tried to

---

17. *ginks*. Persons, mild disrespect usually intended.

18. *motzer eaters*. Truly "matzoth eaters," matzoths are biscuits eaten by Hebrews of the orthodox persuasion.

get even by chuckin' empty lunch boxes over on our side. Well then we come back by scalin'[19] empty pasteboard plates at their nuts when they wasn't lookin'. Us guys sure enjoyed the whole mornin' puttin' their party on the blink, an' Riley's old woman pertended she never seen us.

Now at two o'clock in the afternoon the ice cream wagons show up at the park gate an' ye're s'posed to send a couple o' husky fellers[20] out to get it an' carry the freezers in to the grove. Well us Crapshooters went fer our dessert an' believe me we had spoons up our sleeves when we started. Now after we got it an' started back who does we meet but a delegation o' them kuyks a luggin' their freezer, too.

One o' them looks at me an' I says: "What ye' lookin' at?" He says "Not much!" so I ups an' biffs him. With that one o' his gang picks up a chunk o' ice from the freezer an' wings it[21] at me. I ducked an' it caught Shorty right on the mush. Then we begun another battle an' not havin' any rocks handy we had to use the ice from the ice cream freezers. When it was all gone the Sheenies run an' somebody yells: "Cheese it, the cop!" so we drags off our freezer into the bushes where we refreshed ourselfs after openin' the can, an' then we took it over to our camp. We was a-skared to say nothin' to Riley's mother about the scrap so we put the freezer by the tree with the May pole an' other grub an' batted out fungoes[22] on the baseball field.

Pretty soon the old lady got hep to the freezer, an' thinkin' that them Sheenies swiped the ice an' put salt into our ice cream she puts up a beautiful holler an' goes lookin' fer a cop. She couldn't find none, which is the rule whenever ye' want one in New York so she come back an' rung the bell an' got all the kids round with their plates an' spoons. Well the stuff had all melted an' she had to dish it out with a cup. It was all soup! Well now the funniest think about it is that while we was settin' there drinkin' that ice cream over comes one o' them Geese wimmin'

---

19. *scaling.* Tossing.

20. *husky fellows.* Strong fellows.

21. *wing it.* To throw it.

22. *batted out fungoes.* A practice for outfielders in baseball.

an' makes Mrs. Riley a friendly present o' a brick o' ice cream, froze nice an' solid. Well ye' could a knocked Riley's old woman over with a feather. Inside o' fi' minutes she was chewin' the rag with the enemy an' bygones was bygones. They told her they never done that to the ice cream an' when she come back she was layin' fer us guys, but we kep' shy o' her fer the rest o' that day. When I seen her start a baseball game between them kuyks an' our party I gets our guys together an' we decides to sneak off by ourselfs with our crows.

As you remember Buttsy didn't have no crow so I had to get some dame to stand fer him that afternoon. Well I pipes off a pippin,[23] a crow named Sadie what had moved around our way just a few weeks. "Hello kid," says I, goin' up to her. "I got a nice guy over here what 'd like to get a knockdown to ye'. Ye' on?"

"Who's ye' friend?" she says.

"Oh, he's the goods,[24] believe me," says I, "an' he's no tight-wad.[25] He'll show you a real, good time if ye're on, kid, an' he'll buy kid, he'll buy—anythink from a ice cream soda to a diamon' ta-rar-rer.[26] He's no piker."[27]

"Well trot 'im out," she says an' with that I whistles fer old Buttsy. He comes over sideways, like a horse passin' a automobile, gently lifts his sky-piece[28] like a Willie-boy[29] an' stammers "Pleased to meet ye'." Then he shut up like a clam. I gives Sadie a wink not to kid him too hard, an' off we all go, the whole push havin' a crow. I dont b'lieve Buttsy opened his mush onct all the way from Nort' meadows down to the boat ponds. He just piped off that swell skirt he had on his arm, an' believe me, she took a shine to him, too. She done all the talkin' an' that let Buttsy down light, because he had a repitashun fer bein' a bashful

---

23. *pippin.* A pretty maid.
24. *he's the goods.* He is beyond compare.
25. *tight-wad.* A penurious person.
26. *diamond ta-rar-rer.* Diamond tiara.
27. *piker.* An unsportsmanlike person, a sham.
28. *sky-piece.* Hat.
29. *Willie-boy.* A dude.

gink. Well Red had a young chippy[30] he picked up at the party an' the rest o' the guys had steadies.[31] Well now it was agreed that we'd pair off an' each guy would hire his own rowboat so's no guy would queer[32] the other guy if he wanted to go off an' talk mushy to his crow.

On the boat landin' we didn't have to have no press agent to show folks that we was there. We'd snuk away without chaperones an' we was out fer a real, good time on the lake. Each guy took off his coat an' vest, rolled up his sleeves, spit on his hands an' rowed off like them colledge guys on the Harlem river. Well onct out on the ponds we scattered around an' purposely lost each other. It was a glorious afternoon an' after an hour I stopped rowin' after we drifted under a bridge an' got into a quiet bay, an' I jus' gazed at Big Liz as we floated along. Well soon she puts her fingers to her lips an' we kep' mum. Behin' some bushes we heard voices. We didn't try to rubber, jus' listened. This is what we heard:

"Say, honest Sadie, d'ye think ye're old man 'uld get sore if you was to be me steady?"

"Oh I dont know; me old man dont run me love affairs. I'd like to see him butt-in!" says the dame, defiant.

"Ye' like me? Dont ye?" says the guy.

"Oh you're not so worse. Anyway, ye're all right from ye're head up an' ye're feet down," she answers, sort o' kiddin'.

"Aw, dont kid me; this aint no time fer jollyin'.[33] I want to see where ye're old man 'd stand if I asked him to let me take ye' to dances an' balls next winter," pleads the gink in mushy tone o' voice.

"Oh I can fix that all right, all right. Leave it to me," says Sadie. They set still fer some time. Then Buttsy, fer that's who the guy was, bashful Buttsy, says:

"Oh Sadie, dont ye' wish me an' you was older so's we could get married an' I could woik (he nearly choked sayin' that word) an' we could live in one o' them new flats on Foist avenoo?"

---

30. *chippy.* A girl of loose character.

31. *steadies.* Girls who keep company with certain admirers.

32. *to queer.* To thwart, to interfere with.

33. *jollying.* Teasing, annoying.

"I'm on! That'd be ollygazitsky!³⁴ Ye' cant rush it too soon fer me!" says Sadie.

"D'ye' really mean it?" says Butts, excited.

"Course I mean it," says the dame, an' with that we hears a sound like kissin' an' before them dubs could break away we shoves our boat around them bushes an' queers the performance.

"Say Butts, you're a awful bashful guy, you are!" says Big Liz, from our boat.

"Well Spike aint got nothin' on him or you'd a wore a engagement ring long ago!" says Sadie, "an' let that hold ye' fer awhile!" It looked like a hair-pullin' match was about to commence so we rowed the boats apart an' all went back to the boat-landin'.

Well of all the sensations in high society that there proposal o' Butts an' Sadie had everythink stopped I ever heard of! When the rest o' the push heard me tell it they wouldn't believe it, an' what made it worser again was that Butts was more bashful than before.

We all went up the Mall an' took our crows to the bandstand an' hung around there listenin' to some really good music. They is nothin' like a milit'ry band fer to make the hair stand on end an' puttin' pure, heroic thoughts in a guy's noodle! I come near followin' Buttsy's lead when me an' Liz was goin' back.

We all got back to Nort' meadows jus' when the parade o' Mrs. Riley's May Party was marchin' home, an' we joined in. Now while Buttsy an' Sadie was walkin' along with us Sadie seen a nice rose bush an' yells: "Aint them grand! How I'd love to have them!"

Well now that was a mean idea fer her to put into Butt's nut because he was willin' to hook them fer her. He says "D'ye' like roses?"

"I simply love them. I got a grand rosebush in my yard," she answers. Well Liz let on as how she'd like some roses, too, so me an' Butts drops out'n the procession an' tells the push that we'd see 'em later on.

We went back to where that there rosebush was, an' hangin' around 'til they was a good show we dove into it, yanked off a whole lot o'

---

34. *ollygazitsky.* From "out of sight," meaning superlatively enjoyable.

roses, ripped our fingers open with them spikes on the stems an' dusted acrost the grass plots before anybody seen us. Well we packed them roses nice in our empty lunch boxes, and started home.

Now gettin' out o' Central Park with somethink ye' swiped there aint no cinch.[35] Ye' could sneak diamon's t'rough the Custom House easier than ye' can get by them fly-cops what stand at the park gates an' frisk[36] May Parties. O' course we was hep to that game so instead o' goin' out the Nin'y Sixt' street gate we went over an' slid down into the Nin'y Seventh street transverse. Now a transverse is a street cut t'rough Central Park fer to let wagons cross from the east side to the west side o' the city, because wagons an' trucks aint allowed in Central Park. Them transverses is like subways without no roofs cut t'rough the Park. Well we was hurryin' along whistlin' a happy tune an' was jus' goin' to walk out on Fift' avenue when out jumps a cop and grabs us!

"What ye' got in them boxes?" he asks.

"Flowers," we says, seein' the jig was up.

"Where'd ye' get them?"

"Swiped 'em," says I, Buttsy bein' mum.

Well he took them, tore them all up an' chucked them into the roadway, an says: "Well I caught ye' with the goods on, hay!"

"Ye' nailed us all right," says I.

"I guess I'll have to take you fellers up to St. Vincent," he says. Vincent is the uptown park police station.

We said nothin' an' then he took out a pencil an' notebook an' wanted our names an' addresses. I gave my name as "Bill Weiss" which is Dutch Whitey's name, an' Butts gave some other dub's name. Well he said that a cop would be over the next day to pinch us, hit us a clout[37] over the ears with his leather gloves an' said "scat!" Well we beat it out o' that place like scared mollie-grinders[38] wit' cans tied to their tails.

---

35. *cinch*. Easy task.

36. *frisk*. Search, go through one's garments.

37. *clout*. Blow.

38. *Mollie-grinders*. Homeless cats.

But we didn't catch up with the procession. Oh no! Butts had prom-ised Sadie that he would get her some roses an' it made him pale aroun' the gills[39] not to have none fer his fair lady.

Now by the time we got back to Dugan's cellar it was dark, an' I couldn't console Buttsy in the least. He was fer goin' way back to Cen-tral Park an' stealin' that hull rosebush in the night. The guy was nutty. That dame, Sadie, had turned his nut complete; an' I seen that he'd got to get some roses some way or 'nother. Well we set there in the dark in Dugan's cellar when in comes Mickey. The party had got back an' disbanded.

"Where's the rest o' the push?" I asks him.

"Didn't ye' hear?" says he. "Why, two o' the kids what went to the party this mornin' couldn't be found when he got home, an' there's hell to pay! All them old wimmin what wasn't invited this mornin' is up there tellin' Riley's old woman that they sure fell into the pond an' got drownded, an' if they wasn't in the drink[40] they was surely kidnapped, an' Riley's old woman is havin' fits an' his old man sent Riley, Shorty an' Red down to the Arsenal, the police headquarters in the park, fer to have them drag the pond fer them bodies!"

"Well what d'ye' know about that!" says I, whistlin'.

Butts set there like he was ready to be drownded himself. I told Mickey how we lost our roses.

"Say Mickey, this gink is in love an' he's got to get his mitts onto some roses fer Sadie or he'll die! Aint there somethin' ye' kin suggest?"

He scratched his nut fer a minute, an' sure nuff, he projooced an idee.

"I got it," he says, "Ye' know that sixth yard down from the vacant lot, where I put up two washlines the other day? Well while I was put-tin' up them lines I seen a swell rose bush in the yard which the janitor was just puttin' in, havin' come from the florist. It had a dozen swell blossoms on it an' it'll take about ten minutes an' a sharp cheese-dagger to get next to them!"

---

39. *pale around the gills*. Showing signs of fear.
40. *in the drink*. Overboard.

Butts sprung up in a minute. He an' Mickey sneaks up in the dark vacant lot, takes off their shoes an' crawls down the fences toward that yard where Mickey seen them roses. Ten minutes later they come down Dugan's cellar again. They had the roses! Buttsy earned them roses, believe me! His hands was all pricked an' bleedin' an looked like he had been playin' on a harp wit' barbed-wire strings! That's what a guy'll do fer love!

Well we got him a box an' he gives a kid what knows where Sadie lives a nickel to take 'em up to her wit' his compliments.

•◆•

Well it was pretty late when Riley an' the other guys come back from their search, an' they brung them kids back with them. They had got lost in the ushal way, walkin' toward the west side instead o' toward Fift' avenue an' the cops took them in. We was all dead tired an' after them kids had been duly delivered to them anxious parents Riley's old woman heaved a sigh, handed Riley the old family growler[41] an' a dime an' sent him out fer a pint. She had worked up an awful thirst that day, an' believe me, she punished a terrible lot o' booze[42] in quenchin' it! We said "good night" to each other early, we was so dog-tired, that—as fer meself, I was in dreamland 's soon 's I hit the hay.[43]

Now the worst o' the whole thing is this! Sadie busted off her engagement to Butts! And the cause why was this, that when Butts went up in the dark an' swiped them roses he got into Sadie's yard an' clipped them from Sadie's own rosebush!

41. *growler.* Beer can.
42. *booze.* Intoxicating drink.
43. *hit the hay.* Went to bed.

11.

The Last Raid on the "Cherry Bunk."

Some guys what writes books an' stories often tries to make it appear that us city guys never sees the country, an' couldn't tell a landscape from a fire 'scape! Dont fool yerself on that kind o' bunk.[1] We gets out there onct in a while, an' sometimes twict in a while. That's how we come to find our cherry bunk.

It happened one Sund'y in June that we had enough mazuma in the push to pay ferry an' carfare, so up we goes to Nin'y-Second street ferry an' crosses to Astoria. Well now we walked away out into the country there, got up the Shore road an' foller'd it out toward Long Island Sound. Doin' so we come to a field where we seen daisies by the million, an' before ye' could say "Jack Rob'nson" we had clim' over the stone fence an' was pickin' bouquets. Well, while we was pickin' them flowers Shorty lifts his lamps up into a tree what stood near the fence an' what does he see but some yeller spots which, on closer inspection turned out to be cherries. He gives me a wireless to get hep an' we pipes off the place quiet, fer we didn't want to rouse up the farmer. They was a house acrost the barbed-wire fence on that side, an' four more o' them cherry trees.

Well we worked over that way pickin' daisies but we hadn't much interest in the flowers then. Picked 'em jus' fer a bluff[2] to show we was busy if the farmer come out an' found us near his cherry trees. Well

---

1. *bunk.* Buncombe, also place, resort, rendezvous.
2. *for a bluff.* Pretending, on the appearance that.

when we got under the nearest tree I reaches up, plucks a few an' finds that they aint ripe. But they was gettin' there, an' they looked good to us. No rube come out'n the house so to make sure about it Mickey an' me went over on the bluff to ask fer a drink o' water an' raps on the door. Nobody come, so we tried all doors, hammered and called. But nobody was there so we took all we wanted an' after eatin' enuf to give us all cholery morbus we picks up our bouquets an' starts fer home. Then we seen the farmer come drivin' home. It was Sund'y an' he probaly had been to church.

Well the next Sund'y we went out to that place again. Sure 'nuf the rube was away an' the cherries riper than before was pretty good eats. The trees was loaded an' we was sorry that we hadn't brung pails an' baskets. Well that place we called our "cherry bunk" an' we hit it again next Sund'y. But we seen that the fruit was now nice an' ripe an' wouldn't last much longer. We took hatfuls back with us an' distributed cherries to all the crows on the block. Folks thought we had robbed a fruit stand but we said that Shorty's uncle owned a farm over on Long Island an' gave us all we wanted. I gave Liz me hatful an' she took it up to her old woman. It put me in right with the old lady an' she says: "You dont mean to say that you can get all you want?"

"That's what!" says I to the old girl, throwin' up me chest.

"Well I jus' love cherries. I wish you'd get me a pailful?"

"Anythink to oblige lady," says I, puttin' me foot in it.[3]

They was no chanst to back up, fer she goes to the cupboard an' takes down her favorite growler, a swell agateware t'ree quart can that hadn't traveled enuf to the suds fountain[4] to get a single dent in it. She hands it over to me an' it's up to me to fill it from that minute. I told her I'd go over an' visit Shorty's uncle the next day. Then I went back to Dugan's cellar.

The guys was sprawled on the floor playin' "cherry pits." Did ye' ever play cherry pits? It's a very harmless sort o' game an' has some o'

3. *put one's foot in it.* To get into an embarrassment.
4. *suds fountain.* Beer keg.

the motions o' the crap game. Ye' play cherry pits this way. First ye' go 'round fruit stands if ye' aint got no money to buy none or there aint no chanst to swipe none an' ye' picks up all the cherry pits what ye' can find. Well ye' sucks 'em till they's clean an' then dries 'em. Then each guy puts in, say, ten pits. That makes up the "pot." Then the guy who's first takes all the pits in his hand an' rolls 'em out like he was shootin' craps. Now if he rolled 'em good they'd be separate but not too far apart. Well he picks out two pits what are apart and crosses between them with his pinky[5] an' he aint allowed to touch a pit. He's got to keep his finger on the ground in crossin' an' after he done it safe then he takes his finger an' shoots one pit at the other. If he hits without the "shooter" hittin' any other pit he picks up both an' then crosses two more pits an' shoots again. Well he keeps on doin' it until he misses an' then the next guy does it. Now if they happens to be a odd pit left last then the last feller has the right to squeeze his thumb down on it, make it stick, an' if he can lift it up an' put it down t'ree times he wins it. Now it's a cinch to do this if ye' got a dirty thumb an' ye' blows ye' breat' on it.

Ye' saves all ye're cherry pits until ye' get enuf, an' then ye' gives 'em to ye're crow fer to make a bean-bag. Ye' can also use cherry pits in a bean-shooter,[6] but they shoot crooked. The chanst is that if ye're tryin' to hit a Chinky laundry man's window a cherry pit'll curve an' hit some guy in the eye. The best shots to use in bean-shooters is buck shot or round pebbles.

Well I'm away off'n me trolley![7] I started fer to tell ye' all about the Cherry Bunk an' here I am shootin' hot air[8] about the game o' cherry pits! I turns to the Club members:

"Well, youse guys! I jus' made a contract wit' Liz's old woman promisin' her to fill this growler fer her. What'd ye' know about that!"

---

5. *pinky.* Little finger.

6. *bean-shooters.* A toy made of leather, elastic and crotch on the principle of the sling-shot.

7. *off me trolley.* Off the subject, crazy.

8. *shoot hot air.* To talk about irrelevant things.

"It'll take thirty cents to fill that scuttle[9] wit' suds!" says Mickey.

"Oh it aint booze, but cherries that I got to get," says I. The mob sizes up me kettle an' kids me about it. It was a very dear possession in Liz's family, an' on'y done service at special mixed-ale parties or an occasional wake. Well seein' as how I had told the bluff about Shorty's uncle I decided to take him along with me the next day.

"Tomorrow?" says Shorty. "An' what's the use o' goin' over there on a week-day! That farmer dont leave his joint weekdays like he does on Sund'ys," says he.

"Well them cherries wont last much longer, anyway. The farmer might have 'em all picked by next Sund'y," says I, an' that settles it.

Next mornin' Shorty an' me starts fer the Shore road. When we reached the lot where the cherry trees stood I tells Shorty to lay low on the inside o' the stone fence while I pipes off the place to see what the chanst was. When I gets into the daisy field I drops on me belly an' sneaks up slow toward the trees.

When I come back Shorty lay hid in them daisies, his phyz[10] turned up toward the sky an' chewin' on a grass stem.

"Nix doin'! We aint got a Chinaman's chanst[11] o' gettin' cherries today," says I. "We're too late. That there farmer has ladders up against the trees an' what's more he's right up there in them branches now pickin' the fruit. Dont that beat the Dutch?" says I.

Well we both crawled over in that daisy field where we could pipe off the farmer at work an' talked it over. It didn't seem any use stayin' there, but I was willin' to take a desperate chanst at goin' South with some o' them cherries. Every onct in a while the rube comes down out'n the tree with a basket full an' puts 'em on the ground an' takes up another basket. But he allus put them on the inside o' the barbed-wire fence. We was layin' there wishin' fer the farmer to fall down an' break his neck an' watchin' the Colledge Point ferry boats goin' up Long Island

9. *scuttle.* Beer can, another name for "growler."

10. *phyz.* Face.

11. *aint got a Chinaman's chance.* Absolutely no opportunity.

Sound when a good idea comes into me coco',[12] an' this was it: Wait aroun' till dinner time. Then when the farmer goes into the house sneak up into the tree, work quiet up in the branches where we couldn't be saw an' clean up all we can before the farmer finishes eatin' his chuck.[13] If he leaves a basket o' picked ones where we can get our hooks on it, why, take basket an' all.

Well after watchin' that farmer make trip after trip we finally heard the noon whistles blowin' down in Astoria an' acrost the river in little, old N'York. But the sucker never come down. He went on pickin' an' pickin! At last his old woman comes out'n the house an' calls him, an' he comes down. They both picks up the baskets o' cherries what he had already picked an' goes into the house.

That's our cue. Sneakin' up like Injuns we was lucky in findin' the longest ladder in the daisy lot on our side o' the barbed-wire fence. Well we shinned up out o' sight without bein' saw an' then hustled to beat the band[14] to fill that growler fer Liz an' her old woman. Seemed to me we'd been up there on'y ten minutes when Shorty says: "We'd better be beatin' it fer home."

"Jus' a few more minutes an' I'll be with ye'," says I.

"Remember, too much is plenty," says Shorty, warnin' like.

Then hell broke loose. That rube had come out on his porch pickin' his teet' an' stretchin' hisself when he happened to look our way an' seen them branches movin'. Good night! fer us. He started fer the tree on the run.

Shorty seen him first an' yells "cheese it!" an' starts down the ladder, one round at a time. He was near the bottom when I straddles it like a fireman an' slides down like a shot. I hung on to me kettle but it hit a round, flew out'n me hand an sent a shower o' cherries over the rube who by this time was tangled up in his own barbed-wire fence tryin' to reach us an' yellin' like a Comanche Injun. He sure was not on his way

12. *coco'*. For "cocoanut" and meaning "head."

13. *chuck*. Food, ration. Verb "to chuck" means to throw.

14. *to beat the band*. Intensively.

to church Sund'ys, fer no church guy ever swore like he done. Shorty hadn't reached bottom when I hit him an' we both rolled over like vaudeville acrobats. Thank's to goodness, that rube didn't get out'n his own barbed-wire fence till we got on our feet an' started on a run fer the ferry house miles away. We run an' run, an' the farmer stuck to us. Every onct in a while he'd stop to pick up a rock an' heave it at us, an' we didn't waste no time tryin' to hand him back anythink. I never seen such a persistent cus. He run us over a mile. No cop ever done as much.

We was pretty well winded when he finally quit an' shook his fist at us as we looked back at him. When we was sure he was no longer trailin' us we set down on the sea wall an' took stock while we rested. We'd both lost our hats which fell off, an' worst of all that fancy growler belongin' to Big Liz lay somewhere in that daisy field, 'nless the farmer found it. It wouldn't do fer to go home without our lids[15] much lest without that beer can. So we waited a long time an' then cautiously snuk back.

Well would ye' believe it! That rube had expected us to come back an' was layin' there behind a tree down the lot, an' he had a shillaly[16] ready fer us. We seen him an' dusted again, an' it was more'n a hundred yard dash that time to make our getaway. We never stopped runnin' until we was in sight o' the ferry house an' we caught the boat on the run, an' all out o' breat'.

"Gosh, that's a mean rube," says I, "an' I'd like to get even with him by comin' over some day this summer an' settin' his haystack on fire."

"Or elst by chuckin' a dead cat down his well," says Shorty. We looked like fugitives from justice when we hit Dugan's cellar. Our lids was gone an' with it that agate-ware growler. Well the upshot of it was that the club had all to dig down in their jeans an' help me raise a dollar an' a half to buy Liz's old lady a new kettle an' fill it with cherries bought at the Ginney stand. Gee, but that was a mean rube, though!

15. *lid.* Hat.
16. *shillaly.* Club, stick.

12.

An East Side Excursion.

"If they never was no such think like an East Side excursion fer to make life wort' livin' in N'York I think I'd shake the dust o' Second avenue from me feet an' dig out fer country village life in Flatbush or the Bronx!" declared Shorty one evenin' when the warm summer air drove us out'n Dugan's cellar an' we set back in the vacant lot gazin' up to the stars after somebody had throwed a empty tomato can out'n a flat house window to make us quit practicin' clost harmony. Some of our bunch had the bug-house[1] notion that they could sing. Mickey was a bass an' so was I. Riley thought he was a tenor, but he was on'y a adenoid tenor—he sung like a s'prano sufferin' from the pip! Well we useter practice up an' hoped to get up a quartet, but generally got chased by janitors an' cops when we tried to sing. Comin' back to excursions let me say that no family on the East Side, no matter if they was ready to go into the poor-house ever missed a excursion when the good, old summertime come around.

Excursions may be divided into t'ree classes. First they is them temperence ones conducted by churches an' Sunday schools or charity organizations. They get the respectable East Side patronage an' are too tame fer me. I have went to some o' them jus' to see if I could catch on to some good lookin' Sund'y school dame, but they's too many chaperones on them excursions. They have pretty good hand-outs but they aint no dancin' an' after ye' get to the grove ye' cant go in swimmin' 'nless ye' got a pair o' tights. Now what guy is goin' to take the trouble to carry home a pair o' wet tights!

---

1. *bug-house.* Insane asylum.

Well then they is the second class. This includes all them excursions held by lodges, fraternities an' orders, an' they is held not only fer to furnish a nice day's outin' fer the families o' the members, but also fer to raise a little dough fer the treasury o' the association. Them excursions aint like the others because they aint "dry"[2] an' they runs a bar which opens up fer business 's soon 's the boats has left the dock.

Then they is the third class. Me fer the third class! These is run generally by some club like The Turtle Bay Bachelors, The Asquam Social Club, The Jolly Sixteen, Shamrock Social Club an' so on. Some day The Crapshooters'll run one that'll make folks sit up an' take notice. But we aint got that far yet. An' we wont until we're old enuf fer to vote. Them clubs has got to have backin' an' ye' cant get backin' 'nless they's some votes in the push. To tell the trut' these here clubs in this class is all political, but they calls themselfs "social" or "pleasure" clubs fer a bluff. Go an' find out whose payin' the rent fer them an' ye'll find some alderman or cheapskate politician. O' course they puts in their own mazuma, but when they're in a hole some politician comes acrost[3] an' puts 'em on their feet, an' next election day they're all out wearin' watchers badges an' workin' hard around the polls. Believe me when I go into politics I'll put a social club on every block. It's a good investment an' cheaper than buyin' votes at five bucks a t'row, with a chanst o' gettin' pinched t'rown in.

A East Side excursion consists of two barges an' a tugboat. Nobody rides on the tugboat, which tows the barges to the grove. The barges is lashed together an' a gang plank goes acrost so that excursionists can go over visitin' each other while the barges is bein' towed. It's more sport jumpin' acrost, though, from the upper decks, because ye' liable to fall overboard. It makes the crows all say "oh!" when they see ye' do it, an' ye' make a repitashun fer ye'self.

I been to so many excursions that I'll bet ye' the drinks that I can tell ye' what kind o' excursion is goin' up the Sound, down under the Bridge

2. *dry*. No-license, sale of intoxicants prohibited.
3. *comes across*. Furnishes the money.

or aroun' the Battery jus' be lookin' at the names o' the boats! Will ye' take me on that bet?

Fer instance! If I sees the Grand Republic, Cetus, Sirius, Pegasus or the General Slocum—but no; I takes that back, cut out the General Slocum.[4] I aint forgot what happened to that boat which I useter ride on many's a time when I was a kid, but thank God I wasn't on her that day when she went down with them one thousand kids from Sixth Street Sund'y School. The East Side never got over that tragedy.

If I see any o' them Iron Steamboat company boats or the Crystal Stream, the Blackbird, the Chancellor or the Nassau I makes up me mind it's a Sund'y school excursion, because they generally has the price to hire a real steamboat an' dont have to hire a cheap-skate tug an' a couple o' hay barges all stuck up wit' fresh paint an' flags o' all nations. Any guy what hangs around the docks along the East River can tell ye' all about them boats, what line they belongs to, where they goes to an' in what order they comes up the river on reg'lar schedule. I knows the Glen Island boats, the Bridgeport line, the Fall River an' Providence boats an' even the Joy line, an' what's more I'd bet a three-cent stinker[5] that I could tell the Rosedale wit' me eyes closed by listenin' to the sound o' her engines an' the throb o' the walkin' beam as the sound floats over the water.

I got a kind of away from me excursion spiel in chewin' about these here steamboats. Comin' back to excursion boats I want to say that the steamboat excursions generally go way up the Sound to Cold Spring harbor, or away up the Hudson to Iona Island, or away down Staten Island somewhere. The second an' third class excursions take in Whitestone or Colledge Point on the Sound, up along the Palisades or in the groves above Yonkers on the Hudson, or elst they goes down the Bay,

---

4. [*General Slocum*. The *General Slocum* was a large paddle-wheel steamer that caught fire and sank during an excursion up the East River in 1904 with more than 1,300 people aboard; more than 1,000 died, most of them German immigrants and their children from Little Germany on the Lower East Side.—Ed.]

5. *three-cent stinker*. Cheap cigar, *flor di cabagio*.

on the Raritan an' Jersey shores. I been to nearly every excursion place around New York.

Now what got us guys excited on this partickler night was the quarter-sheet poster what Red brung down. He foun' it tacked on a fence, an' it announced that the grand annual excursion o' the Hell Gate Pretzel[6] Club was to take place the next Sund'y. Well, say, we sure was curious. That club allus pulls off somethink hot in the line o' shindigs[7] an' we knowed that the lid would be off.[8] Ye' could allus enjoy ye'self with the Hell Gates. They puts up special grub, schweitzer-kase sangwidges made out'n schwartz-brod an' real cheese, wit' lots o' mustard, hot dogs an' sauerkraut, leberwurst an' other kinds o' them Dutch eats.

Say it sure is good sport, a goin' to a excursion. Dont ye' like fer to go down by the docks an' smell the river? I could sit all day snoozin' in the sunlight on a dock, wit' the tide goin' along underneat', me fish line with a sandworm bait pulled taut by the current 's I waited fer an eel or a Lafayette[9] to swaller me bait. It's soothin' fer to sit on a dock an' hear the pulleys an' tackle creak an' hear the roustabouts an' longshore men swearin'. Sometimes I think it's jus' as much fun fer to watch a excursion a goin' off 's tis to be one o' the guys that's goin' along with it. It sure is a great sight to see them barges covered with glad rags, flags o' all nations, the band a playin', the whip guys a sellin' their fi' cent whips with a whistle in the handle, an' balloon guys a peddlin' their balloons. Gee, but it's great!

Well Sund'y mornin' bright an' early us guys was down there on the dock. Shorty's big brother belonged to the Hell Gates an' he gave Shorty a extra ticket an' Shorty swiped two more off'n him. They cost one buck a piece. The eats was throwed in.[10] Well they was seven in

---

6. *pretzel.* A German tidbit furnished with beer in beer gardens.

7. *shindig.* Event, excursion, rough gathering.

8. *lid would be off.* All restraint of law would be ignored.

9. *Lafayette.* A small pan fish found in the waters about New York. [A Lafayette is a salt-water game fish.—Ed.]

10. *the eats was throwed in.* Luncheon was included.

our bunch an' we choosed up fer to see who'd get the tickets. Well Shorty, Riley an' Red won. Well soon 's we got down there we seen the Columby an' Susquehanna tied up to the dock an' the three guys wit' tickets goes aboard. Well down the dock comes a brewery wagon an' it begun to unload kags o' booze fer the excursion. Well Mickey pitches right in, helps unload the wagon an' then helps fer to carry them on board the boats. Now when he got near the end o' the load he carries one kag down, leaves it at the bar an' then sneaks up on the top deck where the rest o' the guys was hangin' over the rail, grinnin' at us left-behinds. The way Mickey worked that was some class! Soon 's he seen himself on Easy street up there he amuses himself a shootin' bent pins at them balloon peddlars a bustin' their balloons be puncturin' them.

Well they was meself, Butts, and Blinkey still on the dock an' the tug already had blowed the whistle twict. When it blows t'ree times they throws off the lines, pulls in the hawsers an' off goes the excursion. Well now Blinkey waited till the guy at taking tickets at the gang-plank was rushed,[11] clim' along a string piece followed by me an' Butts an' then when the guys on the barge signalled jumped abord. Butts went next an' I was about to foller when some o' them busybody dames a settin' up there puts up a holler an' gets the committee after us. Well Butts and Blinkey made themselfs scarce be stowin' themselfs in a empty bunk-room on the other barge, an' the committee didn't catch 'em. But there was me, alone on the dock an' the last whistle ready fer to blow. Jus' then I see a old friend o' mine—a dock-rat[12] what was scullin' along a flatbottom[13] in which he picked up wood and other drift what come down the river. I whistled to him an' he come over to the dock. A minute later I was in his old tub an' he rowed me around to the outside barge. [While] Mickey an' Shorty on the upper deck lay keegie fer me an' the other Crapshooters, Riley an' Red went out on the stern end o' the lower deck an' hauled me aboard from the rowboat. They stowed me in wit' Butts

---

11. *rushed.* Very busy.

12. *dock-rat.* A loafer who loiters around docks picking up river flotsam and retrieving lost timber.

13. *flat-bottom.* A flat-bottomed skiff used alongshore.

an' Blinkey until the band hit up a fine tune, everybody yelled, an' we felt the barges movin' down the river. When we was sure they couldn't put us off we come out. We was pretty lucky in sneakin' on board. One bunch o' guys what seen Butts an' Blinkey jump on from the dock got aboard the same way but the committee chased them all over the barges an' in spite o' dodgin', hidin', an' runnin' all over they got caught an' were sent up the gang-plank wit' a good swift kick behin' each guy.

The band was still playin' the first number when us guys mixed in with the excursionists. Shorty, whose family was aboard, had on his best clothes an' besides had brung a crow. She was settin' up with Shorty's brother an' he had to excuse himself from us mugs when he seen we was all safe on board. He was the candy kid, that day. He sported a new, white vest wit' pearl buttons, an' wore a rose what his crow put in his buttonhole. He looked like such a Willie-boy that ye' wanted to slap him on the wrist. He had busted a couple o' crap games the night before an' was flush[14] wit' the coin. He had enuf chicken feed in his jeans to make it click when he come round' dancin' wit' his crow. He sure looked like prosperity. Shorty staked the bunch to half a buck, good fer ten beers. They didn't begin to hand out the grub until noon so we had to forage around the boats an' hit some lunch baskets where we was able to find the old dames nappin'. Well we wasn't hungry fer long. It was no hard job to get next to[15] them lunch baskets, because everybody was rubberin' at the sky-scrapers an' new bridge what we was passin' goin' down the river.[16] Buttsy got into some Dutch family's basket an' found limburg cheese sangwidges. He exposed the stuffin' out'n them sangwidges be smearin' it on the inside rail between them two barges an' people kep' a thinkin' we was passin' garbage scows on the river.

We made our headquarters on the stern end o' the Columby, an' had a nice pile o' ropes to lay on an' pipe off the views. Nobody elst

---

14. *flush*. Had money in plenty.

15. *get next to*. Purloin, break into.

16. [*new bridge what we was passin' goin' down the river*. Spike was likely referring to the Williamsburg Bridge over the East River in downtown New York City, begun in 1896 and opened in late 1903.—Ed.]

went out there 'ceptin' deck hands onct in a while, an' we had a swell time comin' an' goin' whenever they was anythink doin'. What d'ye' spose happened. Why, we hadn't passed the Battery an' was headin' fer Staten Island when out comes Blinkey togged out in an apron an' workin' as a waiter. He was sent out be the guys in charge o' the bar fer to scout[17] beer glasses. They gave him a beer fer every ten empties what he brung back, an' he was hustlin' round pickin' 'em up an' slippin' 'em on a stick like he belonged to the bartender's union. Well he got all the beer he wanted this way an' when he was gettin' pickled[18] I butted in an' told him to quit the job. He wouldn't but he gave his extras to us guys until we thought o' sellin' the extras. Well the first think ye' knowed the hull push was scoutin' glasses an' be the time we reached the grove over in Jersey we'd sold over fifty beers. It was a good graft! Well we was half-edged when them barges swung into the dock there an' it was a wonder that none o' us fell overboard, because we all jumped from the guard rail an' didn't wait fer no gang-plank to be swung acrost.

Well over in that there place there must a been no police department at all. The joint was wide open[19] an' the lid was missin'. Guys got out games from ring-the-cane to the old shell game. Well Shorty an' his white vest broke into the capitalist's game that day, an' this is how it come about. Mickey was a studying them three walnut shells what had a pea under one o' them an' he got so interested that he come over to our push an' said he was sure he could beat that game if he had a couple o' dollars. Well Shorty jumps into him with both feet, fer fallin' fer a con game[20] like only rubes from Hackensack falls fer.

"You poor mutt," he says, "if ye' want to throw away some money go an' drop it in New York Bay, but dont fall fer that old game. Why if ye' got to gamble go an' look fer some guy with an over-even-under seven board. Sometimes the banker loses in that game!"

---

17. *scout.* To search for, to seek.

18. *pickled.* Intoxicated.

19. *wide open.* Lawless, without restraint.

20. *con game.* Confidence game, swindle.

Well Mickey goes a lookin' fer a over-even-under seven game, but they was no guy workin' it there. That puts a idea into Shorty's nut an' he gets a nice clean board, divides it into three squares, marks one "over 7," the middle one "even 7" an' the third one "under 7," gets out his dice an' starts in to run a game. Well the rest o' us guys acted as "come-ons" an' in ten minutes we had a mob around us playin' the game. Well it's one o' them games that works out nine cases out o' ten with the banker makin' all the money an' Shorty run that game all the time we was at the grove. His white vest must o' made them guys think he was another Dick Canfield.[21] He raked in the money so fast he forgot all about his crow, an' me an' Red had to entertain her while her beau was workin' his graft. It was wort' it. When the boat whistle blowed a callin' everybody back fer the home trip Shorty had cleaned up near seventeen plunks. Some day he's a goin' to run some high class Monte Carlo!

Well, like a true sport he divvied up! First he bought his crow about fi' dollars wort' o' souvenirs—jewel box made out'n sea shells, pi'ture frames, glass ship made by the novelty glass blowers in a glass case, purse made out'n pearl shells wit' a real silver chain an' a whole raft o'[22] that kind o' junk. The rest he divvied up with the Crapshooters, an' we didn't have to shag[23] no empty beer glasses a goin' home. We could a bought the bar!

The push got to feelin' so good that one time I found them treatin' a bunch o' Dutchmen. Our guys was singin' "High skilly loben! High skilly loben!" tryin' to imitate them Dutchmen, who wasn't singin' nothin' like that. No sir, they was singin' "Hoch soll ich leben! Hoch soll ich leben!"[24]

---

21. *Dick Canfield.* A noted gambler. [Canfield, who died in 1914, according to the *New York Times*, was "the best known and wealthiest individual gambler in the world" and a "cultured and refined" conversationalist and collector of art. Until 1902 he ran an elegant gambling house on East Forty-Fourth Street near the ritzy Delmonico's restaurant. See "Richard Canfield Killed By A Fall," *New York Times*, 12 Dec. 1914.—Ed.]

22. *raft of.* Great quantity of.

23. *to shag.* To retrieve.

24. [*Hoch soll ich leben!* This phrase means "Long may I live!" and was (and is today) often sung in birth celebrations, with the pronoun changed to "he" or "she."—Ed.]

which is a tune they allus sing at excursions. I dont know what it means but they allus raises their beer glasses, drains 'em, an' has another.

"Well who gave youse guys license to sing that song, youse fatheads!"[25] says I.

"Come on in, the water's fine, you boob!"[26] they yells, an' I joins 'em. Well we sure had a grand time. By the time them barges was pluggin' up the East River again the lights was twinklin' up there on Brooklyn Bridge an' a good many o' them excursionists was ossified.[27] We had got in a row with that there bartender downstairs an' we got square be chuckin' overboard every empty glass we found. Mickey, too, got in a fight with one o' them fellers we'd been treatin' an' they knocked over chairs an' nearly started a panic. The committee locked 'em both in the bunk room an' the poor suckers had to stay there till the boats docked. Now it was pitch dark when we was about to tie-up, an' us guys found the place where the committee in charge o' the lunch counter had done up the grub what was left over. Well we copped some empty-baskets an' down there in the dark we done some awful dirty work. We packed in pies, cakes, soda water in little bottles, hot-dogs[28] an' layer cakes an' when the dock was reached it was a lead-pipe cinch to mix in the crowd an' walk off'n the barges.

Well after all was off'n the boats the committee let Mickey an' the Dutchman out an' it was all we could do to keep Mickey from gatherin' bricks an' cobblestones to heave at them committee guys when they come up from the river. We run Mickey up all the way from the dock an' finally dumped him an' about a barrel o' pies an' other truck down in Dugan's cellar. Well now, most o' us fellers was so dog-gone tired that night that we stayed right down there in Dugan's cellar, et a pie each, an' went to sleep on the mattress.

25. *fatheads.* Stupid fellows.

26. *boobs.* Gullible chaps.

27. *ossified.* Dead drunk, in a state of stupor.

28. *hot-dogs.* Frankfurter sausages.

13.

Burglarin'.

D'ye' know, burglarin' is pretty good sport! That is, if ye' dont get too ambitious an' try fer to crack a crib.[1] Ordin'ry burglarin' without tacklin' a strong-box[2] is really excitin' sport! I leaves it to any guy what ever done it to say whether I aint right! Now I dont mean yeggs![3] That's scientific burglarin'; but I mean boys gettin' into a place at night without no idea o' shootin' up nobody. It tries out a feller's nerve, shows what kind o' a nut he's got on his shoulders an' furnishes more spice an' excitement than a run-in with a mad janitor in a dark cellar! If ye' want to get a real run fer ye' money some night when ye' aint doin' nothin' an' life is dull jus' get a couple o' guys an' try to bust into some joint! Now I aint tryin' to make a crook out'n you! I never tells no guy to do wrong! In fact, my advice is: Allus do like I tells ye' to do, but never do like I do.

Now one evenin' I was walkin' down First avenue when I noticed a mob a kids crowdin' into the doorway an' rubber-neckin' in the winders o' that big double store near Nin'ieth street, an' I piped off the joint meself. Well they no longer was that store-for-rent sign there, but the place was filled with toys, candies an' novelties! A new toy store had broke into the neighborhood. An' maybe it didn't put a crimp into[4] the reg'lar trade! The prices was so low that we called the joint "Cheap Charlie's" right away. I had a couple o' cents in me pockets so I goes

1. *crack a crib*. Blow open a safe.

2. *strong-box*. A safe.

3. *yeggs*. Expert cracksmen who blow open safes with nitro glycerin or other explosives.

4. *put a crimp into*. Obstructed, interfered with.

in to see if the new joint offered any chanst fer hittin' it up. Me lamps traveled over the store an' say, that proprieter sure was green in the business! He didn't have a bit a wire screens over the counters, had the candy trays in plain sight an' clost to the front end so a guy could grab an' run, an' didn't seem to have no protection at all in back o' the counters. I hustled back to Dugan's cellar after buyin' a cent's wort' o' nigger-babies[5] jus' to carry out me bluff that I wanted fer to buy somethink.

"Say bo's, there's a new candy store opened up on First avenue an' it's our meat! I never seen such a show to crook! It looks to me like if we tackles it careful we'll be able to nurse it fer a long time."

Well all the push wanted to see the joint, so we all goes around again an' buys another cent's wort' o' candy. Incidentally we swipes about a dime's wort'. We sized up[6] the joint pretty good an' then went back to Dugan's. As we talked it over we found out that Cheap Charlie's cellar was one o' them under the row o' flat houses where we used to play "Groose-fadder," an' the back alley had a rear entrance to each flat house cellar.

"The best way to hit up that joint is from the cellar, it's a underground job!" says Mickey.

"What's we goin' to be, undertakers?" asks Riley, tryin' to be funny.

Well jus' like them crazy suckers, they wanted to go right around an' rob the joint that very night. Mickey was the o'ny guy that kept his nut! He handed 'em somethink, though! He said:

"There youse go, jus' like I thought youse guys would act! I might as well tell youse right now, that this job aint goin' to be somethink soft, like that hit-an'-run game we works on fruit stands. Youse guys dont seem to have no brains at all. First let me say that if any o' us guys gets pinched doin' a job like this one, burglarin', it means Elmira reformatory.[7] They'll be no Juver' or House o' Ref' about this think, onct we get nailed. Now let's do this careful! First let us pipe off every angle o' the

---

5. *nigger-babies.* Licorice gumdrops in the form of doll babies.

6. *sized up.* Examined the prospect.

7. [*Elmira reformatory.* A state-run institution for youthful offenders (ages sixteen to thirty) in Elmira, New York, which opened in 1876 and, under its warden Zebulon R. Brockway, aimed to reform instead of punish its young inmates.—Ed.]

lay o' the land, fin' out when they's nobody in the store an' if anybody sleeps there, an' let's play 'Groosefadder' there a couple o' nights to get used to the cellar an' find out what we'd be up against."

Well we took that advice an' before goin' home that night we all agreed to rob that joint, stand together an' if any guy got pinched, not to squeal, an' we shook on it![8]

The next night the guys showed up at the club early an' all were on deck when we started out fer to play "Groosefadder." Now Groosefadder is a German word meanin' "grandfather." Shorty says it should be "Gros vater" an' he's Dutch an' ought to know, but us guys called it "Groosefadder."[9] Now one guy who was the Groosefadder is armed wit' a switch or a broomstick, an' he is s'posed to give the rest o' us five minutes start to hide. Then he goes lookin' fer us an' any guy he catches he's allowed to lambaste ye' with his club. The danger o' gettin' a good wallop over ye' noodle puts some ginger into the game, an' it was allus a favorite wit' us guys. O' course we choosed up fer who was to be Groosefadder. He had the most sport, because he was allowed to soak ye' as hard as he wanted, an' nobody could soak back, no matter how hard the Groosefadder hit ye'. On'y a quitter or a squealer kicked if he got caught. The on'y think to do was to keep on runnin' until ye' got away from the Groosefadder. It was a really good game because it learned ye' how to get away from janitors, cops an' others what chased ye'! Well after we played the game fer a while we managed to find out that nobody slept in the store, located the partition in the cellar what separated Cheap Charlie's cellar from the small woodsheds o' the ten- ants in the house, an' got next to all windows, exits an' hidin' places in the cellars in case they come after us. We found out that Cheap Charlie didn't come to the store on Sund'y night so we arranges to pull off the job the next Sund'y night.

Well soon 's it was dark Sunday night we started down from Du- gan's cellar and snuk around into the alley back o' Cheap Charlies'. We

8. *shook on it.* Pledged themselves by handshake.

9. [*Groosefadder.* The actual German word is *Großvater.*—Ed.]

left Butts an' Riley at the back stairway to the cellar to lay keegie, which means to pipe off thinks an' tip us inside workers in case anybody comes. Me an' Red an' Shorty then drops down into the cellar an' starts off on the first trick. We had agreed fer to take turns breakin' in so that all guys could have an equal share. Mickey was up in front o' the store walkin' up an' down in case Cheap Charlie come to the store when Mickey or the guy who happened to be watchin' there was to tip us off.

Well we went slow an' worked our way back in the cellar to the place where the partition was, an' we listened fer a long time to be sure nobody was above us. I had a candle an' lit it an' then Shorty pulls out a nice, steel "jimmy" which he had hid under his coat. Well now, we was sure some burglars! Now the first think to do was to find a crack between two planks in that partition an' cut away some o' the wood wit' a cheese-dagger so that the "jimmy" could be stuck in an' get a purchase fer rippin' out the plank.

We had begun work when we heard somebody comin' down the alley stairs an' Shorty says it's Blinkey. He had just put on a pair o' new shoes an' they squeaked like a rusty car-wheel.

"Fer cripe's sake, one o' youse guys sneak back an' ask Blinkey what'n hell he means to come burglarin' with them $1.98 cent shoes on. Tell him to beat it back home an' put on a pair o' gum-shoes or go in his stockin' feet!" says Shorty. Well Blinkey lost no time takin' off them squeaky kicks,[10] an' worked in his socks.

Well we worked over an hour jus' carvin' a hole fer the tool an' then come the real work. We had blew out an' lit that candle a dozen times on false alarms an' was anxious to hurry the job. Well now we got in the "jimmy" an' put our weight against it. Them planks was nailed to the studdin' with great big spikes an' it seemed like nothin' never would give. Then it begun. Well we ripped a little bit at a time an' then set still waitin' to hear if anybody heard the raspin' sound an' was comin' to find out what made it. But we got along all right. After changin' shifts a couple o' times we finally pulled down the big plank an' laid it aside.

10. *kicks.* Heavy shoes.

There ahead o' us we seen a big black hole where the plank had been. Well we was wonderin' whether we ought fer to go in with the light when all of a sudden heavy footsteps sounded in the hallway above the cellar. They went to the back door leadin' down into the cellar where we was an' before we could make up our minds to beat it they was comin' down the stairway.

We doused that light in a flash, drops on the dirt floor and crowds into a heap at the end o' the corridor down which them footsteps was comin', each guy tryin' to wriggle into the center o' the pile. We sure thought our goose was cooked! We heard the guard in the alley whistle an' knowed that somethink was up!

Well the man come straight down the corridor toward us an' stopped. We heard him fumblin' in the dark an' suspected he was pullin' his gun. Nix! It was another false alarm! The guy was on'y a tenant in the house an' he didn't even know what we was there. He must a been deef, or he'd a heard our hearts beatin'! Well he lit a match, unlocked a woodshed, threw open the door and lucky fer us had it between us an' him, an' after fillin' a basket wit' kindlin' wood from the woodshed locked up an' went upstairs again. Well we got our hearts down our t'roats into our gizzards again, an' after settin' still a little while we goes into the cellar. I goes in first, Shorty follers an' then come the whole push. After that clost shave we got we become sort o' reckless an' when we found ourselfs in that there cellar full o' toys we begun to throw 'em at each other an' cut up awful careless. We found the stairway leadin' up into the store an' me an' Shorty goes up the steps to the top where they was a trap-door. We put our backs up against it an' shoved. It wasn't fastened an' we lifted it gentle so's we could peep into the store an' see what was doin'. A gas light was burnin' so that cops could see inside the store in case they was any crooks in the place. Well the on'y think we could do was to crawl on our belly, an' we done that. We stayed behind the counters an' picked up stuff as we went along. When Butts seen the till[11] he whispers: "Let's open her up!" but me an' Shorty wouldn't stand

---

11. *till.* Cash drawer.

fer it. "Nix on that, we aint no till tappers—yet," says I an' Shorty adds: "An' they's nothin' in it, anyway; that guy Cheap Charlie aint such a dub as to leave his dough in the store over Sund'y."

Well we seen a lot o' league balls up on a shelf an' we wanted them there baseballs for the Dewey Dew-drops nine, but we couldn't stand up to get them because why we would be saw from the street. Well we found a stick an' reached up with it an' knocked down a dozen league balls. Butts found a box o' swell realers done up in cotton an' I got into the counter where the mout' harmonicas was. Well besides this we got penknives an' cheese daggers, pencils, crayons, an' pockets full o' all kinds o' junk. When we couldn't hold no more we backed down into the cellar, lets down the trap door an' clim' out the way we got in. On the way out Blinkey in his stockin' feet stepped in to a box o' Jack-stones an' near punctured his pedals.[12] He's a clumsy cuss, anyway. Gettin' out o' that box he put one foot t'rough a bundle o' paper kites. We had to go back an' cover up the damage, because we didn't want to leave no traces in the cellar as to how we got in. When we clim' out the hole we put back the plank an' put in a few minutes fittin' it in its place. Then we quietly snuk up into the alley, one at a time an' got back to Dugan's cellar all right, each guy loaded with plunder. Well now the back room in Dugan's cellar that night had enuf toys in it to start another store. We divvied up the stuff an' put the baseballs aside fer the baseball team.

Well we done a clean job in that an' nobody never got hep. But as ushal Riley come near havin' us investigated be his bum noodle. Why the very first think he does the next day is fer to go up on the street givin' away the thinks he had swiped an' us other guys found all the kids in the neighborhood a wearin' colored specs an' playin on jewsharps an' mout' harmonicas what he gave them.

"What'n hell ye doin', Riley? D'ye' want to get us all pinched? If ye' do why dont ye' go round wit' a brass band an' tell Cheap Charlie we robbed him?" says I, lacin'[13] him down good an' plenty.

---

12. *pedals*. Feet.

13. *lacing*. Scolding.

"Aw I didn't mean no harm. The kids enjoys 'em so I gives 'em to 'em," he pleads.

"Well they's some guys what can be successful crooks an' philanthropists at the same time, but you aint that kind, so cut it out!" says I, exercisin' me authority as leader.

An' he done it, he stopped bein' a Chris'mas tree fer them kids right off.

14.

Fresh Air Kids.

It was gettin' midsummer, an' cripes, it was hot! Gee, I seen some kids a hangin' round the undertaker's wagon same 's round the ice-wagon waitin' fer a chanst to swipe a piece o' ice. It didn't make no diff'rence to them whether the ice was intended fer a stiff[1] or not.

Now about this time it was gettin' hot fer the Crapshooter's club fer the reason that the cops was makin' inquiries as to where all them kids got them blue spectacles, an' I expected every day fer to see a ding-dong wagon[2] come ridin' up to Dugan's cellar an' make a raid on us guys. We all made ourselfs scarce as much as we could waitin' fer that affair at Cheap Charlie's to blow over, an' as luck would have it along comes a nice Sund'y school dame to help us out.

It was this way. Up on Lexin'ton avenue they was a Sund'y school what none o' us went to except to rough-house[3] or fer to ring-in on[4] the Chris'mas entertainment. Now we heard around the street that that there Sund'y school was a goin' to send a party o' Fresh Air kids up to the country fer two weeks, an' nobody what went had to pay a cent fer nothin'! They gave ye' everythink an' all ye' had to have was ye' duds[5] an' carfare to the ferry. Now that there Fresh Air graft was a mighty good graft, an' I says to meself, seein' as how us Crapshooters had better keep out o' sight fer a time: "Why wouldn't it be a good plan fer us

1. *stiff.* Corpse.
2. *ding-dong wagon.* Patrol wagon.
3. *to rough-house.* To disturb.
4. *to ring-in on.* To participate in.
5. *duds.* Clothing.

to take a trip with them there Fresh Airs?" Well now I puts it up to the club an' they appoints me an' Shorty a committee to try an' fix it with that Sund'y school dame.

Well it was no sooner said than done. Up goes Shorty an' me to the old dame's home an' puts up a song-an'-dance[6] that got her right away. We told her we was a club o' hard workin' boys what had never seen no country an' that we was all in poor healt' an' that we would like fer to join that Sund'y school when we come back an' belong to the Watchful Eye Society. Well she fell fer it, all right but Shorty come near queerin' it by sayin' that we was all sufferin' from the con.[7] I give him a good kick in the shins fer to get off'n that stuff because they dont take no lungers[8] on them Fresh Air trips. Well the old dame says: "I'll see what I can do an'll speak to the committee. We've got a big party goin' next week but I'll see what I can do. Youse guys come around on Tuesday an' if we can take ye' we'll examine ye're noodles an' look down ye're t'roats an' if ye' pass I'll try an' find room fer ye'." Well we thanks her an' ducks back to Dugan's cellar.

"Examine me noodle?" says Riley, "What fer does she want to examine me noodle?"

"Not fer brains," says I, "but maybe to see if ye' got fleas!"

Well the upshot was that the whole push got their hair cut, went down to the free bath,[9] an' washed up like they never done before. On Tuesday afternoon we marched into the Sund'y school rooms an' set down with a whole mob o' kids. Well the nice dame sees us an' takes our names an' says we can go if we pass the examination. Well first a guy what was a doctor shoved a shoehorn or a can-opener or

6. *song-and-dance.* A plausible but untruthful story.

7. *con.* Consumption.

8. *lungers.* Persons suffering from lung trouble.

9. [*the free bath.* Concerns about public hygiene prompted philanthropies and eventually municipal governments in New York and other American cities to provide bath facilities in the 1890s. In New York the Association for Improving the Condition of the Poor opened the People's Baths on the Lower East Side in 1891, with twenty-three showers, charging five cents. See its *Forty-Eighth Annual Report* (Oct. 1891), 19–20.—Ed.]

somethink like that down our t'roats an' squints down fer to see if we was sufferin' from some disease. We was all ollygazitsky on that. Then they looked over our noodles, but as we had our hair cut they was nothin' to be saw on our nuts. They was lookin' fer any kids what was lousey an' they gives them the bum's rush an' dont let them go to the country. Well now we passed successful, an' the dame told us to appear at the church on Friday night at seven o'clock with enuf clothes fer two weeks an' a nickel carfare.

We was there wit' bells on[10] at the strike o' the clock, an' it sure was a great mob. If you never was a Fresh Air kid ye' dont know nothink about raisin' Cain. Everybody was laffin' because he was a goin' away an' everybody was cryin' because they was homesick. Well things was doin' right off the bat.[11] First they took our names an' pedigreed us an' then give us each a tag which they tied on us like we was a bag o' oats. On each tag it said what your name was an' what was the name o' the rube what ye' was goin' to stay with. Well now Riley seen that Shorty's tag said that he was to go to a rube named Riley an' he swapped with Shorty so's he could stay with a guy o' the same name. That got the rest o' us to swappin' tags until we was all satisfied. Now about eight o'clock all was ready an' we lined up on the sidewalk an' marched to the Elevated road, took a train down to the Battery, transferred up the west side an' got off near the ferry fer Hoboken. Well a bunch o' ministers an' church dames was in charge an' they keeps us from gettin' run over an' after we gets a nice ride acrost the ferry we all gathers in a corner o' the railroad waitin' room. Now the place what we was goin' to was called Dansville,[12] Livin'ston county, N'York an' it was on the D. L. & W. railroad. Well them guys up in the country called it the Delay, Linger & Wait railroad but it wasn't nothin' like that. They was

10. *there with bells on.* Ostentatiously prompt.

11. *right off the bat.* Immediately.

12. [*Dansville.* This small city in Livingston County, on the Delaware Lackawanna & Western Railroad, according to local newspapers, hosted Fresh Air children in the 1890s. The church where Shorty caught the pigeons (p. 173) was likely the United Methodist Church on Chestnut Street.—Ed.]

swell trains an' they flew jus' like the Grand Central trains what we use-ter heave rocks down on in the Park avenue tunnel. Well we had to set around in the waitin' room a long time an' then the guy opens the gate an' all marched t'rough an' got on the train. We had two whole cars all to ourselfs, an' each kid had a whole seat. Well we had to ride all night to get there an' it must a been pretty near Chicago. Well now after that there train started an' them kids begun to re'lize that good old N'York an' their poppers an' mommers was left behind they begun to get home-sick. First one would begin to blubber an' then another an' them Sund'y school guys had a awful time tryin' to make 'em laff an' cheer up, be tellin' them about the green fields, the apple orchards an' brooks in which they would be playin' the next day, with cows an' sheeps an' calfs. They shouldn't a brung such guys along. They was one big yapp,[13] about fifteen years old. He was cryin' all the time fer his mommer. Well Shorty goes up to him an' pretends to feel sorry fer him an' starts him up every onct in a while be sayin': "Maybe ye're mother's dead" or "It's a sign o' bad luck to travel on Friday nights."

None o' us guys was homesick! We didn't have no time to be home-sick. We had brung along some o' them mout' harmonicas what we swiped at Cheap Charlie's an' takin' up one end o' a car we had a swell time playin' ragtime.[14] Me an' Butts took a sneak outside on the plat-form one time an' we set there with our feet danglin', smokin' butts, an' enjoyin' the night air until a brakeman seen us an' chased us inside. Well some o' us guys tried fer to get to sleep after awhile, but there was nix doin' in that line because we spilt ice-water from the cooler down the necks o' the guys what was sleepin'. Well it must a been after midnight an' we all finally got to snoozin' when all of a sudden Shorty wakes up the whole party be yellin' "fire." He points out'n the winder an' says a whole town was burnin' up. Well the kids got to yellin' an' the conduc-tor comes t'rough an' says it was on'y blast furnaces an' that we was passin' t'rough the towns where they was steel mills in Pennsylvania. It

13. *yapp.* A childish, stupid fellow.

14. *ragtime.* A vulgar form of music in syncopated notes.

was some time before all the kids got to sleep again, an' when we woke up it was gettin' daylight. Well pretty soon we come to the place where we was to get out. Say, that was swell country. The trains there run way up on the mountain an' all the rubes what we was to stay at lived in the village an' on farms down the valley. Well we piled off'n the cars an' all got roped in while the head minister read off the names o' the diff'rent rubes an' called the names o' the kids. Well now that swappin' o' tags what we done had got everybody tangled up an' they had to t'row all us tangled guys into the discard an' wait until the good ones got delivered to the farmers what was to have them. Then we got handed around. Well when they started fer to separate the crowd they was hell to pay! Some guys wouldn't leave each other an' brothers an' sisters refused fer to be parted, an' famers what had ordered on'y one kid had to take two or t'ree an' some rubes what wanted some didn't get none.

Butts an' Red gave a line o' con[15] to one rube an' he took both together, but the rest o' our push was scattered to the four winds. We promised to visit each other soon's we got settled, jus' like we lived on the same block. Well them farmers lived miles apart an' it was on'y be luck or when we happened to go to the village post office that we seen each other. Well them two weeks past awful quick to us Crapshooters, although I guess them poor, homesick dubs thought it was life imprisonment fer them.

Well on the mornin' when we was to return it was a happy bunch o' kids that them rubes brung up to the station. The mob looked like they'd been foragin' on the fat o' the land, an' say, believe me, ye' wouldn't believe what two weeks in the country done fer that push! We was all fat an' sun-burned an' all had all he could carry. Them farmers sure was kind hearted in the hand-outs an' no guy went back to the city without a big load o' truck o' some kind. Well all what come up didn't go back. Some stayed longer, because the farmers liked 'em, an' some stayed forever, because the farmers adopted 'em. None o' us guys stayed up there because we'd a died if we had to stay outside o' N'York.

---

15. *line o' con.* A false story.

We could easy got a job up there but we had got 'nitiated in that there farm work an' we didn't believe in that eight-hour day, twict a day.

Well when our bunch got on the train wit' all our baggage we looked like a immigrant gang jus' come in at Ellis Island. Us Crapshooters got together in seats by ourselfs an' told what we done durin' them two weeks. This was Mickey's story:

"Well that mornin' the rube what had charge o' me come up an' said: 'Hey, sonny, come along with me.' He chucked me clothes in his carriage, set me on the seat with him an' off we went. Well we got away out until I thought I'd never get back if I didn't like it an' wanted to run away. We got to his house which was a nice little farmhouse with barns an' chickens an' a farmyard. Well we went in the house an' he intreduced me to his wife. What d'ye think she had the nerve to do? Well, she kissed me like I was a kid an' says: 'Oh you poor child o' the city streets.' I didn't know whether she was callin' me names or not! Well they took me upstairs an' put me up in a nice little bedroom an' told me to wash up fer grub. Well I washed up to satisfy her an' then come down; an' maybe I didn't do a thing to that grub! Say fellers, they's nothin' nowhere like eats up there in the country! While I was at table the old woman asked me if I could do chores! I didn't know what them was an' when she asked me again I told her I didn't know. Well then she says: 'Do you like Johnny cake?' an' I told her I never met the guy. Well she thought I was kiddin' her an' I thought she was kiddin' me. Then she says: 'I should think ye' could do chores, all right; caint ye?'

"'Come again?' says I.

'Chores,' says she."

"Well I got mad, an' I ups an' says: 'Say missis, I dont get next to ye' rube langwidge.[16] Ye'll have to talk N'York to me,' an' with that her husband jumps up an' makes a pass at me, an' says he'll learn me manners before I goes back to N'York. Well dont think I was asleep durin' this. I grabs a chair an' raises it an' tells him I'd knock his block off if he hit me. I told him that his wife couldn't jolly with me no such lingo, nor

16. *get next to ye' rube langwidge.* Understand.

neither could nobody elst. Well after that scrap he sort o' took a shine to me an' we got to be friends. The next mornin' he asked me if I could work an' I says 'sure' an' so he put me out on a field to hoe corn. He showed me some growin' stuff what he said was weeds an' then some other stuff what he said was corn, an' told me to dig out the weeds. Well after he went away I forgot which was which an' I dug up a whole lot an' found out I was yankin' up corn with the weeds. Well he fired me from that job an' swore to beat the band an' took me to the barn an' asked me if I could curry a horse. I said 'yes' an' he left me on that job. Talk about city nags bein' dirty! They aint in it with them country horses! I jus' took 'em down to a creek an' gave 'em a good wash an' put 'em back in the barn. The rube said it was a good job an' gave me a pleasant look onct in a while. Well I'd have chucked up that place in a hurry if I hadn't been hypnotized by the eats that farmer's wife put up; it had anythink stopped I ever shovelled into me face. An' she never put up no kick an' kept a fillin' ye' plate 's soon 's ye' put away one helpin', so who could flew-the-coop[17] from a place like that? O' course I had more troubles, like when the old dame tried to get me to make butter. She had a box full o' milk an' set me a turnin' it an' told me to keep on 'til she come back. She told me not to stop fer nothin'. Well, after I cranked the handle until me back was near broke I got a hankerin' fer a smoke so I sneaked into the orchard an' burned up a couple o' the coffin nails.[18] When I come back I went to turnin' the handle again. When she come she squints into the box an' says: 'You didn't turn this as I told you to.' How she ever got hep I dont know. Well she told me to quit an' called in the old man an' he set there swearin' an' turnin' the crank while I set in the hammock an' et apples. After that it was a cinch. I made out as how I didn't know nothin' about work o' any kind. The old guy got mad about it but the woman stuck by me an' blamed it on the city. I used to string her wit' stories that was all bull con,[19] an' she thought I

---

17. *flew-the-coop*. Escape, desert.
18. *coffin nails*. Cigarettes.
19. *bull con*. Lies.

was a victim o' circumstants. I useter get next to them hen-coops an' suck eggs, eat meals all day long an' apples between times. Ever since I made a bum job o' that butter churnin' they didn't trust me fer to do any more work an' it was one, long graft. Now that I'm on my way I guess the rube is glad I went. My two weeks was a cinch!" declared his nibs, Mickey, the Son o' Rest.

"Dont you talk about no cinch!" says Shorty, buttin' in to tell his story. "I bet none o' youse had a cinch like me! Lis'n till I give youse guys an idea about somethink real soft. I was met by a young feller who pipes me off like he was sizin' up me muscles, an' he takes me down to the village on Main street an' trots me into a big candy store an' bakery, which his old man run. Well he took me into the kitchen an' gave me a hand-out, an' after I stowed away some mighty fine eats, he takes me around an' gives me a knockdown to his brother an' sisters an' some other rube dames. Well he took me around town as his chum an' he sure was a real sport. Treated me white all the time. He useter treat me to some kind o' soda water what they called 'pop' an' he gave me a knockdown to all the big guys around town. I learned 'em how to shoot craps an' got in wit' them on the ground floor.[20] They said I was the candy kid, an' I showed 'em how to tear off a few stunts before me two weeks was up, believe me! Fer instance. One night I was down like the rest o' them rubes rubberin' at the post office. Well one o' them village cut-ups thought he'd get fresh to me, jus' to amuse the crowd. He says: 'Say you, Fresh Air kid, run over to the hardware store an' ask 'em if that carload o' post-holes is in yet!'

"Well I made a bluff that I was goin' over, an' after I got outside they all laffed. When I come back I went up to the rube an' says: 'They aint got no post-holes but here's a left-handed monkey wrench!' an' with that I plugs him a left hook on the jaw that spilled him on the floor an' he near took the count.[21] Well a bunch o' rubes come to his aid an' wanted to do me up, but all them guys what I had learned to shoot

---

20. *get in with on the ground floor.* Intimately.
21. *near took the count.* Nearly knocked out.

craps come to my side an' the fresh guy dug fer home when I offered to fight him bare-knuckles or boxin' gloves. Well doin' that to the fresh mug got me solid wit' the whole town. It put me in right with everybody! Even the fresh guy come around after a few days an' shook an' made up. He wanted me to learn him how to use his mitts like I done an' I handed him so much josh[22] that he wanted fer to know what the chanst was o' his gettin' a job if he come to New York. I told him he could easy get a job makin' holes in Schweitzer cheese or pickin' fly-specks out o' pepper in the grocery stores around where we lived. I told him I'd send him the address on a pi'ture postal card. He fell fer it, too. Well them guys in that village took me around like I was a dook visitin' America fer the first time. One day I'd go fishin' an' one day huntin' an' sometimes crookin'. When we went fishin' we caught a kind o' fishes called 'suckers' what had big scales an' looked like them moss-bunkers[23] what we catch in the Nort' river, on'y they had Sheeny noses. An' say did any o' youse guys get took up to that there swimmin' hole couple miles from the village? Not the one by the paper mill but one away out? Gee, that was a swell place. Didn't have to wear no tights, an' nobody 'uld chaw roast beef wit' ye're duds![24] I showed them rubes some real swimmin' an' divin'. I hadn't dove from the highest lumber piles on the East River[25] fer nothin' an' them guys thought I was a wonder when I clim' out on trees an' dove on'y about twenty feet. I showed 'em floatin', treadin', dog-paddle, overhand, side-stroke, fetchin',[26] partin'-ye're-hair,[27] an' all kinds o' stunts.

"Then nights that guy where I stayed an' his brother an' me useter go to bed an' read a crackerjack story paper, tellin' about a guy what

22. *handed him so much josh.* Told him so many lies.

23. *moss-bunkers.* Menhaden.

24. *chaw roast beef with ye' duds.* Tie knots in your clothing and wet them.

25. [*highest lumber piles on the East River.* This reference is likely to the Heucken & Willenbrock lumberyard at the foot of Ninety-Fourth Street on the East River (see Figure 3).—Ed.]

26. *fetchin.* Swimming under water.

27. *parting your hair.* Diving so that the impact with the water parts the swimmer's hair.

run away from home an' worked on the towpath, an' it made ye' cry, an' then when we finished we soaked each other wit' pillows until one busted when we'd all duck under the covers an' quit raisin' hell fer that night. O yes, we useter sneak down to the store too, an' cop a pocketful o' chocolate creams an' eat 'em in bed.

"But the greatest think I run into was the Methodist church. It had a steeple an' away up there they useter be a flock o' pigeons what flew away every day an' come back at night an' roosted up there. They was wild an' nobody owned 'em, so the guy what I lived wit' says so, so I showed them guys how to get next to them birds. I found a side window one afternoon where the latch was busted so I shoves it up an' sneaks into the church. Then I went upstairs, finds the box in which the ladder to the belfry was kept, opens it an' goes clim'in' up, an' up, an' up! Well say ye' never seen so big a pigeon coop in ye' life. They was any number o' nests, some with birds settin' on eggs, others wit' squabs in 'em an' it was me fer that place every night after that. Well before I went down I seen hundreds o' swallers a stickin' on the walls up there an' I picks off a dozen' an' shoves 'em in me blouse. Well I clim' down again, shut up everythink so's nobody would get next that I had been up there an' goes over to me friend's house. Well he near throwed a fit when I begins fer to pluck out live swallers out'n me shirt. Well we writ our names on little tags, tied 'em on them birds legs an' let 'em fly away. Well that night me an' the guy an' his big brother goes over to the Methodist church after them pigeons come home an' the whole flock was roostin' an' we sneaks through the window an' goes up into the steeple. It was pie-meat fer us. All we had to do was to pick them pigeons off'n their roosts in the dark an' shove'm into our shirts. We got all we wanted an' et pigeon pot-pie every day. Well last night we went up again an' copped all we could get our mitts on. We got ten an' I got 'em over there in a box under that seat. I'm goin to make home-knockers[28] out'n them. I'll show 'em to ye' afterward when I feeds 'em."

28. *home-knockers.* Pigeons that always return to their coops.

Short was sure "bug"[29] on the pigeon game. He useter keep birds in New York but pigeon crooks cleaned out his roost so often he give it up. Pigeon flyin' is pretty good sport. Ye go to the bird store or meat market when they gets in a crate o' live birds an' ye' buys a couple dozen. Then ye' take 'em home an' put 'em in a coop with a large screened yard so they can come out an' exercise in captivity. Ye leave 'em at least two weeks in the cage makin' home-knockers out'n 'em. Sometimes it takes even longer. Well now after they been there two weeks ye' takes a few out an' throws 'em up in the air near the coop. Well they fly around awhile an' if they come back an' light on the coop they's "home-knockers" but if they fly away ye' got to work to get 'em back. Generally a guy what keeps pigeons allus has some good home-knockers an' if a new bird flies away he throws up a home-knocker who flies with it an' keeps it company until it gets night an' then, sure 'nuf, ye' find the home-knocker an' the stray a settin' perched on the outside o' the coop waitin' fer to be let in. Well now ye' have a drop trap ready an' with cracked corn sprinkled inside an' a few grains outside as a teaser ye' watch till the stray and the home-knocker goes in an' then ye' drop it. Now it's great sport flyin' pigeons, 'specially after ye' got a good flock o' home-knockers. Ye' goes up on the roof wit' 'em an' releases all. Then wit' a bamboo fishpole wit' a long tail tied on it ye' drives 'em up into the air where they flock an' follow the motions ye' make with the stick until they have made a long flight over the city. Now while they's up in the air all strays what happen to be on roofs fer blocks an' blocks sees 'em an' flies up an' joins 'em. Now when the flight is over all come down on your roof an' your home-knockers lead all into the trap an' ye' sure to catch a few strays every day. Well ye' pick out the strays an' confine them until they become home-knockers. It's quite excitin' sport when ye're up on the roof tryin' to coax in a stray what's hangin' round ye're drop, because all the while ye're liable to fall down a airshaft or off'n the roof. Many a guy's been killed flyin' his birds down there on the East Side. Well Shorty had some fine birds in that box. They was one fantail, couple ruffle-necks, two or t'ree

29. *bug.* Crazy over, passionately fond of.

antwebs,[30] some bull-eyes an' pearl-eyes an' a couple wit' lots o' crust on their bills which he said was homers. He didn't know whether there was no tumblers[31] in them because he hadn't seen them up in the air. They was a swell lookin' lot o' birds, though, an' the rest o' the guys was sore because Shorty didn't write a couple o' postals an' put us all wise to the joint before we left that town.

Well I gives my spiel when Shorty got t'rough. I got put up in a quiet joint, church folk—all 'ceptin the old man. They treated me pretty fine, didn't expect me to do no work although I manicured the lawn[32] a couple o' times 'thout bein' asked. They sure made me feel I was a guest an' I'll give them a recommendation any time if they feels they want to entertain any more dead-heads[33] like meself. I got took to a Sund'y school picnic. I put in most o' me time eatin' cake. They was about 57 different varieties an' I sampled all. The finest time I had was when I was took be the old guy to the County fair. Let me say right here that they was some class to them shows, even if they was got up fer rubes. I didn't have to sneak in neither—the guy at the gate made no charge fer any o' us N'York kids what showed up at the gate. If youse guys missed that there fair ye' missed half o' ye' life. Us guys from N'York think we're a pretty fast bunch o' thoroughbreds when it comes to the cards, chips an' roulette wheels, but say, them rubes know a think or two. They had more gamblin' devices than a church fair! They had anythink from the paddle lottery up to roulette an' fan tan, an' the big attraction was horse-racin' with real bookmakers who wore reglar Sheepshead Bay clothes an' flashed stones[34] that blinded ye'! Talk about Broadway bein' wide open! If ye' want to see somethink that'll give Ant'ony Comstock an' Doc. Parkhurst[35] the blind staggers ye' want to go to a County fair!

30. *antwebs.* Antwerps.

31. *tumblers.* Pigeons that tumble while in flight.

32. *manicured the lawn.* Cut the grass.

33. *dead-heads.* Persons who receive anything gratis.

34. *stones.* Diamonds.

35. *Anthony Comstock and Dr. Parkhurst.* Noted reformers. [Anthony Comstock was founder of the New York Society for the Suppression of Vice (1873) and led a movement

Do the Midway! They was a balloon guy who went up every day. He was some class. I never seen none o' them before. This guy went up an' when he got away up he dropped wit' an umbrulla an' did handsprings an' bend-the-crab up in the air. The old guy what took me to the fair bought me a lot o' throws on them gamblin' macheens, an' I won about fifty three-cent stinkers. I took 'em out among the crowds at the race-track an' sold 'em at a nickel a throw![36]

They was one guy dressed like a clown an' he got a crowd by throwin' away real money. Then he sold anythink from a paper o' pins to silk neckties. I seen from his lingo[37] that he was a New York guy, an' winked at him an' he winked back.

"Yea bo, what's ye' game a throwin' ye' chicken feed aroun' like this?" I asks him, when business got dull.

"How'd you come to get ditched[38] in this berg?" he asks me.

"I'm the guest o' the town, Fresh Air kid," says I.

He got hep an' put up a proposition fer me to beat it with him, follow the County fairs for the summer an' promised to land me back on First avenue in the fall wit' fifty bucks clear. It listened good,[39] but I couldn't stay away from Dugan's cellar fer that long, so I says: "Nothin' doin', bo." He gave me a nice necktie when I left him.

They was all kinds o' side-shows, jus' like a big chunk o' Coney Islan'[40] got moved up to that there rube town. They had all from hot-dog stands

---

for federal antiobscenity legislation, henceforth known as the Comstock Law (1873), which criminalized the distribution of "obscene" materials (including information about birth control) through the mail. The Rev. Charles H. Parkhurst used his position at the Madison Square Presbyterian Church in New York City to campaign against the Democratic Tammany machine and corruption in the city government.—Ed.]

36. *nickel a throw.* Five cents apiece.

37. *lingo.* Language, talk.

38. *ditched.* Located, stranded.

39. *it listened good.* Sounded attractive.

40. [*Coney Islan'*. Coney Island, the southernmost edge of Brooklyn, was a crowded summer resort area of beach bathhouses, massive hotels, cheap amusements and, after 1903, magnificent amusement parks.—Ed.]

to shoot-the-shoots an' loop-the-loops. If they didn't I'll eat me hat! When we come home from the Fair I put in most o' me time eatin' pie an' fried-cakes. They calls dough-nuts "fried-cakes" up here in the country.

"Gee, youse guys was lucky," says Buttsy, speakin' fer himself an' Red. "Me an' Red sure got handed a lemon! They was no chanst fer us to pose as parlor car sports,[41] believe me! The day we hit this berg[42] the rube what took both o' us guys puts us in his rig an' drives away over the hills an' out in the backwoods about ten miles. I didn't like that idea an' when I seen where he was takin' us I says to Red, when the guy wasn't lookin': 'Let's take a sneak back to that there town, first chanst we get.' 'I'm on,' says Red, but the farmer didn't give us no chance. He kep' makin' us more sour on his proposition all the time be talkin' about all the work he had fer us to do. Final'y I says:

'Say Mister, if them Sund'y school ginks put the idea in ye're nut that us guys come up here to work, ye' got the wrong dope. We was told that we was on a vacation, so ye' better get off'n that stuff about work fer us to do. Nix on that, see! If them guys told ye' we was willin' to work they was handin' ye' bull-con!'

"He looked at me like I was givin' him some kind o' funny mono-logue an' said nothin'. Well while we was drivin' along he had to stop an' go in a farmhouse fer somethink' so I says to Red: 'Here's our chanst, let's turn these nags around an' swipe the rig, sell it after we make our getaway an' take the train back fer old N'York.'

"'All right, you drive,' says Red, an' with that we turns them nags around, hits 'em a cut with the whip an' before that rube knowed what was up we was racin' to beat hell back toward the place what we come from. We made the nags go faster be Red lambastin' them with the tail-board. We flew acrost country like a young cyclone. When we got a couple o' miles we turned off on a side road, because we knowed the rube would hitch up an' dig fer that there town. We drove t'rough one town after another an' when it got to be afternoon the nags couldn't

---

41. [*parlor car sports*. Parlor cars were the deluxe first-class cars of passenger trains.—Ed.]

42. *berg*. Village.

run no more an' we had to walk them. Well after we give them a rest we tries to sell the outfit in one town fer thirty-five dollars. Well nobody would buy them so we gets out o' that cheap skate berg an' drives on to another town. Well in some way the guys in the next town got hep that we swiped that there outfit. How they done it I dont know, fer we was miles an' miles away from the place where we swiped it.

"'Dont ye' s'pose them rubes know how to use telephones?' asks Shorty.

Butts goes on: "Now when we got into that next jerk-town,[43] Red opens his mush wit' such a crazy question like this: 'Mister, can' ye' tell us how far it is to N'York?'

"The old gink looks us over an' says: 'Ye're in New York. If ye' mean how far is't to Pennsylvany I cal'late it's about fifty mile'.' Then he spoke to another guy an' he come over an' got fresh. He says: 'Boys where'd ye' get that rig? Aint ye' the two Fresh Airs 'at run away from Dansville?'

"'Fresh Airs nothin',' says I, an' with that he grabs the horses' lines.

"'We're pinched, Red. Let's beat it!' says I, an' we both jump out on the other side an' hike it acrost lots. The guy puts up a holler an' before we go out o' sight the hull danged town was chasin' us. We run into a woods but they surrounded us an' soon collared us. We was probaly the biggest sensation that ever hit that berg, old dames an' young crows come out to rubber at us when they took us up Main street an' locked us in the jug. The jug was in [the] fire department an' the fire department was in the town hall. We was chucked into a cell made out'n planks wit' iron pipes fer bars. They asked us a lot o' questions but we gave 'em floats[44] fer answer. We was kep' in that cooler two days an' was makin' up our minds to break jail when the rube what owned the team come to see us. He brung along another rube, an old guy wit' spin-nige on his chin[45] who was the justice o' the peace. He said he'd let us go if we promised to go back with the rube whose team we swiped, an' we

---

43. *jerk-town*. Backwoods village.
44. *floats*. Nothing.
45. *spinnige on his chin*. Chin whiskers.

said 'sure think' an' cut us loose an' the rube put us in the same rig what we swiped an' off we started again. He said it was about eighteen miles to his farm so we had a long ride. He said that if we tried any funny business he'd press the old charge against us an' we'd sure go to prison. He said up there they hung horse thieves.

"When we got to his farm all the farmhands come out fer to see us. They was a big house an' five barns, eighty cows, a whole mob o' pigs an' fifteen farmhands, besides other animals. We seen it was a case o' work, good an' plenty. The rube put us up in a room an' said if we done the right think by him he'd pay us each five bucks when we come to go back home. He seemed to be a nice enough guy, but he allus talked o' work, work, work!

"Well now in the middle o' the night that rube an' his farmhand got up an' wakes me an' Red an' says: 'All up, time fer chores.' 'All right,' we yells down the stairs, an' then lockin' the door we goes back to bed an' sleeps out the night. We made up our mind he'd have to bust in the door if he wanted to get us out o' bed at that time o' day. Gosh, it was fierce! About eight o'clock we got up an' went down stairs. We asked the farmer's wife when they was goin' to have breakfast.

"'Tomorrow mornin',' she says.

"We savvied.[46] Then we says: 'We'd like to have some grub, missus.' She says that we'd have to get up early if we wanted to eat wit' the family, she wasn't runnin' no boardin' house. Then we went to the orchard, knocked off a lot o' green apples an' then went to the barn where we et apples an' bran. Well we got a bellyache an' the rube's wife took pity on us an' when dinner time come we set down with the rest o' the crowd an' et some real eats. Well when all went out to work again the farmer come to us an' gave us a heart-to-heart talk an' when he got t'rough chewin' the rag we promised to work, on'y we thought the hours was long. We didn't hedge,[47] though, an' the rube said he'd do the square think by us.

46. *savvied*. Understood.
47. *hedge*. Quibble.

"We went out to the barns that evenin' when the cows come home an' the rube learned us how to milk cows. Say bo, did ye' ever milk a cow? It's a cinch! All ye' got to do is to pull an' squeeze an' aim at the can. When one tit is done ye' try another an' sometimes ye' come back to the first one. I learned the first time, an' I helped a farm hand to learn Red how. After that me an' Red useter have lots o' fun squirtin' that there cow juice in each other's eye instead into the kittle.

"Well that rube was a pious gink. On Sund'ys he hitched up the horses an' took us all to a town near there to go to church. They sure have hot churches out there in the country—no organ but t'ree rubes playin' a fiddle, trombone an' a flute. I'd a helped out wit' me mout' harmonica if I'd a knowed them tunes. They was no altar-boys nor no nuttin'. Gee, it was punk! Red an' me got up an' went out to the sheds an' smoked butts until the rube was ready to go back home. Then we went back an' had dinner. Well that afternoon Red found a pocketbook on the floor upstairs. He says: 'Findin's is keepin's' an' shoves it into his pocket. Well I says: 'Findin's aint keepin's when ye' find it in the house. Findin's is keepin's on'y when ye' find it on the street; an' then ye' liable to get pinched.' So Red took out fifty cents, fer reward, an' then took the pocketbook back to the lady an' she got sassy an' says he found it in the bureau drawer, which was a lie, because I seen Red when he done it. Well he had the fifty cents reward on'y the old dame didn't know it, so we waited till afternoon an' then hitched up a nag onto a buckboard without permission an' drove to town. When we got there we seen a lot o' the farmhands from our farm an' some o' them had on half an edge.

"'Where 'd youse guys get next to the booze?' says I. At first they wouldn't tell us, but one o' them told us fer to go into a barber shop there an' ask the guy fer 'hop sody.'[48] Well we done it an' fer a nickel a t'row the guy handed out bottles o' beer. They called it 'hop soda water' but it was nothin' o' the kind; it was straight lager beer, an' after we drunk four bottles each we found out that it had a kick like a mule. We took our last nickels to buy cigarettes, an' after smokin' up we clim' into

---

48. *hop-soda.* A brew of beer sold in the disguise of soda water.

the buckboard an' drove home plastered.[49] One more swig o' that stuff an' we'd a been paralyzed. Gee, the rube was mad when he seen us. He was goin' to fire us an' have us took up fer hoboes, but he cooled down an' said he'd put that barber shop guy on the blink soon's he could see the district 'torney. Cripes, we had a barrel o' fun out there. Well today when we got packed an' ready to go back the rube slips us t'ree bones[50] each an' says he was sorry we hadn't earned five apiece. We was satisfied because we thought he was goin' to give us the hook![51] Well he also gave us each a big sack an' told us to go out an' fill 'em with spuds[52] or apples or anythink we wanted on the farm. Well we took punkins because ye' dont see none o' them in the grocery stores on First avenue."

"Well you're a dumm-kopf,[53]" says Shorty. "Dont youse guys know that them little punkins ye' got aint ripe? Aint youse ever heard about the 'frost on the punkin?' That means they aint ripe until the frost is on them."

Sure 'nuff them guys had fell[54] fer unripe punkins, hard as brickbats. Well they wouldn't t'row 'em away, though, an' lugged 'em all the way N'York. We all give 'em the merry ha! ha!

"Well now's youse guys have got t'rough wit' ye're spiel maybe ye'll let me get in a word edgeways!" says Blinkey, snuffin' his butt an' slippin' it into his pocket.

"The place where I stayed was all to-the-peaches-an'-cream! Honest fellers! I'm really sorry to be a goin' back to N'York! I'd probaly die if I didn't go back but jus' the same, that joint was dandy an' I'll miss it, manys the time! It was jus' an old woman an' her daughter, who was a old maid. They had a dorg an' a fat, old molly-grinder an' flowers an' a vegetable garden, an' they lived in a great big house all alone. The old woman had money to burn an' she slips me a quarter or a dime every time I goes up to town an' tells me to buy meself candy. They fed me

49. *plastered*. Intoxicated.

50. *bones*. Dollars.

51. *give us the hook*. Reject, expel.

52. *spuds*. Potatoes.

53. *dumm-kopf*. German for block-head.

54. *had fell*. Were fooled into.

the best o' eats an' had a hired man that come an' done the work. It was about the softest proposition I ever run up against! Why that old dame was better to me than me old woman ever was. She asked me fer to promise her not to smoke no more cigarettes when I got back to New York an' said she'd send me ten dollars fer Christmas, but I wouldn't promise her because I knowed I'd bust me promise an' then I'd probaly lie to her to get them ten bucks. She give me a box o' writin' paper an' envelopes an' a bunch o' stamps an' I'm goin' to write to her every mont', maybe, probaly, perhaps! She told me if I was a good guy while in New York next year I could come up fer the whole summer. She bought me new kicks, a new suit, couple a shirts an' a lot o' duds. It was jus' like I fell into a Chris'mas tree, strikin' that there joint! She wanted me to stay longer but I wanted to come back to N'York wit' the old bunch o' Crapshooters."

Well Riley was the on'y guy left an' he happened to be up at the end o' the car a pourin' ice water into a big wooden box he had there. We called out to him to spin his yarn. Well he come down the car an' says: "I'm afraid he'll croak!"

"Who'll croak?" we all says in chorus.

"Me woodchuck," says he.

"What's that?" says we.

Then he shows us. Down there in that box he had a fat wild animal what they calls a "woodchuck." Then he tells us about it.

"Well," he says, "the house where I was took was owned be a farmer wit' two daughters. They sort o' took me fer a freak an' laffed all the time at me lingo. They tried to kid me, too an' asked me if I could milk hens or thrash punkins. I told 'em I could put the kibosh on fresh hayseeds,[55] an' might be induced to try it if they didn't cut out their kiddin'. Well while I was up there I learned how to plant corn an' pertaters an' how to kill a chicken. Ye' cut the head off an' then t'row the chicken on the ground an' let him run till he's dead. The first one I tried I held

55. *hayseeds.* Rustics.

onto his feet tight an' wouldn't let him go an' I got me clothes covered wit' blood an' looked like them rabbi slaughter house guys down on Forty-Fourt' street an' East River.[56]

"Well a couple o' day ago the farmer caught a woodchuck in a trap an' was a goin' to kill it but I asked him to gimme it so he made a box an' put it in fer me. I'm goin' to take it to N'York an' try an' train it to do tricks. Then we can use it fer a show an' charge admission. The on'y think is that it wont eat no grub. Whenever I goes near it it grunts an' shows its teet'. I have to watch it clost an' rap it when it bites at the wooden slats. Its teet' goes t'rough wood like it was paper. I was jus' tryin' to make it take a drink o' ice water but it's a stubborn cuss."

Well all us guys had fer to go down to the end o' the car an' take a look at it. It was a hairy animal about the size of a spitz-dog an' it stunk like the small mammal house in the Bronyx Zoo. It was homesick an' wouldn't eat nothin'.

Well all the luggage in the car was piled up on Riley's woodchuck box, because he wanted to have it dark fer the animal. Ye' see them woodchucks live in holes in the ground an' so Riley thought it would be sort o' homelike to pile all that baggage on top o' the box.

Well the kind lady what had took us up into the country from that there Sund'y school come around in the cars an' we all shook hands wit' her. Well after them bundles o' clothes, fruit, vegetables, flowers, lunches, pigeons, woodchucks an' Lord knows what was all piled up, the names called off an' all counted the train starts an' we're off fer N'York! This time we rode all day instead o' all night. Well by night we got to Hoboken an' half an hour later we was in good, old N'York onct more. Us guys took the elevated railroad an' got up to our homes all right an' say it was awful punk back there in Yorkville again. The streets seemed to be narrower an' Dugan's cellar was worse than a woodchuck hole. An' that reminds me o' Riley. The poor kid got his box home all right an' then found that his woodchuck had croaked. He showed the

56. *Forty-Fourt' street and East River.* Abattoirs.

dead critter to all the kids in the block an' then we had a funeral up in the vacant lot. Riley took it awful hard. He made a real grave. Ye' can see it over near third base jus' off'n the baseball diamond where the Dewey Dew-drops play ball. Riley allus seemed to have hard luck! Anyway he didn't carry home a lot o' no-good punkins like them city rubes, Buttsy an' Red!

15.

Mickey Sent to the George Junior Republic.

We was back from the Fresh Air trip jus' one week an' Riley an' Mickey was walkin' down Second avenue one day when a kid to what Riley had gave some Jewsharps at the time we busted into Cheap Charlie's joint come along with a man. Mickey seen 'em first an' nudgin' Riley says: "There's a plain clothes cop, let's beat it before he puts his lamps on us." Well they was too late. That there kid pointed at Riley an' the man starts fer both o' our guys. They turns back up Second avenue an' digs, hopin' to get down Dugan's cellar where they could lose the bull.[1]

The flatty[2] was comin' along hot foot when Mickey an' Riley scattered. Riley shot down a flathouse cellar an' Mickey, who was a pretty good runner, digs fer the middle o' the street. But that there detective was some runner himself an' he nabbed Mickey when a car blocked his way. Riley made his getaway.

Well this was a good sample o' what a bonehead Riley was. If he had never give away none o' them Jewsharps an' spectacles nobody would never got wise that we robbed Cheap Charlie's an' they couldn't a run it down to us guys. They had been workin' on this case ever since it happened an' they never found out how the burglars got inside, because they never went back in the cellar. They thought it was a job pulled off be professionals an' that the guys what done it had skeletin keys. They didn't know it was a cellar job at all.

1. *bull.* Detective.
2. *flatty.* Detective.

Mickey was pinched fer keeps this time. They took him to the police station an' gave him the third degree[3] but he was game to the core. He wouldn't let out a peep against the rest o' the crowd. Riley got all broke up about his bein' the cause o' Mickey gettin' pinched, an' felt so bum about it that he was ashamed to come around to the club. Inside o' two weeks his old woman took the family an' moved downtown again to Cherry street where they had lived before they come uptown. Riley's old man worked downtown when he wasn't soused.[4] So the club lost two members, Riley movin' away an' Mickey—but that's a whole story in itself.

When Mickey was hauled up in court they charged him with burglary, but they didn't have no evidence. When they gave him that third degree it made him mad an' he made up his mind that he wouldn't puke up nothin' about nobody. Well us guys raised $15 an' hired a Sheeny lawyer to appear fer him, an' we kep' out o' sight ourselfs. Well the lawyer advises Mickey to keep his mouth shut, to plead not guilty an' stand trial. He says, "Them cops aint got nothin' on you unless you caves[5] on yourself. Jus' keep a stiff upper-lip an' say nothin' to no one," says the lawyer. So Mickey wouldn't squeal an' they finally fixed up a deal by which 'stead o' Mickey bein' sent to prison he was to be sent to a joint upstate called the George Junior Republic. They said it was a school, an' cripes, there aint no walls around it! A guy can escape if he wants to. But the funny think about it is that a guy don't want to run away after he gets there. From all I heard about that there joint since Mickey got railroaded[6] up there I feel like gettin' sent there meself. Honest, maybe ye' wouldn't believe, but Mickey has wrote that he wouldn't leave that joint 'nless they kicked him out. Now the on'y way I can tell ye' about that Junior Republic is t' let ye' read Mickey's letters what he has sent to us guys after he got sent away.

3. *third degree*. Stiff police examination to force a confession.

4. *soused*. Intoxicated.

5. *caves*. Yields information. "Peaches," "squeals."

6. *railroaded*. Unjustly sent away, committed.

Letter No. 1.

Dear Spike—

You must be surprised to hear from me. I aint in no State's prison. O no. When I got nabbed by that flatty on Second avenue I thort my hash was cooked, because of the many times I ever got pinched. Well that lawyer what yous guys got to butt in for me done the business all to the candy. He told the judge there was nothing on me and he could prove a lullaby for me wich means I was not there when it happened. But the judge said I had a bad record so he discharge me on the condishon that my old woman sine me over to a guy what is named Mr. George, wich is the gink what started this here camp where I am now staying. I got to stay here until 21 only if I do the rite thing he says I can go home sooner. He seems to be a nice guy and all the kids here call him Daddy. Well this joint is on the Levi valley railrode in Freeville, Thompkins county, New York about midway between Auburn prison and Elmira reformatry. They call it junior Republic because it means government by kids, for kids and of the kids, and I aint kiddin at that!

Well on the train coming up hear the man what brung me toled me a hole lot about it. He did not have no braselits[7] on me and nobody on the train know it that I was a yung burglar being took up there. Well I was expect to find a place with a 20 feet wall all around it but when I got there I seen only a little villige up on a hill and all the inhabants was kids, guys like you and me. Nobody said "What did you get sent up for?" or nothing. That there big guy they call Daddy come over and seen me and he says Well Mickey dont you think we have got a nice lots of boys and girls up here, and I looked around and said "sure." I had to admit that they seemed to be a nice bunch althouth I could see some fine rough house artists there. I was surprised becaus he

---

7. *bracelets.* Handcuffs.

called me Mickey becaus I thort they was not aloud to use tough names. I called him Daddy like them other guys done.

Now the junior Republic is a place where every guy has got to work for his living. They have got a motto wich is on their money. They have alumium money and their motto is on it in Ginney langwidge. It says NIHIL SINE LABORE. That means Nix without you work for it. Well a guy works up here and gets paid in alumium money and checks and pays his bills and voats and you can run for offis and get elect. Also you can get pinched for vilating the laws, and all these here guys wich are called citizens make the laws themself. Well there is a school too and all kinds of trades and stores and government offis and bank and police and court, and any guy has a right to be anything if he can get to it.

When I got brung up here I was thinking they would chuck me into a prison and put a uniform on me, cut me hair, line me up and make me get up, eat, work, go to bed and be like all them poor kids in the Juvernial asylum. I think I'would die if I had to be one of them guys till I was 21. Well sted of doing that I'll eat me hat if they did not cut me loose when I got here. That guy Daddy says to me Now Mickey I am sure you are going to like it here. You are free to do what you like except going away. There are no gates or walls to keep you here, but if you run away we will be able to get you back and then the citizens will punish you as a deserter. But I know you wont run away because after you have found a job that you like you will want to stay and become one of our leading citizens. By the way do you play baseball. We have got a pretty good team here. "Sure" says I.

Then he staked me to two dollars alumium wich will board me for a cuple of days and told me to find a job and go to work because I would have to ern my own living. Well I sure like this joint, so far anyway. It is lonesome without none of you Crap-shooters up here but there is lots of kids here and they all treat a new guy white, and dont ask no questshuns about what you ever done and they tell you how to get along. I will write again first chance. I think I am going to like this joint very much. Tell Riley I aint got no hard feelings against him becaus I got pinched on account he gave them specs and jews harps to that there kid what sqeeled. I'will wrote to youse guys all about this place when I have time. I got to get me eats now and look around.

So long,

MICKEY.

P.S. If yous guys write to me you need not be a frade to say nothing because they dont read your letters up here. That is what I like about this joint. They are on the sqare.

Letter No. 2.

Dear Fellows—

I suposen you got my first letter in wich I wrote about this place. Well I dont think I am going to stay here if I can beat it. the reason is becaus I got pinched after I been here only three days unjustly. When that guy daddy gave me 2 dollars in republic money I done what he toled me and looked for a job. Well there was no jobs I liked becaus they all had hard work to them like hammering, or digging diches or carrying things. Anyway they had toled me if I did not want to work I need not work but I would not eat neather. Well it was a fine day and I did not want to work so I went down to a swiming hole where all the citizens go. We had a swell time and it was great fun. The guy we called Daddy seen me when I come back and he says Hello Mickey, having a good time. I said "sure" and he said have you got a job yet. No, I said, I aint, becaus I aint going to work until I find something soft. Them jobs they got dont look good to me. He said any job should look good to a fellow out of work. You will get into trubble if you dont find work soon he says.

Well next day them two dollars alumium he staked me to run out and I was broke. It costs 25 cents lodging and 25 cents a meal for grub so I seen I was up against it hard because I thort what that guy said to me, if you dont work you dont eat. And believe me it is a great place to give you a apetite.

I scratched me nut a long time and then I found a skeem to make more money. Now up here in Freeville candy is skarce and if a guy has caramels he can get a nickel a piece alumium for it. Now them caramels cost two for a cent U.S.A. money in the villige at Freeville which is a mile away. Now I had a fifty cent piece of U.S.A. money which I had hid in me shoe becaus you aint suposed to have any U.S.A. money when you come there. You have to deposit it in a bank and they give you credit for it. So I took a sneek down to the villige and bort 100 of them caramels wich at 5 c would make me $5 in alumium. That would keep me nearly a week without working. Well I brung them up the hill into the Republic bounds and after I et a cuple I begun to sell them. Well they was going like hot cakes when a citizen guy come along and says did you pay tariff on them caramels. Pay what says I. Pay tariff says he, duty of fifty percent on all candy brung in. Well what do you know about that. A guy with his own money aint aloud to bring in candy and sell it without paying the government half of it for tariff. the hell you say says I. Well you better quit selling them he says. Then along come a boy cop and he says you are pinched for smugling goods into the Republic, come with me. Come with you nix says I and when he laid his hands on me I smashed him on the jaw. With that all them citizens come to the cops assistans and they pasted me and smeared me all over the ground good and plenty. They put real handcufs on me and put me in their jail. Honest its a real jail with steal cage inside and you cant make no getaway without you have saws. I put up a good fight but they got me in there all rite and serched me. They found a pack of butts in me pocket and took them away becaus its against the law up there.

Well what do you sposen they done to me they charged me with smugling and confistickated all me caramels, charged me with swaring and resisting a offiser and with the crime of having tobacco in me poseshun. Think of that, all them trumped up charges for nothing at all. would not that frost you. Well I made up me mind not to stand for such a raw deal like that.

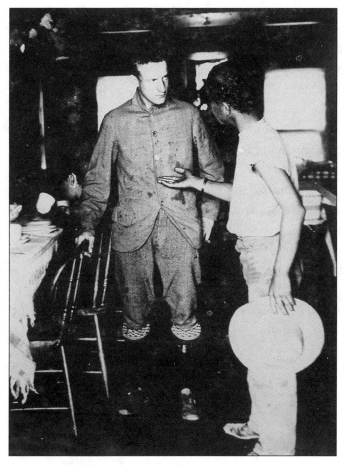

10. A new citizen, trying to beg for a meal at the Republic's restaurant, is shown the door and told to get a job and earn money to pay for it. The photograph was posed to illustrate the Republic's motto, "nothing without labor," and its intolerance of pauperism, ca. 1901. William R. George Family Papers, no. 800. Division of Rare and Manuscript Collections, Cornell University Library.

When I got hauled up before the boy judge I pleded not gilty to all them charges. He toled a citizen to be me lawyer and I had a jury trial. I toled them juryors that I did not know them laws up there and that kid judge says to me igerance of the law aint no excuse. I would have biffed him only there were too many of them citizens around and they all sided with the court. Well the jury said I was gilty of smugling, swaring, fiting a cop and having tobacko in me poseshun. outside of that Im all rite aint I I says to them juryors. What do yous fellows think of such a joint like this where the fellows themself make a law against smoking tobacko. Some punk, hay. Then that there jury reckermended mercy for me. The judge done the rite thing he gave me a week for resisting the ofiser and suspended sentence and he let me go on all the other charges. That let me out again but I made up my mind I would flew the coop first chance. So I am writing yous guys for to say that I will see you soon. I been asking questshuns and I found out wich way is the tracks of the trains for New York. I am goin to jump a frate and ride the rods[8] or brake-beem[9] or else make it "blind-baggage."[10] So long I hope to see you soon.

MICKEY.

Letter No. 3.

Dear Fellows—

You may be surprised to hear from me up here yet. but I did not make my getaway. the reason is that I was pinched again. This is the esiest place in the world to get pinched seems to me. It was like this—

When I was loafing around after that boy judge let me go on suspended sentence and while I was waiting for night to

---

8. *ride the rods*. Straddle the rods under a freight car.

9. *brake beam*. Beam at end of a freight car on which tramps steal rides.

10. *blind-baggage*. The "blind" or doorless end of certain types of baggage cars on fast trains.

sneek away in the dark a boy citizen come along and asked me if I wanted a job. He said I will give you fifteen cents a hour. So long as I was going to beat it I was not going to work there if I could help it so I said Nix on the job.

Well five minits later a boy cop come along and asked me if I was working. I toled him no and he says have you got 25 cents. No I says. Then you are pinched says he, what for says I. Being a vagrint says he Come along. Of all the nerve. Well now thats the law up here. If a guy is out of work and aint got a quarter in his pocket he is a bum[11] and they pinch him and up he goes to the workhouse. Well I did not think it wise to resist after that boy judge showed how sour he could be over a guy what resists a ofiser so I went along. I was found gilty of being a vagrint and it reelly made me ashamed becaus there was little kids up there what erned their own living and did not have to get pinched for vagrints. So I got sent to the workhouse for two days. Well now as soon as I got sentence the keeper come to me and says, I got work for you to do come along. so I had to go over to that guy what offered me fifteen cents a hour and now I had to do the same work for the government for nothing. He paid the government ten cents a hour for services of their prisoners and all the government give the prisoners was thre bum meals and lodging in jail. Well I thinks it all over in jail that night and I seen that I was a real bonehead, solid ivory. Here I was working for the government at no pay only me meals and lodging. The government was gettin $1 a day for my work and if I had took the job myself I would a got $1.50 a day and would not a been arrested for a vagrint and would not be disgraced. I found out that it dont pay to be a bum. so when my two days was up I stayed rite on that job and hired out to that fellow for fifteen cents a hour. Am I rite? I guess yes. I worked for that hotel guy a cuple of days and forgot all about

11. *bum*. A tramp, idler, worthless fellow.

my skeem to run away. So long as I had money coming to me I did not want to beat it and at the end of the week I was ahead of the game[12] a little so that I begun to get intrested and I made up me mind to stay just to see what I could do in compatishun with them other ginks. Besides this I found when I was ahead of my debts I had time to go out and play baseball and I seen I could make a place on the team they got. In fact I begun to get proud and made up my mind that I could show some class myself. Well I done my work so good that the hotel guy made me manager and paid me $1.75 a day and now I have hired another guy to do the dirty work I done.

I am thinking of studying to be a lawyer here. You can go into the libary and study it up. Lawyers make slathers of money here.

I will write more when I get more time. I am going to save some money because you can start a business here. I wished yous guys would be here. Cant yous all get pinched for something and have them send you up here. honest its great.

MICKEY.

Down in Dugan's cellar we didn't think that that there joint was so rosy like Mickey wrote it and we didn't believe half the stuff he wrote. Anyway we didn't care to quit N'York fer that there joint up there in Freeville. If we got pinched—well then it was a different matter. We did not care to go no place where a guy learned to love work, no sir, not 'nless we was sent there fer punishment.

---

12. *ahead of the game.* Prosperous, improving.

16.

Hallowe'en.

Blinkey was bendin' the crab[1] on the meat hooks in front o' a meat market near Second avenue one night, an' the rest o' us was doin' gymnastics or settin' on the steps makin' remarks at women what come down the street when all of a suddent Blinkey drops to the ground with a yell. I thought he must a run a hook into his old carcass like I onst seen a poor Ginney organ grinder's monkey do when he clim' up the meat hooks to get a penny from a woman upstairs over the store. But that wasn't it at all. Soon's Blinkey got on his feet after his big drop he yells "Cheese it, the cop!" an' with that the whole gang digs fer Second avenue. We wasn't any too quick. Acrost the street "Blood" O'Connor, the fresh cop what was new on our beat, slipped out from behind a party o' men an' digs after us. [Blinkey] had piped off his shiny shield in the dark an' seen him in time. We run down the avenue an' that sucker of a cop trailed us four blocks. We went back to Dugan's cellar by way o' First avenue. Well we peeked out o' the cellar window that led up to the street an' there sure enough, right in front o' our clubhouse stood that fathead[2] cop lookin' up and down the street fer us guys comin' back. He stood there wipin' the sweat out 'n his helmet when Paddy, the Devil, come along. He knowed Paddy because he allus passed out the side door beers[3] to the cop up on the corner.

Paddy seen that somethink was up and says: "Anythink doin'?"

---

1. *bending the crab.* A gymnastic stunt.

2. *fathead.* Stupid, ignorant.

3. *side door beers.* Glasses of beer passed surreptitiously to policemen by saloon keepers to silence them and keep them from noticing liquor law violations.

"Ho, I'm only after them loafers that hang out over in front o' that there meat market. I got orders today to clean up that gang. I'd give a month's pay to capture them lads. I get reprimanded every day fer not breakin' up that bunch. What I'd like to know is how they make themselfs scarce so easy."

"They go over in the vacant lot," says Paddy, puttin' in a bum guess. He didn't know nothin' about Dugan's cellar. Well the cop decides to sneak up the street an' hid in a doorway acrost from the lot waitin' in vain fer us guys to come out an' get pinched. We near laughed out loud when we heard him talkin' to Paddy, but we didn't, jus' the samee. It was gettin' warm, though, around our headquarters. Some kids was gettin' inquisitive an' asked us if we had a den, an' as we still had a lot o' plunder hid down there we sure couldn't run no chanst o' havin' some guy get wise to our joint.

We lit lights on'y in the back room what had no window an' then on'y after closin' the door an' shadin' the candle. Well when we seen that "Blood" was after us we made up our minds not to hang around outside that night any more. Some o' the guys laid down on the mattress an' read dime novels an' the rest played whiskey poker.[4]

"Say fellers! It's on'y t'ree nights from Hallow Eve," said Shorty all of a sudden. Well that busted up the game right there. All got to chewin' about puttin' up jobs on all the guys that we owed scores. Now Hallow Eve is a holiday what's celebrated on'y at night. I dont know who the guy is what is honored by it, but he must a been a hell-raiser! Well now the way ye' celebrate Hallow Eve is this. Ye' play all kinds o' jokes an' put up jobs on anybody ye' want, an' ye' cant get pinched fer it. The chief way it is celebrated though is to go around with a stockin' full o' flour, turn ye' coat inside out, an' paste any guy ye' see. Ye' get pasted ye'self too an' the sport is to see which guy can soak the most guys. When the flour is used up ye' get more. Also ye' get hold o' yapps[5] an' make them "it" in playin' snide tricks[6] on 'em.

---

4. *whiskey poker.* A common card game.

5. *yapps.* Stupid fellows who make easy victims for practical jokes.

6. *snide tricks.* Mean, malicious tricks.

The first think we voted to do was to go out on Hallow Eve a soa-kin' guys wit' stockin's filled wit' flour. But we had to get them.

"Well we dont want to get left behin' the hearse[7] about gettin' stockin's an' flour, so I moves that we swipe some tonight," says Shorty. His motion was carried so I takes the deck o' cards, shuffles 'em an' hands 'em out, face downward, one at a time to each guy. "The guys what got most red cards goes to Davey's fer flour an' the guys what has most black cards goes up into the backyards an' swipes the stockin's from the wash lines. That's square enuf, aint it?" I asks. They nods "yes" an' looks at their cards. Me an' Riley had most black cards an' Shorty, Butts, Red an' Blinkey had reds. Well fer half an' hour the joint was empty. We was all out on strange ground tacklin' our jobs. Me an' Riley, wash line crooks,[8] soon came back with a fine collection o' stockin's. They was short ones an' long ones an' fat ones an' lean ones, an' we was laffin' fit to bust when we come down. The other guys was there ahead o' us an' Shorty butts in an' says:

"Cut it out! Cut out ye're laffin! D'ye' want everybody to know where we hang out, after we been here nearly eight months!"

I couldn't stop laffin an' he got so mad he wanted to resign from the club. But I kep' thinkin' o' that there poor mutt[9] away up in the air—cripes, it was funny!

It was this way. When them other guys went to steal the flour me an' Riley got onto a back fence an' went down the street a ways. There was a nice moon shinin' an' we could see a nice string o' stockin's han-gin' from a fourt' story window out to the pole abou' nine houses down toward First avenue. Well we clim' along the fences until we got there an' Riley says: "Who's goin' up, you or me?" I says: "I'll go up, an' you lay keegie." Well I clim' up the pole slow an' quiet an' when I reached the line I pulled. But it got stuck an' wouldn't run t'rough the pulley. I pulled hard an' bing! Down come the whole line, havin' pulled the staple out o' the window. Well as I clim' down I took off the

---

7. *left behind the hearse*. Missed, neglected, forgotten.

8. *wash line crooks*. Thieves who make a specialty of robbing wash lines.

9. *mutt*. Dog, also low-down fellow.

stockin's an' had cleaned off the whole line 'ceptin' the part that hung in the yard. Well Riley went down in the yard to do that an' was ready to come up on the fence again an' make a getaway wit' me when that danged Hibernian spitz-dorg owned by that Dutch janitor come runnin' out. It was too late fer Riley to get up the pole an' I whispers: "Kick the mutt in the gut." Riley done it an' knocked the wind out'n the cayute.[10] It near croaked the poor [word illegible]. Well to do the job up brown we tied a couple o' stockin's around the mutt's belly, hitched him to the rope an' pulled him up the pole. He come-to before we was very far away an' set up a howlin', an' every window on the block opened up to find out what was up. Sounded like the yards was haunted. We made our getaway all right, an' here we are.

With that we dumps down a pile o' stockin's an' sizes up what them other ginks had got. They had brung back eight packages o' flour. It's a cinch to swipe flour. All them groceries have it piled out farthest from the doorway because no kids never steal it. O' course we got it fer Hallow Eve or we wouldn't swipe none neither. All that kids swipe is stuff ye' can eat. Ye' cant eat flour 'nless ye' cook it.

Well it come Hallow Eve an' us guys got ready to make a real night o' it. We turned our clothes inside out, so in gettin' soaked wit' flour it wouldn't soil our duds,[11] filled our stockin's wit' flour an' throwed in a handful o' pebbles to keep the flour mixed an' let the guys what we soaked know what we was handin' 'em somethink juicy. Shorty an' me was the main gazayboes[12] an' we each took up one side o' the street wit' our guys. Well it wasn't ten minutes after we got to swingin' our stockin's that we left a trail o' blubberin' kids. We smashed right an' left an' lambasted all who didn't sneak into their homes. So many kids was fell by the wayside that they was about fifty o' their mothers yellin' at us from out'n the windows an' shakin' their fists at us, an' yellin': "Wait till my old man comes home, he'll fix youse fellers or I'll have the police on

---

10. *cayute.* Dog.

11. *duds.* Clothing.

12. *gazayboes.* Leaders, proprietors.

ye'!" Well we swatted kids until they was no more sport in that so we rigged up a tick-tack[13] on Terro Camillo, the Ginney shoemaker.

He was an awful mad Ginney an' useter jump an' threaten to hit us wit' a hammer even jus' when we stood in front o' his window an' stuck out our tongue at him. He sure was a peevish wop an' we allus looked out fer him. He had such a bad temper that he'd kill ye' if ye' didn't skidoo[14] right away after ye' put up a job on him. He played trombone in a Ginney band an' we useter kid him when he was practicin'. Well we seen Terro this here night a blowin' his trombone so we knowed he was our pie-meat.[15] Because it is easy to rig up a ticky-tack on a guy if it is some kind a noise goin' on while ye're riggin' it up. Well we tossed up to see which guy had to do the hard work, drivin' in the tack an' stringin' the thread. Riley lost but he didn't care anyway, because his family was movin' down town an' he'd be away soon an' nobody could get him pinched. Well he got a rock, rigged the tick-tack, strung the thread acrost the street an' we got busy.

We was out o' sight behind a cellar railing an' it was great sport a watchin' Terro blowin' his trombone. The first time he heard the tick-tack he looks up an' quits playin'. Then he come out an' looked up an' down the street to see where the kids was what done it. When he got inside again we let down the iron nail what ticked on the window an' started it a goin' again. He come out on the run again but seen nobody. Then we seen him go back an' when we got busy he pretends he didn't hear it an' edges towards the front o' the shop. Then he dusts out[16] again, but nix doin'! He looked all over his window but we had pulled up the tick-tack an' he couldn't see it in the dark. Then he searched the doorways of the houses nearby but he didn't get hep to us. Well that Ginney got so mad he put on his hat an' coat and then made a bluff that he was goin' away. We seen everythink he done an' we kep' our

13. *tick-tack*. Prank involving tapping on the window.

14. *skidoo*. Flee, escape.

15. *pie-meat*. Prospective victim, ready victim.

16. *dust out*. Run out suddenly.

eyes peeled all the time. Gee, but we sure had that Ginney's alley![17] After bein' away fifteen minutes he come back, gum shoein'[18] down on our side o' the street an' we laid low an' quit tick-tackin' while he was around. After awhile he gave it up an' went inside again. He put off his coat an' hat an' put on his apron an' begun to fix shoes when we started the think agoin' again an' say, that Ginney knocked over his bench in a hurry to get out an' cop the ginks that was annoyin' him. He looked all over the window again an' then went inside. Soon he come out with a light an' we got hep in time to yank down the tick-tack an' beat it. He never knowed to this day what done that tappin' on his shop window.

Well the next guy what was on our list fer rough house was Sing Lee, the Chinky[19] laundryman. Now there was a big meat market down on Avenue A an' we knowed where they kep' their rotten meat in a side alley where the board o' health wagons got it. Well we went down there an' found a lot o' old beef livers waitin' fer a free ride to Barren island,[20] so we cops a couple o' them an' drags 'em to the Chink's joint. It was down a basement an' all ye' had to do was to heave them down an' run. Well we run apast in a line an' each guy let fly his liver or heart or rotten meat an' it scared that Chink so bad that he hid behin' his counter till we was out o' sight. Then he complained to the landlord an' the landlord complained to the cop. But nobody knowed who done it.

When we got back to our own neighborhood again all the kids was out again, an' when they seen we didn't hit them with our stockin's anymore they come out an' we let them play wit' us. Well we played horseshoe the mare, hide the straw, deliver the black puddin', fire, fire an' so on.

Ye' play horseshoe the mare like this. Ye' get some green guy who is choosed fer mare, another guy is blacksmith, an' another guy is driver. Well the driver takes some good stout cord or rope and ties it on the mare's arms pretendin' she's a balky nag an' must be tied tight. Then he

17. *had that Ginney's alley.* Succeeded in enraging.

18. *gum-shoeing.* Speaking quietly.

19. *Chinky.* Chinese.

20. *Barren island.* The city dumping ground.

drives off to have her shoed. Well the guy who is blacksmith has his shop in front o' some house where a cranky janitor[21] lives. Well the driver comes along an' says to the guy what is blacksmith: "Mister, I want my mare shoed." "All right," says he, "back up." Then he backs up the mare near the door, an' while the blacksmith is busy pretendin' to shoe the mare the driver ties the lines tight to the door bell an' yanks it fer all he's wort'. Then the driver an' blacksmith dust, an' the poor mare is tied an' cant get loose an' when the janitor comes runnin' out the mare gets lambasted. It's good sport, an' aint nowhere near as bad as Hide the Straw. Now ye' play that a good deal like Deliver the Black Puddin'.

In deliver the black puddin' ye' get some particlar fresh guy[22] what dont know it. Then ye' chooses up, appointin' a Good Judge, a Bad Judge, a Cop, a Villain an' a Crowd. Now the guys what's in on the game tells the fresh guy what he must do. They name him as Good Judge. That gives him a swelled head! Then they go out an' scatter fer awhile. Then the Cop grabs the Villain an' says "You stole the Black Puddin'." The Villain is brung before the Bad Judge. "You stole the Black Puddin'!" says that Bad Judge. "I didn't," says the Villain. Then they argue an' the Bad Judge lets him go. Then the crowds go out again an' the Cop grabs the Villain an' brings him before the Good Judge. Well when the crowd comes back ye' notice that they all got somethink behin' their backs. The Villain generally has somethink ripe an' juicy. Well now the Good Judge says: "Officer bring the prisoner." The Cop brings in the Villain, an' everybody gets around so the Good Judge is up by himself. Well the Good Judge says to the prisoner: "Sir, you stole the Black Puddin'."

"Sure," says the Villain.

"Have you it with you?" says the Good Judge.

"Sure," says the Villain, fingerin' somethink behind his back.

"Then," thunders the Good Judge, "Deliver the Black Puddin'!" An' he does! Every guy in the crowd delivers that puddin', an' it aint no

21. *cranky janitor.* Irritable, irascible.
22. *fresh guy.* Unpopular person, bombastic or self-centered person.

speshal recipe on'y it must be somethink ripe an' juicy. Well the game ends there wit' the Good Judge runnin' home covered wit' mud an' garbage, an' he gets licked[23] by his old woman. It's one o' the best games ever invented an' every new guy has to be a good judge if he dont know the game.

In playin' Hide the Straw the guy what is "it"[24] hides a piece o' straw somewhere, an' each guy takes one guess where he hid it. If ye' guess wrong he's got to say so, an' show that ye're wrong. Well at that right time some guy says: "I know where it is, ye' hid it in ye're mout'." The guy says "No" an' the feller what's guessin' says "Open ye' mout' an' let 's see!" Well when the dub[25] opens his mush every guy standin' round tries to throw somethink in it. The easy mark[26] gets all plugged up wit' mud, an' ends up be runnin' home.

Now Fire, Fire is another game o' this mud-slingin' kind. Ye' go where they is an empty truck standin' somewhere, ushally near stables. Well ye' get a sucker an' appoint him Chief. The other guys is firemen. Well the Chief waits until a guy yells "gong, gong! gong, gong!" which is a fire alarm an' he climbs up on the seat o' the truck an' yells "fire, fire! fire, fire!" an' wit' that every one o' the firemen fires somethink at him an' keep soakin' him wit' rotten apples, vegetables an' other stuff from the ash barrels until he beats it home. Well we quit playin' them games when they was no more suckers to be found an' we went down the street puttin' out street lamps, dousin' lights in flathouse hallways, stickin' pins in electric push button bells to keep them ringin', dumpin' ash barrels an' gettin' our money's wort'[27] fer Hallow Eve.

We was down on First avenue when we seen a wagon in front o' a saloon, an' Shorty jerks his thumb at the wagon to tip us all off. Well it was the sissidge wagon, an' the driver was in that there saloon deliverin'

---

23. *gets licked.* Thrashed.
24. *it.* The duly chosen victim.
25. *dub.* Foolish fellow.
26. *easy mark.* Victim, butt of the joke.
27. *getting the money's worth.* Going the limit.

bolognies an' hot-dogs[28] fer the free lunch counter. Well while one o' us watched him inside the rest o' the guys clim' up the back o' the wagon, stuck in their paws an' pulled out a string o' hot-dogs, an' we cleaned up a big mess o' them sissidges. Well it was gettin' pretty late so we went back to Dugan's cellar chewin' hot-dogs. We had lots left after we et all we could, an' we cut 'em into little pieces the size o' corks an' used 'em to plug up the speakin' tubes in the houses on our block. On the way back to the cellar we swiped a couple o' bottles o' soda water from Dutch Miller's grocery store. The way we done it was this: Dutch Miller had a greenhorn named Peter workin' fer him, an' Peter was a fly sort o' guy[29] an' when we robbed Dutch Miller, who was deaf, he allus told him. Well we seen Peter go down in the grocery cellar fer a hod o' coal, an' when he got down there we throwed over the cellar door, stood on it, an' before Peter could come up we throwed the hasp an' put a plug in the staple. Well he made a racket but Dutch Miller didn't hear him because he was deaf, so we took all the filled soda water bottles that was left in the crate outside the store. We took it down Dugan's cellar an' drunk it fer to wind up Hallow Eve. Peter was locked in there near an hour!

To show what nerve Shorty had—the next day he took seven empty soda bottles what we had in the cellar up to Dutch Miller an' collected two cents on each bottle, bein' what they allows ye' fer empties. Shorty has sure got a reglar gambler's nerve!

28. *hot-dogs.* Frankfurter sausages.
29. *fly sort of guy.* An obnoxious person.

17.

Letter from Mickey in the George Junior Republic.

Freeville N.Y.

Dear Spike:—

It has been some time since I wrote to yous guys becaus the reson is I was to busy. They are going to have a lectshun here in November and I am getting in rite with the citizens and I wuld not be suprised if I run for some job. I am lerning to be a lawyer but I got to go some yet to no enuf but I am going some, believe me. Now I no you wont believe it but I can prove it I sware it on a stack of Bibels. I am a Cop![1]

Of corse I aint a reglar only a speshal but I can pinch guys that vilate the laws. aint that going some? I am lerning a whole lot in the libary and will try sivil service. You got to pass it to get in. the worst I am up against is my spelling Im a bum speller but I think I can pass soon. Then I will be a reglar cop.

The way I got speshal is this. there was to big guys in jail last week and they was tuff nuts.[2] Now they got sent on the gang wich means convict prison for one month each for stealing things from a guy's room. well one night they broke out of jail and beat it from this here place. When I seen that them guys escaped after stealing another guys propety it made me awful mad, cheaf

---

1. *cop.* Policeman.

2. *tuff nuts.* Incorrigible characters.

becaus it was my propety they swiped. Well I did not like the noshun of them blokes making a getaway without punnishment they desurved. I asked the boy president here to let me help capture them. He sed yes and the cheaf of police swore me in speshal. they sent two cops out in every directon and I went with another guy to the south and we traled them as far as a little jerk town called Harford mills a place on the way to New York. Well I got a clue in that place becaus a farmer sed I seen them boys hiding near my barns. So I run in there and yelled hey you guys surender. You are surownded so dont put up no fite. I sed it jus like Nick Carter[3] used to when he pinched guys in his dime novels. Well them two big dubs sed all rite. The guy who was with me had a pair of real braselets[4] and we ironed them to guys together. Then we took a trane back to the Junior Republic and we was given a glad hand[5] for capturing them tuff propositions. it put me in rite and I can be a reglar cop as soon as I pass sivil service. so I am putting in lots of time in the libary. Them guys we pinched will get put on the gang[6] more now than if they had not snuk away.

Well this joint looks gooder to me every day. Im intrested in that there lectshun but Im afrade that I dont look good to the crows. they have voats for wimmin here, all the girls voat and a guy toled me that they voat only for the guy what is good looking and a fellow with a fiz like mine aint got no show. They say if a guy has got the ginger[7] and wares good clothes the dames voat for him. Well now Im against wimmin voting. but I wont not say it up here till after lectshun. We have town meeting here and it

3. [*Nick Carter.* Between 1890 and his death in 1922, Frederick Dey, according to the *New York Times,* wrote more than 1,000 stories for dime novel publications featuring the master detective hero Nick Carter. See "Creator of 'Nick Carter' Kills Himself, " 27 Apr. 1922.—Ed.]

4. *bracelets.* Handcuffs.

5. *given a glad hand.* Congratulated.

6. *on the gang.* In the convict gang.

7. *ginger.* Money, wealth.

decides laws and any citizen has a right to move anything. I was going to move that all big guys can smoke butts but they advised me not to do it becaus it will get me in wrong[8] and I would not stand no show of having it pass. This here town meeting makes taxes and you got to pay them. Taxes is money collected to run the government. You got to pay it and if you dont the guy takes your clothes and sell it and keeps the money for the government. Besides taxes they have a bank here and I got some dough[9] there alreddy. They pay off in checks and I pay my bills by writing a check. It lerns you to keep a counts and you no where your dough goes to. I never saved a red cent in me life till I come up here. since I been here I have saved about twelve dollars good mazuma. Say you could not get me to leave this joint now without you pry me loose with a jimmy and a monkey rench. I made that there baseball team and I play first base and we travel all around this here country. We trim anything from Sqedunk to a semi-pro team[10] and could beat the Deweys hands down.[11] Dont think I am knocking[12] yous guys I aint. I wish yous was here. I no yous would like it even if yous cant smoke or sware or go on the crook or scrap or lofe or pull off rough stuff on nobody. You get used to be without that sort of fun and there are so many other things that keep a guy busy you get sour on the old stuff. I tell you when you have got to work and you are able to spend your own money what you erned and you hire your own room and eat in your own grub joint and buy your own clothes and have to pay taxes you lern that money is worth something and it feels pretty good to a count to nobody but your self. Well I wished I had more time for to write. So long, remember me to the bunch.
    MICKEY.

8. *get me in wrong.* Make me unpopular.
9. *dough.* Money.
10. *from Sqedunk to a semi-pro team.* From a backwoods to a semi-professional team.
11. *beat . . . hands down.* Defeat without effort.
12. *knocking.* Saying mean things about, holding low opinion of.

P.S. I aint quit using butts yet. I no a place down over the hill near a swamp where I take a sneek every few days and lite up a butt. I got a pack hid there inside a tin can under a bush. There is a peper mint bush there growing close to the ground and when I get through smoking I chew big gobs of the leafs. They pinch you here even if you smell like smoking.

18.

'Lection Time.

The gink in the cigar store on Second avenue was tackin' up signs "Register Here" in front o' his joint when me an' Blinkey come along one day. We piped him off till he finished. We knowed them signs meant that 'lection was soon here.

"Hey, mister; when is 'lection?" said Blinkey when the guy got t'rough.

"Same day as last year," he says, gettin' fresh. He laffed an' went inside thinkin' that he put somethink neat over on us. Well we met another guy an' he told us it was the Tuesday after the first Monday in November. We thought he was a kidder, too; but he was right. Blinkey felt sore over that first guy's answer, though an' after lookin' in the cigar store window a couple o' minutes he says to me "Got a pencil?"

"Sure," says I, handin' it over. Well now in that window there was a big arch o' cigar boxes stacked up in a fine display, an' it must a took that fresh guy a whole day stackin' up them cigar-boxes fancy like that. Under the big arch was a big jar o' gold fishes. Well Blinkey run his hand along under the window until he found a little round hole in the bottom of the window where the water ran out when the guy washed the window on the inside. Well now after he looked into the store and found a good show Blinkey shoved my pencil up the hole, took a brick from the gutter an' drove the pencil up good an' plenty. It hit the boxes standing at the bottom o' the arch an' sent the whole danged collection tumblin' down. Then we dusted an' was safe down in Dugan's cellar before the guy reached the sidewalk. We got even wit' that fresh mug, anyway!

Well the days was gettin' cold an' we found the bunch down in Dugan's cellar when we got there. We told the guys how 'lection was

208

soon comin' an' how it was gettin' time we started to collect stuff fer our big fire. Now on 'lection night every year each block on the East Side has its own 'lection fire, an' one gang scraps wit' another to swipe stuff to make the biggest fire. Well now we hadn't opened our mugs[1] when Shorty butts in an' says that the guy what Tammany[2] put up this year was his uncle.

"What's ye're uncle's name," says I.

"Jake Bender," says Shorty.

"That's the guy," says I, because I seen that there guy's pi'ture in store windows. He was a Dutch guy[3] but Tammany put him up fer Alderman because the Republicans run a guy named Goldstein to get all the kuyks an' Dutchmen in that there ward. The Harps was Tammany anyway. Well now Goldstein was onct a Tammany grafter but he got trimmed good an' plenty, an' now he was runnin' on the reform ticket. A good bestin' has made many a graftin' polytishan turn reformer.

"Hurray fer Bender!" says I, an' the club voted right away fer to get up a big fire fer him. But the first think to be did was to find some cellar to put our barrels an' boxes an' stuff. We could not use Dugan's cellar because that was our club house an' we paid no rent, an' anyway it would put outsiders hep to our hangout. Well me, Shorty an' Red was appointed a committee to see Shorty's uncle, so we went down to his saloon on Avenue A near East River park. Well he was a wise guy an' seen that it was wort' while to have such a lively bunch like us on

1. *mugs.* Mouths, faces, persons.

2. [*Tammany.* Tammany Hall was officially a social club of the Democratic Party in New York City, but in actuality operated as a powerful political machine, using patronage and a vast network of influence to hold power in the city and reward its followers. For reformers like Thomas Osborne and William George, Tammany was the darkest evil force in the city because it ran the city for its own interests rather than the good of the people. They saw Tammany as the principal obstacle to improvements in tenement housing, more effective policing, fighting prostitution and the saloon evils, and they believed that muckers learned early to follow the machine's orders instead of their independent consciences.—Ed.]

3. *Dutch guy.* German-American. The word "Dutch" is always applied to German-Americans.

his side an' he goes behind the bar, opens up the till, an' comes across wit' a five spot.[4] We knowed where they was a good empty cellar up the block from Dugan's cellar an' we soon had a receipt fer five dollars as one month's rent. Then we begun to gather stuff fer the fire. Every day we got the kids in our neighborhood an' we'd go out stealin' empty boxes, dumpin' wooden ash barrels an' swiping 'em, confiscatin' empty baskets, tubs an' sometimes we got empty beer kags. We'd come marchin' home with 'em an' the cops never butted in because they was afraid to make the politicians mad. When a cop seen our gang comin' he looked the other way an' over would go somebody's garbage barrel, zip, some guy would empty it, an' then two guys would take hold of it on each end an' we'd take it to our cellar. The hard work was to fight our way when we had a run-in wit' some other gang out swipin' stuff fer the 'lection fire. Now it's a rule that ye' can swipe whatever any other guys have when ye' meet them, so it's allus best to take a big gang with ye' when ye' go out. Now in the night time we useter get the older guys when they come home from work an' we'd go out an' swipe some real classy fuel. We'd go where they was a store closed an' before a guy could wink his eye down come the sign an' half a dozen husky guys was scootin' down the Avenue wit' it an' ten minutes later it would be piled up with the boxes an' barrels in the cellar fer 'lection. Now it's a rule that no kid can join ye' gang fer 'lection 'nless he gets his license. If a kid comes around ye' say to him, "G'wan, beat it out o' here 'nless ye' gets ye' license!" Well then he goes out an' steals a couple o' boxes an' barrels an' brings 'em in an' says: "Is them enuf license?" and then ye' sends him out again if he aint got enuf. If he got enuf then ye' let him join ye' gang an' he can come round the fire on 'lection night.

Now when ye' go out swipin' barrels ye' take clubs wit' ye' an' if ye' meet another gang ye' try an' take their barrels away an' if they scrap ye' beat 'em up good an' plenty till they drop their 'lection stuff an' run. Well we done that an' inside o' two weeks we had that there cellar full o'

---

4. *Five spot.* Five-dollar note.

stuff. Now would ye' believe it we got in right[5] wit' Shorty's uncle. Why he got so's he never said nothin' when we walked right into his saloon an' cleaned house wit' his free lunch counter, an' he fixed it so that we each got a torch light fer the big parade one night. We was some class that night. I was captain an' all the Crapshooters marched in one line in front with the band. Gee, how sorry we was fer poor Mickey up there in that joint called the Junior Republic an' poor Riley, downtown in Cherry Hill! Them was great times they missed! Shorty's uncle seemed to know that I was the leader an' he give me orders to give to the guys. Well we paraded all t'rough the ward an' finally disbanded at a big truck all lit up wit' torches and wit' seats on it an' bunting an' lithos wit' Bender's fiz pasted all over it. The band played an' then they was fireworks an' me an' Shorty was put in charge. We touched 'em all off, sendin' up sky-rockets wort' half a dollar apiece, blowin' up flower-pots an' mines, and shakin' Roman candles by the armful. Gee, but it was great to shoot off them twenty-ball Roman candles an' then when they was dead to chuck 'em down among the kids who knocked each other's blocks off to get 'em. If Big Liz'd a seen me she'd a said I was some class, all right, all right!

Well while we was touchin' off the fireworks an' the band was hittin' up thinks the grand stand filled up wit' all the biggest ginks in the ward from the janitor o' the Tammany clubhouse to has-beens an' never-wases in polyticks. I seen guys on that there platform that hated each other so bad they'd paste each other on sight if the crowd wasn't too big. They say that polyticks makes strange bed-fellows, an' I thinks it's because they is all bit be the same bed-bugs. They wants a good, soft place fer to rest an' finds they's plenty o' vermin to keep 'em busy. Well they was many pikers up there on the platform an' I went up there meself.

They was a whole lot o' speeches an' our bunch was there wit' the cheers an' applause when each guy done his little spiel. East Side chewin'-the-rag[6] aint as classy as them Carnegy Hall speeches but they

5. *getting in right.* Making oneself popular.
6. *chewing-the-rag.* Speaking.

got more punch to 'em. Y'ort to heard the yell we let out when Shorty's uncle got up to say a few words. He never spoke more than twenty words to onct in his life. All he said was, "Gents the hour is getting late and you have all heard the remarks of these here gents on this platform. I will not delay you no longer. Gents, I thank you." Now what d'ye' know about that fer a speech to run on! Aint that the limit! Well, believe me, that's all what Shorty's uncle said at every meetin' o' that campaign. They allus kep' him to the last after every other guy had shot his hot-air[7] an' then they let him chop his own short an' so get all the applause. Then while they was cheerin' him he'd jump down among them bums, strikers,[8] political yeggs an' highbinders, shake han's wit' 'em, an' says: "Gents, if any of yez ever get around by my saloon just drop in an' have one on me!" That caught 'em an' he made manys a vote be passin' schooners[9] over the bar instead o' slippin' the velvet[10] to 'em on 'lection day in big chunks o' cold cash. Never be stingey with the booze—one kag o' beer tapped at the right time 'll get more votes than a roll o' greenbacks big enuf to choke a cow! Buy bums with booze, but blow ye' boodle[11] on'y on them strikers what's waitin' around the polls half an hour before closin' time, that's the on'y time ye' really have to bid high. The pikers[12] has all clim' aboard ye're band wagon[13] early in the campaign, but the strikers an' high-priced graters hold out 'ntil the 'lection 'nspector is ready to say: "Hear ye, hear ye; these here polls is closed!" That's the time ye' got to come acrost an' ye'll have to peel off more than a two-spot to land 'em, too. Them guys want the kale![14]

7. *shot his hot-air*. Made his speech.

8. *strikers*. Political strikers must be distinguished from labor strikers. Political strikers wait until voting time and sell their votes to the highest bidders.

9. *schooners*. Large glasses of beer.

10. *velvet*. Money.

11. *boodle*. Ill-gotten gains, money used to corrupt voters.

12. *pikers*. Shams, small-fry.

13. *climb aboard the band wagon*. To take definite sides.

14. *kale*. Money.

Well now honest, if you'd a been there an' listened to them hot-air pushers[15] that night you'd a believed that the Republican party was composed entire of yeggs,[16] secon'-story men,[17] dips,[18] bank-wreckers an' fifty-seven varieties o' grafters. Why they'd a had to have a game law to pertect Republicans around that ward that night! An' the funny think about it is that I never knowed what a great man Shorty's uncle was. I useter think he was a plain, little Dutchman peddlin' his booze an' rakin' in nickels fer a livin' an' here he was tryin' fer to break into a seat in the Board o' Aldermen when he didn't know the diff'rence between a subway an' a elevated.

The Tammany bunch had a clubhouse down there near the park an' that's where our meetin's wound up. All hands would pile in, an' us guys hung out there a lot before 'lection time. They'd a give us the bum's rush durin' the rest o' the year. We useter go in there an' cop what was left in the glasses when guys put down their beer glasses while they was talkin' polyticks, an' we'd spit on the carpets an' spill cigar ashes around like them big guys done. We met lots o' "heelers"[19] there an' onct Shorty took me down there because his uncle wanted to see me. He was wit' a party o' guys that was throwin' in a couple o' schooners an' chewin' polyticks, but he broke right away when we come in an' put his mitt out fer me to shake. Ye' ort to see them guys look at me. They must a thought I was some class. Well he says:

"Young man, how would you and your friends like to drive a few wagons around the district from now until Election day?"

"D'ye mean 'lection wagons?" says I.

"Yes."

15. *hot-air pushers.* Bombastic speakers.

16. *yeggs.* Safe crackers.

17. *second-story men.* Burglars.

18. *dips.* Pickpockets.

19. *heelers.* Political workers who will undertake anything, from bribery to strong-arm work, to obtain votes.

"I'm on, an' so's the rest. Leave it to me," I says. Well he comes acrost wit' one buck[20] a day, two guys to each wagon—one to drive an' one to keep the bell agoin'. It looked good to the Crapshooters when I put it up to them, an' the contrac' was closed. We was there wit' bells on the next mornin' at the stable where he had his 'lection wagons.

A 'lection wagon is a reglar truck or delivery wagon wit' a big framework built on it. On the frame they nails canvas transparencies with signs sayin' "Vote For Bender" an' such like words. In the inside sits a guy ringin' a bell all day long as the wagon goes t'rough the ward, an' at night the inside is lit up be torchlights an' the wagon goes a clangin' t'rough the streets o' the ward advertisin' ye're candidate. Sometimes ye' put his litho on the wagon, but it aint wise if ye' drive t'rough streets where the opposition is strong. They allus rough-houses[21] ye'. We had t'ree new wagons an' we was told fer to drive along in one-two-three order an' keep clost together to avoid trouble. We let a lot o' the kids up our way ride in the wagons wit' us an' made them ring the bell an' drive the nags while we set around an' draw'd the pay. We made a fine appearance goin' down Second avenue an' when we passed our own block we made enuf noise fer to be heard in the backyards.

We was agoin' down Third avenue an' the kid what was drivin' the first wagon turns into Eighty-Fourt' street an' 'efore we knowed any-think we had a run-in with a bunch o' Republican kuyks. We sure was in-wrong, an' zip, zip come a shower o' small stones, empty cans an' dirt. I seen a kid t'row a old shoe, grabs me whip jumps down off'n the wagon an' chases him. While I was down a cellar lookin' fer him a gang o' kids runs out'n an alley, heaves a dead cat at Shorty an' knocks him off'n the seat. By this time I got back an' slashin' around wit' me whip I scatters most o' them kids. They gives their gang yell, though, an' in two minutes the street was full o' kids throwin' bricks, tomado-cans, an' assorted garbage so we turns the wagons around an' beats it as fast as them poor nags could run.

20. *one buck a day.* One dollar a day.
21. *rough-houses.* Assaults.

Cripes! We was a fine sight when we got back to Second avenue. They near put us completely on the blink! The screens was torn an' covered wit' mud an' on our wagon, the first one, them kuyks had ripped off one side entire. Not a one o' our guys come t'rough that there battle wit'out gettin' decorated. Some o' us had our eyes in mournin' from hand-to-hand scraps, an' we all had cuts from stones or clubs. Maybe Shorty's uncle wasn't mad when he seen our caravan. We looked like we come t'rough a cyclone. He was for puttin' the cops on them kuyks right away. Tammany had the cops an' it would a been easy to pinch the whole opposition. We fixed up the wagons an' was told not to drive around that there street no more.

Now in that there ward they is a lot o' Germans, all Republicans, because they was old soldiers in the war an' fit fer Lincoln. Well they allus voted fer Republicans an' give Tammany the hook every time. That's why Tammany stood fer Bender, he was a German Democrat an' they thought he'd cop some o' that German vote. Well now they got up a slick game. It begun to look very clost an' jus' before 'lection day the guys in Bender's clubroom got the names o' all them German Republicans an' sent out letters to 'em. They put the letters in plain envelopes, wrote the addresses on them an' me an' Shorty took them around an' delivered them the day before 'lection. We was told fer to put them in the letter boxes, an' if anybody asked us where we got them to say that a Sheenie wit' lilacs all over his fiz[22] hired us to deliver 'em. We spent all day deliverin' them letters.

Nex' day was 'lection day! It's one o' the best days in the year, an' they's excitement all day long. Well our workers kep' on the go, an' brung in the voters steady. Guys what never even had the price o' a ride on a trolley car come ridin' down in hacks an' automobiles pervided by Bender or Goldstein, an' bot' candidates come around wearin' a Kelly[23] an' shakin' hands wit' everybody. Then they drove on to some other pollin' place an' give the glad hand to the ginks hangin' around there.

---

22. *lilacs all over his fiz.* Whiskers all over his face.
23. *Kelly.* High, silk hat.

At five o'clock the polls closed, but nobody went home fer supper. Ye' get ye're eats at them politikal clubs on 'lection night. They has a hand-out fer anybody. Well Shorty's uncle paid off us guys fer runnin' the 'lection wagons that afternoon an' we then collected our gang an' got guys from other gangs to join us, because we was goin' to raid them kuyks that put our 'lection wagons on the blink when we was out that day. Red knowed some good scrappers[24] from the Car Barn gang up on Nin'y Four' street an' with a bunch from the East River park gang we went over to where them Republican kuyks was buildin' their fire soon as it come dark. Well soon the sky was red wit' bonfires in all parts o' the city an' while the voters was busy gettin' returns us kids was pilin' on stuff on the fires. Now we had sent a spy over an' found out where them kuyks had their fuel so when our mob crossed Third avenue we swept down through the street, raided their cellar an' copped nearly a wagon load o' barrels, boxes, old sofas, chairs, signboards, cellar doors, mattresses, an' I'll be gang-danged if I know what all! We brung it back to our fire and piled it on. We had made our bonfire on the side street because it was cobble stone pavement. If ye' build on the asfelt they send the firemen to put it out because it burns big holes in the pavement. Well our fire was lit jus' opposite the alley an' facin Sing Lee's Chinky laundry. We had slathers o' wood an' other fuel an' along about hap-past eight the guys begun to get fresh an' piled on the stuff until it got dangerous. No cop was around an' I couldn't stop them. Well now first think we knowed the panes o' glass in Sing Lee's laundry window cracked from the heat an', 'fore a guy could move, the red curtains inside was burnin' an' the joint was on fire. Then them guys lost their noodles[25] an' went up in the air 'stead o' gettin' buckets o' water an' puttin' out the Chinky's fire. Someone pulled the alarm an' the Fire department soon come up on the run, an' it was good night fer our fire! They run a line into the laundry an'

24. *scrappers*. Strong-arm fighters.
25. *lost their noodles*. Lost their heads, became panic stricken.

put that fire out an' then pulled our bonfire apart an' wet it down so's it wouldn't burn again in a week. By this time the police had got hep that our fire started the laundry fire an' the ding-dong wagon[26] come along full o' cops. Then we dusted an' run down near the park an' went up into the Tammany club where Jake Bender an' the other guys was receivin' 'lection returns.

The place was packed wit' men but they wasn't much joy in that there joint. Bender set there wit' his collar all sweat down, his hair all ruffled, chewin' nervous on a cigar an' grabbin' bulletins what a guy brung in from a ticker every little while. The reason was that the race was pretty clost, an' it looked bum fer our side. We had jus' got there when a bulletin come in sayin': "Goldstein, Republican, leads in the —th Ward over Bender, Democrat, by four hundred."

"I guess it's all off, boys," says Bender, lookin' sick.

Then comes another: "Tammany sweeps the city with large majorities in Board of Alderman, and Assembly delegation. Close race between Bender, D. and Goldstein, R. in the —th Ward."

Then we hears a yelp out in the other room where them guys was operatin' the telegraph and telephones. A guy comes runnin' in with this:

"Five districts missing gives Goldstein lead of 14 votes over Bender in the —th Ward."

Some more figures come in, an' them guys with the pencils an' pads got busy. They let out another yelp when they writes out this an' sends it in to Bender an' the crowd around him:

"Goldstein leads by three votes over Bender, three districts missing."

Then everybody asks what them three districts are. Someone says they're in the German section an' Bender t'rows up his han's in despair. He knowed them Dutchmen was all Republicans. He was ready to turn out the lights an' go home.

---

26. *ding-dong wagon.* Police patrol wagon.

"Dont t'row up the sponge,[27] old man!" yells the crowd, an' they runs to the telephones to telephone to the pollin' places in the Dutch neighborhood fer unofficial counts. It seemed like they'd never get the count in when along about ten o'clock the guy at the telephone ticker tears off a strip o' tape an' comes runnin' into Bender like he was nutty.

Bender reads it wit' his face all white an' like he was all in.[28] He tries to stand up but he could not, the crowd hung over him all excited. A guy takes the tape, stands on the table and reads:

"Complete returns for the —th Ward give Bender, Democrat, a plurality of 168 over Goldstein, Republican, for member of the Board of Alderman."

Well now that mob went crazy, an' they danced around Bender an' near smothered him with congratulations. The poor Dutchman couldn't believe he was elected. "How can it be?" he asked. "Them Germans wouldn't vote for me just because my name is Bender. Them guys is all black Republicans,[29] I tell you!" he said. "How do you account for them turnin' down Goldstein?" he asks.

"This is what done it!" says a guy on the committee, wavin' a copy of a letter. It was one o' them letters like me an' Shorty delivered. I got a copy of it an' it read:

Dear Sir:—

The time has arrived for all of OUR PEOPLE to stand together against these here German and Irish.

This year we have nominated a man who is of OUR OWN FAITH—a man who, if elected, will stand up for the Jewish people against all others.

A VOTE FOR BENDER IS A VOTE FOR THE UNBELIEVERS.

A VOTE FOR GOLDSTEIN IS A VOTE FOR OUR OWN FAITH.

The Germans and Irish are increasing in this ward. They are of a different faith. Here is your opportunity to give them

---

27. *throw up the sponge.* Give up the fight.

28. *all in.* Exhausted, about to faint.

29. *black Republicans.* Loyal, dyed-in-the-wool Republicans.

a blow at the ballot box. Vote early for GOLDSTEIN. Get your friends to vote for GOLDSTEIN. Let the watchword be
"UNSER EINER"[30]
Signed: The Jewish Committee.

Ye' see it was a fake! But them Dutchmen fell fer it. They thought that the letter come from Goldstein, raisin' a religious issue. It made them hoppin' mad an' they voted against him an' fer Bender. That letter sure done the trick, all right, all right! It's an old Tammany gag, at that!

30. [*Unser Einer.* Translated in context the phrase means "We the Jews," and here is used by politicians to stir up ethnic hostilities.—Ed.]

19.

Mickey In-Wrong Again.

I knowed that Mickey wouldn't like that there joint up in Freeville, Junior Republic, Thompkins county. Look at this here letter what I got from him today. The poor sucker 's pinched—just fer smokin' cigarettes.

Dear Fellow members of the Crapshooters club:—

Yous will probaly be suprised to hear that insted of me being elected to offis I am in jail. Me, only last week a cop in this here boy's government and trying to break into office now pinched and on the workhouse for smoking. Well I might of been wise to meself[1] and cut it out. Yous remember I wrote yous that I had a bunk[2] out of bounds where I hid me butts and how I chewed peper mint what growed on a bush there after I took a sneek down for a smoke once in a while. Well I done that day befor yesterday and when I come back me breth smelt of peper mint and tobacco. I happened to speak to a cop about something and he asked me to talk to the district attorney. Well they said youre pinched, you been smoking. I said you cant prove it. well they pinched me and got a whole lot of citizens to smell me breath and charged me with circumstanshal evidence and railroaded me to jail. They give me five days in jail. I got three more to serve. I would like to beat it again but how can I because I got now nearly $17 dollars in bank and besides I gettin to be a prominant citizen. I guess I take me medesin and cut

1. *wise to myself.* Accepted the inevitable.
2. *bunk.* Hiding place.

220

out the butts hereafter. Sorry I cant write more now, but being a prisoner I got to go now and mop the jail floor. I did not get run for offise because they said they was wise that I was breaking the law by smoking on the sly.

Remember me to all the felows.
MICKEY.

20.

Ragamuffin Day.

Ragamuffin Day ought to be called Grafters Day. But instead it is called Thanksgiving Day. In some places they say that the people go to church on Ragamuffin Day but I never seen nobody go to church here on the East Side, on'y to get a hand-out. Some churches ye' know give out free turkey dinners. The reason it is called Thanksgiving Day is because ye' suposed to say thanks when ye' get a hand-out. But if ye' dont get no hand-out ye' blow ye're horns at 'em.

Well on Thanksgiving or Ragamuffin day—same think—ye' get a gang together, dress up crazy in any kind of costume or dippy outfit,[1] each guy diff'rent, and ye' go around with masks on ye' faces, tin horns, baskets, and ye' go to a door way, ring the bell whether ye' know the people in the house or not, an' when they come to the door ye' say: "Missis what ye' goin' to give us fer Thanksgivin'?" Well she'll go back an' come out with a pie, cakes, money, fruit or some kind o' hand-out an' if ye're satisfied ye' say: "Thank you" and go on. But if she turns ye' down[2] ye' all blow ye' tin horns, cuss her, ring the bell and raise the dickens until she throws a quarter out'n the window. Well all the stuff ye' get ye' put in the baskets an' the money ye' hand over to the leader an' it is divvied up when ye' quit panhandlin'[3] and so is the stuff divvied up too. Well ye're suposed to go in stores, houses, shops or anywhere the graft looks good. The funnier ye' dress up the better chanst ye' got

1. *dippy outfit.* Grotesque costume.
2. *turns you down.* Denies, rejects.
3. *panhandling.* Begging.

to get a big hand-out. But sometimes ye' get a good, swift kick at that, if ye' happen to ask some grouchy sucker what he's goner give ye' fer Thanksgivin'. The rule is that if a guy dont give ye' nothin' ye' keep on annoyin' him until a cop chases ye' away. On'y tight-wads an' stingey misers turn ye' down, an' the best way if they dont give ye' nothin' is fer to get even wit' 'em some day by playin' some trick on 'em.

"The oily boid gits the woim," says Buttsy, talkin' real N'York, so we was out wit' sun-up on Ragamuffin Day. We had copped come crazy duds from some trunks that we busted open in a flathouse cellar, an' we made a hit. We went over to the Fift' avenue an' Madison avenue houses an' them swells over that way come acrost pretty good, givin' us mostly silver.[4] In our own neighborhood they give us mostly grub o' some kind or other. We quit before noon an' had four baskets o' pretty good eats, an' about t'ree dollars in real money. We took off our funny duds an' put the grub away in Dugan's cellar fer to be et some other day. On Ragamuffin Day ye' put away ye' grub what ye' panhandle, because they is manys a place where ye' can get a hand-out in a turkey dinner. They give hand-outs in missions, Salvation Army, churches, sometimes newspapers, an' even the polytishans. All ye' have to do is to find out where they serve their grub, drop in an' get ye're eats deadhead.[5] Well ye' aint suposed to be dressed up when ye' tackle them joints so us guys looked as bum as we could when we started out at noon. We went down the avenue to the Guiding Hand Mission. In that there joint we had rough-housed manys a meetin' an' put it on the blink, an' we expected maybe them ladies down there would keep us out. But they didn't. They smiled like they knowed us, led us in to tables an' served us wit' roast turkey, cranberries, salary, mashed podadoes, buttered rolls, ban-annas, oranges, grapes, an' then some. Well we didn't waste no time readin' them there Scriptur' signs hangin' on the walls. Instead we cleaned house wit'[6] all the grub in sight an' shoved all what was loose

4. *silver.* Small silver coins.

5. *deadhead.* Without cost, complimentary.

6. *cleaned house with.* Made away with.

down inside our shirts on which we had opened the buttons so that we could slip in them extras without bein' saw by them dames servin' the grub. We emptied the fruit plate t'ree times before they got hep an' they wanted us to deliver up what we had stowed. We said hell no, an' they sent fer the man-minister so we dug out.

We took our graft back to Dugan's an' then went to a place on another street where they was feedin' newsboys wit' a Thanksgivin' dinner. Well there was a big guy in the doorway an' he said: "Are youse newsboys?"

"Sure," we said.

"What papers do youse guys sell?"

"The Joinal," we all said. Well we was wrong. It was another news-paper what was givin' out them eats.

"Well where's ye're tickets?" says the guy.

We sure was stumped but we all swore that we lost 'em. Well the guy laffed an' let us in without them. Ye' see it pays to lie even when the guy gets wise to ye'! If ye' lie hard enuf he'll laff at ye're bluffs an' ye'll get by. Well we put away another square meal in that place an' come out pretty full. We was near bustin' when we hit the Salvation Army barracks an' joined the bums there. Well we didn't have no trouble get-tin' in there an' 'stead o' eatin' we shoved everythink in our pockets an' when we got outside dumped the stuff in paper bags what we left wit' Red while we went back an' repeated. Well we cleaned up a lot o' tur-key legs, oranges an' fruit before they got wise to us comin' in so often an' when we started back fer Dugan's cellar we was filled to the snoot[7] wit' highclass eats. Well we spent the rest o' the afternoon takin' naps an' restin' on our mattress in the clubrooms.

They's no place like a old mattress fer restin' a bellyful o' grub, an' we all fell off to sleep on it as it come dark down there in Dugan's cellar. I dont know how long we slep', but when we woke up it was pretty well into the night. It was darker than a nigger's coal bin, an' was quiet jus' like Sund'y night.

---

7. *snoot.* Mouth.

"Cripes sakes! Let's tell ghost stories!" says Riley. With that Shorty leads off. It was like this. If youse guys can make head or tail out'n it ye're good ones. Ye' can search me! If I could make up stories like that gink Shorty I'd be a orther.

"Onct upon a time they was a certain guy what croaked. It was said that he was moidered. Well he left a will which was not fer to be opened until one year after his deat'. Well they took the dead guy an' buried him under a block o' granite weighin' four tons, which was accordin' to his wish. Well now he had a guy what he called his best friend on eart', an' before he died he asked that guy to come to his grave at midnight t'irteen days after he was planted[8] fer to get a message from the dead. Now the guy went to that there cemet'ry at midnight t'irteen days after the funeral an' was scared to deat', almost. Well at midnight as he set there in the dark watchin' that grave he seen the four-ton block o' granite lift up on one corner an' while he begun to get the cold shivers a voice comes out'n the grave sayin: 'Fear not.'

"Well while the best friend was starin' at the spot a white skelykin hand comes slidin' out from under the rock an' a voice says: 'The name of the guy who will inherit my fortune is that of the first man who follows out the directions I have here wrote in me life blood.'

"Wit' that the skelykin hand shoves out a note on which was wrote in blood these woids:

"To win the prize go to the cellar of my earthly mansion at the hour of midnight, and when the clock has struck the last blow run around a post there recitin' these woids.

> Raw head an' bloody bones![9]
> Raw head an' bloody bones!
> Raw head an' bloody bones!
> Cant catch me!

8. *planted.* Buried.

9. [*Raw head an' bloody bones.* Shorty's story was derived from a well-known and ancient bogeyman tale that the *Oxford English Dictionary* finds circulating as early as 1564.—Ed.]

"Well that there guy thought this was a lead pipe cinch fer to come into a fortune so he whispered to the skelekon that he was on, an' slowly the hand slid back into the grave an' the big rock come down flat again.

"The very next night the man went to the cellar wit' a party o' friends an' all set there silent until the clock begun to strike the hour o' midnight. Then he got up an' leavin' his friends begun to run around a post yellin' 'raw head an' bloody bones, cant catch me!' Well now the moment the last woid was out o' his lips they was a deathly silence. When he didn't come back his friends went over to where the post was an' lit a match. They jumped back in terror, for there laid the guy, stone dead!

"Well now at the funeral the undertaker found that there note in the dead man's pockets tellin' how to come into a fortune. He tried the same gag, an' he too was found dead. An' to this day nobody never got that man's fortune!"

Now Shorty told that story wit' plenty o' gumshoe whispers an' creepy moans an' when he got t'rough we was all pretty much askared. Bime by we got bold, though, an' Red pipes up:

"Say Shorty, that yarn listens good,[10] but dont tell me that a guy is goin' to drop dead jus' fer runnin' around a post yellin' such drool[11] as that! You dont b'lieve that stuff, ye'self!"

"I dont, dont I? Well I sure do. I knowed the undertaker's brother who tol' me the story himself! It's a true story an' I can prove it!" says Shorty, gettin' hot under the collar.[12]

Well we all chewed the rag an' it fin'lly come about that Red said he'd test the raw-head theory if us guys would go down some cellar wit' him an' stand by him in case—well in case any ghosts did show up.

They was no posts down in Dugan's cellar so we went down the block to the flathouse where "Savage" was janitor. It was gettin'

10. *listens good.* Sounds plausible, seems to be agreeable.
11. *drool.* Nonsense.
12. *hot under the collar.* Angry.

midnight an' we knowed that he'd be in bed by this time. Savage was a vicious, ugly sucker an' he run a row o' flats which had cellars connectin' by arches an' many posts, an' they was over a hundred ways to beat it. We useter play Groosefadder there because they was so many ways o' gettin' out in a hurry.

Well we was all pretty pale around the gills when we snuk down there an' poor Red looked like a corpse when we all shook his hand so that everythink would be straight in case he kicked the bucket[13] in doin' that raw-head stunt. It was awful solemn an' I fer my part, was ready to call it off. Red was a game cuss, an' wouldn't take back a word.

Well we all patted him on the back an' told him we'd stand by an' if any spook put in his mush[14] we'd knock the puss[15] off'n him. Red set down beside the post what we picked out, an' the rest o' us guys set down in another part o' the cellar, quite near to the alley stairway by chanst. Well we huddled together an' whispered to pass the time away while we waited fer midnight. Onct in a while one o' us would call over: "Red, are ye' there?"

"Sure think!" he'd answer back, kind o' husky.

Well it come midnight an' at last Red's time had come fer to shout out them deadly woids. The bell up on the orphan asylum tower begun to strike the hours an' we counted them breat'less. All of a suddent us guys heard a strange sound in another part o' the cellar. It was sneeky, like a cat steppin' on loose sticks. We was about to warn Red when it was too late. The last blow o' midnight had struck an' Red had started his run around the post. We heard the strange sound comin' nearer an' at the same time we heard Red, his voice gettin' louder as he run around yellin': "raw head an' bloody bones, raw head an' bloody bones." He almost reached the end when they was a dull thud an' we heard him go down wit' a moan. We all got terror struck an' Blinkey, leadin' off the hull push, dug up fer the street wit' some mysterious bein' chasin' us. We

13. *kicked the bucket.* Died.

14. *put in his mush.* Appeared.

15. *puss.* Face.

got out all right an' run fer half a block before we stopped to look back. Red was nowhere in sight an' we decided to arm ourselfs wit' clubs an' go back to that there cellar an' get him out dead or alive!

Well as we got near there again we wasn't so brave as when we was up under the street lamp but we poked our nuts down into the cellar an' shouted in: "Red, Red, where are ye?"

They was no answer at first but soon we heard footsteps approachin' an' every few steps they was a groan. We backed out an' hid in the alley. In a few minutes out came "Savage" in his night-shirt wit' a broom stick in one hand an' holdin' Red by the other. Well that janitor was the ghost, an' he had hit Red a wallop on the noodle that laid open the scalp an' sent the blood all over his face. Red was groanin' an' pretendin' that he was near killed an' finally dropped on the sidewalk.

Savage then thought that he had committed murder an' he run in his night-shirt to the corner drugstore an' told 'em to send fer the amb'lance.

Well we found Red after Savage had run to the drugstore an' lugged him down First avenue to another drugstore where they patched up his nut, an' we sneaked back to Dugan's cellar. When the amb'lance come an' didn't find nobody they wanted fer to pinch Savage. Well ever since then we have called Savage by a new name, "Old Raw Head." An' make out we wont do a think to him some day! He's got a legacy comin' to him all right, all right—an' he'll get it good an' plenty!

21.

Spike's Comment on Religion.

Them Sund'y school people on whom we useter deadhead fer Chistmas gifts, Fresh Air excursions an' ice cream festivals useter say sometimes that us guys was barbarians. An' cause why? Jus' because we didn't go reglar to them churches, an' stand up an' give testimony. Now they's manys a kind o' churches, an' in our bunch they was many ideas. Us ginks found so many argymints against all religions that we passed all'n up. We went to church when we felt like it an' that was on'y when they was somethink doin', like a strawb'rry festival or a magic lantern show.[1] But that dont say that we never chewed religion. Why we useter have more scraps over religion down there in Dugan's cellar than we did on sports an' polyticks put together!

Now because I'm tellin' ye what we useter say about religion dont youse guys get sore at what us guys said. We didn't never tell no guy not to go to church, but we never went ourselfs 'nless they was a hand-out. We didn't believe in rabbi, priest nor minister, fer the simple reason that we believe they's all nursin' a soft graft, an' shootin' hot-air an' bull-con fer to keep it agoin'. But youse guys needn't think that we mean any partickler religion if we roast[2] it. Speakin' fer meself, they's on'y one religion I reconnize, an' that 's me own religion. No sky pilot[3] can teach it an' no red devil can skare it out'n me. It's jus' this: Follow ye're noodle.

---

1. [*magic lantern show.* Lantern, or stereopticon, shows were the PowerPoints of the turn of the century, only more impressive. Jacob Riis transferred his images of the slums to glass slides and projected them on a screen.—Ed.]

2. *roast.* Ridicule, argue against.

3. *sky pilot.* Clergyman.

Ye' noodle tells ye' when ye' done wrong. Ye' noodle tells ye' what's right. Some guys calls it conshince. Same think. When ye' done wrong, ye' noodle tells ye' to do right. Turn a backflip. Dont be afraid, ye'll find that ye' land on both feet every time. An' the crowd 'll give ye' the glad hand 'nstead o' the cold shoulder.

Now if ye' plug up ye're noodle with all that bunk[4] that them perfeshinal sky pilots hand out it wont work, ye' get rattled, an' ye' find ye'self argyin over how it's to be done, an' onct ye' get that far ye' forget all about that reverse-English[5] what ye' was agoin' to put on ye're downward career, an' first think ye' know ye're takin' another drop!

Most guys think religion is shoutin' halleluya, an' bein' saw often inside a church. But it aint. Take Mickey fer example. He allus goes to church—wears the biggest cross o' palm on Palm Sund'y, swabs his mush wit' oceans o' holy water an' knows the 'postle's creed frontwards, backwards, an' upside down. An' what good does it do? Mickey's as tough a nut as any o' us what dont go to no church. Look at Riley! He dont never go to church an' yet aint he allus gentle? Kind to the poor? Dont he respect the aged? Does he ever steal from a guy what needs more than himself? An' he gives away all the stuff he swipes, at that! If a poor guy croaks an' they's takin' up a subscription, dont Riley dig down into his jeans an' come across with somethink? Wouldn't he take the shirt off'n his back fer ye' if ye' needed it! Well, he's what I call a real Christian. He didn't stand posin' on the end o' the dock a crossin' himself an' waste time makin' zigzags over his face the time he dove over an' saved the little Sheeney baby what fell off'n the stringpiece on Nin'y-first street dock!

Religion is good fer people when they think its good. Ye' remember old Mrs. Dunn? Well she useter think holy water cured her rheumatiz. Every week reglar she sent some kid down with an empty bottle an' a quarter to the priest's house to get it filled. It took Mickey to get next

---

4. *bunk.* buncombe.

5. *reverse-English.* The impulse that causes an object to follow a different ultimate course than the apparent course.

to a graft in that errand. He got her to let him run the errand. Now he knowed that the priest holied the water by chewin' Latin over it in blessin' it. So Mickey comes down here to Dugan's cellar, fills the bottle at the pump, chews the on'y for'n words he knows over it, which is the Ginney words: "chinkarrasol, aberygotz, festamongule," pockets the quarter, an' takes the bottle o' water to the old dame. The funny think is that she kep' a tellin' the neighbors that it was great stuff fer her rheumatiz. Christian Science aint got nothin' on that![6] An' it aint no better wit' ministers. They ask ye' more questions than a Sheeney lawyer, an' then when ye' think ye' got religion they scare it all out'n ye be askin' ye' to stand up an' say somethin'.

No, the on'y kind o' religion that counts is that which tells ye' the difference between right an' wrong. That's ye're noodle!

---

6. [*Christian Science aint got nothin' on that!* Spike's disrespectful reference here is to the Christian Science practice of praying for the ill to be healed rather than seeking medical help.—Ed.]

22.

Not to Be Opened
until Christmas.

A racetrack sport what useter call on the Fairy stopped Shorty on the street one afternoon couple o' weeks before the holidays. The Fairy was the fat, old yaller-haired actress in the apartment house up at No. 231. The gink hands Shorty a dime an' a nice package done up in ribbons, an' asks him to deliver it to the Fairy. Shorty took it, read the address an' his lamps fell upon a fancy label. He piped it off a couple o' times. It was printed in red, an' said: NOT TO BE OPENED UNTIL CHRISTMAS.

"A Christmas present, hey?" says Shorty.

"You're on. Some class to it, too," says the tout, addin', "Dont lose it, an' if she asks ye' who sent it say a man sent it, didn't leave his name."

Well Shorty delivered that package o.k., bought a dime's worth o' candy an' come down Dugan's wit' it. He passed his sweets around an' set there chewin' a caramel a few minutes without sayin' nothin'. Then he picks up his lid an' starts out'n the cellar like he was on important business.

"Where ye' goin'?" says I.

"Oh, up around," says he, diggin' out before we could ask more questions.

Now when a guy is thinkin' hard, picks up his hat, starts fer somewhere, an' answers—"Oh, up around"—when ye' ask him where he's bound fer, ye' can make up ye're mind they's somethin' up! We couldn't get next to his game an' found it hard fer to forget his impoliteness.

It come ten days before Christmas that I went down Dugan's cellar that afternoon fer to get a drink o' water in the sink in the rear room.

I was a bumpin' around in the dark there when I run up against a pile o' packages. They was all done up neat, tied with tough twine in hard knots an' plenty o' sealin' wax. I hefts[1] 'em, sizes 'em up an' rubbers hard at the neat printin' on each parcel. They was all addressed to people up here in Yorkville.

Cripes! It looked like some o' the guys had robbed a Christmas express wagon an' buried the loot down our cellar. I was examinin' the packages when down comes Red.

"Pipe off this lay-out o' Christmas packages," says I.

"Gee, where'd ye' swipe 'em!" says Red.

"Ye' can search me," says I, "I never seen 'em before. Let's open 'em up."

We was tryin' to bust the strings when Shorty slides down the cellar followed by Blinkey. When he pipes us monkeyin' wit' them parcels he near throws a fit.[2]

"Dont open 'em!" he yells, "Me an' Blinkey has got to deliver them fer a guy."

We dropped the packages an' waited fer some explanation. There was nothin' doin'. Shorty ties 'em up in two big bundles, an' he an' Blinkey sneaks out o' the cellar wit' 'em fer to deliver 'em. Before they beats it I yells:

"Hey Shorty, what's the answer?"

"I'll tip youse all off soon enuf!" he says.

They was mystery there!

•◆•

The next Saturday night, come one more before Christmas, we was down Dugan's fer reglar meetin'. Shorty come in smilin', an' lookin' like ready money. Blinkey looked happy, too.

"What's ye're errand boy game, Shorty?" says I, recallin' them packages they delivered durin' the week.

"I'm ready fer to put youse all next to a new graft," he answers.

---

1. *hefts.* Judges the weight of.

2. *throw a fit.* To get into a rage, become excited.

"Spill it," says I, an' he gives out the game. He says:

"When I carried that package up to the Fairy the other day I got an idea. I seen a paster on the package sayin': NOT TO BE OPENED UNTIL CHRISTMAS. Well now, I got me noodle a goin' an' I says to meself: 'If ye' cant open that until Christmas how do ye' know that somebody aint handin' ye' a lemon?' Then I asks meself: 'Why cant a guy go around deliverin' packages wit' them pasters on an' a bag o' sawdust inside?' When ye' delivers 'em write on each parcel: 'Collect 25 cents,' or as much as ye' think the guy 'll stand fer? Well now I gets Blinkey, an' me an' him tries the game out. First we wraps up an' old shoe in a box, puts nice clean paper around it, ties it up tight, seals it wit' sealin' wax, an' goes up to the stationery store on Eighty-Sixth street an' buys a package o' them pasters readin': NOT TO BE OPENED UNTIL CHRISTMAS. We stuck one o' them on our shoe box an' writin' on the outside: 'Collect 40 cents.' We addresses it to the Fairy an' tries it. I sent Blinkey up to deliver it, because she knows me. Well she was tickled to deat', forks over the mazuma an' gives Blinkey an orange fer deliverin' it. Then we made a couple more an' tried 'em on others. All bit easy. We put 'Collect 25 cents' on them what we delivered in this neighborhood, an' boosted 'em to 40, 50 an' even 70 cents over on Madison avenue. All ye' have to do is to make a noise like[3] a express delivery boy, have 'em sign a receipt book, an' hang on to the parcel until ye' get ye' collect charges. Be sure an' let 'em see the label: DO NOT OPEN UNTIL CHRISTMAS. That keeps 'em from rubberin' in the parcel after ye' go, an' it wont be until Christmas mornin' that them ginks 'll wake up an' find out that they have been gold-bricked.[4] It's the slickest game I ever tried an' works like a greased axle. Even if they should catch ye' all ye' have to say is that a man sent ye' with it an' told ye' to keep the money fer runnin' the errand. The cops cant fasten ye' on that!"

Well now Shorty an' Blinkey had made more than twelve dollars in two days sellin' them kind o' gold-bricks, an' believe me we all lost no time breakin' in on that graft.

---

3. *make a noise like.* Imitate, appear like.

4. *gold-bricked.* Swindled.

We decided not to be so mean as to give the victims nothin' at all, so we got out all the old Jewsharps an' blue specs what we had left from our raid on Cheap Charlie's cellar last summer an' we done them up in packages o' all kinds, big, little, fat an' lean. Shorty onct worked as a shippin' clerk fer four days an' he showed us how to tie 'em up wit' some class. He furnished the labels, an' believe me we went all over Harlem, gettin' names out'n the city directory, a peddlin' them dont-get-stung-til-Christmas-mornin' packages! An' maybe we didn't start a lot o' fights! Everybody what got one o' them lemons made up his mind that his nearest enemy sent that package, an' we heard o' more than one case where neighbors pasted each other. We had our nerve wit' us—apassin' off them phony Christmas presents!

But talkin' about nerve! Jus' fer the fun o' it we tosses up, an' Red loses, an' he has fer to deliver a parcel to Cheap Charlie in his home over on Lexin'ton avenue. He collects 30 cents fer a pair o' Cheap Charlie's own blue spectacles. Aint that goin' some! Next year we'll do that graft up right—hire a truck an' peddle 'em by the gross!

23.

Christmas Graft.

Us guys was pretty busy wit' religion about this time! Every Sunday fer t'ree Sund'ys runnin' we went to church an' Sunday school, wit' Epwort' league an' Christian Endeavor[1] t'rown in durin' the week-days. I mustn't ferget to mention the prayer meetin's neither.

Ye' see every Christmas them churches gives a handout to all who belongs. First ye' get a ticket to the Christmas entertainment an' then at the entertainment ye' get a box o' candy, a bag o' cake or fruit an' sometimes a book. They's lots o' chanst fer pinchin' stuff, too. Some churches gives swell handouts an' some gives bum ones; but, at that, they're all wort' panhandlin' an' ye' dont ring in on them 'nless ye' belongs. That's why we was so reglar in attendance, because they gives out the tickets a couple o' Sund'ys before Christmas. We went reglar fer a whole mont' nearly to the Baptist an' t'ree weeks to the Methodist. We went near ever other night to the Guidin' Hand Mission because they had the repitashun o' givin' out the swellest handouts of any. That's how we called it the Golden Handout Mission. On Ragamuffin Day they give ye' nearly a whole mincepie wit' the dinner. Some rich ducks[2] supported that mission an' they done it up brown, comin' acrost wit' real Christmas presents—toys, clothin' an' plenty o' swell eats.

---

1. [*Epwort' league an' Christian Endeavor.* Both evangelical Protestant organizations enlisted young men and women in their mission activities. The Epworth League was affiliated with the Methodist Episcopal Church, and the United Society of Christian Endeavor recruited Protestants from all evangelical denominations. William George was active in Christian Endeavor.—Ed.]

2. *rich ducks.* Wealthy persons.

Now churches an' missions aint the on'y Christmas graft. They's Christmas funds raised by the newspapers where they gives out a lot o' junk that aint wort' taking home. They's benev'lent societies an' lodges. Lodges is private, but they put up a pretty good handout. If ye' can get a ticket to them ye' pretty sure to come away wit' a fine handout. Them lodge Christmas parties is on'y fer members an' their friends, an' sometimes fer friends o' friends.

We rung-in[3] as friends o' friends. That's how we come to go to one on Christmas eve. Shorty's old man belonged onct on a time but had got canned[4] fer not payin' his dues. Every Christmas Shorty still kep' up the old connection, an' went. He tipped us off to it, an' some way or other got tickets fer all.

Well the entertainment was fer to begin at eight o'clock so us guys went over to the hall before seven. It was so early there was no guy at the door to take tickets, an' the lights was low. We went right on in, an' never minded it in the least that there was no ticket taker. An' the cause-why I'll be a tellin' ye' later.

As long as it was dark we went up in the balcony an' set in a dark corner waitin' fer somethin' to turn up. The curtain was down on the stage an' we could hear guys behind it shoutin' at each other as they got everythin' ready. Down on the ballroom floor we could see a big Christmas tree, reachin' near to the ceilin' an' loaded wit' goodies. They was a million candies an' cakes, an' apples an' Lord knows what else in them branches. Gosh, we could hardly set still up there in the dark. We wanted to go down on the floor an' clean house with that tree. It was a peachy show[5] an' they wasn't a lodge member around. But we didn't tackle it, though; because if we went down on the floor an' was seen they'd ask us fer our tickets. So we kep' quiet an' waited.

Well soon the ticket taker put his table in the doorway an' people begun to come to the show. Pretty soon they come in so fast ye' couldn't

---

3. *rung-in.* Gained admittance.

4. *canned.* Expelled, suspended, discharged. Sometimes means drunk.

5. *peachy show.* Splendid opportunity to steal.

count 'em, an' then they turned on the lights. Then the musicians showed up an' the orchestry got busy a sawin' away at the music. Then us guys come down an' mixed in with the audience. Shorty asked us fer our tickets, tellin' us that he had a idea they would be useful later an' askin' us to let him keep 'em. We coughed up[6] the tickets an' Shorty pockets 'em.

Well they put on a great vaudeville show wit' clog an' wooden shoe dancin', buck an' wing, an' some other fancy stunts, an' at hap-past nine they put on the last act, Punch an' Judy. We'd seen that over at the Globe museum so often we didn't care much fer that, an' roasted it. All the kids there enjoyed it, though, an' they was laffin' all the time so we quit roastin' it so long 's they enjoyed it. Then the curtain come down fer a few minutes, an' when it went up there was two big piles o' heavy paper sacks, one on each side o' the stage. Well each bag was filled wit' cakes, candies, nuts, raisins, fruit, an' all sorts o' good thinks. We knowed what was inside because we stole a bag durin' the evenin' an' divvied it up in the gents toilet room.

Then out steps Santa Claus on the stage an' a committeeman asks all kids in the hall to line up, two by two, fer the grand march an' distribution o' gifts. Santa Claus comes down an' steps inside a sleigh which was drawed by six ginks dressed up in reindeers' costumes what walked on their hind-legs. Well the little kids was all afraid an' thought they was real reindeers but us guys wasn't afraid an' Shorty went up to one reindeer an' took it by the horns to show a little kid what was cryin' that it wouldn't bite.

"Whoa reindeer!" says Shorty, givin' the reindeer a kick in the shins like it was a horse, an' demonstratin' fer the cryin' baby.

"You do that again an' I'll knock ye're block off!" says the reindeer to Shorty. Shorty bowed off an' let the kid cry.

Well when he come back to us guys as we was scrappin' fer front places in the procession, he pulls out the tickets an' says "Each guy cut his ticket in half. Dont let the committeemen see the halves, an' remember that each half is good fer a bag."

---

6. *coughed up.* Surrendered.

Ye' see, Shorty had piped off the system, which was the same as in the past two years. After the kids was lined up the orchestry hit up a tune an' all marched through the big hall. In passin' one end the committee handed out a check, consistin' of one-half of a admission ticket, an' good fer one bag o' handouts. Well the procession marched around twict an' then Santa Claus got out'n his sleigh at the head an' clim' back on the stage where he handed out the sacks. He give one to each kid as the kid handed up his check. Well them tickets we cut in half was a soft think[7] fer us. That procession was endless fer the Crapshooters. We kep' on repeatin' so much that Blinkey had fer to drop out o' the line an' sit on the back stairs guardin' the common prope'ty o' the club, twelve fat bags to which we later added about a dozen more. We hid 'em under the stairs 'ntil we was ready fer to beat it home. An' we didn't stop when our checks run out, neither! There was some bags left an' we was pretty good reachers,[8] too.

It was while everybody was clamorin' fer the extra bags that Red wiggled his way t'rough a lot o' committeemen an' got on the stage. He was buttin' in on Santa Claus who was takin' off his costume behind the scenes when he thought that Red was tryin' to swipe some o' the bags he had set aside fer himself. He hit Red in the face wit' his staff. No guy, not even if he is Santa Claus, can do that to Red. He grabbed that staff out'n his hand before he could move an' pulled his whiskers off with such vi'lence that he took along a fistful o' Santa's real hair. Well there was a fight an' it ended by Red gettin' the bum's rush out'n the hall. We found him shiverin' out on the sidewalk when we come out half an hour later. The poor mucker got trun out[9] without'n his overcoat.

We got even fer Red before we left that hall, all right. All we done was to gather around the Christmas tree an' start pickin' presents off'n it. That started all the other kids a goin' an' pretty soon the grown-ups joined the scramble. The floor committee tried to stop it, but they was

---

7. *soft thing.* Advantage.

8. *reachers.* Petty larcenists.

9. *trun out.* Ejected, thrown out.

swept along in the rush. We tipped the tree over an' down it come, an' when the whole danged lodge fin'lly got it up again they wasn't a thread o' tinsel or a fancy glass ball left on it. The floor manager, sergeant-at-arms, an' other ginks was soon on our trail so we collects our bags an' digs out. We took Red's overcoat out to him, an' then all went back to Dugan's cellar. It was midnight an' it was snowin', an' we all felt hellish happy.

It was cold an' cheerless when we got back an' slipped quiet down into Dugan's cellar, an' wit' all that truck what we had got our hooks into we was now wonderin' what to do wit' it. There was more than any o' us wanted to take to his home an' somehow after all the happy sights we seen that night an' the lighted Christmas candles in many windows what he passed we all got to feelin' mushy an' soft-hearted. We had so much stuff there that would make some poor dubs happy, an' with the toys left in the cellar from manys a raid we made up our minds to play Santa Claus.

Callin' the ginks together after we had lit some candles I says: "Take a slant[10] at them thinks, fellers an' after ye've piped 'em off let's vote on who is to get 'em! Let's give some poor family a Merry Christmas!"

Shorty took the floor. He said:

"I moves that we take this stuff an' give it to some poor family what aint got no Merry Christmas. Fer instance, Yens, the Yanitor! He's got a sick wife an' four hungry kids. He stand's the the gaff[11] from us guys all the year round, works hard, aint no booze fighter,[12] an' never busted no bed-slat over any guy what teased him. I moves we elect him fer to have this here stuff fer a Merry Christmas."

"Secon' the motion," puts in Blinkey. The other guys called fer the question. By this time, ye' know, us guys was gettin' hep to parlemantery rules.

"Are youse all ready fer the question?" I asks.

---

10. *slant*. Look.

11. *stands the gaff*. Is made the butt of pranks.

12. *booze fighter*. Drunkard.

"Question! Question!" they yells.

"All in favor o' Shorty's motion that we donate this stuff to Yens, the Yanitor, an' family, fer a Merry Christmas, say Aye!"

"Aye! Aye!" says the whole push.

"Carried!" says I. "Get busy!"

Now Yens, the Yanitor, was the name we give to Hansen, the Swedish janitor down the block a ways. He lived wit' his family in the basement under the front stoop of No. 237. We goes tumblin' down there makin' enuf racket to wake the dead.

We rapped pretty loud an' long on his door before we heard a movement inside. He thought we was playin' pranks.

"Get away fon dere!" he yells.

"Open up!" I says. "Us fellows come down fer to give you an' ye're kids a Merry Christmas!"

He unlocks the door an' peeks out cautious, like he was expectin' us to heave somethink at him like we done sometimes. Then he opens wide, lit a light an' gets rattled when we pile in an' t'row down our presents.

"Dis ban a mistake!" he says.

"Hell no, this is a Merry Christmas from us guys," says I.

Wit' that we each shakes his hand an' says "Merry Christmas!"

By this time his kids had woke up an' comin' runnin' in to rubberneck they digs right in to the bags o' good eats we had brung. Us guys didn't know no more to say so we says good night.

"Tank you!" says Yens.

Then we dug out.

24.

New Year's Callin'.

Dat neat little trick we done on Christmas Eve give us guys a swelled head.[1] The way dat Swede janitor bowed to us when he seen us on the street after dat made us feel like we really amounted to someting. It was a busy week, believe me. We had bids an' tickets fer holiday shows an' graft parties that kep' us on the go all week. We felt so sorry fer Mickey, up there in the country, an' Riley, who'd moved away downtown.

Butts had a uncle livin' down on Cherry street an' he got Riley's address fer us an' we wrote an' got his promise fer to spend New Year's day uptown wit' us guys a goin' callin'. On the East Side every guy goes callin' on New Year's day an' ye' aint suposed to get pifflicated[2] until night. Ye're suposed to allus have ye're hack handy an' do ye're callin' real classy. Then when ye' all get stewed up to the ears ye' have the hack driver take ye' home an' ye' show off when ye' hit ye're own block.

We fixed up our party at a speshal meetin'. Our Crapshooters Club by this time was holdin' its meetin's like reglar clubs, an' I lerned them guys a whole lot about makin' motions an' aye an' no votes. I sent out notices on real postal cards sayin': "Special meeting tonight. Come."

When they showed up I says: "I called youse guys together fer to take due reconnishun o' the comin' event, New Year's day. Now I'll give youse the dope, an' if any o' youse guys got diff'rent plans I'd advise ye' to cut 'em out. The plan is dis.

---

1. *swelled head*. Inflated with one's importance, conceited.
2. *pifflicated*. Mildly intoxicated.

"Each guy can hand in his list o' joints where he wants us fer to make a club call, we'll pick out the best an' t'row the rest into the discard, hire a hack, an' do our callin' up in Fifth avenue style."

"One hack aint enuf!" says Blinkey.

"Hire a funeral outfit if ye' need to!" says I.

"Yea bo!" says the rest o' the push, gettin' joyful.

"We'll tog out swell an' take along a case o' booze in each hack," says Red.

"An' what's more," says I, "Riley has sent up word that he'll come uptown an' spend New Year's day wit'us. We got a letter from him a week before Christmas that he was a dyin' to take a slant at the old crowd an' that we could expect him up here fer to pay us a New Year's visit. If Mickey could on'y run away from that there George Junior Republic up there in Thompkins county, New York, an' find his way back here we'd have a swell reunion! Hey!"

Tell the trut' I had me doubts about Mickey ever comin' back again to see our old gang. Cripes, his letters showed that he was gone clean-to-the-bad up there! There he was a willin' to obey the law, a willin' to quit smokin', a willin' fer to be a cop! An' worse yet, he was willin' to work! Fer the love of Mike—dont never send me to no such a joint! I didn't say this to them guys, though. They'd a passed resolutions con-demin' Mickey as a traitor.

"Say you, Spike, that 's a good line o' dope you jus' handed out," says Shorty, an' he moves to make me plan unanymous. It went t'rough wit' a rush.

"I had been plannin' fer to go with me old man to Brooklyn," says Blinkey, "but I'll be wit' youse guys so long 's Riley'll be here. It would make me feel good to put me lamps on the kid, again!"

Then we passed out pieces o' paper an' each guy wrote down his list o' joints fer us to pay New Year's calls. When they was done we put 'em together, an' then made out one list from all. After chewin' the rag I makes the announcement o' the programme.

"Now fellers, I got these here joints picked out from all the lists, an' if ye' want any added on wait 'ntil I get t'rough me announcement!

"First we go up to pay a call on Big Liz! She was me steady an' I didn't want to take no chanst o' comin' up to her home after some o' us guys got a skate on,[3] so I decided that we make them calls on our dames first. If we went a New Year's callin' on our crows in an intoxicated condishun it would a been good night fer us. They'd a t'rowed us down good an' hard.

"After we leave Big Liz we go to visit Shorty's crow, then we give Yens, the Yanitor, a call, cross the street to see old Widow Hogan who has invited us to drop in an' taste a new mixture o' hot punch, then to Mrs. Crayton who punishes[4] six cans o' booze a day, back here to visit the Fairy an' her puppy dorgs, up the next block to call on Terro Camillo's joint, then down to Alderman Bender an' then if we aint got pinched yet, or landed in Bellyview horspital[5] we wind up at Shorty's home."

"Some class to that skeem," says Blinkey.

"I think it's all right, but I would like fer to have ye' add me boss[6] on that list," says Red. "He's a rich Sheeny an' lives in bachelor apartments on Eighty-Sixt' street near Fift' avenue, an' I think he'll show us a good time if we drop in over there. Put him on the list fer an early visit, we dont want to go there half edged."[7]

"Wake up! Wake up! Come out o' it!" says the crowd, joshin'[8] Red fer his nutty plan.

"We'd have a fat chanst o' breakin' into any swell joint wit' our push!" says I.

"Why not? Aint we goin' to travel in hacks? Aint we goin' to wear glad rags!"[9] put in Red.

---

3. *got a skate on.* Became intoxicated.

4. *punishes.* Drinks.

5. *Bellevue Hospital.* The largest municipal hospital on the East Side. [In 1895 Bellevue Hospital on East Twenty-Sixth Street was a large institution (700 beds) where the city's destitute were sent for serious medical care.—Ed.]

6. *boss.* Employer.

7. *half edged.* Partly intoxicated.

8. *joshing.* Making fun of.

9. *glad rags.* Best clothes.

"Have it your way! We go to the kuyk's, too," says I, puttin' it down. Then I told each guy to be ready wit' five bucks assessment an' meet at Shorty's home on New Year's day at four in the afternoon. Glad rags was the rule.

• ◆ •

On New Year's day we was all there wit' bells on! All but Riley! He broke his promise an' never showed up! It was the first time Riley ever welched on the gang.

The rest o' us was there all right, all right; an' we certainly showed Yorkville a few points on swell get-up. Me an' Shorty had done a mean trick, at that! We, as committee, had hired two hacks from an under-taker an' rode over in them to Shorty's house from the livery stable. Well now when we stepped out'n the rigs we near started a scrap wit' the other guys, because we had got up real swell an' hadn't tipped 'em off. Ye' see, the day before New Year's me an' Shorty went down to the Bay[10] off'n Chatham Square an' after tryin' a few o' them Baxter street joints we hired dress suits from a kuyk that rents clo'es. I had on a swell pair o' new tan shoes an' Shorty had pat'nt leathers, an' we had a pink rose pinned on our coats. While we was downtown we had run into some bargains an' now we blossomed fort' in all the best regalia. We had swell brown derby lids,[11] fancy shirts an' real Arizony diamon'[12] studs. Say we was sure some class! I knowed it would get the other ginks sore, an' maybe they didn't rave when they seen us.

"Cripes sake! Spike, why d'n' ye' say ye' was goin' the limit when ye' give out the orders?" says Blinkey, awfully peeved. He was no slouch, himself, neither. He had on a black cutaway that looked like a hand-me-down from his old man's weddin', but his pants had some pretty gay stripes, at that; an' as fer socks! He had it over all o' us like a bushel basket! He turned up the bottom' o' his pants twict, jus' so 's he could advertise them red silk socks he wore.

10. *the Bay.* Old clothes section of Chatham Square.

11. *lids.* Hats.

12. *Arizona diamonds.* Imitation diamonds.

Blinkey dug up a cutaway somewhere, too, an' he must a had help in coppin' the rig he had on. He had a white vest wit' real pearl buttons, but he spoilt it wit' wearin' golf pants. He didn't have no classy stockin's so we waited while he took off the golf pants an' baseball stockin's what he had on, an' put on long pants what Shorty lent him. He had a Kelly but we wouldn't let the crazy sucker wear it!

Well we got started an' Shorty, Red, an' Butts took the first hack, an' me an' Blinkey took the second. We had a case o' beer in each hack, an' each guy had a pack o' swell New Year's cards. Mine was great big ones with silk fringe all 'round, an' on it was a pi'ture o' a farmhouse in the forest wit' real, glitterin' snow pasted on where the snow ought to be an' the words A HAPPY NEW YEAR done on it in white snow. They was a little envelope in the corner inside o' which was a card on which I wrote me name. Ye' suposed fer to leave o' card at every place ye' call. Mine cost ten cents apiece, on'y I did not buy mine. I swiped 'em. Buttsy swiped his'n, too. But the other guys didn't get a good show an' had to pay real money fer theirs.

Well after the hacks got a goin' we drawed some notice, believe me. Shorty had brung along his accordeen, an' he was practicin' tunes in the hack while we drove along.

Now it didn't take us more 'n five minutes to get to the home o' Big Liz, an' there she was, dressed up like a doll waitin' fer us. "Happy New Year, Liz! Happy New Year!" we all yells an' goes a pilin' into her rooms. She took us into the parlor an' she puts out chairs, an' we all set down in a circle. Cripes, it was like a minstrel show! We guys didn't need no knockdown[13] to Liz's family an' we got busy, believe me. I sung tenor but I sure was no Caruso![14] Shorty hit up his tenement house piano[15] an' I sung Ben Bolt, with the whole push comin' in chorus. Then fer a oncore I sung a comic, I'd Leave My Happy Home Fer You! Then Liz's old man come in an' passed around the glasses wit' real wine in 'em an' after we

---

13. *knockdown.* Invitation.

14. [*Caruso.* Spike meant Enrico Caruso, the famed Italian star of the opera.—Ed.]

15. *tenement house piano.* Accordion.

drunk a toast to Liz we got Blinkey to oblige wit' a buck-an-wing. Now if youse ever seen Blink ye' know he weighs about two hundred. Well soon after he got to dancin' a breakdown, Shorty playin' Turkey-in-the-Straw on his accordeen, the people down stairs come up an' asked us please fer to stop as the plaster was fallin' down from their ceilin'. That put a crimp into any more rough house so they passed around the cake an' wine a couple o' times again an' then we says good bye. Now before ye' take ye' lids an' say good bye ye' gotta come acrost wit' ye're New Year's cards. So our push lined up, give out our swell cards an' ducked. Say, I got in-right wit' Liz's family that night! She told me afterward that the neighbors all piped me off wit' me dresssuit an' asked her old woman who that "fine tall fellow with the fine clothes" was. Liz says that her old woman said "Him? Why he's Liz's young man!" I guess I did make them Harps sit up an' take notice, at that!

We give our drivers orders to drive on a couple o' blocks to where Shorty's crow lived. His skirt put on more airs than Liz. Her old man was a cop, but he was away on duty. They had a piano an' Shorty's dame could tickle the ivories,[16] some. They was much bowin' an' scrapin' when we hit that there joint, fer we had to get a knockdown to quite a bunch o' dames we never seen before. They must a thought we come there to make a night o' it. The hand-out almost come to a square meal. An' they was port, sherry an' Rhine wine where ye' could hit it wit'out makin' any noise. The bunch was some bashful when they first struck that joint but they got over it soon after the glasses clinked a couple o' times. Well we sung Ben Bolt, I'd Leave Me Happy Home Fer You, On a Bicycle Built Fer Two, an' all the lates' pop'lar hits, woids an' music, price ten cents, one dime, as the guy yells out in the theayter lobby after the shows. Shorty's accordeen, the piano, an' a couple o' mout' harmonicas what us ginks shoved acrost our mugs furnished enuf music to notify the neighborhood, an' tell ye' the trut' we had a real swell time up there! They was some dancin' an' games, too. One cock eyed scarecrow wit' a face that 'd stop a clock says "Oh boys an' goils, let's play t'row down

---

16. *tickle the ivories*. Play the piano.

the pillow!"[17] Shorty pipes off her fiz, winks at me, pulls out his dollar Waterbury[18] an' announces: "Say boys, it's after six o'clock an' we got to get a move on." It was the signal to pull out our cards an' we dropped 'em into a hat as it was passed around an' then beat it. In the hall way while puttin' on our coats Butts managed to slip a bottle o' sherry under his coat. I called him down good an' plenty when I heard what he done, because he was li'ble to queer Shorty wit' his crow be doin' that. I advised him to say nothin' to Shorty an' leave it in my hack.

We had promised Hansen, the Swede, to give him a call an' we went there next. Well now all that poor guy had to offer us was lemonade! Think o' it! Lemonade on New Year's day! I was curious fer to see how us ginks would treat that Sund'y school drink. I'll eat me hat if every one o' us didn't gulp it down, an' make believe he liked it. We et big chunks o' cake, though. Then we started on our way. I got a chanst to sneak down an' present Mrs. Hansen wit' that bottle o' sherry. She needed it, too, bein' sick in bed half the time. Shorty aint never knowed to this day how Buttsy outraged the hospitality o' his prospective father-in-law, the cop.

It wasn't until we struck Widow Hogan's joint that trouble begun. I gotta tell ye' somethink about her so's ye'll understand how she come to put up the drinks. She was janitress, an' upstairs was a family o' rich Ginneys. They run a wholesale store where they sold Ginney wines, Ginney macaroni, an' Ginney cheeses. Now 's you know on'y one family in a house can have one woodshed. Well in this here house Widow Hogan run thinks to suit herself, an' she give them Ginneys the use o' t'ree woodsheds. They in return, knowing her fondness fer the booze, allus kep' her supplied be givin' her a small kag o' imported Ginney booze that had a kick worse 'n Jersey lightnin'.[19] Well now she had recently turned over another woodshed to them Dagoes an' in return had got a

17. *play throw down the pillow.* A kissing game.
18. *dollar Waterbury.* Cheap watch.
19. *Jersey lightning.* Cheap whiskey.

small cask o' ratgut.[20] Well o' course we had to accept her invitation to call on New Year's day an' taste her new punch.

It was some punch, believe me! Solar plexus punch! We dropped in there ten minutes after leaving Hansen's place an' she was overjoyed to see us. She told us to make ourselfs at home while she put on the hot-water kittle, an' we kep' thinks lively singin' tunes an' feedin' parlor matches to her parrot.

She didn't pride herself wit' a swell punch bowl an' when she got the dope[21] all ready she dumped down a big dishpan an' mixed the booze. She put in a couple o' quarts o' that strong Dago booze, a couple o' pounds o' sugar, sliced lemons, an' hot water. Then she stirred it up, an' say bo; ye're mout' would water at the smell o' the steam. She passed around empty beer-glasses an' told us to dip in. We did. It's a good think that booze was pipin' hot. We had to drink it slow. That stuff was so strong it would corrode a concrete cistern. We was all pie-eyed when we clim' out o' Widow Hogan's basement an' started fer Kelly, the car conductor's joint. They seen we was plastered before we got out o' the hacks an' wouldn't let us enter. Shorty started in fer to slug the janitor an' I was hardly in condishun meself fer to be a peacemaker. All I know is that I heard a crash o' glass an' us guys all pile into our hacks ayellin' to beat the band, an' the drivers whip up their nags an' we dug fer other territory. Some one' o' the push had heaved a rock t'rough the plate glass in the street door.

Well we drove over to Central Park an' remembered that Red's boss lived over that way. It took us half an hour to find the apartment house an' half a minute to get-the-hook[22] there. Then we all clim' out o' the hacks in front o' that swell place everybody rubbered. One guy asked us if it was a masquerade party, an' I think the sucker was makin' fun o' us. Well inside the hallway we met a gink in buttons.

20. *ratgut.* Whiskey made chiefly of wood alcohol.

21. *dope.* Mixture.

22. *get-the-hook.* Ejected.

"We'd like to see Mr. Whats-his-name," says I.

"Who'll I say, sir," says the bellhop.

"Who'll ye' say? Why say Red an' the whole push!" says I. He left us waitin' in the hall. That's as far as we got. The guy in buttons come back right away.

"Will you give me your cards?" he says.

"Not be a danged sight!" says I. "Us guys dont leave no cards until we gets a decent hand-out."

Then he gives us a plain card an' a pen an' asks us to write our names on it. Well I dont know what it looked like after we wrote on it. None o' us could write sober so ye' can imagine what it looked like pie-eyed. The guy took it up again. He come down lookin' sorry.

"Mr. Whats-his-name is not at home, sir," he says.

"You gang-danged liar!" says Red, squarin' off fer to paste him. Well now it stands to reason that it wasn't that poor guy's fault an' we butted in an' wouldn't let Red punch him.

"You go up an' tell my boss that tomorrow he can look fer a new office boy. Tell him I resign me job, an' that I'm sorry I ever worked fer such a cheap-skate piker!" says Red, boilin' mad.

"Yes sir!" answers the bellhop. Poor sucker! He was a polite guy!

We then drove back over to the East Side an' voted to visit the Fairy. I might a told ye' somethink about her before. She was a short-haired, yaller-haired, peroxide blonde an' onct on a time had seen better days when she was a actress. She was a pretty old gal now, an' spent her declinin' years in the companionship o' six ki-yies[23] an' a battered old growler. That growler must made at least a hundred trips to every grog-shop in the neighborhood. She useter give us guys a nickel every time we took it out fer a scuttle o' suds. The ushal fee fer runnin' fer a can o' beer was two cents. She was a true sport an' she opened her doors wide when our push come in yellin' "Happy New Year!"

When she was on the stage she useter play banjo, an' I'll be gosh-darned if she didn't dig up her old banjo an' sing the old songs fer us.

---

23. *ki-yies.* Lap-dogs.

Her voice was pretty much to the Coney Island concert hall, but it sort o' made ye' feel like cryin' to see the old dame tryin' to sing the old time successes wit' us kids settin' round, an' her puppy dogs locked in the bedroom an' whinin' fer to come in an' join us. The trouble wit' the Fairy was that she couldn't let the booze alone. She kep' a hittin' the decanter on the sideboard until she got half-shot, an' wit' us guys up there ready to muss things up it was a bad combination. She got to dancin' an' it was somethink like the houcha-ma-couche,[24] 's near 's I can remember. We got tipped off that neighbors sent fer a cop so we dug out.

Me memory fails me on the rest o' that night. All I know is that we got to Terro Camillo's, an' the Ginney shoemaker poured out a new kind o' booze from rattan-covered bottles. We tried to get into Alderman Bender's house but there was nix doin'. Then we had some kind o' a fight wit' Sheenies. I dont know how it started but I know how it ended, so far as us guys was concerned.

Shorty arrived home in the hack, accordin' to schedule. But he was badly damaged. His rented dress suit was full o' rents an' th spiketails was torn off. His nut was laid open an' it took four stitches to close it up. Red had a broken arm. He didn't know it till the next day. Widow Hogan had took him in after the fight an' it wasn't 'ntil next day that they found it was busted. He was laid up a mont'. None o' us was pinched. Take it all-in-all, it was the happiest New Year we ever celebrated. The only disappointment was that Riley had welched on us.

24. *houcha-ma-couche.* Oriental dance of a vulgar kind. [Usually spelled "hootchy-kootchy," it refers to the exotic dancing—"suggestively lascivious contorting of the abdominal muscles"—of "Little Egypt" (and her imitators), first on the Midway of the World's Columbian Exposition in Chicago (1894) and later at Coney Island.—Ed.]

25.

Riley's Christmas.

Say! It wasn't Riley's fault that he never showed up to go out callin' wit' us guys on New Year's day! I learned about it later. He didn't welch. No sir! He was true blue an' proved that he was what we allus thought he was—a prince! It's a long story but I guess I'll tell it, because youse guys ought fer to know what a good-hearted kid Riley really was!

Now it happened that time that when Riley's family moved downtown back to Cherry Hill it was because they had to move. They hadn't paid no rent fer a long time an' the landlord put 'em out. Riley's old man had been hittin' up the booze a lot an' lost his job. Uptown they couldn't find a place to live cheap enuf fer the family an' so back they goes to Cherry Hill. O' course Riley never told us the real reason why they moved, but I found it out.

Well Riley's old woman took in washin', worked nights scrubbin' in office buildin's downtown near Cherry Hill an' Nellie, the oldest girl, she looked after the kids. They was a pretty big assortment o' them Rileys, seven or eight, I guess! Our Riley was the oldest boy, couldn't a been a day over fourteen. Well he pitched in an' sold papers to help out. He was such a pinched little runt that he couldn't get no job in a factory because nobody would believe he was fourteen. He couldn't stand no inside work, anyway. Ye' remember how I told ye' in the beginnin' how I thought he had the con?[1] Well Riley sold enuf papers every day to furnish the supper fer the family an' have enuf left over fer

---

1. *con.* Consumption.

the next day's stake an' a little extra. The old man was plastered[2] all the time an' was goin' from bad to worse. That's the way affairs was goin' when Christmas was comin' along, an' it was a dead cinch[3] that the Riley family wasn't agoin' to have no Merry Christmas that year!

But they did have a Merry Christmas, but not A Happy New Year! Mrs. Riley told me the whole story how it all come about. Two days before Christmas, she says, Riley run up Frankfort street to Newspaper Row[4] to wait fer the afternoons as ushal. His old man had took the lad's overcoat an' hocked it fer the price of a couple o' schooners o' beer, an' all that the poor kid had to wear was an' old sweater. Well Riley stood smellin' the steam from hot soup in a beanery an' then crossed over an' roosted wit' other shiverin' kids on a iron gratin' where a cloud o' ink-laden steam come up from the printin' offices. They was settin' there comfortably, an' Riley was a dreamin' an' thinkin' that he was suddenly rich an' had money to burn, an' was agoin' to blow the whole family off on Christmas an' that he wouldn't spend nuttin' on himself. Well his pipe-dream was short, fer all in a bunch the kids jumped up an' made a dive fer the first editions.

Riley's happy dream didn't vanish right away, an' when he come out'n his trance all the other kids had beat him to it, an' were a flyin' down to the ferries an' over Broadway an' Park Row wit' their papers. The rule is first come, first served; an' poor Riley found himself pretty late when he got away wit' his bundle.

Riley useter dig fer Fulton Ferry 's soon 's he got his hooks onto his daily stock o' papers but a mob o' other newsies had trimmed him that afternoon. That's what he got fer settin' there in the steam a dreamin'!

He started fer the ferry but in every place he seen that it was no use. Reglar customers held up papers an' waved him off when he run into stores an' cafes on the way down, so, almost cryin', he goes back to

---

2. *plastered*. Dead drunk.

3. *dead cinch*. Absolute certainty.

4. [*Frankfort street to Newspaper Row*. At the turn of the century, Newspaper Row in downtown Manhattan was home to the *Times, Tribune, Sun, World*, and, nearby, the *Staats-Zeitung*, the major German-language publication.—Ed.]

Park Row. In spite o' the rule that no guy can butt in on any other guys territory he made up his mind that the Brooklyn Bridge entrance was anybody's, just like the outside o' the ferry house. Well he hadn't been there two minutes before a big guy gives him a dig in the jaw an' tells him to git! An' the old wimmin sellin' papers were jus' as ugly. They told him to beat it, an' they was nothin' to do but try elsewhere.

Riley shoves his papers under his arm, dodges trucks an' cars, an' goes diggin' up the Bowery[5] yellin' his wuxtries. He hadn't got to Chatham Square when he found his papers goin' pretty well. He goes on up past Steve Brodie's an' wit' his runnin' an' good luck he was soon all warmed up. Then the dirty sky begun to drop snowflakes—first little ones that fell on Riley's sleeve an' stayed long enuf fer him to look at the pretty little flakes. Then they come down thicker an' fell into the cracks between the cobble stones where the wind drove 'em an' fashioned the street into a white lined checkerboard. Riley run on. Soon the snow come down like feathers an' crunched soft under foot, an' deadened the clink o' the horse's hoofs on the pavement an' put the soft pedal on the truck noises an' car-bells. Well be the time he got to Grand street[6] everythink was white, an' everybody seemed happy, fer it was the first real snowstorm o' the winter. Riley had on'y a few papers when he got to Grand street. He stopped to rubber.

Say, you ever seen Grand street at Christmas time? They's no place in the world like it! It's got it on Fourteent' street like a bushel basket! Why it's jus' one mass o' tinsel an' toys! Window after window chock full, an' street booths crowdin' each other so's the hawkers is allus scrappin' wit' each other fer space. Inside an' outside they was miles o' tinsel, gilt balls, paper chains, rosettes. Candy stores with mountainous piles o' sweets, menageries o' red an' yaller candy animals that a guy wanted to suck, candy canes an' baskets, snap-crackers, mounds o' French mixed, tubs o' chocolate creams dumped over, an' boxes an' boxes o' plain an' fancy sweets, an' then some!

5. *Bowery*. Famous old thoroughfare of the lower East Side.
6. *Grand street*. Center of lower East Side shopping district.

Riley's eyes bulged when he seen this. He run along kickin' in the snow, happy, an' wonderin' why God made it so cold 'nstead o' warm like the snow in the windows, that was sprinkled on the toys. He swiped a little branch from a Christmas tree so's he could carry it in his pocket an' take it out every onct in a while an' smell it. D'ye ever notice how it makes ye' feel happy jus' to smell the odor o' Christmas trees? Try it an' see!

Riley soon run into a crowd that was comin' an' goin' in a big department store an' he seen a sign what said that Santa Claus was inside an' was givin' away free a pi'ture book to every good boy an' girl. Riley knowed that there was no chanst fer him gettin' a book, because he was a bad guy. Everybody but his mother had told him that. He got the notion, though, that if he could get in to see Santa he could put up a argymint an' get one fer little Jimmy, his third littlest kid brother. Everybody said that he was sure a good kid. Riley took a chanst. He dodged a floor walker near the entrance an' sneaked upstairs where Santa Claus set on a t'rone. The cash girls an' sales ladies an' clerks was too busy waitin' on customers to t'row him out, an' Riley lines up wit' other kids that went up to shake hands wit' Santa an' receive a book. O' course Riley knowed he was a phony[7] Santa Claus, but that made no diff'rence so long as he was handin' out presents.

Well, his nibs wit' the white whiskers[8] gives Riley a book, an' it tickled the kid to deat'. He thanked the old guy an' come out o' the store before a floor walker could nab him an' take it away. They'd a done it, too; because them books was suposed to be on'y fer customers' kids. Why Riley couldn't a bought a shoestring!

He tucked his precious pi'ture book inside o' one o' his papers an' went back to the Bowery happy. It was gettin' night, an' he took a stand at the uptown entrance o' the "L" road. There he met another newsy who hadn't had much luck a sellin' his papers, because he had been shootin' crap. He offered to sell his bundle to Riley fer a quarter. Riley shook his head.

7. *phony.* Counterfeit.

8. *his nibs with the white whiskers.* Santa Claus.

"Twenty cents an' they're yourn," says the kid.

Riley comes acrost[9] wit' two dimes an' takes the bundle. Then he hung out at the "L" station until the six o'clock rush was ended. His shoes was busted an' snow got inside an' he was pretty cold by now. He decides to go on up the Bowery to where he seen the street widened out. Droppin' in at saloons he managed to sell a dozen papers an' copped enuf free lunch to make up his supper. He managed to keep warm be stayin' in the saloons 'ntil they told him to beat it. Then he dug out—wit' his fist full o' sliced bologna or cheese an' crackers. Well d'ye' know? That kid kep' on until he got way up to Cooper Institute[10] an' he never'd thought fer a minute what time it was got to be. He looked up at the big clock that kep' its eye on the old Bowery an' asked a guy what was passin' what time it was.

"Twenty after eight," says the guy, plowin' on t'rough the snow.

"Cripes almighty! I ought a been home long ago," says Riley. They allus depended on him to be home with enuf money fer supper at eight. He turned back down the Bowery an' took it on the run. His nut had been filled with the idea all that day that he could give the whole family a Merry Christmas an' the extra pennies he kep' pickin' up from customers who handed him nickels an' said: "Never mind no change, keep it fer a Merry Christmas!" had made him feel sure he could put that plan over.[11]

Now he was a runnin' down the Bowery an' makin' good time when a guy run out o' a booze joint an' yells: "Hey kid, d'ye' want a job?"

Riley stopped. He'd forgot all about gettin' home an' thought on'y o' earnin' money fer Christmas. He was all out o' breat'.

"D'ye' want t'earn half a dollar or so, settin' up pins fer a little while?" says the guy.

Riley didn't have no time to answer. The guy took him down into the basement an' back to the place where he heard the poundin' an' tumblin' o' tenpins. The job looked a cinch. All Riley had to do was to

---

9. *comes across.* Accedes.

10. *Cooper Institute.* Building at extreme north end of the Bowery.

11. *put that plan over.* Accomplish that plan.

set up the pins, dodge them when them Dutchmen bowled 'em over, drop the ball on the incline, an' set 'em up again. The kid started in without takin' off his sweater. It was play, at first. Then he got to sweatin' an' he took off all the duds he could. Well believe me, it was awful work. Them guys had the ball rollin' down on Riley before he had fairly got up out o' the alley an' they kep' him at it a long time. He was gettin' dizzy when they quit fer a short time. He was agoin' to beat it home then, but they jollied him an' told him they'd make it right fer him if he stayed 'til they finished their matches. Well the poor kid was game an' stuck it out. They quit about midnight an' besides payin' him the half-dollar they promised they passed the hat[12] an' slipped him about a dollar more. They liked his gameness an' told him to come again some other time. He picked up his pi'ture book an' left over papers, put on his sweater an' this time dug fer home fer keeps.[13] He run most the way an' when he got to familiar places down near Chatham Square he found out that it was one o'clock. Now it had quit snowin' an' the night was bitter cold. Well the poor little sucker's clothin', damp wit' perspiration when he left the bowlin' alley, was now frozen near stiff, an' when he crawled upstairs in his own tenement he was near exhausted. His old woman set there asleep wit' the lamp turned down, patiently waitin' his return an' when he come in she give him hell.

He sure gave them an awful skare. When he didn't show up at eight o'clock his mother sent Nellie acrost the hall to borrow the supper money from Mrs. O'Rourke, who often helped out in a pinch fer the Rileys. When it come nine o'clock she begun to get skared. She sent Nellie down to the ferry an' back to Park Row an' when the girl come home wit' no news Mrs. Riley herself went to Oak street police station an' Roosevelt hospital,[14] an' all over Chatham Square lookin' fer the kid. When his old man come home she told him all the kids was in bed an'

12. *passed the hat*. Took up a collection.

13. *for keeps*. Without further interruption.

14. [*Roosevelt hospital*. Opened in 1864, the large hospital at Fifty-Eighth and Ninth Avenue offered care to poor patients.—Ed.]

when the old guy fell asleep she got up an' kep' quiet watch fer Riley, fer she knowed somehow he'd show up.

Well she sent him right off to bed an' five minutes after the kid got home the tenement was dark an' silent. Riley dropped off to sleep wit' his ears ringin' "pel-lunk! pel-lunk!" like them tenpins was tumblin' all night long. He got to coughin' a lot, too an' when daylight was comin' his mother woke up, got out o' bed, raked the coals in the stove an' made a hot punch. She woke Riley up an' made him swaller it! "I'm afraid ye're sick," she said as she tucked him in bed an' went back to her own broken sleep.

When it come to gittin' up time Riley was goin' to dress, but his mother said nay. He pleaded, said he had most important business that day an' jus' had to go.

"Why lad, ye're sick, an' I cant let ye' out," she said, an' took his clothes away from him. Riley covered himself wit' his beddin' an' cried. Then he got his noodle workin'. He had been brung up in a school where he learned how to use his nut to get thinks done 's he wanted 'em, an' he was good all day. He stayed in bed an' took his medicine,[15] an' was allowed to get up to eat supper wit' the rest. Now wit' six kids to keep track of Riley's old woman discovered soon after supper that he'd swiped his clothes an' skipped out. He'd made his getaway so quiet nobody knowed nothin' 'ntil his mother wanted him to get back to bed.

Along about eleven o'clock—it was Christmas Eve, mind ye'—Riley come pantin' upstairs strugglin' with a big bundle an' he soon tumbled a big swishin' Christmas tree into the kitchen. He took his old woman down to the woodshed in the cellar where he had hid his Christmas presents.

"Here, help me git these upstairs. They's fer all o' us. I earned 'em meself to have a Merry Christmas. They's somethink fer every one," he said.

---

15. *took his medicine.* Submitted to treatment and discipline.

His mother near dropped the candle in her suprise. They took up the packages an' laid 'em on the kitchen table.

"Now I'm goin' to bed an' be good. I wrote the names on 'em, so ye' can tell who they's fer," says Riley, shakin' wit' chills. He hit the hay[16] right off an' left his mother to trim the tree an' arrange the Christmas presents.

The kid woke up onct that night. He found his mother bendin' over him. He knowed that she had just kissed him, an' he wondered why. She had never kissed him before. Nobody had never done that to him. He was sort o' dazed an' rattled. She'd been cryin', too. Her tears had wet his cheek when she kissed him. Riley thought it was because his old man was drunk again down there in Callaghan's booze joint. He made up his mind he'd be good now an' get well an' grow up till he was big enuf to knock his old man's block off. He told his mother o' that ambition. She said nothin' but set there till he dropped off to sleep.

Christmas mornin' the whole tribe o' Riley kids rough-housed each other out'n bed an' run into the kitchen fer to see if what Riley had been tellin' them all week about Santa Claus was true. Sure enuf, the good old guy, Santa Claus, had visited them. There stood a swell Christmas tree floodin' the stuffy kitchen wit' its sweet balsam smell. It was covered wit' chains made o' colored paper, candies hangin' to tempt ye' to swipe 'em from every twig, sugar coated popcorn bustin' out at the end o' every little shoot, a reglar [fake?] zoological collection runnin' wild in them there branches. They was little an' big packages done up an' hid in the branches an' up on top was old Santa hangin' like he'd been lynched, an' angels, an' colored glass balls, an' roses, an' stars an' crescents made o' tinsel, an' lighted candles, an' crystal snow an' flitter-gold, an' a t'ousand other thinks what on'y the kids could spy out. Under the tree stood a dish o' cakes an' a dish o' oranges an' apples, an' a dish o' candies an' nuts. Cripes, them kids never seen nothin' like it in their life!

"Merry Christmas! an' help yerselfs!" yells Riley from his cot.

16. *hit the hay.* Went to bed.

"Merry Christmas! Merry Christmas!" answers the kids as they went to it.

After breakfast Riley's mother let him git up fer awhile, an' he had a swell time playin' wit' the kids. He had gave Mikey, his next-in-size brother, a live white rat in a box wit' pink eyes. Y'understand the rat had pink eyes, not the box! All played games an' they tried to learn the rat how to do tricks, Riley allus liked kids an' animals. Ye' remember how he brung home the woodchuck the time he was a Fresh Air kid!

• ◆ •

It come New Year's Eve. Upstairs in that Cherry street tenement Riley's old man an' Mrs. Riley set beside his bed waitin'. It was near midnight, an' they knowed they'd be an awful racket when the watch-night crowds up there on Brooklyn Bridge cut loose when the old year went out an' the new year come in. Riley was awful sick an' they was afraid the racket would make him worse. The Free Dispensary doctor[17] had been up there to see Riley twict that afternoon.

They was settin' there in the silent tenement gazin' out over the white roofs. Up above the tenements they seen the lights twinklin' on the big bridge an' the black mass o' humanity up there was flowin' back an' fort' waitin' to celebrate the arrival o' the New Year. The on'y sound they heard was the loud ticks from the tin-can alarm clock out in the Riley kitchen. The clocks begun to strike twelve.

Then hell broke loose! Fact'ry whistles shrieked, river an' harbor craft bellowed, fire crackers shot off, revolvers was fired, tin horns an' brass trumpets put in their din, bells rung, drums was pounded an' anythink that made a racket was used be them wild guys celebratin' downtown. It lasted until steam, lungs an' strengt' become exhausted, an' ended be leavin' the field all alone to them sweet chimes o' Trinity.[18]

17. [*Free Dispensary doctor*. Dispensaries, located throughout the city and usually supported by philanthropies, offered outpatient medical care for the poor.—Ed.]

18. [*sweet chimes o' Trinity*. The bells rang at Trinity (Episcopal) Church at Broadway and Wall Street.—Ed.]

The next mornin', New Year's day, the muckers on Cherry street come over an' looked silent at the white crepe an undertaker hung[19] on the doorknob o' the tenement. They knowed that Riley had croaked. That's why he didn't show up fer our New Year's callin'. Now dont ye' think, takin' all in all, that he was a little prince! There was no welcher[20] about him, was there?

19. [*white crepe an undertaker hung.* White crepe ribbon signaled that a child had died.—Ed.]

20. *welcher.* Traitor, one who fails to make good.

Index

Italic page number denotes illustration.

Abbott, Lawrence F., 42, 43
Adams, Samuel Hopkins, 42
Adventures of Tom Sawyer. See Twain,
   Mark
alcoholic beverages: "beer boy," 88; brew-
   eries of, 22; consumption of, 60, 84, 85,
   104; and Germans, 18, 101; intoxica-
   tion, 44, 114, 121, 156, 181, 237n4; and
   police, 195; and politics, 212–13; and
   tenement life, 77, 81, 84–86, 141, 143,
   151, 186, 252–53, 257, 259. *See also* Crapshooters Club
Aldrich, Thomas Bailey, 43
Alger, Horatio, 42
Atlantic (magazine). *See* Scudder, Horace
   Elisha
Auburn State Prison (New York), 187

baseball. *See* Crapshooters Club
Beefsteak John's (restaurant), 97, 108
beer. *See* alcoholic beverages
Blackwell's Island, 53
bonfires. *See* politics
Bowery entertainments, 97–110
Brodie, Steve, 110, 110n65, 254
Bum's Rush, 45, 66, 108, 166, 213, 239

Canfield, Dick, 155, 155n21
Carnegie, Andrew, 133, 133n16
Central Park, 22, 131–40, 249
Century Dictionary (1897), 46
Century (magazine). *See* Gilder, Richard
   Watson
Child, Lydia Maria. *See* Jacobs, Harriet
childhood: attitudes toward, 7–8, 13–14,
   23, 28; children's play, 24
Christmas, 38–39n46, 45, 95, 182, 232–35,
   236–41, 252–61
cigarette smoking, 32, 56, 62, 80, 94, 109,
   121–22, 167, 170, 180, 182, 190, 206–7,
   220–21
Comstock, Anthony, 175, 175–76n35
Coney Island, 176–77
consumption (tuberculosis), 165, 252–61
Coogan's Bluff, 113n5. *See also* Polo
   Grounds
Crane, Stephen, 10, 45, 46
Crapshooters Club: and alcohol consumption, 66, 122, 153–56, 180–81,
   242–51; attitudes about education, 58;
   attitudes about parents, 58; attitudes
   about rural life and folk, 142–47,
   169–71, 175; attitudes about work, 58,
   62, 87–88, 94–95, 189; and baseball,

Crapshooters Club (*cont.*)
111, 113, 118, 119; clubhouse (Dugan's cellar), 63–65; crimes and swindles, 45, 130–31, 157–63, 223–24; and dime novels, 61, 94, 97, 196; ethics of, 162; formation, 62–68; and girls, 136–41, 143–44, 149, 153, 195; and hygiene, 88; and loyalty, 159, 186; and making money, 58, 130–31; nicknames of members, 56–57, 59–62; and pigeon-keeping, 42, 173–75; and police, 63, 65, 66, 125, 139, 185, 195, 217; and poverty, 77; pranks and vandalism, 76, 197–203, 208; and religion, 76, 229–31; rules of, 67; and scavenging, 25, 56, 130; and social pretensions of adults, 77–86; and theft, 61, 65, 69–75, 85, 96, 98, 128, 130, 142–46, 152–53, 154, 156, 158, 164, 210; and women, 129–30

Dapping, Mathilda Lauterbach. *See* Dapping, Wilhelm (William Sr.)
Dapping, Wilhelm (William Sr.), 14–19, 22; Civil War service of, 15–16; disability of, 14–16; marriage to Mathilda Lauterbach Dapping, 18–21; veteran's pension of, 16
Dapping, William O.: attitude toward social reform, 11; authorship of *The Muckers*, 4, 12, 38, 40–47; career at George Junior Republic, 33–34; childhood and youth, 12–13, 19–20, 21–22; death of, 47–48; desire for respectability, 11; education, 9, 10, 24; efforts to publish *The Crapshooters Club*, 38–40, 45–46, 47; gangs, causes of, 10, 54–56; gangs, character of, 53–57; and George Junior Republic, 9–10, *10*, 26, 29, 32, 33–34, 47–48; relation to William R. George, 26, 33–34; relation to Thomas M. Osborne,

36–38, 47; relation to Progressive Era reform, 8, 9–10; religion of, 24–25, 47
Davey's store, 69
Deadwood Dick, 97, 106–8
dialect literature, 45–46
dime novels. *See* Crapshooters Club; *Deadwood Dick*

election day. *See* politics
Elmira Reformatory, 158, 158n7, 187
Epworth League, 236, 236n1
ethnic conflicts, 44, 56, 78, 100, 153, 175–76; toward Chinese, 66, 98, 144, 200, 216; toward Germans, 73, 89, 90, 98, 155–56; toward Irish, 98; toward Italians, 58, 69, 70, 71, 89, 90, 123, 147, 188, 195, 199–200; toward Jews, 63, 69, 89, 90, 134–36, 186, 214–15, 216, 218–19; racist terms, examples of, 44, 100, 158, 224

Fabian, Ann, 39, 41
Fass, Paula, 8
free baths (People's Baths), 165, 165n9
"Fresh Air" charities, 27–28, 164–71, 229. *See also* George, William R.

games: cards, 196; cherry pits, 143–44; craps, 55–56, 94–95, 130, 144, 153, 171; gambling, 154–55; Groosefadder (*Großfater*), 159, 227; hide the straw, 202; horseshoe the mare, 200; marbles (miggles), 125–27; at parties, 79–80, 85
gangs, 9, 28–29, 216; attitudes of police toward, 53
Garrison, Frank W., 38
George, William R., 9, 10, 21, 22, 25, 26–27, *27*, 55, *60*, 112; Fresh Air camp

in Freeville, 28–30; interest in gangs, 28–29; and political corruption, 209n2; and problem of pauperism, 31–32; religious instruction of, 26–27; and United Society of Christian Endeavor, 236n1. *See also* Dapping, William O.

George Junior Republic, 29–33, 55, 55n7, 181, 185–90, *191*, 192–93, 211; attitude toward girls, 31–32, 55n7; boy-centeredness of, 31; and dime novels, 93n28; and entrepreneurialism, 190, 194; Mickey at, 186, 190, 204–6, 220–21, 243

German immigrants, 14–16; Little Germany (*Kleindeutschland*), 18–19; stereotypes of, 16. *See also* ethnic conflicts

Gilder, Richard Watson, 46

Gilfoyle, Timothy, 6

girls. *See* Crapshooters Club

Globe Dime Museum, 97–108, 97n22

glossary (*The Muckers*), xvi, 11, 51n1

Governor's Island, 98

Hall, G. Stanley, 28

Halloween, 195–203

Harlem, 79, 113

Herring, Fannie, 104

Heucken and Willenbrock lumberyard, 22, *23*, 172n25

Jacobs, Harriet, 39

jails, 121–24

Jones, Gavin, 45–46

juvenile justice system, 30

Lauterbach family, 18–19

Lewis, Edward Herbert, 46

Maggie: A Girl of the Streets. *See* Crane, Stephen

marbles (miggles). *See* games

May Parties, 129–38

McClure's (magazine). *See* Adams, Samuel Hopkins

Methodist Episcopal Church of the Savior (New York City), 26

miggles (marbles). *See* games

Miles, Johny, 25–26

minstrelsy, 238; "buck and wing" dance, 82, 82n31, 246–47

Mintz, Steven, 13

Muckers: A Narrative of the Crapshooters Club, The: absence of sentimentality in, 6; and "bad boy" literature, 43–44; contribution to social reform literature, 11; and dialect literature, 45–46; ethnic hostilities and racism in, 44; profanity in, 44; representation of corruption in, 44–45; slang in, 44, 46–47; structure of, 7. *See also* Dapping, William O.

Murphy, Kevin, 29

music: accordion, 61; popular songs, 82, 246–47

Nasaw, David, 25

New York City, population of, 8. *See also* German immigrants; Yorkville

New York Evening Post, 38

New York House of Refuge, 89, 89n11, 96n14

Osborne, Thomas M., 9–10, 34–36, *35*, *37*, 46, 47, 48; friendships with Republic boys, 36–37; and political corruption, 209n2; sponsorship of Dapping

Osborne, Thomas M. (*cont.*)
  sketches, 39–41, 43. *See also* Dapping,
  William O.
Outlook (magazine). *See* Abbott, Lawrence
  F.

Parkhurst, Rev. Charles H., 175, 175–76n35
pauperism, 16–18
Peabody's (restaurant), 109
pigeon-keeping. *See* Crapshooters Club
Pittenger, Mark, 36
politics: campaigning, 214; election day
  festivities, 210–11, 216–17; and ethnic
  conflicts, 214–15, 218–19; Germans
  and Republican Party, 215; political
  corruption, 212, 215, 218–19; Tammany
  Hall, 11, 63, 209–15, 209n2, 217–19
Polo Grounds, 113
Progressive Era reform. *See* Dapping,
  William O.; social reform

Rafter's store, 69
Ragamuffin Day, 222–24
Riis, Jacob, 9, 12, 13

scavenging. *See* Crapshooters Club
Scudder, Horace Elisha, 42
Sing Sing Prison, 53, 61
slang. *See Muckers: A Narrative of the Crap-
  shooters Club, The*
Socialist Labor Party, 95
social reform: "child-saving," 17–18; lit-
  erature of, 1, 7; problem of slum, 8–9;
  Progressive Era reform, 7–8, 17–18, 36.
  See also Dapping, William O.
Stanley, Carrie, 97, 104, 104n47

Story of a Bad Boy. See Aldrich, Thomas
  Bailey
Stowe, Lyman Beecher, 29
street boys, 5–6, 9; popular representa-
  tions of, 3. *See also* Crapshooters Club;
  George, William R.; Osborne, Thomas
  M.
summer excursions, 148–56; *General
  Slocum* disaster, 150; and political
  machines, 149
Sunday schools, 12, 65, 81, 82, 148, 150, 236.
  See also Dapping, William O.; George,
  William R.
Syracuse University Libraries, 6, 48

Tammany Hall. *See* politics
tenements, 8; daily life in, 70, 130–31;
  description of, 81
Thanksgiving. *See* Ragamuffin Day
theft. *See* Crapshooters Club
Tony Pastor's Theatre, 94
Twain, Mark, 43, 45

United Society of Christian Endeavor,
  236. *See also* George, William R.

Washington, Booker T., 42–43
Weber, Joe, 104

Yorkville, 20–24, 23, 45, 48, 59, 86, 111, 113,
  132, 183, 233, 245
Youth's Companion, 43

Ziff, Larzer, 43

Woody Register is the Francis S. Houghteling Professor of American History at the University of the South, where he teaches US history and American studies. He is the author of *The Kid of Coney Island: Fred Thompson and the Rise of American Amusements,* and he is coauthor with Bruce Dorsey of the two-volume series *Crosscurrents in American Culture: A Reader in United States History.* He lives in Sewanee, Tennessee.